CAN I STEAL YOU FOR FOREVER

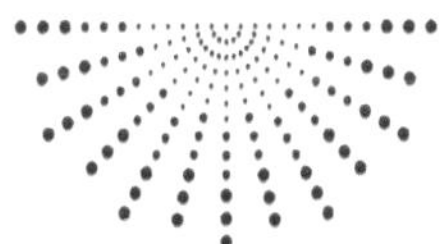

KYLEE SUMMERS

Sequential
House

For Emily and Eliza Partridge

FOREWORD

For clarity's sake, I refer to members of the Church of Jesus Christ of Latter Day Saints as Mormons throughout this book since that is still what they are most well known as. While I love the people and community I grew up with, the teachings, culture, and systems of the church can hurt people. This book isn't here to try and convince people to leave the church. Instead, it's here to accurately depict what it can be like growing up in that environment.

This book is an open door romance containing explicit sex scenes. If you prefer to skip such scenes, you'll want to skip pages 208-210, 234-238, and 309-310.

Chapters 21 and 27 contain brief scenes of bishop interviews, which could be triggering for some. OCD is discussed, and a panic attack is described. Please read with care.

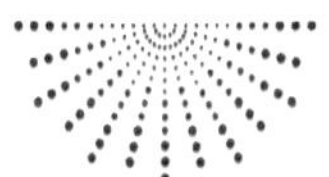

$\mathcal{A}$fton Hayes knows perfection is unattainable—screw you Matthew 5:48—but she needs to get as close as possible tonight. Which is why she spent two hours in traffic to get the last pebble ice maker in the area. Any good Utah girl knows the most underrated element for a dirty soda is the ice. Rectangular cubes water down the soda, cream, and syrup concoctions while ruining the aesthetic. Crunchy or pebbles are the only way to go.

Afton double checks the soda bar one last time, rearranging the tiny ice spheres with the metal scoop until they're just right.

"This is what you've been so busy with? Come on, that's production assistant work," a familiar voice says from the doorway.

Afton flips Chelsea off without looking up.

"Rude," Chelsea scoffs, crossing the room and standing on the opposite side of the table. Afton's seen her best friend's familiar work uniform of black athletic wear and white sneakers hundreds of times. But seeing Chelsea with her headset *and* a clipboard, standing in this ornate and perfectly lit room? Her stomach twists.

Afton is here, rearranging ice on the set of *Ready for the Ring*. Even after a decade working in TV and traveling the world, being in *this* room is surreal. The built in bookcases she's lusted after for years are behind her, re-stained a beautiful walnut. She flicked on the decorative lamps in every corner and checked for visible fingerprints. Instead of wondering if the velvet couches are actually comfortable, she carefully tried them. Season after season, Afton watched hundreds of people enter this room filled with hope, only to leave with crushed dreams. She won't be one of them.

"Do I need to remind you that you're a producer here, not a PA?" Chelsea asks, scooping up the pebbles, then watching them fall slowly back into the bucket.

"This is important."

Chelsea raises an eyebrow. "It's soda."

"Did you ask me to be your Mormon whisperer?"

Chelsea nods, her messy bun of auburn hair bobbing.

Afton leans across the table dramatically. "Then let me whisper."

Chelsea rolls her eyes before handing Afton the clipboard. "You're ridiculous."

Afton flips through the pages filled with pictures and summaries of the thirty contestants. Usually she would have memorized the cast bios, but the faces of the women blur together. In her defense, her previous shows were never this large, and she only started here a month ago.

Then the leading man–ridiculously called the Fiancé-to-be– was arrested for drug possession and production scrambled to replace him. A new Fiance-to-be meant different ideal women to date, so the final contestants weren't finalized until yesterday. She meant to stay up memorizing the women's backgrounds, but got sucked into watching videos of power-washing drive-ways while doom scrolling.

Two PA's flit through the doorway, adjusting candles. A dirty-blonde cameraman follows them, looking through his lens as he positions himself in a corner.

"Have you all met Afton?" Chelsea asks the room.

The PA's quickly incline their heads. The cameraman sets his equipment on the floor before walking over and extending a hand. "Luke. Nice to meet you."

She returns the gesture, doing her best not to gawk at his biceps and calves. Hauling a camera around all day takes strength. "You as well."

"Did you know Afton likes WWE? Has the voice of an angel? *And* she's–" Chelsea starts.

"More than capable of introducing herself," Afton cuts in.

Luke chuckles. "If you're the same Afton Chelsea's been talking about the past few years, you're going to fit in just fine."

There's no time to worry what stories Chelsea's told because a voice crackles through all of their headsets. "The first limo is pulling up."

Luke gives a reassuring smile, then jogs back to his camera.

Afton turns to Chelsea. "What are you doing?"

"Helping you make friends."

"By listing my hobbies like a dating profile?" Afton hisses.

Chelsea's eyes light up. "Luke *is* single if you're interested."

Afton folds her arms across her chest and glares.

Chelsea sighs. "I want you to enjoy it here since, you know."

Since Afton got herself epically fired from her last production? And is now digging into her…unique background to create drama for tv?

"I'll be fine. You can stop treating me like your toddler who's learning to make friends. Pretty sure I've got it."

"That's debatable," Chelsea mumbles.

Afton fakes a lunge at her and Chelsea runs out of the room, cackling. Her headset crackles again, announcing the first contestant is emerging from the limo. Afton clutches the sides of her clipboard, damp hands wrinkling the edges of the paper.

Two more PA's file in, and Afton gives them a small wave and a smile. They look her up and down and keep walking. *Okay then.* Maybe it's nothing, or maybe they're friends with crew members from her previous show and hate her in solidarity. You've got to love the small world that is television.

New voices echo through the hall and the first woman crosses the threshold. She's white with long blonde extensions styled in Utah curls. Her shimmering navy-blue gown hugs all her curves, complete with cap sleeves. Ghostly white veneers flash in a smile. Did the casting team type 'Perfect Utah Mormon Woman" into AI and then 3D print the results? Considering Jonah Partridge is being advertised as the Mormon Fiancé-to-be, this woman is exactly what he should be interested in.

Afton skims the woman's bio—Jacie Taylor is from Provo, a former BYU cheerleader, and now she's a nurse. The fact that she was the first out of the limo means production thinks she'll go far. Jacie stares at Afton expectantly, tipping her head to the side.

She should be brainstorming possible questions for Jacie, but her mind completely empties. She's not Afton the producer who can do this in her sleep. She's a teenager clawing her way out of the same mold that created Jacie.

It's work. You can do this.

"Make yourself comfortable. It's going to be a long night," Afton finally says, forcing a smile.

Jacie flashes her veneers, then emits the tiniest of squeals when she sees the soda bar. She starts mixing a diet coke with creamer and lime, heavy on the pebble ice.

Afton sticks to the walls as women keep filing in after meeting the Fiance-to-be. They naturally congregate in two groups—those with soda, and those with wine. *Yes.* Afton approaches a woman on the edge of the wine group. She's black with braids down to her chest. Emily, 29, an accountant from Seattle.

"Why are all the girls with soda sitting over there?" Afton asks Emily before stepping out of the shot.

Emily quickly surveys her group on the couch. "Why *are* all the girls with soda sitting over there?"

The other women on the couch look around, noticing it too.

"Are you all under twenty-one?" a white woman with her black hair up in a clip calls out to the soda couch. Bentley, 26, from Flagstaff, Arizona.

"No, why would you think that?" a white, blonde woman replies. McKinlee, 22, Rexburg Idaho.

"None of you have wine," Bentley replies.

"Because we don't drink," a different white, brunette woman replies slowly. Rileigh, 24, Sandy Utah.

"That's cool. I respect that," Emily smiles.

"Thanks," Rileigh says, turning and rolling her eyes at her friends. One snickers.

It's already starting, just like Afton knew it would.

There's a commotion on the headset. Multiple voices calling for the medic. An authoritative voice announcing they don't need EMS. Then, nothing. She keeps her face carefully neutral, not wanting to alert any of the women that something is going on outside. Needing a medic on reality TV is normal thanks to the combination of nerves, alcohol, and dehydration. It doesn't make it any less unsettling when someone needs help. She waits three minutes before texting Chelsea, but there's no response. Probably because the Fiancé-to-be himself is walking in, carrying a woman dressed up as a pioneer in his arms.

Afton completely freezes. No. No. *No.* This was not supposed to happen. She was supposed to be in here; asking her questions, reading the room, and searching for storylines. There was going to be ample warning before the Fiance-to-be walked in so she could disappear into the shadows, only reappearing when he was busy with someone else. Rinse and repeat for the whole season.

Was it a slightly delusional plan? Yes, but when she'd been fired from her last show, she'd been desperate. Most shows had already started production, and her favorite backup serving jobs didn't need any help. Chelsea literally screeched when Afton called her panicking about what to do. There was an opening for a producer on *Ready for the Ring* and Chelsea could vouch for her. *Ready for the Ring* had been her dream show since she'd decided to work in television, but things never aligned. Now she got to work here and spend more time with her best friend. Her teenage self would have thought it was all arranged by the Lord himself.

Except.

The sudden recast. The higher-ups wanting someone with a squeaky-clean past. So they'd chosen Jonah Partridge, beloved Mormon boy from Utah and fan favorite a year prior. The one who'd been sent home tearily confessing his fear that he'd never be someone's first choice. People flocked online with break-downs of every throat bob, declaring him the world's most handsome crier. The internet rioted when Jonah wasn't announced as the next Fiance-to-be. He was here now, and everyone on this set was here to help the world fall even harder for Jonah Partridge.

The same Jonah Partridge who had been Afton's first love.

When he'd been announced, Afton panicked. She could tell the truth and maybe production wouldn't care. Or, they'd give her job to the next producer in the lines of them wanting her spot who didn't have a personal history with the lead. She knew what the job market was like and after pissing off the crew on her last show, her reputation preceded her.

She was a run-of-the-mill producer whose job was to interview the women about their thoughts in tiny closets and awkward spaces. This was the largest production she'd ever been on; she still hadn't met everyone. She could keep her head down for a few weeks, show everyone what she was capable of, and keep the stable job she'd always wanted without Jonah ever knowing she was here.

Or, she could tell the truth and risk being jobless. When she'd weighed her options, there hadn't even been a real choice.

Now, not even an hour into filming, Jonah stands mere feet away. From here she can see the subtle highlights in his chestnut hair from the sun. The stubble on his cheeks already forming. The way his tailored navy suit perfectly hugs him; showing off the hint of his biceps and wide shoulders. She used to daydream about what he'd look like as an adult. Her dreams were nothing like this.

She covers her face with the clipboard as Jonah carries the woman to a plush armchair, setting her down gently. Afton scans her papers, trying to match the woman to a bio. Her long dark hair is in two French braids, a lavender bonnet hanging down her back. Her pioneer dress is more authentic than the Target ones. Did she sew it herself? The outfit makes it harder to match her to a profile, but Afton finally finds her.

Bea. 28, from Colorado. Founder of a non-profit that works to prevent foster youth from being trafficked. With that background and this dramatic entrance, there's no way Bea doesn't make it to the final four this season.

Jonah kneels next to the chair as a PA carries an ottoman over. They carefully prop Bea's ankle on top of it, and the medic approaches from the side, handing Jonah an icepack. He gingerly places it on her ankle.

"Does that help at all?" Jonah asks.

That voice; so familiar, yet foreign. Goosebumps crawl up Afton's arms. *Traitorous body.*

Bea winces. "Yes. I'm so embarrassed."

"Don't be. Who hasn't twisted an ankle while pulling a hand-cart solo?" Jonah asks Bea, stroking her wrist with his thumb.

Afton tears her eyes from Jonah, studying the other women's reactions. Some look concerned. But Rileigh and her new bff Maylee look downright furious from their spot on the couch. *Perfect.* She'd bet money one of them accuses Bea of twisting her ankle on purpose to get more attention from Jonah. She'll make sure when it happens, it's on camera.

Jonah finally leaves Bea's side and heads outside to meet the rest of the women. As chatter slowly starts up again, Afton pulls Rileigh and Maylee into the hall for an interview, along with Luke the cameraman. Rileigh is just as petty as she'd hoped, and Maylee easily follows Rileigh's lead.

When she returns, Bea and Emily have made friends with a redhead from Chicago named Tessa. Afton positions both of them on the arms of Bea's chair and has Bea recount how she tripped on a rock while pulling the handcart up the driveway. Then Afton chats with McKinlee who shares she's hoping to get her first kiss ever tonight.

When she's wrapped up, Chelsea has returned from outside. "This is going to be a good season. I can feel it."

"You say that every season," Afton teases.

Chelsea elbows her. "I do not. Last season I distinctly remember calling a dud from night one."

Someone on the headset warns that the host–Brian Tims, the retired football star with multiple Super-Bowl rings crowding his fingers– is about to enter the room.

"Alright ladies, Jonah's coming for his welcome speech. Grab a glass of something, look excited about whatever he says, and let's get the rest of this night started," Chelsea calls out.

PA's circle the woman, handing out glasses of champagne and sparkling cider. The women rearrange their dresses and ask their newfound friends to check for lipstick on their teeth. Afton fades into the corner, next to the French doors that lead to the back garden. Once everyone is settled with their drinks, Chelsea silently pulls Afton outside to a tiny tent on the side of the mansion. Inside monitors show everything happening in the great room. Right now Brian Tims is introducing himself and comparing the women's journey to love to winning a Super Bowl.

"Afton, meet Richard, my co-executive producer," Chelsea says, gesturing to a man sitting in the tent. Specks of hair dye are visible on his scalp and hairline. She's tempted to offer to help remove them with the vaseline in the emergency backpack she carries on sets, but he's already scowling. Best not to potentially embarrass him and piss him off further.

"First impressions of the women?" Richard asks, drumming his fingers on his thigh.

Jonah's voice floats through the tent and her eyes flit to the monitors. He's in the great room, champagne glass in hand. She turns so her back is to the screen, focusing solely on Richard who is shooting daggers at Chelsea for recommending her in the first place. Yet another obnoxious man she needs to prove herself to.

She starts listing off all the potential threads she'd like to explore: the drama over drinks, who might be catty, and McKinlee's first kiss. The longer she talks, the more Richard's expression clears. Then she stops.

Working on sets has made listening to multiple conversations second nature. From the constant chatter on her headsets, to zeroing in on the juiciest conversation in a group while also talking with co-workers. Normally she can file them Her decade of experience isn't enough to stop her from turning her back to Richard to face the monitors, needing to double check what she heard. Did Jonah say what she thought he did? She had to have heard him wrong.

Everyone else in the tent has gone silent too.

"Oh no," Chelsea breathes.

Richard's face has gone white.

Oh, Jonah *definitely* just said that.

CHAPTER TWO

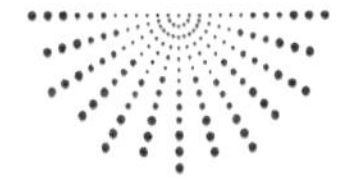

*J*onah Partridge was raised to endure to the end and it's the only reason he doesn't turn around and run. That, and his pushy sisters. The three of them were the ones who'd convinced him to accept the last-minute offer to be on *Ready for the Ring* in the first place.

"A once-in-a-lifetime opportunity is still a once-in-a-lifetime opportunity," Sarah had said.

"Even if you are their second choice," Ruth had added.

"He probably wasn't even their second choice. I bet he was the only one who could leave work on such short notice and they assumed he doesn't have a substance abuse problem," Naomi finished.

If he turns around and runs home now, the three of them will roast him within an inch of his life. He has quite a few things he'd like to do before dying, so he stays put in the front of the room. The champagne glass trembles between his fingers and his stomach churns. The features of the thirty women sitting across from him all blend together.

He closes his eyes to clear away the swimming faces. When

he'd been a contestant on the show a year ago, he'd thought night one was stressful. How naive he'd been. All he'd had to worry about then was how to stand out in a crowd of handsome men while sitting around. Now, his brain is mush from making small talk with thirty strangers while taking directions on how to do the next intro better. How is he supposed to get to know each of these women and decide who to send home already with said mush brain?

He opens his eyes and the women are still there. All of them stepped away from their lives to meet *him*. A regular guy who gets roasted by his sisters and whose knees ache from standing too long in dress shoes. Quite a few of them came here specifically for who they *think* he is. A version of him that doesn't exist anymore.

The room starts to spin again. If he doesn't relax, he's going to pass out. *Just give the easy speech.* The one where he simply invites everyone to go on this journey to find love with him. He knows what he's looking for in a partner, and can easily weed out those the truth will bother. There's no need for dramatic declarations tonight.

Brian Tims lays a supportive hand on Jonah's shoulder. When they met, Brian likened himself to a sherpa here to guide Jonah up the Everest that is finding a wife. Jonah never liked him as a player, but right now his heavy hand weighed down with rings is the only thing grounding him.

"Speak from the heart. If you mess up, you can try again until we get it right," he murmurs in Jonah's ear.

He'll have multiple chances. Even if production doesn't approve of his first attempt, he can try again, but the women won't forget what was said. He exhales shakily, forcing a careful smile as he surveys the room.

"Thank you all for being here. This is an incredible group of women, and I'm genuinely excited to get to know you all more.

Before we begin, I need to be honest with you. Honesty is something I value, along with the ability to make informed choices."

He sucks in a deep breath, trying desperately to calm his racing heart. It's good they took his smartwatch because it'd be ordering him to seek medical attention.

"When I was on *Ready for the Ring* over a year ago, I became known as the Mormon boy sobbing in the car about never being someone's first choice. I've spent the last year working through past hurts and hangups and realized what's truly important to me. At a young age I learned time is never promised. I want to spend the time I'm given with people I love, exploring this world we're lucky enough to live in."

He's talking too fast, but he's almost finished. "Your time is equally important to me. Since it was a large part of my identity previously, it's only fair to let you know I am no longer a member of the Church of Jesus Christ of Latter-Day Saints."

The women had been quiet, but crew members were whispering and walking throughout the house. Now, everything goes deafeningly silent. Women look back and forth among each other. Some cover their mouths with their hands. One is… crying? He digs deep, trying to dredge up sympathy for her. He can't find any. His personal faith journey is not worthy of tears from a stranger.

"I know some of you came here hoping you'd find a partner who checked that box, so I want to be straightforward from the start. Other than that, I'm the same Jonah. I still love emo music. I prefer swimming in the ocean over a pool. I'm obsessed with my dog, Millie, and I'd do anything for my little sisters. If my faith is a dealbreaker for you, please be honest and don't waste either of our time. Time is a gift and I'm looking forward to spending mine getting to know you all, and hopefully finding my future wife."

Whatever's been squeezing his chest loosens. It's out there. If they kick him off the show and recast, he doesn't care. He's lost worse from confessing before, and if he's going to go on this journey, it'll be as his authentic self.

"How do you feel about mixed-faith relationships?" Bea finally asks, breaking the silence.

He smiles at her. "I'm entirely open to it. I can respect and support someone else in their faith, if they're willing to respect and support mine. I'm not a missionary project though. Please don't waste both of our time by thinking you can convert me back."

Bea nods. Even though she'd been injured, she'd made him laugh the entire time he'd carried her. If she chooses to go home, he'll be bummed, but understands. Mixed-faith marriages have their own struggles with boundaries that have to be constantly renegotiated. He's watched his best friend, Henry, navigate his. He and his wife are happy now, but it took years of work.

"What's a member of the church of, whatever you just said?" Emily asks from where she's perched on the arm of the couch. She'd brought him a gold medal to wear, referencing his worry that he'd never be someone's first choice, saying that he was hers.

"I'm no longer Mormon," Jonah clarifies.

"That doesn't bother me," Emily says.

Several other women murmur in agreement.

Maybe he panicked for nothing. He'd spent the last year mourning the life he'd missed out on. The people he'd written off because there was no chance of being sealed for eternity. The things he'd believed with his whole heart were necessary to be a good person, and the hurt he'd inflicted because of it. He learned the constant policing of his thoughts and need to confess was actually OCD and attended therapy. He was climbing out of that fog of anger, grief, and regret that comes from feeling like you've wasted the best years of your life. He'd decided he was going to live life to the fullest when he was approached by the show. He doesn't believe in signs, but it was the closest thing to one he'd had in a while.

Production reassured him they understood the change and they wouldn't advertise him as the Mormon Fiancé-to-be. Talking about his beliefs was fine; they only asked that he not make grand declarations that might offend viewers. That sounded reasonable; what were the odds they'd get more than a couple actively believing Mormons applying for the show, especially when he was the replacement lead?

Turns out, they were high. Woman after woman thanked him for giving them the opportunity to come on the show to date a fellow member.

Brian Tims reappears, clapping Jonah on the shoulder. "Thank you for being vulnerable and sharing that. Let's take a quick break before continuing on with our evening." Brian leaves his hand on Jonah's shoulder as he leads him out of the room to Barb, Jonah's personal producer. Her entire job is managing him. She doesn't smile much, but she's kind with a dry sense of humor. Her expression is blank now as she leads him down the halls of the mansion to an office.

Inside the two executive producers, Richard and Chelsea, wait. Richard is scowling with crossed arms while Chelsea leans against the wall. Barb stays next to Jonah, fiddling with her wedding band. Richard and Chelsea are in charge of the day to day operations. If they're waiting, who's coming? The head of the entire network?

The door finally opens and an asian woman and white man walk in, Hannah and Karl. He can't remember their job titles, but knows they're a level above executive producers, and they're who extended his invitation to the show. Karl had talked Jonah through all his worries on a video call. Now, Karl's face is red all the way up to his bald spot, while Hannah's expression is unreadable. Barb tenses slightly next to him.

"What was that?" Karl spits.

"You promised me I wasn't going to be the Mormon Fiancé-to-be when I agreed to the show. It's obvious from the women you cast, and their entrances, that was a lie."

Chelsea's mouth opens in an o, her eyebrows raising. Richard and Hannah both gape at Karl. Was Karl the only one who knew about this?

"I didn't promise anything and I can't change people's preconceived notions of who you are," Karl sputters.

"Which is why I decided to let everyone know from the get go. You said this was my journey; this is how I want to do it."

That was the wrong thing to say. Hannah raises a brow while both Richard and Karl's faces darken. Although in Richard's case, it might be hair dye running down from his hairline.

"We can easily recast you. I have a whole list of men who would love to be in your shoes right now," Karl says.

So that's it. He's already done. At least he can say he didn't run.

"Hold on," Chelsea says. "Only thirteen of the women identified as Mormon. That's less than half the cast. Religious affiliations have drastically changed post-pandemic, and people are talking about it. Not even all the women on *Secret Lives of Mormon Wives* are practicing Mormons. You'd be losing out on an opportunity for a unique audience here."

Chelsea had only been a producer last time he was on the show and they'd hardly interacted. Why is she sticking up for him now?

"How do you know all this?" Karl asks.

"My best friend is a former Mormon. We have weird late-night discussions."

Hannah cocks her head, studying Chelsea.

Karl grumbles. "We can't get rid of half the women on night one. I doubt they'll want to stay after your little declaration."

Jonah can't blame them. Since he's not an active member in good standing, he isn't eligible to be married in the temple—the pinnacle of being Mormon. Many people can't understand why having different religious beliefs could be such a dealbreaker. With the idea of an eternity spent alone on the line, it's everything.

Chelsea moves out into the hallway, talking into her headset. Her voice is too low to eavesdrop, but she comes right back.

"Only three of the women want to leave because of what Jonah said. The rest are willing to give him a chance," Chelsea says with a smirk.

Karl glances between Hannah, Chelsea, and Richard. "What do you think?" he finally asks.

Richard clears his throat. "If we're already this far off track, what's next?"

Chelsea scoffs. "This is reality tv. You're supposed to be able to roll with anything."

"Not from the *lead*," Richard says.

Chelsea faces Hannah. "We know recasting doesn't work well, and if only three women want to leave, that's great. This has the potential to be the most interesting season yet, which we desperately need."

Hannah presses her lips together. "Let's chat," she finally says, gesturing for Karl to follow her into the hall.

"Thank you," Jonah says to Chelsea once the door closes.

"Don't thank her yet," Richard mumbles.

Chelsea rolls her eyes before turning back to Jonah. "Don't make me regret it."

"You're mad because your idea sucked. Get over yourself," Hannah says firmly from the hall.

Chelsea barely stifles a laugh and the corner of Barb's mouth twitches upward. Whatever happens next will make a great story for his family. They're fascinated with all things behind the scenes of *Ready for the Ring* after years of watching the show religiously.

Afton would be too.

He shudders, shoving the thought away.

The door flies open and Karl storms in, getting so close Jonah can see his untrimmed nose hairs.

"This was your one thing for the season. From now on, you obey. There will be no hopping fences to run away, or refusing to choose someone. If we want to keep the two worst women on for drama, you ask how long? If we decide to bring a contestant you sent home back, you welcome her with conflicted arms. Can you agree to that? If not, I'm recasting you and saving all our time."

Barb steps forward, crowding Karl. Karl glares at her, then takes the tiniest step back.

There's no way to predict the future, but he shouldn't need another thing. Now that the truth is out there, he plans to fully trust the process of this journey. He has Barb, Chelsea, and Hannah on his side; at least for now. There are women in that room he wants the chance to know, and he's not a quitter.

"Yes, I can."

"You let middle schoolers look through your dating profile as a reward?"

Tessa laughs, her freckled face scrunching adorably. "By the end of the school year, you have to get creative to keep their attention. My students were so disgusted with the options; they nominated me for the show."

"That's a lot of pressure, trying to compete with the fine men of…"

"Hinge," Tessa says.

"Hinge in Chicago."

"I have faith you can handle it." Her gaze drags down to his lips, then slowly back to his eyes.

His heart speeds up. Four women kissed him right after walking out of the limo, saying they wanted to be his first of the evening. Two more in the garden used this exact move. Here with Tessa will be the first kiss *he's* initiating tonight. Leaning in feels natural instead of expected.

"Can I steal you for a moment?" a voice asks.

He startles. Tessa's cheeks go pink, and she immediately stands up, making room for the new girl. Jonah glances over at Barb, silently questioning. The producers decide who gets time with him. It's a mixture of those with interesting stories and those he might actually have chemistry with. Why did they let this woman interrupt his almost kiss with Tessa?

Barb's only answer is a shrug.

He focuses on the new woman in front of him, white with strawberry blonde hair and piercing blue eyes. She settles down on the stone bench, fiddling with a loose thread on her dress. If she wanted to interrupt him, she could at least say something.

"Remind me of your name again?" he finally asks.

"McKinlee. You two were about to kiss, weren't you? I'm so sorry. It took everything in me to walk over here, so once I started there was no stopping. Do you want me to get Tessa back?"

His annoyance lessens. McKinlee seems young, she can't be over twenty-five. Why did they choose to cast her? Do they genuinely think they could be a couple? Or is there another reason?

"It's all good. Where are you from?"

"Sandy, Utah. What about you?"

"I moved to Orem when I was eleven—"

He's cut off by McKinlee shoving her face at him, her teeth clinking against his own. The coppery tang of blood fills his mouth as she pulls away.

"I'm so sorry!" McKinlee gasps.

"I'm fine. No big deal."

"That was my first kiss," McKinlee says, starting to full-on sob. Barb appears with tissues, ready for his every need. Jonah hands one to McKinlee before pressing another to his lip. How can it be bleeding this much?

A memory surfaces. The creak of swings. Snow biting against his ankles. Another brush of lips. Flying backward, pain, then blood. He chuckles.

"Don't laugh at me," McKinlee cries.

"I'm not laughing at you, promise. My first kiss was worse than this."

"How?" she sniffs.

"We were sitting on swings and I was so surprised I ended up flying backward and cutting my head."

The corner of McKinlee's mouth twitches.

"We'll have to make a bloody first kisses club," he jokes.

She lets out a single breathy laugh. "I'll make matching bracelets."

"I can't wait." He removes his tissue and licks his lip. It's stopped bleeding. "Do you want a redo?" If this is her first kiss, she deserves more than tears and blood.

She gives the tiniest of nods. Jonah cups her face with one hand, partially to make sure they don't slam into each other again. Then he leans in slowly, stopping a hairsbreadth away, eyes flicking to hers.

"Still okay?" he whispers.

"Mhmm."

He presses his lips to hers softly, lingering for a moment before pulling away. It's the same as the rest of his kisses tonight, lacking that spark. It's because he barely knows these women, it's past midnight, and he's emotionally exhausted. Right?

McKinlee presses her fingers to her lips before getting up from the bench without a word.

The night drags on and he laughs, kisses, and stumbles through conversation after conversation. He barely has time to analyze his feelings before jumping into the next encounter. Now it's 2AM and time to make what could potentially be the most important decisions of his life—who to send home. It would be impossible if it weren't for Chelsea and two other producers furiously taking notes of his interactions with everyone. It reminds him of being in the temple and the workers—dressed all in white—there to help you through the ceremonies. Here his helpers are all in black with headsets.

As Barb leads him back to the mansion, someone approaches from the french doors.

"I couldn't let you go without doing this," Tessa says, looking up at him. The lights strung through the greenery illuminate the glitter on her cheeks as she comes closer. When their chests are inches apart, she steps up on her tiptoes, wrapping her hands around his neck, her eyes searching his for permission. He closes the distance between their mouths in answer.

This.

This was what he came here for. This instant chemistry with someone. He moves his mouth against hers, drinking her in.

Tessa finally pulls away, smiling up at him.

"Wow," she breathes, eyes glittering.

"Wow."

She giggles and presses one last quick kiss to his lips before disappearing back into the mansion.

Barb reappears next to him. "Glad that worked out. Let's go eat."

Eat and decide who's going home. His stomach twists for the millionth time tonight. They turn down a hallway and a producer in black turns toward him. Brown eyes he knows better than his own stare back.

No. It can't be.

He stumbles a step, bumping into a vase. It topples off the table and he barely catches it before it hits the floor. Once he's placed it safely back on the end table, he searches for the woman. She's long gone.

Rubbing hands over his eyes, he tries to picture her face again. She'd had thick, black-framed glasses, and brown eyes. Were they *those* eyes? The harder he pushes, the more her features swim, morphing with the thirty other women he met tonight.

It can't have been her. He's just tired. His therapist told him the harder you try to resist a thought, the more it comes up. He must have shoved his memories of her earlier down so hard he's hallucinating. It makes sense she's on his mind; they grew up watching the show together. She was the person he thought he'd spend his life with. He simply pasted her features on the first stranger he saw with the same color of eyes.

He needs to get through the promise ring ceremony where he hands each woman who's staying an adjustable promise ring to wear for the week. Then he can finally sleep. After a good eight hours he'll be clear headed and the memories will stop. He'll focus solely on the present. This is his chance to find the person he wants to spend his life with. He won't let the past get in the way, again.

CHAPTER THREE

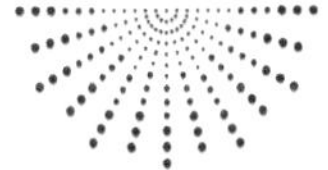

TWENTY-TWO YEARS AGO

"You're not a girl," Afton said, not bothering to hide her disappointment.

The boy with messy brown hair standing across the driveway from her frowned.

Afton's dad nudged her with his elbow, a silent warning to be quiet. She couldn't help it. She'd watched eagerly as twin girls with lopsided pigtails were unloaded from a minivan. They looked to be five. An eight-year-old girl climbed out next. The last person to emerge from the van was a boy the same height as her.

She didn't want a boy to move here. Her house was stuffed full of them. They were the reason she'd thought hiding a whoopee cushion on her best friend's chair would be met with laughter. People had laughed all right, but her best friend had cried in embarrassment. Now her former best friend, along with all the other girls in their class, were shunning Afton. When she dared approach the boys, they'd screamed "cooties" at her and thrown gravel.

Afton had prayed day and night for weeks, begging God for

a new girl to move in. One who would like Afton and think the other girls were mean. When her dad announced a new girl her age was moving into the house down the street, she knew her prayers had been answered.

God and her dad had both lied.

A blonde-haired woman and dark-haired man appeared behind the three girls and boy on the driveway.

"I'm Carrie Partridge, and this is my husband, James. These are our kids Jonah, Sarah, Ruth, and Naomi," the woman said.

Brother and Sister Partridge Afton reminded herself. That's what she was supposed to call them.

Afton's dad shook hands with the Partridges before introducing them. "This is my son Dan, he's thirteen. This is Afton, she's eleven. We have three other boys at home."

Sister Partridge beamed, focusing on Afton. "Afton, you and Jonah are the same age." She pushed a furiously blinking Jonah toward her. Everyone stared at her, waiting for a response. Her dad nudged her with his elbow again.

"Hi," she said quietly.

"We'll have to have a playdate," Sister Partridge said.

Jonah rolled his eyes at the word playdate. Afton started to smile, then remembered that Jonah wasn't her friend. He'd probably join the rest of the boys yelling cooties at her, so why waste her time?

More fathers and sons started filing out of their homes, coming to help the Partridges move in. Afton was the only girl here. Normally she didn't help with moves, but she'd come in hopes of meeting her new best friend. Which wasn't happening. No one was paying attention to her so she could sneak back...

Sister Partridge handed Afton a box. "Can you take this upstairs to Jonah's room? He'll show you which one it is."

The box was small, but surprisingly heavy. Afton followed Jonah up the stairs of the house to an empty room, almost dropping the box when she got there. Then she followed Jonah back to the moving truck. To her dismay, the only boxes that she was strong enough to carry were more of these tiny ones labeled JONAH.

After her fourth silent trip up the stairs with the tiny boxes, she couldn't stay quiet anymore.

"What's in these?"

Jonah studied her. "Books," he finally answered.

She eyed the eight boxes they'd brought up. "What kinds of books?"

"Ones about witches, wizards, and dragons."

Her eyes went flared. "You're allowed to read about those things?"

His thick eyebrows pulled together. "Why wouldn't I be?"

Afton shifted her weight from foot to foot. "My mom doesn't let me read anything that's about witchcraft."

"Why?"

"The bible says it's against the church."

He scrunched his forehead. "My parents have never said that, and my dad is a college professor."

What did being a professor have to do with reading the bible? She was too embarrassed to ask.

The top flap of the box she'd carried was starting to open. She bent down to close it, then paused, intrigued by the sliver of dark blue peeking out. She peeled the flap back, revealing a blue cover with a dragon on it. Its single blue eye studied her. She ran a hand over the cover, loving the contrast between the textured paper and the gold foil. She traced each letter of the title with her fingertip. *Eragon.*

"The bible doesn't say anything about dragons, does it?" Jonah asked.

She startled, momentarily forgetting where she was. "I don't think so."

"Maybe you should read that one," he pointed.

Afton studied the blue dragon longingly. "It's a big book. I don't know if my mom will have time to read it first." Her mom pre-read all of Afton's library books. With the new baby, she was always busy.

"My parents read it, and they didn't think there was anything bad in it."

She clasped her hands together. "Really?" If Brother and Sister Partridge told her mom there was nothing wrong with the book, then her mom would have to let her read it, right? She practically bounced down the stairs to grab another box of Jonah's belongings.

She beat him to his room this time, setting the new box next to the one with the book. She didn't realize she'd been standing there, staring, until Jonah dropped a heavy box, making her jump. Wordlessly, he crossed the room and grabbed the book from the box. She bit her cheek. He was going to hide it, just like her brothers whenever there was something she wanted. She couldn't blame Jonah; she was being a total weirdo standing here staring at his things.

He stood up and pressed the book into her hands.

"You can read it right now if you want. I'll keep moving boxes."

"What?"

"You can read it. If you want. You don't have to…"

"I want to," she interrupted.

"Go for it," he said before heading back down the stairs.

Afton clutched the book to her chest, waiting for the Holy Spirit to warn her. She'd felt the warm tingling of it when doing something nice for her brothers, and the sickening pit in her stomach when she did something wrong. If reading this was truly wrong, it was the Holy Spirit's job to guide her.

All she felt was excitement. She settled on the floor in an empty corner, then opened the book.

Jonah stopped carrying in boxes at some point, moving onto hanging clothes in his closet. She offered to help him, but he waved her off. She kept reading; moving corners whenever she was in his way.

"Where are you?" he asked while putting sheets on his mattress lying on the floor.

"The egg just hatched."

"Keep going, it's about to get really exciting."

Afton's dad yelled up the stairs for her just as Eragon had to flee with Saphira and Brom. Reluctantly, she set the book down before going to the top of the stairs. Brother and Sister Partridge stood next to her dad at the bottom.

"She's helping me put my things away. Can she stay for dinner?" Jonah asked.

"Of course," Sister Partridge smiled.

"We don't want to intrude, it's your first day here," her dad said, flaring his eyes dramatically in silent warning. That look was usually reserved for when her brothers were rowdy in public. Head hung, she started toward him.

"We're ordering pizza; it's not an intrusion. Jonah's friends are always welcome," Sister Partridge said.

Afton's dad looked between Afton and Jonah again. She tried not to look too hopeful. If he saw how much she wanted to stay, would he take it away?

"Come home right after dinner. And leave his bedroom door open," he added.

Jonah's parents both frowned.

"Of course," Afton said, hardly believing her luck.

Her dad left, and Jonah and Afton immediately ran back to his room. She kept reading, Jonah peeking at the pages over her shoulder while arranging his bookshelf.

"A fellow fantasy nerd?" Brother Partridge asked from the doorway a bit later.

Afton blinked up to him. Adults didn't talk to her often, not when her older brother the basketball star existed. "This is the first one I've read."

"Hopefully the first of many," Brother Partridge smiled.

Afton carefully placed the book on Jonah's bookshelf when dinner was ready. Brother Partridge was dishing the pizza on paper plates. Sister Partridge walked in from outside, giving him a kiss on the cheek, and he handed her a plate as well. Afton couldn't think of one time her dad had helped with dinner. Or kissed her mom in front of them. She grabbed her pizza and settled next to Jonah on a wooden bench. His younger sisters fidgeted on the other side of the table.

"Thank you for inviting me Brother and Sister Partridge," Afton said, remembering her manners.

Sister Partridge smiled at her. "You can call me Carrie. I hate being called Sister Partridge."

"Call me James," Brother Partridge added.

What was she supposed to do? Call them by what she was taught to, or what they asked her to? She was glad her dad wasn't here.

"Mom, is it against the church to read about witchcraft?" Jonah asked.

Sister Partridge/Carrie frowned. "There's a verse in the bible that says to stay away from witchcraft, and there are some evangelical churches that think that means in all forms, even media. But no, the prophet has never said you can't read about it."

"There's actually quite a bit of fantasy that teaches about Christ. *The Lion, the Witch, and the Wardrobe* for example is a straight allegory. You could make the argument for *Lord of the Rings*, or Harry Potter as well. Stories are helpful tools to help us better understand what the Savior did for us," Brother Partridge/James said.

"How do you know about all of this?" Afton asked.

Sister Partridge/Carrie smiled again. "James is a college professor so that's all he thinks about. I love to read too. It opens doorways and gives perspectives we'll never experience otherwise."

The way they talked about reading was beautiful.

"I wish my parents liked to read," Afton said solemnly. "All my dad does is watch sports and play them with my brothers."

"What about your mom?" Sister Partridge/Carrie asked.

"She's just a mom."

Sister Partridge/Carrie frowned. "No one is just a mom. What does she like to do for fun?"

Afton had to think about it. "She's an amazing singer. Her dream is to be in the Mormon Tabernacle Choir one day. She used to teach voice lessons, but she doesn't anymore because she's so busy with all my brothers."

Sister Partridge/Carrie's face fell before she pasted the smile back on. "I look forward to meeting her."

Afton froze. "Please don't tell them about the book."

Jonah's parents studied her. "What do you mean?"

Afton considered lying. The Spirit hit her like a brick, unease squeezing her chest. She looked at her lap.

"I'm not supposed to read books my mom hasn't read. Or books about witchcraft. But she's so busy with the baby, she'll never have time to read this one." Afton's eyes started welling up with unshed tears. "Maybe you could tell her what you told me earlier, about the Bible."

Jonah's parents were quiet for a long moment. "You read books at school, right? In class? Does your mom read all of those?" Sister Partridge/Carrie asked slowly.

Afton frowned. "No."

"We could talk to her. But none of us really know what you read at school," Sister Partridge/Carrie said slowly.

"Carrie," Brother Partridge/James said, resting his arm on the back of her chair.

"What? I'm simply pointing out facts," Sister Partridge/Carrie said with a wink.

All weekend Afton couldn't stop thinking about the book and the Partridges. She desperately wanted to know what happened next, and why the Partridges smiled so much. They were so different from all the other families she knew. She was bummed when Sister Partridge/Carrie didn't talk to her mom at church, telling her about the book.

On Monday, she was ecstatic to find Jonah was in her class. She volunteered to be his desk buddy and show him around the building. Before lunch, she found *Eragon* shoved inside her desk. Jonah pretended not to know how it got there. That's when she figured it out. Sister Partridge/Carrie wasn't going to talk to Afton's mom. That's why she'd mentioned school. She sat under a tree with Jonah at recess, both of them absorbed in their own books.

God did work in mysterious ways. Maybe it wasn't so bad that Jonah was a boy after all.

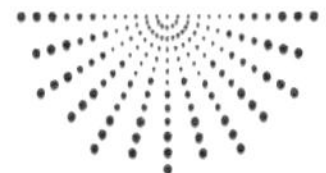

CHAPTER FOUR

"For the first group date, we've decided to go with Jello wrestling," Karl announces.

"Another one of Afton's ideas," Chelsea interjects.

Richard rolls his eyes and a few PAs exchange looks.

Afton kicks Chelsea's foot under the table, glaring at her. Chelsea's already mentioned the ingenuity of the soda bar and the instant drama it created between the women who drank and didn't. Then she'd gotten Karl to begrudgingly acknowledge that if Afton hadn't been there, they would have been in deep shit having to recast so many women, or find a new lead that those same women wouldn't be interested in due to the religious differences.

On any other day she'd be thankful to have someone who had her back, making sure she was recognized for her contributions. Especially with someone as revered as Hannah Choi in the room. Hannah Choi was the brains behind multiple hit shows and beyond connected. A good word from her could erase Afton's reputation for causing problems. After her run-in with Jonah in the hall last night though, the last thing Afton wants is attention.

She'd barely slept before this meeting, playing the moment over and over. Had there been enough time for him to recognize her? Was she even recognizable now with her thick glasses, shorter hair, and woman's body? *Hello hips and slower metabolism.* She'd paced her room, debating whether to even come back to set today. With two run-ins on night one alone, there was no way she was going to be able to hide from Jonah for a whole season.

She'd fully decided to quit while she was ahead, until she fought with Indeed to upload her resume, only to be forced to enter every. single. item. by hand. And then she learned that half the jobs posted there weren't even real. The minuscule chance she wasn't getting fired today and wouldn't have to apply for jobs was worth coming and facing the wrath of the network and their lawyers.

So far, so good. But every time the door opened, she panicked, thinking it was someone coming to out her. Jonah could realize who she was at any moment, and the suspense was eating her alive.

"Here's a tentative schedule for the rest of the season. Obviously, there could be weather delays, but we should wrap up filming in Costa Rica the last week of October," Karl says, passing a stack of paper around the table with locations and dates printed on it. She scans them.

Mexico City, Mexico (September 22nd-September 29th)
Salt Lake City, Utah (September 30th-October 6th)
Toronto, Canada (October 7th-12th)
Family Visits (TBD) (October 13th-October 20th)
Papagayo Peninsula, Costa Rica (October 21st-25th)
She stares at the dates, the room around her completely

disappearing. She hasn't believed in signs in over a decade, but today might change that.

"You good there?" Chelsea asks, waving her fingers in front of Afton's face.

Afton startles, dropping the paper covered in finger sized divots from gripping it too hard. The meeting room cleared out while she was busy disassociating.

"I have to quit."

"Excuse me?"

"I can't do this."

"Did you not sit through the same meeting I did? Where Hannah, woman of few compliments, praised you twice? And Karl even gave a begrudging grunt of recognition?"

"This is a sign I need to leave," Afton says, waving the paper in Chelsea's face.

"Because we're going to Salt Lake City? Your family lives an hour away."

"Utah is a small world. A friend of a friend will see us at the airport and they'll call my parents and they'll appear."

Or, someone will recognize her with Jonah and post about it online. Both options are equally bad.

Chelsea huffs. "Seriously?"

"We're starting family visits the day of Naya's baby shower. I can't miss that; her family will kill me."

Her best friend since middle school, Naya, had specifically planned her baby shower for when she'd be 38 weeks pregnant. Naya's family begged her to move it in case the baby came early, but she wouldn't budge. Why? Because Naya wanted Afton there and that's when she would be returning from filming off the coast of Spain. Everything *would* have been fine, if Afton hadn't gotten herself fired and ended up in this mess.

"It's a baby shower, not a wedding. Who cares?"

"Sadie's flying in. I can't miss it." Sadie was the other part of their friendship trio, and Afton hadn't seen her in years.

Chelsea gapes. "For the shower? You can't even meet the baby yet. We'll be back once the baby is here and you'll have weeks to be there as much as you want."

To outsiders it might seem like simply missing a party. But thanks to work she'd missed Naya's engagement and bachelorette parties, along with Sadie's death-to-her-twenties party. The only reason she'd made it to Sadie's law school graduation and Naya's wedding was thanks to red-eye flights. Afton didn't want to spend another night in an uncomfortable airport chair, looking at everyone else's pictures of the celebration. Imagining what the food tasted like, the sound of their laughter. She wanted to *be* there. She'd missed out on so many things for work, with what to show for it?

"Do they come to any of your parties?" Chelsea asks.

Afton snorts. "I haven't thrown any."

"That's the true crime here. You need to throw one."

"Why? The only people I'd invite would be you, Naya, and Sadie."

Chelsea frowns. "Another problem. You need to make more friends."

"That requires being somewhere for more than a few weeks. Kind of hard with our jobs."

"You're supposed to make friends with the crew, dumbass. They're the ones going everywhere with you."

"I do, but then we're hardly on the same shows after."

Chelsea stands abruptly, pulling Afton up from her chair and outside the garage-turned-meeting-area. Chelsea gestures dramatically to the grounds. The infamous mansion that now houses all the contestants. The stone outdoor patio filled with benches, exotic plants and flowers. The shimmering pool surrounded by chaise lounges.

"This is the beginning of your next chapter. You're working on your dream show; you won't have to constantly be hustling. You'll make good friends here and we'll throw parties for them all to attend."

Except, Afton won't be here for a long time. Because her original plan of hiding from Jonah is going to fail, or her heart will from the constant stress.

Afton's phone starts ringing. When she sees who's calling, she's dizzy. It's her mom.

"She knows," Afton hisses.

"You know she can't hear unless you accept, right?" Chelsea asks at a normal volume, but starts chewing on her lip nervously. Even Chelsea knows this is abnormal.

"That's my third sign from the universe. I have to quit."

The phone stops ringing. Afton waits for the voicemail notification and when it doesn't come, she opens her text conversation with her mom. The last message was from three months ago, a picture of a relative she'd never met in a casket. You know, the absolutely essential things your estranged daughter wants to see. The three dots bounce across the screen.

MOM

Have you talked to your brother?

Which one? Mysterious, but not an emergency. If it was, the message would say something more provocative to make sure she'd call right away. She'll deal with it later.

"Everyone okay?" Chelsea asks.

"As far as I can tell." Afton blows out a breath, trying to shake off the message. The sun glints off the pool in the distance. "What's the policy on us dipping our feet in the hot tub before everyone starts making out in it?"

"Very pro."

Chelsea expertly removes the cover on the tub and turns on

the jets. The two of them perch on the edge, clinking their water bottles. The hot water is marvelous and Afton relaxes for the first time in weeks.

"Want to catch up on Monday Night RAW?" Chelsea asks, pulling out her phone.

"Duh."

In college Chelsea and Afton had bonded over their love of reality TV. When you work in the industry though, it's no fun to watch. So they'd switched over to wrestling. It has the same dramatic storylines with the fun of costumes, music, and smashing tables. The best part of wrestling is Afton has absolutely no idea how they produce it. How do they decide who gets to win each match? Or to choreograph them so no one gets hurt week after week? She loves not knowing.

"I could do that," Chelsea says as one of the women does a power-bomb.

"You say that every week."

"This time I mean it. Let me try."

Afton hears something and pauses the show. It's the sound of trickling water.

"Something's leaking."

Chelsea listens, and they both climb out of the hot tub. They inspect every side, but there's no water on the ground besides their wet footprints on the stone. The sound isn't coming from the pool, but from somewhere below them. They follow a path of stone steps surrounded by palm trees and agave plants that leads down a gently sloping hill. With each step down, the sound of water grows louder. At the bottom of the hill, the path veers to the left, a wall of pampas grass blocking their view. The sound is coming from behind it.

"If there's a body over there, do you think they'll let us play ourselves in the Dateline re-enactment?" Chelsea asks.

Afton laughs. "We're on the wrong network for that."

Together they walk past the grass. Afton freezes. There's not a body, but an outdoor shower that's currently on. There's a camera crew positioned in front of it...

With Jonah inside.

At least he's wearing swim trunks. These aren't the trunks of their youth, the long ones that covered his knees and would balloon around his legs in the water. No, he's wearing the current style, tight fitting and tiny. If it weren't for the water repelling fabric, Afton would assume they were boxers.

"Stop staring directly at the camera. Close your eyes and run your hand through your hair," Richard yells to Jonah.

Threaded between her worries last night were questions about him. What caused him to leave the church after all this time? How did his family take it? How is he when there isn't a camera pointed at him? What did the rest of him look like under that tailored suit?

Tearing her gaze from Jonah's muscular legs, drifting past his defined chest, she has the answer to one of her questions. Her eyes finally meet his face. He's gawking at her, droplets of water falling into his open mouth. His eyes lock on hers, burning into her soul.

She spins and sprints back up the hill, Chelsea calling after her.

CHAPTER FIVE

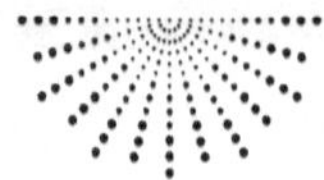

*A*ll Jonah did was ask to go for a midafternoon run. After the whirlwind of the night before, he needed to clear his mind. Barb had agreed, on one condition. That's how he'd found himself hosing off in the outdoor shower with a camera crew. Richard was shouting directions on how to run his hands through his hair while simultaneously flexing.

He could practically hear the squeals and gagging noises his sisters would make back home when they finally saw this footage. The little old ladies from his hometown church might watch and ogle him. His boss might see this. Jonah knows America will discuss his sex life and whether he's a loud kisser. He draws the line at this.

He breaks the first rule of shower thirst traps and opens his eyes to yell that he's done. That's when he hears the laugh. His entire body goes cold despite the hot water pouring down. He'd recognize that laugh anywhere. It was the laugh of terrible dad jokes, surprise rain storms, spilled bowls of popcorn. Awkward kisses, avoidable sunburns, interlaced fingers. It was a sound he thought would fuel him through the ups and downs of life. A sound he'd lost and never expected to hear again.

He swipes at his eyes to see better. The same crew members are staring back at him, none of them so much as smiling. Where did the laugh come from? Did he hallucinate that too? He's been in the heat too long; he needs to sit down. He's reaching for the tap when Chelsea and another producer appear on the path.

He scans the woman. She's wearing thick black framed glasses. Her hair is up in a bun, little pieces falling out on the sides. A golden nose ring glints in the sun. Her black tank and bike shorts hug her curves.

The woman is a stranger, and not. She's older. She's seen, learned, and lived through things he has no idea about. But it's Afton. He knows those eyes, the ones she'd always called mud brown, but are actually dozens of shades of brown and gold, the mixture mimicking scales. They were home, and he'd been trying to forget them for over a decade.

Now they were here, staring at him while he filmed a thirst trap for cable television.

Afton's eyes lock on his and someone must have thrown a toaster in the shower. It's the only way to explain the current of electricity that shoots through him. Her eyes widen before she bolts in the opposite direction, erasing any shred of doubt it's her. Afton is here, and she's running as far as she can.

Again.

He can't get out of the shower fast enough. Everyone is talking all at once but he can't understand them over the pounding in his ears. His legs are unsteady and he braces against the outer shower wall as he passes a towel over his wet skin. He hasn't seen Afton in fifteen years. He's dreamed of running into her, preferably when he was put together. Calm, cool, collected. Not while posing in the shower.

These shows always pulls tricks. He'd expected them to bring his ex from *Ready for the Ring* since she'd recently broken up with her fiancé and moved to California. The number of videos he's tagged in daily asking if the two of them are going to meet up again is obnoxious. But Afton? His first love? How had they found her? The number of times he checked social media for accounts in her name, and then googled Afton Hayes theater, Afton Hayes musicals, Afton Hayes California, Afton Hayes obituary, was embarrassing.

Had she heard that he was going to be on the show and reached out? Did she want to reconnect with him now as an adult? He hadn't been hard to find through the years. His mom still mailed Christmas cards to her parents. His sister Sarah is TikTok famous and would have gladly passed on a message.

Is she here for fame?

He's going to be sick. How could they be so cruel to dangle her in front of him, now? When he's finally ready to step into his future?

"You okay?" Barb asks, crouching down next to him to look in his eyes. She presses her wrist to his forehead.

"Got dizzy for a second there, but I'm fine now," he says.

She purses her lips. "They kept you in that hot water for way too long. Take the rest of the day and rest up for tomorrow." She hands him another towel and walks him back to his casita. She checks that his fridge is still stocked with water and the snacks have been refilled.

"Radio if you need anything. I mean anything," Barb says.

"I'm feeling better now. Don't worry about me," he lies. It must be convincing enough because Barb finally leaves.

He gets dressed in a hurry, throwing on one of the collared shirts wardrobe provided him with. It's tighter than he'd normally wear, straining slightly against his pecs. He adds chinos, new loafers, and actually styles his hair. He needs to look his best, in case he runs into one of the women. Who's he kidding? It's so Afton can see the semi-successful adult version of him before he tells her to get lost. He's not wasting time on an ex simply for juicy television.

He walks the grounds, searching for her. Is she a full-blown contestant, staying in the mansion? Or somewhere else? When he was a contestant, he hadn't had access to the full property, so there could be places he doesn't know about. Why did he waste time on his hair? He should have run after her the second he saw her. She's slipped away, yet again.

He's careful as he walks in front of the mansion, not wanting any of the women to see him and alert production. There's laughing from the east side where he knows there's a balcony, but no one says his name. Except for dozens of cars parked up and down the winding driveway, he's alone. He's about to give up when a beam of sunlight reflects off something, nearly blinding him. He follows the beam and is instantly lightheaded. Afton is leaning on the hood of an old Toyota, her back to him, the sun reflecting off her phone case.

"So everyone's fine?" she asks, then pauses. "No, I haven't. Why do you care?" She tips her head up to the sky, still listening. "He's an adult, he's probably just busy." She pulls the phone away from her ear, flipping it off before putting it back. "Sure, I'll let you know. I've got to get back to work. Mhmm. Bye."

She hangs up and slides the phone back in her pocket before running her hands over her face.

This is it, his moment. He approaches, the gravel crunching beneath his feet. She whips around and opens her mouth as if she's about to scream. He sprints to her and places a finger on her lips. "Shh, it's me."

She relaxes into his touch. Then her eyes flare wide, and she backs away, climbing onto the hood of the car.

"What the hell are you doing?" she hisses, eyes blazing.

"Me?" Is she serious right now? "Not sure if you noticed, but I'm kind of the Fiancé-to-be."

Afton rolls her eyes. "Congratulations. Why are you creeping up on me?"

All awe at finally seeing her after all this time instantly dissipates. "Oh, I don't know, I just wanted to find out why the woman who disappeared off the face of the earth is here. On a show. Where I'm looking for my wife. Did you come to fuck with me?"

Her eyes flare when he says fuck, the corner of her mouth twitching. Then her expression turns serious. "I work here."

Even though she's dressed in all black, the thought of her actually being on the crew never crossed his mind. "You what?"

"Do you need my W-2 or something? I. Work. Here," she says, making a circle with her finger.

"Why?"

She tilts her head. "Because I've been in television for nine years and I'm good at my job."

His mouth opens and closes. She's been working in television this whole time? That had never been on his list of possibilities where she'd disappeared to. He'd been leaning toward a CIA agent, undercover cop, or a farmer on a remote island in the Philippines. Never a television producer.

"Congrats. You can't be here," he says.

She scoffs. "Last I checked, you're not actually in charge. You're just the talent."

Annoyance flashes through him. She thinks this is funny. Breaking his heart and completely disappearing wasn't enough?

"Do you have a personal vendetta against me being happy?" he asks.

Emotions flit across her face so quickly he can't catch them all. It's been so long since he's read her and he's rusty. He swears the last one is hurt, which is ridiculous.

"Of course not. How could you think that?" she asks quietly.

He blocks out the instinct to instantly comfort her. "You weren't here the last time I was. When did you start?"

She wraps her arms around her bent legs. "A month ago."

His jaw clenches. "A week before they asked me to be the lead? Did you convince them to ask me?"

"Of course not! You were my last choice."

"Then why are you here?"

"I wasn't going to give up a good job because the last guy had a drug problem."

He folds his arms, glaring and waiting. There has to be more.

"I didn't think you'd see me," she mumbles.

He barks out a single laugh. "What was your plan? Wear a mustache and hope I was too busy to notice you?"

The door to the garage slams shut, people talking. Afton slides off the hood, grabbing his arm and pulling him to crouch behind her car. His skin heats everywhere her fingertips touch. He tries to wriggle out of her grasp, but she holds tighter as the voices grow louder.

"How much do you think they paid Hannah to come here?" one asks.

"However much, it's not enough to deal with Karl," the other replies. They both laugh, their footsteps coming closer to where they're hiding. The footsteps stop and Jonah holds his breath. They should have sat inside the car. That would be far less obvious than crouching on the ground. If he's discovered with her, they're both screwed. Karl is still pissed at him from yesterday. Getting caught hiding with his ex-girlfriend is the perfect final straw.

Afton's fingers dig into his arm and he studies them. Her ring finger is bare, not even a tan line. Either she doesn't like jewelry, or she's not married. Is she single? With a partner? What has the last decade looked like for her?

It's none of his business.

The steps start up again, continuing down the driveway. When they're no longer audible, Afton abruptly lets go, turning to face him.

"I'm here to do my job, that's it. I'll stay as far away from you as possible and you can pretend I don't exist."

Afton is here. Crouched behind a car. Telling him to pretend she doesn't exist. "I'm trying to find my wife. I can't do that knowing my ex is standing in the production tent listening to every word I say."

"I'm usually nowhere near that tent. I'll mostly be doing one-on-ones with the women."

He gapes. She'll be behind the camera asking the women prodding questions to help process what they're filming.

"That's worse. You're going to cause drama with all the women I like. You'll make them doubt me."

She once knew every vulnerable thing about him. She'll know the right buttons to press and things to bring up with the women. He'll constantly be worried about what her and the productions' motivations are, and how to stay a step ahead.

"Whoa, stop spiraling," she says, placing her hand back on his arm.

The feeling of her touch startles him from his doom spiral.

"I know you have no reason to trust me, but I want you to be happy. You deserve the best."

He studies her. Why would she want that? "We should talk to production. They could have you work somewhere else—"

She fiddles with her nose ring. "We can't."

He hates it, but he's intrigued. "People are going to be digging into my past, and they're going to find out who you are to me. We should come clean now."

Her eyes dart everywhere. "No, they won't. There's nothing

about me online for them to track, and as long as you keep your mouth shut, they'll never know."

"Afton, this is ridiculous. You can't seriously want to stay; or think this will work."

She exhales, shoulders sagging. "Not sure if you noticed, but the job market sucks right now. My entire career has been in production and everything in this industry is word of mouth. I was fired from my last show and was lucky to get hired here thanks to my friend Chelsea. I'm desperate. I'll stay out of your way, promise. You won't even know I'm here."

She was the friend Chelsea had been referring to in the office last night, the one who'd convinced the majority of the women to stay. Why would she do that? To make sure his season went forward so she could mess with him more?

"Why'd you get fired?" he finally asks.

"One of the men on the project was clearly emotionally abusive, and I couldn't stand watching it anymore. I... intervened."

"How?"

She looks down at the ground. "I showed the woman clips of what he was saying behind her back. When he tried to spin it, I yelled that he was a worthless piece of shit that only felt better by tearing others apart."

He raises both brows.

"All off camera of course, so the show couldn't even use the drama," Afton adds.

Working in reality television, he expected she'd love the drama. Instead she'd gotten fired for standing up for someone? His chest loosens.

Afton's eyes light up. "Let's make a deal. What do you need most?"

"You, somewhere else."

Another eye roll. "Besides that. Hypothetically."

He actually thinks. He has a short amount of time to get to know twenty plus women without access to the outside world. "More insight into the women. To know what's real and what's production manufactured. Or, if anyone's here to be an influencer."

A slow smile creeps across her face. "I can be your spy. I'll let you know which of the women are being fake, and what production is up to."

"How?"

"I have access to social media. I'll go through everything again, see who has skeletons in their closet. I'm going to be in the house with the women so I'll see that too. And I'm in production; I'll be in the meetings where they decide what direction to take things. It's perfect."

An inside look into all the women? That would be invaluable. Then he wouldn't risk leaving engaged to someone with a boyfriend back home, or who's secretly racist. He'd be able to stop second guessing everything production does.

No. This can't happen. The price would be Afton here, always watching. If he'd struggled with thoughts of the past popping up before, they'd be even worse now.

"I feel for you with your job, but I can't do this—"

She puffs out her cheeks, blowing out a slow breath. "I didn't want to use this, but you owe me."

He huffs. "For what?"

Her expression is pained. "For confessing."

He physically recoils. He'd rather have her slap him. This was the other reason she couldn't be here. Seeing her was a constant reminder of his past. Who he had been. To go on this journey, he needed to focus on who he was now.

"Give me the week. Let me show you what it'll be like. I'll get you intel by the first cocktail party. If you still can't stand me, then I'll quit." She scoots backward before standing up. She looks around, then extends a hand to pull him up.

He grabs it without thinking, mind and body instantly warring. Why does every touch feel electric even though he wants nothing less?

"It'll be worth it, promise," she says before opening her car door. She waits a beat, maybe to see if he says something. When he doesn't, she climbs in and starts the engine. He stands there even after she pulls away, trying to sort through what the hell just happened.

He's in deep trouble.

CHAPTER SIX

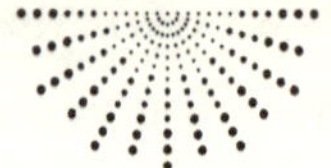

TWENTY-ONE YEARS AGO

Middle school was weird. When she wasn't struggling with her locker during the day, she had nightmares about it at night. She had no classes with Jonah so she only saw him at lunch and after school when they walked home together. It wasn't enough time to tell him everything she thought of throughout the day, or to discuss the books they swapped.

Lonely in class, Afton wrote Jonah a letter, beginning their pen pal phase. They'd swap letters every day once they reached their street. Afton would fall asleep reading about how he had to sit next to Henry Owens and Chad Perkins in all his classes. (Henry was cool, but Chad smelled like BO.) About *Legends of Zelda*, the video game his dad let him play now. And how all he wanted was to take a shower without clumps of his sisters' hair all over the walls.

She wrote about being annoyed with taking care of her little brothers. How she was nervous to make new girl friends because of the whoopee cushion incident. She could be herself with Jonah and not worry that she was going to scare him away. When she'd covered everything in his bedroom with googly eyes, he'd laughed so hard he'd choked on his spit.

He told her the next morning that anyone would be lucky to be friends with her. She'd lived off that high the whole day.

Things started changing slowly. Henry joined them for lunch. He didn't like to read, but he did play Zelda, so he'd interrupt her and Jonah to talk about that. Henry brought another friend he played basketball with, and that friend brought more, filling the table with boys. Even though she sat next to Jonah, he could barely hear her over his friends' loud conversations. It was exactly like her brothers bickering. They still had the letters and walking together after school though, so she endured lunch.

Halfway through the year, all the youth and their parents gathered in the chapel. Her older brother Dan was sitting with his friends, but she was next to her parents. She spotted Jonah sitting a few rows ahead, and when he looked in her direction, she waved. He didn't wave back, but did a head nod.

"Can we go sit with the Partridges?" Afton whispered.

Her mom pursed her lips and her dad's forehead wrinkled. The Partridge's had invited her entire family over for dinner and games after they'd first moved in and it'd been a disaster.

"You don't even have to talk to the Partridges since we'll be listening," Afton added.

"This isn't the kind of meeting you want to be sitting with your friends for," her dad finally replied.

Afton frowned. What kind of meeting was this?

Henry went and sat in the pew next to Jonah, the two of them talking animatedly while their parents chatted.

"Why's it okay for them to sit together?" Afton whispered to her parents.

"They're both boys," her mom said.

"So?" That made no sense. If it was about being reverent and respectful, her and Jonah would have an easier time next to each other. Henry pulled a tiny skateboard from his scripture case, and Jonah had one too. The two of them started driving them up and down the wood of the pew, doing little flips at the end. *Seriously?* They were almost thirteen years old. Her little brothers didn't even bring toys to church anymore.

"Drop it," her dad replied, voice low.

Afton knew that tone, stomach instantly sinking. She rested her elbows on her knees, leaning forward.

The Stake President, an intimidating old white man with wispy blonde hair, finally approached the microphone. The bustling in the chapel immediately stopped. Her parents sat straighter in their seats. Behind him a white screen lowered.

"Thank you all for being here. As Stake President, I am charged with making sure the people under my care make their way back to Christ. Being a teenager is one of the most fraught times in our lives, filled with temptations at every turn. As such, this meeting is one of the most important things I do each year."

A PowerPoint projected onto the white screen, the first slide reading:

Necking

French kissing

Petting

Heavy petting

Sexual intercourse

AFTON STARED AT THE WORDS, cheeks flaming. What did half of that list mean? All she knew was that whatever sex was, it was where babies came from and only referred to in whispers and giggles.

The Stake President cleared his throat. "We are all born with the tendencies of the natural man, and part of our test on this earth is to rise above it. The Lord gave us commandments to act as guide rails through this mortal journey and keep us from falling off the path. Sexual immorality is one of the most tempting acts in this life, and is a sin next to murder in the eyes of the Lord." He paused.

"The sacred powers of procreation are to be employed by man and woman, lawfully wedded as husband and wife. Tonight I will provide you with guardrails to keep you from ever getting close to falling off the cliff of temptation that is sexual immorality." He scanned the room dramatically.

Her stomach churned. Why would she ever be tempted to do something as bad as murder? She tries her best to be a good person, to help her parents and brothers when they needed it. Is she going to struggle with whatever this is? Why did God make it so hard to get back to him?

"When you are dating, you will naturally want to express affection to each other. That affection should always be a chaste kiss. A kiss that you would feel comfortable giving your parents."

Afton made the mistake of glancing at her parents. They stared straight ahead, stiff as statues. She barely hugged them, much less kissed them.

"Necking is kissing passionately, especially on the neck. French kissing is kissing while putting your tongue in someone else's mouth. It is a sin that mirrors the act of sex and stirs feelings that should only be awoken once you are married."

Why would she ever kiss someone with her tongue? That was disgusting. Afton kept her gaze forward, avoiding eye contact with her parents. Except, Jonah and Henry were sitting in front of her, straight backed in their pew, toy skateboards put away.

"Petting is touching breasts over clothing," the Stake President continued. "Heavy petting is touching private parts below the waist or anything under clothes. You should never touch where someone else's underwear covers. If you touch the sacred parts of another person, you must confess it to your bishop. You have sinned, and only confessing to the bishop can cleanse you."

Why would she ever want to do something like that? She pictured Jonah walking up to her and touching the aching nubs that were her breasts. The thought made her stomach hurt. She folded herself in half, trying to shrink away from the crowd.

Did her parents do those things? She silently began singing a primary song in her head to clear her mind of those images.

"Last is sexual intercourse. Sex is when a penis enters a vagina. If you are unmarried, this is a sin next to murder. You must confess this to your bishop to do the work necessary to cleanse your soul. If you do not stop having premarital sex, you risk being excommunicated."

Her stomach flipped. So that's what sex was. That meant that her parents had… That meant that every couple in this room who had kids had done that. And the Stake President was worried about people doing that for fun?

What was wrong with people?

The Stake President began crying, and she wanted to join him. "I know how powerful the natural man is and how hard it is to be a teenager. I pray every day that we do not lose one of your souls as you journey through this perilous time. Please know the atonement is always there. Our Savior bled and died for our sins, and there is hope. If you avoid these activities, you will be safe on your journey. But if you make a mistake, your bishop and I are there to help you."

She watched from a far away place in her mind as she was asked to hold her right hand up with all the other teens in the room and pledge they would stay pure. Her parents were asked to do the same as they vowed they would help her on that journey. Everyone hurried out of the building after. Afton kept her eyes on the ground, especially when she could hear Carrie talking in angry whispers with Jonah's dad. That meant that Jonah was behind her and she couldn't look at him, not now.

The next day at lunch, Jonah was surrounded on both sides when she got to their table. Neither of the boys moved, too focused on their conversation. Jonah met her eyes, glanced away for a moment, then back at her.

"Sorry," he mouthed.

He was quiet on their walk home. Afton was too, her mind wandering back to the chapel and the horrors she's learned there. She started singing that primary song again, trying to banish them.

Jonah was surrounded the rest of the week. She brought a book to lunch and read as soon as she finished eating. Jonah would still ask her questions about the books, but they were decreasing in direct proportion to how many times she'd get whacked by a random elbow or leg when the boys started messing with each other. At least Jonah always gave her apologetic looks when he finished play-fighting.

The invitations to come to his house for dinner slowed. Jonah joined the basketball team and when he didn't have practice, he was at his friends' homes for dinner instead.

One day Jonah's friends were stuck in the lunch line longer than usual. Afton had just started the first in a nine-book series about wizards and started telling Jonah about it. He listened intently, nodding along.

"I'll tell you when I'm returning it so you can check it out right after," Afton offered.

"I don't have time to read anymore," he said quietly.

That was her first true heartbreak. She'd desperately been holding onto this friendship, but now she knew it was a lost cause. Books were the thing that had always been theirs. And now there wasn't even that.

She didn't sit with him at lunch the next day. Instead she sat at the end of an empty table with her book. To her surprise, another girl plopped down across from her with her own book. The girl had black hair, dark skin, and warm brown eyes. Her book had a girl in a miniskirt on the cover, threatening to kill someone.

"I'm Naya," she said.

"Afton."

"I'm not Mormon, so if that's a deal breaker for you, let me know now," Naya said.

That was not at all what Afton expected her to say. "Why would that be?"

Naya tilted her head. "Did you just move here?"

"No, I was born here."

"People have been canceling playdates with me over it since preschool. They're scared I'll be a bad influence or whatever," Naya explained.

"That's messed up."

"Yep. So what brings you to my table?" Naya asked.

She hadn't realized this was Naya's table. "Do you want me to leave?"

"Not at all. Now the lunch ladies won't make small talk with me out of pity when all I want to do is read."

Afton relaxed. "I'm tired of being jostled by boys while I'm reading."

Naya sighed. "At least they let you read."

For the first time in weeks, Afton laughed. "What's your book about?"

Naya's eyes lit up. "Girl spies."

"Can I read it with you?" Afton asked.

Naya grinned. "I'd love that."

Afton caught Jonah's eye as she got up from the table and moved to sit next to Naya. He looked almost sad. How dare he when he'd been slowly moving on from her for weeks? She tossed her hair over her shoulder and looked away.

CHAPTER SEVEN

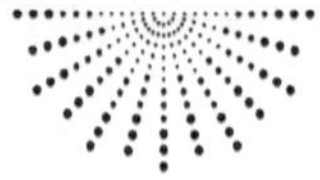

"Are you sure we can't put in the carrots? It would make it more authentic," Afton says, staring down at the giant inflatable pool filled entirely with green Jello. On another show, she would have been the one tasked with filling the pool with gallons of powder and hot water and stirring until her arms ached. Here, that's someone else's job so she can focus fully on creating drama.

Chelsea makes a gagging noise. "Just because some people think that qualifies as food doesn't mean the rest of us have to subject ourselves."

Afton sighs, then starts eating one of the raw carrots she brought.

Chelsea watches in horror. "Is eating them plain a Mormon thing too?"

"Nope. An 'I'm too lazy to go get ranch but I'm hungry' thing."

"You wouldn't have to eat raw carrots for breakfast if you hadn't hit snooze four times."

"I still made it on time, mom."

Chelsea frowns. "That's not like you."

Afton exhales quietly, trying to blow away her building annoyance. Chelsea has never commented on her snoozing habits before. Granted, Afton usually only presses it once, if that. Just because Chelsea got her this job, doesn't mean she needs to monitor her.

Then again, Afton is a liar, so she has no room to talk.

"I'm okay, promise," Afton says.

Chelsea presses her lips together. "What drama are you going to cause today?"

"The women are causing enough on their own. Did you hear about the hidden coffee yesterday?" Afton asks.

She'd spent most of yesterday with the saga. In the middle of the night someone had hidden all of the coffee *and* the coffee maker. Fingers were pointed, tears were shed, one woman was taken by ambulance to the hospital because of a debilitating migraine from caffeine withdrawal. They were barely a week into filming and they'd already gotten their classic ambulance shot to tease audiences next year.

"Yes. That's pure evil. Did they figure out who did it?"

"No. The crew was thinking about installing night cams in the kitchen to see if they catch anything."

"I love this job," Chelsea grins.

Afton forces a smile back. She should be ecstatic. Jonah hasn't turned her in yet. She gets to work with her best friend. This group of women is unique and push each other in ways that haven't been explored on television yet, and she's the most qualified person on set to do it. Yet her mind feels like it's crawling through Jello. Green, with carrots.

Car doors slam shut, announcing the women's' arrival. She rolls back her shoulders to snap out of her funk while appraising everyone's outfits. Tessa and Emily are wearing matching halter tops in jewel tones and high-rise daisy dukes.

Maylee and Rileigh have monokinis and rolled down the waist of their unbuttoned shorts. Bea is in a vintage style polka dot two-piece, while Tage is in a bandeau tankini.

Whoever decided to keep Bea on the wrestling date needs to explain themselves. Her ankle is still wrapped and she's on crutches. Tage's bandeau tankini though? That's entirely Afton's fault. She'd been so focused on the hilarity of the green Jello she hadn't double checked their outfits before they left. Now they're a good forty minutes away from the mansion, and Tage's bandeau top is a nip slip waiting to happen.

She grabs her emergency backpack from the ground and digs inside. There isn't an extra bikini top, but she does have various kinds of body tape and adhesive bras. She runs and intercepts the women before they get close to production.

"Tage, can we chat for a second?" Afton asks.

Tage freezes, pointing at her chest and mouthing 'me?' Maylee and Rileigh let out low "oohs" like Tage was called to the principal's office. Afton grabs Tage's arm gently and pulls her to the side of the group.

"This is completely my fault; I should have prepared you better. We're Jello wrestling today and I'm worried your top might fall down. I have body tape to secure it so it has no chance of moving. Or I have adhesive covers we can slip on underneath. Whatever makes you the most comfortable."

Tage bites her thumbnail. "Is that tape strong enough to withstand Jello though?"

"This is the stuff that celebrities and models use, it's really strong," Afton says.

"They're not actively wrestling. Do you have a t-shirt I could throw on?" Tage asks.

Afton starts digging through her backpack looking for the black t-shirt she keeps. She was so grateful for it after a contestant vomited on her last project...

Shit. She hadn't replaced it after that. She taps on her phone, finding a drugstore two blocks away.

"I can get you one."

Tage's body instantly relaxes. "Thank you."

"Of course, this was my fault in the first place."

Afton sprints over to the production tent, searching for Chelsea. "I need to grab someone a t-shirt for the actual wrestling. I'll be gone twenty minutes tops. Why don't you," she trails off. Jonah is standing under the tent, halfway through buttoning up a striped referee shirt. It has to be two sizes too small from the way it's hugging his arms. It's plain rude to remind her how much of a man he is now and not the boy of her memories.

"Why don't we what?" Chelsea asks.

Afton whips her head back to her where the rest of the crew stare at her. She'd stopped talking mid-sentence because she was too busy ogling Jonah. Whoever told her that boys think about sex all the time and girls don't was a liar. She'd worried something was wrong with her in high school because of how often she'd thought about it. With Jonah in particular. Now Jonah is a man standing feet away, and she has a far richer imagination.

Jonah meets her eyes, then quickly turns away. *Way to be subtle.* At least she doesn't have to worry about hiding from him anymore.

"Why don't you film them explaining the rules? A dramatic moment where Bea has to sit out and the women get mad because they think Jonah is favoring her. I'll be back by then."

"Do you really need to get her a t-shirt? Just tape her up and call it good," Richard says.

Afton frowns. "I already offered that, but she'd be more comfortable with a shirt."

"Who cares about–" Richard starts.

"I do," Afton snaps.

She can feel Jonah watching her as she grabs her keys and bolts across the grass before Richard can respond. Her heart thrums the entire drive to the drugstore. Hopefully her outburst doesn't reflect poorly on Chelsea.

She hurries through the drugstore, grabbing white t-shirts in various sizes. She also grabs swim caps, satin headbands, baby wipes, and hair-ties. The checkout line winds through all the impulse buys thanks to an elderly woman arguing with a bored cashier about a sale item. When her phone starts buzzing incessantly in her pocket, her lungs squeeze. This is it. She's getting fired again. She should have known better than to accept this job in the first place, especially with Chelsea vouching for her. She's lost her ability to stay quiet around asshole men.

The phone buzzes again and she resists the urge to chuck it. It won't make this go away, and she won't have money to replace it.

It's not Chelsea or work. It's a group message with an unknown number.

> Hi! Naya said you were all willing to help organize the baby shower with me. I thought it'd be good to start brainstorming ideas. What are your emails so I can share my Pinterest boards with you?

Afton's eyes slide closed. She'd called Naya the other day to start breaking the news gently that she wasn't sure if she'd be able to make the shower. In that call she'd failed to tell Naya

A) she'd been fired from her previous job

B) she was working on *Ready for the Ring*

C) yes, *that* Jonah was the lead

D) she needed everyone to pretend that they'd never dated so she could keep this job that

E) would be filming the week of her baby shower

INSTEAD, she'd agreed to be added to the planning group chat Naya's cousin was starting. Maybe she could make up for the fact she wouldn't physically be there by helping organize whatever it was that Naya's cousin deemed needed a Pinterest board.

Sorry, boards. Plural.

She's sending her email back when another text comes in from an unknown number starting with 801, a Utah area code.

UNKNOWN

New Number, who's this?

AFTON CHECKS THE GROUP MESSAGE, but the Utah number isn't in it. Who is this? She copies the number and asks Naya if she knows who it is. When Naya doesn't immediately respond, Afton texts back

Pretty sure that's my line.

Now I'm stealing it.

Who is this?

Guess.

AFTON DOESN'T HAVE time to play games. She shoves her phone in her pocket and moves up with the line. A clearance rack of colorful pool inflatables catches her eye. Specifically the whale ones. There are various blue whales, grey whales, and orcas. She snatches them and adds them to her pile. Jonah is going to be *so* annoyed. Everyone makes jokes about him watching out for whales thanks to the bible story behind his name. Why not hide whales in plain sight all over the set? Maybe an eagle-eyed viewer will catch it and start a whale watch.

Her phone buzzes again as she's walking out of the store.

UNKNOWN

Typical. Not even trying.

HER HAND SHAKES. There's only one person who talks to her like that. Her littlest brother, Noah. Getting a new phone number just to remind her of how much she'd failed him was new though. Usually he muttered his snide remarks under his breath at Christmas. Did his new number have anything to do with her mom wanting to know if she'd talked with him recently? Interesting. She definitely can't respond now. A clear head is a prerequisite for messaging her family.

If she was at karaoke she'd sing "Run Away Girl."

When Afton reaches the production tent, completely winded from running, multiple women are complaining that Bea gets to sit next to Jonah while he referees. Turns out she does possess self control because she doesn't say, 'I told you so,' to Richard. When she gives Tage her shirt, two other women ask for one as well. The hair ties and headbands are snatched up too. She might always let her brother and Naya down, but at least she can help these women feel more comfortable.

Rileigh and Maylee whisper on the edge of the group, heads bobbing up and down as they look over everyone's outfits. Afton catches the eye of Luke the cameraman and motions for him to follow her.

"Maybe if they weren't so worried about showing off their bodies, they wouldn't have to wear those ugly t-shirts," Maylee says.

"Hopefully Jonah is smart enough to see through them," Rileigh says.

"He's a man. He can't help himself," Maylee says.

Afton wants to gag. This is the exact rhetoric she grew up with. Every time there was a swimming activity at church, there was a pile of black t-shirts for any of the girls who weren't dressed modestly enough to wear. Yeah, she just bought her own pile of shirts, but it's not because she's scared of them showing skin. It's for comfort.

Now that Luke's filming Rileigh and Maylee, this kind of thinking will get airtime. She's tempted to drag the camera elsewhere. Or, she can work with this.

Luke stays with Rileigh and Maylee while she goes to where Bea is sitting on the grass, braiding strands together. From Afton's sleuthing to get insight for Jonah, she knows Bea is the exact woman for this job.

"Do you want to argue with some women on purity culture?" Afton whispers.

Bea immediately pushes to stand. "Let me at them."

"Follow me. I'll get them talking, then you go right ahead."

Bea grins like a shark.

"What's wrong with their suits?" Afton asks Rileigh and Maylee.

Rileigh's face brightens as she turns to face the camera. "The prophets have warned us not to wear bikinis. Men are visual creatures, and it's our job as women not to tempt them. I'd much rather a man love me for who I am, than how my body looks."

Crutches swing into the frame. "Are we talking about the girls in two-pieces?" Bea asks.

Rileigh and Maylee both nod.

"And how if we did an inch per inch comparison of how much skin everyone has showing, you two are showing way more in those pieces of floss you call a one-piece than everyone else here?" Bea asks.

Rileigh's cheeks go red as Maylee steps back as if she was slapped.

"How Christ said that a man should carve his own eye out if he's struggling with lustful thoughts and nothing about what women were wearing?"

Rileigh and Maylee frown.

"Or how it's sad to go around spending time and energy policing what other people are wearing because of our own insecurities, instead of just living?" Bea finishes. "If you don't want to wear a two-piece, then don't. But don't pretend that you're better than anyone else because your suit is harder to pee in."

Bea swings around, the clacking of her crutches the only sound.

When Afton brought Bea over, she expected it to be good, but not this good. If she has to stand in the editing booth herself to make sure they air every single second of that conversation, she'll do it. Or bribe someone to get her the footage so she can rewatch on hard nights.

Rileigh and Maylee merge with the crowd to watch the first of the wrestling matches. Luke hangs back with Afton. "How did you do that?"

"I have my ways." Namely a lot of internet stalking, knowing exactly how these women grew up, and the best way to mix it all together.

"Afton, can you come to the tent?" Chelsea asks over the headset.

All her confidence instantly evaporates. Now it's time to pay for earlier. When she gets to the tent, she's surprised to see Chelsea sitting in a chair next to Hannah with Richard and Karl nowhere in sight.

"I saw that little altercation you orchestrated there," Hannah says.

Afton's not sure whether that's good or bad, so she stays silent.

Hannah's lips quirk. "And you stood up to Richard."

"I'm sorry for how I spoke, but—"

Hannah holds up a hand. "Don't apologize. Heaven knows he never will. Sit."

Afton settles into the chair next to Chelsea.

"You're the one who brought her on?" Hannah asks Chelsea.

Chelsea nods. "I told you she'd be perfect, especially for this season."

Afton shifts uncomfortably in her chair.

Hannah's lips quirk at the sides, almost in a smile. "How long have you both been in the business?"

"Nine years," Afton and Chelsea say in unison.

"What are your aspirations?" Hannah asks.

"I want to be a show-runner one day. I have a whole notebook of ideas," Chelsea says.

Hannah dips her chin, then turns to Afton.

"I'm just happy to be here with my best friend."

Hannah's lips return to their usual flat line.

That was the wrong answer. Hannah creates careers and is

known for mentoring women with ambition. And Afton said *that*.

"Keep up the good work," Hannah finally says before looking back at the monitors.

Dismissed, Afton gets up, Chelsea following behind her. Once they're a good distance from the tent, Chelsea whirls on her. "What was that?"

"I panicked," Afton says.

"You think? You could have said show-runner, or EP."

"But I don't want to be a show-runner."

"Then what do you want?" Chelsea asks as if that's a simple question one just knows the answer to.

"Tacos. World peace."

"Is this about getting fired? You know you weren't in the wrong, that set was toxic. Getting let go says nothing about your skills."

"I know," Afton sighs.

"Then what? I can't help you if you don't talk to me," Chelsea says.

She owes Chelsea something, a single thread she can pull from the knot she's made of her life. Chelsea's putting her job on the line every day and not even knowing it.

"It's been fun brainstorming unique ways to bring Utah culture to the show, but it's also bringing up a lot of old stuff from growing up."

Chelsea's expression softens. "I'm sorry, I hadn't even thought of that. Do you want to talk to the therapist?"

"No, I'll be fine. We're truly making the most dramatic season ever. No one will ever be able to top this."

"It's not worth it if you're not okay. Would a different position help? Maybe less time with the 'lee's?"

"I'll be fine. Promise. Please don't worry about me," Afton says.

"But it's my job to, literally."

That stings. She's never wanted to be a burden. "I don't want to be your job. I want to be your friend."

Chelsea's expression flits to something before she smooths it out. "You are," Chelsea says, wrapping Afton into a hug.

When they pull apart, they turn just in time to see Tage take Rileigh down, instantly pinning her in the Jello. Jonah dramatically waves his hand three times, then blows his whistle, the match over. Tage jumps to her feet, pumping her arms in the air triumphantly. Jonah offers her a hand and helps her get out of the pool. Rileigh on the other hand has gelatin stuck in all the nooks and crannies of her monokini.

"Imagine if you'd let me put the carrots in. She'd have to pull them out of her boobs," Afton says.

Chelsea snorts. "The poetic justice would be even more authentic."

The two of them get into the rhythm of filming, the awkwardness dissipating. Afton interviews each of the women after their matches, getting sassy sound bites. Some women are super into wrestling, while others want to get out of the Jello as soon as possible.

The last match is between Maylee and Emily. Maylee fights dirty, trying to snatch the satin scarf protecting Emily's braids. Emily ducks out of her reach, wrapping her arms around Maylee's middle, and tackling her to the ground. She pins Maylee for the count of three until Jonah blows his whistle. When Jonah reaches to pull Emily out of the pool, Emily pulls on him until he topples into the Jello himself. He emerges, sputtering. Emily laughs, helping him wipe the Jello off his face.

"It wasn't fair that we were doing all the dirty work," Emily quips.

"I agree," Jonah says.

Afton has the perfect view of Emily perfectly executing the

triangle stare, looking between both of Jonah's eyes, then to his mouth. He must clock it because he's pulling Emily closer to him, then kissing her in the middle of the Jello pool. With Maylee still in there. In front of *all* the women.

She knew that him being on *Ready for the Ring* meant that he would be kissing people. She'd watched him make out with another woman on last year's season. But standing up close and personal, watching him kiss someone else versus on a screen? Something boils within her; suffocating and heavy. She desperately needs to look away but can't.

What the hell? They broke up fifteen years ago. She's beyond moved on: there's been over a decade of boyfriends, flings, and situationships since then. She'd started to forget Jonah existed until she saw his face all over social media last year. Granted, her highest time period not thinking about him was six days, but still. This level of jealousy is inappropriate. She has no claim to him, and this is what he's here for. To kiss beautiful women and fall in love.

It's because it's so close. You'll get used to it.

Afton's not the only one struggling with jealousy; she's just the best at hiding it. The women around the pool are murmuring. Some turn their backs, others hug each other. Maylee starts wailing from the other end of the pool. It's a sight that will be etched in the annals of television history.

Rookie move, Jonah. You don't kiss someone in front of the group, especially on the first group date. He was worried about her manipulating the women for drama, but he should have been more concerned with himself. Now it's her job to get the juiciest soundbites from the mess he's making.

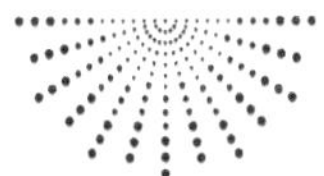

CHAPTER EIGHT

Jonah keeps his limbs loose so he won't startle too hard when Afton jumps out of a bush or drops down from a balcony. Knowing her, she's probably figured out how to rappel down from a ledge *Mission Impossible* style, simply to hand him a sheet of paper. She'll ruin all elements of surprise by laughing as someone pulls her back up though.

At least, that's what the old her would have done. Who knows if the new her is just as silly? Certainly not him, and he's not going to find out. All he wants is this supposed secret intel on the women she promised him. If it isn't worth his time, then there's no deal. She'll quit and he'll never have to see her again.

He'd be lying if he said he wasn't curious about what she'll say. He's barely had a chance to interact with half these women. What if the best fit for him is someone he hasn't gotten to know, and he sends her home? Or what if he's started falling for someone who's secretly awful? This information could change everything. Why does it have to come from *her*?

He wishes he could text or call Henry, but they took his

phone. Although, Henry has a habit of choking on his spit and breaking into violent coughing fits whenever he's shocked. If he heard that Afton of all people was here, he might not live long enough for Jonah to finish telling the tale. Best to break that news in person, when he can make sure Henry's not eating and has someone nearby for the Heimlich.

He makes it all the way to the pool and Afton hasn't appeared. What's he going to do if she doesn't fulfill her part of the deal? Turn her in? She hasn't exactly stayed in the background, going head-to-head with Richard right in front of him, then setting up a confrontation between Bea, Rileigh, and Maylee. And then there's her words constantly replaying every night as he tries to sleep. *You owe me. For confessing.*

It'd taken a whole decade of growth and therapy to forgive himself for that moment. What made it worse was not being able to talk to Afton and apologize. To see if she ended up okay. Now she was here in front of him. Confident, capable, smart as hell. Laughing. She seemed happy from afar and he wanted to believe all was forgiven.

But she'd still said it. He owed her.

She told him he'd barely notice she was here, but her presence is everywhere. He spots her car in the driveway every morning. Gets directions from her best friend. Constantly hears her laugh. And now he's wasting time wondering if she's going to uphold their tentative deal instead of focusing on the women right in front of him. Who are all in swimsuits.

Normally that wouldn't warrant a second thought. After having Maylee and Rileigh cry to him about Bea chewing them out, and then having Bea explain what actually happened, he's nervous. Some women actually believe he is incapable of seeing them as people and only as objects. The lessons from church echo in his mind. Look away. You are weak. Even thinking about it is a sin. You can't control yourself. You are an addict.

He rolls his neck to the left. He isn't here to lust. He doesn't see these women for their skin, and couldn't care less about what they want to wear at the pool. He's here to find his wife, and if she happens to be hot and he notices, does that make him bad?

He rolls his neck to the right. Thoughts are thoughts. Trying to control them gives them more power than they deserve. He can simply let them pass by. He shakes his head, then scans the pool. Women are playing volleyball on one side, others relaxing on loungers. A few are laying on floaties in the water. He does a double take. They're all whale floaties. It could be a coincidence... It better be.

He walks to the closest group of women. They start laughing and waving as he approaches; McKinlee turning bright red while Bentley gives him a wide smile. He settles on the edge of the pool between Bentley and Tage.

"How're you doing?" he asks them.

"Great. Although I wish there was a zip-line here," Bentley says.

He laughs. He'd had a one-on-one with Bentley, driving a Bentley, down the Pacific Coast Highway. "Is that the only reason you're here?" He knocks his shoulder into hers playfully.

"Maybe." She pushes him right back.

"Is that from a show?" McKinlee asks.

"Yes, it's called *I Think You Should Leave*" Bentley says.

"What are your favorite shows?" Tage asks him.

He kicks his feet in the water. "I grew up watching reality TV with my mom and sisters."

"Seriously?" McKinlee asks, twirling a strand of hair around her fingers. "Did you like them?"

"I'd pretend not to, but yes. My favorite was *Survivor*."

"Is that why you applied for the show in the first place?" Tage asks.

"My sisters actually nominated me the first time, then talked me into accepting the Fiancé-to-be position."

"They sound like good people," Bentley says.

His heart squeezes thinking of them. He can practically picture them sitting on the chaises, watching him over their sunglasses. If everything goes to plan, they'll be meeting two of these women in a matter of weeks to help him pick the woman he proposes to.

"They are."

A PA approaches and taps him on the shoulder. "Emily is waiting for you over there," she says, pointing to a lounger on the other side of the pool where she's sitting next to Tessa. Seeing the two of them, something that feels suspiciously like butterflies flutter in his gut. This is his first time seeing them both since the electric kisses they shared. Unfortunately for Emily, he'd gotten carried away and kissed her in front of everyone. Hopefully she isn't paying for his lapse in judgement.

Halfway there, he stumbles slightly as he spots Afton walking with a camera behind her to another group of women. Her hair is in two French braids with little buns on the bottom. She's wearing a black cropped tank/sports-bra/shirt thing. Whatever it is, there's a sliver of her stomach showing above the top of her biker shorts. His eyes trail over her hips, the curve of her ass. That inch of skin. What would it feel like to trail his fingers along it…

What the hell? Most thoughts are neutral, but those ones are inherently bad. He can't think about her like that. He focuses back on Emily and Tessa. Two women who are both sexy as hell, give him butterflies like a teenager, and whom he's been dying to talk to again.

As he settles onto a lounger, Tessa gives him a small smile before getting up. Did the producers tell her to leave so he could talk to Emily? Or is something wrong? Does he go after her, or talk with Emily first? Is this a test?

Poor him, having all these women wanting his attention and not knowing how to handle it.

"How have you been?" he finally asks Emily, perching on the edge of his lounger so his knees almost graze her feet.

She smiles at him. "I'm sure you keep hearing this, but better now that I'm seeing you."

"You're actually the first to say that today," he says, scooting even closer.

She sits up, appraising him. "If this is going to go any farther, I have some important questions for you."

His mouth goes dry. It's time to get serious. "Hit me."

"Do you believe in dinosaurs?"

He laughs, relieved. "What? Of course I do, why wouldn't I?"

"You'd be surprised. Next question, do you celebrate Halloween?"

"It's one of my favorite holidays," he says. "My mom would get my costume super early and I'd wear it every day after school for months."

"What was your favorite costume?" Emily asks, her eyes dancing.

"Power Rangers."

"Solid choice. I was Hermione Granger three years in a row until I couldn't get my arms into my robes anymore. My mom sewed them by hand."

"Really? Did she make all your costumes?"

"Until I was ten. Then she taught me to sew, and we made them together."

"That's incredible. I can sew a button, but that's it."

"Hmmm. Maybe I can teach you," Emily says, leaning in. He pulls her toward him, and then they're kissing. It's so easy, the way their mouths fit together. She deepens the kiss and makes the tiniest moan that has him instantly hard. The compression shorts under his trunks better be doing their job…

He's smacked in the back of the head by an inflatable beach ball.

"Sorry!" voices shriek from the pool.

He pulls away from Emily, drinking in the blush on her cheeks.

"I shouldn't monopolize your time. It was good seeing you." She stands and reaches for his hand, giving it a quick squeeze before walking away.

"Give it back," a woman yells.

It takes three seconds too long for him to process that they're talking about the ball. Instead of standing and showing off his boner, he leans carefully to grab it.

"Bea's stuck in a cabana over there, you should chat with her," a familiar voice says next to him.

He startles, folding in half and covering his crotch with his arms. Afton stands above him holding a clipboard, lips pressed together so hard they're turning white. Is she mad? Or trying not to laugh?

She finally opens her mouth again, then drops her clipboard.

"Whoops," she says, making no move to pick it up. He leans down reflexively to grab the pile of papers. On top is a handwritten page.

Bea, Bentley, Emily, Tage, and Tessa are clean.

Maylee & Rileigh have horrible socials.

McKinlee is convinced you are her soulmate.

Those you haven't had lots of time with are the wannabe influencers/suffer from all the -phobias.

The women are still pissed you kissed Emily in front of them.

Someone keeps hiding the coffee and coffee maker.

"Are we good?" she asks.

Who would be evil enough to hide the coffee maker? If you don't drink it, it doesn't mean no one else should be able to.

He reads through the points once again. The women he's felt the biggest pull toward are ones Afton was able to clear. The past year has been an exercise in trusting his own intuition versus the idea of having to earn guidance from a higher power. This tiny validation that he can trust himself buoys him.

He hands the clipboard back, careful to avoid brushing her skin.

"Are we good?" she asks again, voice low.

He takes a slow breath. If he says yes, he'll go on this journey watching the shadows, constantly wondering where she is. She'll see every kiss, every confession, every vulnerable moment. His thoughts might wander down forbidden paths, and old memories will come to the surface. Is this information worth the trade?

He's tried to get over her for a decade. To rid himself of the parts of him she'd touched. Once he wrote on a reddit board asking if anyone else struggled to forget their first love. Hundreds of anonymous people assured him it was normal; your first love is a formative experience during a simpler time in life. Thinking back with rose-colored glasses is normal.

He'd never seen Afton as an adult. Never fought with her over dishes, laundry, money. Hell, he's never seen what she looks like first thing in the morning. Shoving down the thoughts of her hasn't worked. Maybe her being here gives him the opportunity to move on once and for all. He'll see that she's just a woman, not an unattainable ideal from his memories.

Not confessing instantly would also count as an exposure for his OCD. An opportunity to show himself how far he's truly come.

"Under one condition," he says, slowly.

Her eyes flash and she scans the pool. Everyone is waiting

for him, and probably wondering what's taking so long with the producer. His lips slowly work their way into a smile. For the first time since he saw her in the shower, he's the one with the power.

"What is it?" she asks quickly.

"You have to answer whatever questions I ask honestly. If you can't, the deal is off."

She frowns at him. "Absolutely not—"

"That's my last condition. Otherwise I'm out. Having you here is too hard." He stands up from the lounger, looking down at her. Her forehead wrinkles as if she's thinking hard.

"What kind of questions?" she asks.

He'll give her a softball to start. "Are you behind all the whale floaties?"

Her lips quirk then press together. "They were on clearance. I couldn't help it."

He bites the inside of his cheek. Growing up he'd told her how annoying Jonah and the whale jokes were. She'd been appalled, saying it was too easy of a joke and she'd never stoop to that level. Why's she doing it now? Having her answer things honestly is to help him move on, not come up with even more questions.

"Do you accept the deal?" he asks.

"Yes," she says easily.

He turns toward where Bea is waiting for him with her ankle propped in the cabana.

"Great. Next question, did I ruin your life?"

She stumbles, dropping the clipboard again. This time she immediately kneels to pick it up.

He crouches down next to her. Her chest is rapidly rising and falling. Good. Her words have been haunting him; she deserves to squirm. "Answer honestly."

She closes her eyes for a long moment. "Yes, and no."

"Not good enough. I need a real answer."

Her eyes flutter open, boring into his own. The sunlight glints in her irises, illuminating that familiar scale pattern of gold woven throughout the shades of brown.

"At first, I would have said yes. But if it hadn't happened, I wouldn't be here. I wouldn't be free." She clutches the clipboard to her chest and stands, slowly walking away.

Free? What does she mean? From the church? Her family? Him?

Despite his new questions, he swears his shoulders feel a tiny bit lighter as he walks to Bea.

CHAPTER NINE

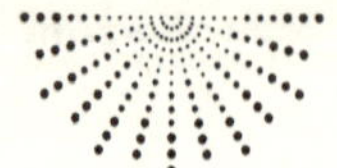

TWENTY YEARS AGO

When Afton turned fourteen, she was officially old enough to go to the church dances. It wasn't even a question that Naya would go with her. They got ready in Naya's bedroom, applying layers of glitter and walking through clouds of Love Spell perfume. Afton instantly felt sexier knowing she smelled like Victoria's Secret. Maybe her fantasy of meeting a handsome older boy who'd instantly fall for her would actually happen.

Walking into the dance, a large poster hangs at the entrance with the dress code listed on it.

"Why does the boy's section say they need to wear clean clothes and brush their teeth, while the girl's section is a novel?" Naya whispered as they waited in line.

Naya did have a point; the girl's side of the dress code was embarrassingly long. Naya had tagged along with Afton to various church activities the past two years. She knew the drill: no saying 'oh my god,' no swearing, no hanging out on Sundays. Yet every time she came, she asked questions that made Afton squirm.

They approached the check-in table where two elderly men were sitting. They looked Afton and Naya up and down once, then twice. Afton was wearing one of her church dresses while Naya shimmered in a sparkling dress she'd found at the thrift store.

"Your dress is too short," the elderly man said to Naya.

"What do you mean? It goes to my knees," Naya said.

"It's above the knee cap," he said, staring at her legs.

"She's not a member. This is her first dance," Afton said. Her own cheeks were burning. Why were they treating her friend like this?

"It's your responsibility to make sure she's dressed appropriately. We'll let it slide this time," one of the men finally said.

Afton and Naya pushed through the streamer-clad doorway of the church gym before the men could change their minds. Inside the room was lit entirely with white Christmas lights. Naya's watery eyes reflected the lights of the disco ball in the middle of the room.

"I thought this dress was nice," she sniffed.

"I'm so sorry they did that; I thought you were fine. Your hot older boy is going to love it."

Naya snorted and Afton wrapped her into a hug. "Let's get snacks."

From the safety of the snack table with plates loaded with chips and candy, they surveyed the room. She spotted Jonah standing with his guy friends, all of them jumping and trying to touch the top of the doorjamb. There were a few girls from church, but Afton wasn't going to subject Naya to them.

When a rowdy group of boys started play fighting next to the snack table, they found a secluded corner of the gym to listen to the music. Not only had Naya introduced Afton to contemporary books, but she'd opened a world of music for her. Afton's parents only played church produced artists or the

Mormon Tabernacle Choir. Hearing "Umbrella" by Rhianna was an awakening.

Naya made it her personal mission to give Afton a music education, burning mix cd's. Afton listened to them with headphones from the safety of her room, silently mouthing the words so she wouldn't get caught. Her studying paid off because Afton knew every single song that played, able to finally sing aloud with an invisible microphone in hand.

"You have a voice," Naya commented.

Afton blushed. Her mom gave her a few voice lessons when her brothers were less chaotic than usual. It'd been awhile, but apparently she still had it.

At the end of "Don't Stop the Music" the DJ tapped on a microphone.

"I'm about to play the first slow song of the night and I need to say something to the young ladies. If a boy has the courage to walk over and ask you to dance, please don't say no. It's scary to ask someone to dance, especially when you're all standing in groups. These dances are about meeting other youth your age, so go and dance!"

"Chasing Cars" started playing, and Naya and Afton exchanged a look. This was it. The chance for boys to notice them. Afton scanned the gym nervously, searching through all the boys in white shirts and slacks. Some had colored button ups with rolled up sleeves. She spotted one cute boy, but he was walking toward a different girl. She made eye contact with her older brother Dan and looked away. *So awkward.* Then her eyes met with Jonah's.

He was on the other side of the gym with his hands in his pockets. His eyebrows raised when their eyes locked. He looked around him, then back at her. He took the tiniest step forward when Henry grabbed onto his arm and yanked him out the doorway into the hall. Of course he did. Jonah and Henry were too immature to be thinking about crushes and dancing. That's why Naya and her needed older boys.

While she'd been looking at Jonah, her brother and his friend Brennan started walking their way.

"Is he coming over here?" Naya breathed.

Afton glared at Dan, silently begging him to walk away. He didn't see her because his eyes were focused on Naya. *Seriously?*

"I forgot you were old enough for these now," Dan said when he reached them.

"You don't notice much, so that's not a surprise," Afton said.

Dan rolled his eyes. "Naya, would you like to dance?"

Naya swallowed before answering. "Yes."

Dan grabbed her hand and led her farther into the gym, holding Naya's right hand, his left on her hip. Afton wanted to be happy for her, but she felt like a sitting duck standing by herself.

"Would you like to dance?" Brennan asked.

She jumped, not realizing he'd still been there. "Sure."

She'd hoped an older boy would notice her. Brennan was sixteen with long blonde hair. He knew how to snowboard and all the girls at church had a crush on him. He was probably only asking her to dance as a favor to her brother. There was no way he was actually interested in her.

Brennan grabbed her hand, and placed his other hand on her hip. She flinched when his fingers rubbed against the seam of her embarrassingly high-waisted underwear. *Was this heavy petting?* His hand was where her underwear was. She waited for him to move it, but he left it there. She dutifully placed her other hand on his shoulder as he swayed them to the beat.

He began asking questions, but she couldn't focus. Wasn't this wrong? All of them were in the same meeting about not touching where someone's underwear was. Yet everyone else had their hands pressed on hips too while the chaperones stood on the edges smiling. If the whole room was doing this, then it must be okay.

She tried to sway back and forth in time to the music, but Brennan's hand kept moving on her hip, the tip of his middle finger sliding the waistband of her underwear down slightly from over her dress. She stopped moving, and Brennan's hand shifted higher on her waist where it stayed.

Maybe this was her mom's fault for buying Afton granny panties. Brennan's fingers wouldn't keep brushing her waistband if it wasn't so high. That had to be it.

The song finally ended, Brennan releasing her with a smile as Dan and Naya returned. Afton studied the floor until the boys left.

"That was amazing," Naya breathed.

"It was something," Afton said.

She felt shaky when the next slow song started. She'd barely registered the slow tempo when a new boy was asking Naya to dance. *No. Not again.* Naya mouthed, "sorry," before following him to the middle of the gym. Once the two of them were swaying, Afton bolted to the hallway.

A chaperone stood there. "Go dance with someone. It's fun," the woman smiled.

"Bathroom," Afton said, hurrying down the hall. As she turned the corner, someone ran into her and knocked her to the ground. She looked up to see Henry.

"Sorry, I didn't see you," Henry said.

"Probably because you were running like a child," Afton snapped.

The other boys he'd been running with oohed. A hand appeared in front of her. It was Jonah's.

"Are you okay?" he asked.

She ignored him, pushing up from the ground herself.

"I'm really sorry," Henry called as she escaped into the bathroom. Her throat burned and her eyes watered. What was wrong with her? She wasn't going to cry because Henry knocked her over. Or because she was terrified to dane with someone again. She wanted to go home, but she'd brought Naya here and she was having a blast. She splashed water on her face to try and shock the tears out of her system. When she opened the bathroom door, Jonah was standing there, leaning against the wall.

"Creeper much?" Afton asked.

Jonah blushed. "I wasn't trying to be creepy. I was making sure you were okay."

"I'm fine." She walked right past him, down the hall.

He kept up with her. "Are you sure? You look pretty upset."

"If I wanted to deal with crazy boys, I would have stayed home."

Jonah winced. "Yeah, they're annoying. You're the third person they've crashed into."

"Then why are you hanging out with them?"

Jonah stopped walking. "Great question. Can I hang with you and Naya?"

"You'd have to sing Taylor Swift with us," Afton joked.

"Good thing I know all the words." They were next to the doors to the gym, and Jonah parted the streamers for her. She hesitated.

"Why do you want to hang out with me?"

"Because my friends are idiots and…" he cut himself off.

"And?"

"I've missed talking with you."

She scoffed. "That's your own fault."

"I know, I messed up. Henry's a great guy when he's not running, and he introduced me to his basketball friends. And then…" he trailed off.

She tapped her foot, waiting. When he stayed silent, she turned to walk away.

"Then we had that weird meeting, and it freaked me out. Everything was changing so fast, and I didn't know what to do."

Weird meeting? The one about sex? "I was there too, but I didn't feel the need to stop talking to you."

He ran a hand through his hair, the damp strands sticking up. "I know. I was scared of my thoughts and what might pop in my head. I didn't want to think about you like that because you're my best friend, and you deserve respect, and..."

The more he talked, the more he pulled at his hair, clearly upset by this. She sort of understood; she'd felt weird seeing him the next day too. The feeling quickly evaporated, but apparently it hadn't for him and he'd needed a human shield between them at lunch.

"So you're saying you stopped being my friend because you were scared I have cooties?"

The tips of his ears turned bright red.

"You totally did!" Afton laughed.

"That's not, I didn't say," Jonah sputtered.

"The only way I can forgive you is if you admit that you stopped talking to me because I'm a girl and you were scared of me," she said gravely.

Jonah covered his face with his hands, muttering something.

"I can't hear you," she singsonged.

"I may have overreacted after that meeting and I have regretted it every day since. Can you find it in your heart to forgive me and let me sing Taylor Swift with you?"

Afton pretended to think about it. "On a trial basis."

He smiled and it stung how much she'd missed it. She walked through the streamers, Jonah trailing after her. When they reached Naya, he held out his hand to introduce himself. Naya frowned.

"You have some explaining to do," she told Jonah.

"He was scared of my cooties," Afton said.

Naya laughed while Jonah blushed all over again.

"Do you promise not to break her heart again?" Naya asked.

Afton elbowed her.

"I won't," Jonah promised.

"Then we're good," Naya said.

The three of them people watched, sang, and saw who could come up with the worst dance moves. The final slow song of the night started playing and Afton's stomach dropped. A boy approached the group, looking between Jonah, Afton, and Naya. He pointed between Jonah and Naya, and Jonah held his hands up as if he was surrendering. When the boy asked Naya to dance, Afton breathed in relief. She scanned the gym, searching for Brennan. He was on the other side of the room, his back to her.

"Do you want to go dance with him again?" Jonah asked.

Afton shuddered. "Absolutely not. Want to go wait in—"

"Do you want to dance?" Jonah interrupted.

"Aren't you still scared of my cooties?" she asked.

"Absolutely," he said, completely serious. He held out his hand to her though. She grabbed it, surprised at how warm his skin was. She stepped in closer to him, placing her other hand on his shoulder. He smelled like cologne and the tiniest bit of sweat.

She waited for his hand to land on her hip and start messing with her underwear. Instead his hand floated next to her side, barely touching her. Her whole body relaxed as they swayed to the music, both silent.

"What's this song?" she finally asked.

Jonah tilted his head, listening intently. "If I had to guess, I bet it's called "I Don't Want to Miss a Thing.""

"Is it supposed to be romantic or creepy? He said he wants to watch her sleep."

"Doesn't the guy in those vampire books watch the girl sleep?" Jonah asks.

Afton gasped. "You read *Twilight?*"

"No, but my parents love to discuss it at dinner."

"What do they say?" she asked excitedly.

"Umm, it's not their favorite." Jonah's voice cracked.

When did his voice start cracking? "What do they even know about good books?"

"Oh, you know, just enough to get a PhD."

"Psh, that's nothing."

Jonah laughed. "When did you get so into music? You knew every line of every song before this."

"Naya's been sneaking me mix CDs. Did you know there's a whole world of music out there besides the Mormon tabernacle choir?"

"Who are your favorites?"

She listed her favorite bands. Jonah nodded enthusiastically with most of them, making a face when she mentioned Maroon 5.

"His voice is awful and he can barely perform live," he said. "I'm making you a mix cd too."

"Do it," she challenged.

"I will. I'll give it to you at school on Monday."

He wanted to extend this moment of... friendship? Past tonight? Maybe getting plowed down by Henry in the hall was a blessing in disguise.

"The song is over," Naya said, having appeared out of nowhere. Henry and Jonah's other friends stood on her other side, grinning mischievously. They jumped apart.

"Thanks for the dance. It was great meeting you, Naya," Jonah said before walking off with Henry.

"What was that?" Naya asked.

"Probably nothing." She didn't dare hope. She'd been crushed by the loss of his friendship before. Tonight was a fluke. He'd gotten her through some awkward moments, and she was grateful for it.

On Monday morning, Jonah appeared at her locker, mix CD in hand.

CHAPTER TEN

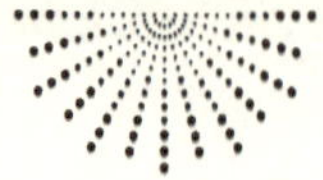

*A*fton finds Chelsea sitting on a bench out back, eyes closed, massaging her temples. When she sits next to her, Chelsea's eyes fly open.

"Is that?"

Afton holds out the bag of McDonald's and diet coke. "Eat up before you get a full-blown migraine."

"How'd you know I was getting one? I didn't even know until a few minutes ago."

"You keep rubbing your neck like you do before a migraine."

Chelsea wraps Afton into a tight hug. "I should get you registered as my migraine-detecting-support-human."

"This wasn't solely for you. Barb's already mysteriously late for work and you can't leave me alone with Richard. Eat up."

Chelsea salutes her with a fry. Today should be a chill day for Afton. The group date was yesterday and she already got plenty of in-the-moment interviews. Today Jonah is taking Tage on a one-on-one date. There shouldn't be too many snide comments about it; Jonah and her haven't done anything for others to be jealous of yet.

"Chelsea, we need you in the great room" Richard's voice crackles over the radio as Chelsea takes the last bite of her burger.

"I think we caught the migraine in time," Chelsea says before standing. Inside the mansion a full camera crew is already at work, along with Richard's favorite PAs. Tension fills the air, and Afton can't pinpoint where it's coming from. All of the women are sitting on the couches, staring at each other silently. The coffee maker is visible on the counter so it's not that. Richard leans against the wall, looking smug. Chelsea goes straight to him while Afton scans the women again. One is missing.

"Where's McKinlee?" Afton asks.

"Where's McKinlee?" Tage repeats, a touch forcefully for the cameras.

"She left ten minutes ago," Bentley says, pointing to the back door.

Richard is pleased with himself, not panicked, so she's not missing. A PA is probably walking McKinlee down the hill to the casita where Jonah's staying. But why? They talked a bit yesterday at the group date, but nothing dramatic happened.

Chelsea and Richard talk in low voices, and Afton joins them.

"Why weren't we told the plan?" Chelsea murmurs.

Richard squints back at Chelsea. "You know how fluid things are. She asked if she could talk to him about something she didn't get to address yesterday, and I decided to let her."

"Her? Of all the women?" Chelsea asks.

"I know what I'm doing," Richard says, crossing his arms.

Is he causing chaos to try and gain back some control? He's been visibly annoyed by the praise Chelsea and Afton have been getting for their ideas.

"Why would you do that when Barb isn't here?" Chelsea asks.

"It's not my fault she's late to work," Richard huffs.

The back door opens, and McKinlee walks in. She's in a flowy dress, face flushed.

"Where were you?" Rileigh asks.

"It's none of your business," McKinlee says as she takes in everyone staring at her.

"It seems like you want it to be," Tage says, leaning on the back of one of the couches.

Bea barely conceals a snort.

McKinlee looks at each of the women one by one. "I was with Jonah. We had sex." She holds her head high.

Tessa was taking a sip of water and does the perfect spit take. Chelsea gasps. Afton scrutinizes McKinlee, something hot slithering through her chest. Did he really sleep with her? McKinlee of all people? During the second week?

The heat is gone by her next breath. There's absolutely no way. McKinlee was gone for maybe fifteen minutes. While this Jonah may be a puzzle to her, she can confidently say he wouldn't hurt all of these women to have a quickie with McKinlee. So why is McKinlee saying it?

The women start gasping. "What?"

"He's a fake."

"If he slept with you, I'm out."

McKinlee's face is smug as she surveys them all. "I knew he was my soulmate. He just proved it to me."

Someone starts crying. Tessa's hand covers her mouth. Bea's brow is furrowed; her lips quirked to the side. Luke, the cameraman, is walking backward slowly toward Afton, capturing everything. She pushes off the wall, ready to get to work. She pulls the nearest crying woman off the couch, leading her down the hallway to a quieter room.

"How did you feel hearing what McKinlee said?" she asks.

Woman after woman confess their anger. It's the second week. How could he have already done that? Many say that they came here for a man with high morals, and the fact that he did that shows he's a fake.

Afton knows the exact questions she should ask. She could easily push and prod to make them angrier and play into Richard's plan.

"Do you believe McKinlee?" she asks instead.

This gives most women pause. Only the few women in McKinlee's clique instantly say yes. Others take a moment to think.

Bea immediately snorts when Afton asks. "No. Her hair is too perfect, and she wasn't gone long enough."

Afton covers her laugh at that and Bea's eyes dance with amusement.

Emily shakes her head emphatically when asked. "McKinlee came here saying that she was saving her first kiss until her wedding. Then she kissed him not even an hour later, claiming he's her soulmate. The story keeps changing."

Tessa bites her lip at the question. "I want to say no. The man that Jonah's shown me wouldn't do that. But I've been tricked by men before."

Afton tries to keep her face neutral. There are two paths she could take. She could play into Tessa's insecurity with this; create doubt. It's obvious she and Jonah have a connection and could go far. With enough doubt, Tessa will be on track to have a sobbing moment outside her parents' home during home visits, confessing she's not ready to say she loves Jonah yet because she can't trust her feelings. Jonah will have tears in his eyes as he carefully tries to reassure her without revealing which woman he's actually going to choose, followed by a one-to-one where he pulls his hair while pacing in circles.

That's what she should do. Exhaustion creeps over her.

"It's hard to trust our judgement when we're hurt by people who should have our best interest in mind," Afton says, thinking of all the times she was told to ignore her intuition growing up. How long it took to trust herself.

Tessa nods. "I'm a science teacher. I rely on data and facts to make decisions, but when it comes to love, that's not enough."

What a soundbite. "Let's look at the facts then. How long was McKinlee gone?"

Tessa looks upward, as if she's calculating, "Fifteen minutes at most."

"Is that enough time for her to get over there, convince him to sleep with her, kick out the camera crew, have sex, get dressed, and come back?"

Luke makes some sort of noise behind the camera. Afton turns to look at him, but his face is engrossed in his screen.

Tessa laughs softly. "McKinlee was only gone for a few minutes, and still in her dress. That doesn't seem like enough time for something like that to happen. I want to get all of the facts and hear Jonah's side of the story before I jump to conclusions."

Yes. This will be a great touchstone for Tessa's scenes going forward.

Richard's plan thwarted, Afton returns to the living room where everyone is gathered. The cameras are trained on the women's faces and the front door as Jonah enters. His smile slips as he looks around the room. Those who meet his gaze fiddle with their promise rings while others frown with their arms folded.

"Hey ladies," he says slowly. "What's going on?"

"McKinlee told us what happened," Maylee says.

Jonah's brows pull together. "I'm sorry, I know how hard— "

"She said you had sex. Either you're a two-pump chump or someone's lying," Bea calls out from the couch.

Afton wants the sound that comes out of Jonah's mouth as her ringtone. It's a mix of a gasp, a laugh, and a groan. The look of utter shock that accompanies it is definitely going to be a meme. She could use it to respond to the heinous things her family texts for years to come.

Jonah turns to where McKinlee is standing. Her head is held high, hands on her hips, and her hair rests perfectly across her shoulders. She doesn't back down from his gaze.

"McKinlee did come to my room, but we didn't have sex," Jonah says calmly.

Everyone whips around to look at McKinlee. "Oral sex counts as sex," she screeches.

His brows raise. "McKinlee, can we speak privately?"

She shakes her head. "No. Anything you have to say to me, you can say in front of them."

He closes his eyes, blowing out a slow breath before opening them. "McKinlee, what do you define as sex?"

"You kept putting your, you know what in my you know what."

Jonah presses his lips together. "Where I'm from, we call that French kissing."

The room is silent. Then Bea starts laughing, starting a chain reaction that soon has everyone giggling.

"Why would you say you had sex when you didn't?" Bentley asks.

"Because, I thought," McKinlee starts breathing heavily. Then she runs out of the room, Richard chasing after her with the cameras.

The women all speak at once, the rest of the cameras swooping in. Jonah stays where he is, looking lost.

"Why would she think that was oral sex?" Chelsea whispers to Afton.

"I was told not to French kiss because it mimics sex. The church tried to ban oral sex briefly in the 80's. Maybe someone actually taught her that's what it is. Anything is possible."

"Wait till she finds out what it really is," Chelsea says.

Afton feels sympathy for McKinlee. Yeah, she was trying to make everyone jealous. But this was made possible thanks to a church culture terrified of healthy sexuality using shame as their weapon. Old hurts twinge inside her at how that same shame completely changed the direction of her life.

Jonah approaches her and Chelsea.

"Where's Barb? What do I do?" he asks.

Chelsea frowns. "I'm going to find out. Can you do an in-the-moment with him?" It's not really a question because Chelsea walks away, phone pressed to her ear.

Jonah rubs at his temple and Afton gulps. She can't protest; there's no one else here to do it. She grabs Luke and leads Jonah down the hall to the nicest office. He's the talent so he doesn't get shoved in closets for this. She pulls an armchair into a corner, ordering Jonah to sit and grabbing a folding chair for herself. She closes the door and the smell of his soap and cologne fill the room. He'd been about to pick Tage up for a date and has to deal with this instead.

"How are you feeling?" Afton starts, like it's her first week on the job and she has an EP watching over her shoulder. It's one thing to push a relative stranger to answer her prying questions. But him? Barb better have a good excuse for not being here.

Jonah runs a hand through his hair, leaning back. He focuses on a spot above her head. "Confused. Hurt. Annoyed. McKinlee showed up wanting to talk. She opened up about feeling insecure about being in her twenties and not experiencing things.

We started kissing, and yes, I deepened the kiss, but that was it. There's camera footage of everything."

"Do you believe she thought that was sex?"

"I have no idea. She either thinks I would sleep with her with a camera crew watching, or she said it to make everyone jealous. Both options aren't great."

"Are you sending her home after this?"

He takes his time choosing his words. "I need to figure out what just happened, and why she did it. If it was an honest mistake that's one thing. But if it was to hurt my relationships with the other women, I'm not okay with that."

She tries to think of a follow up question, then realizes something. She has to answer his questions honestly as part of their deal. But right now *he* has to answer her questions, no matter what they are.

"Would you have slept with someone during week two if given the chance?"

Jonah glares at her. She doesn't back down. His eyes flit to Luke standing behind the camera, and he sighs.

"Absolutely not. I take intimacy seriously. That's not something I'm willing to jump into with someone until I really know them."

"Is it something you're willing to do before marriage now, considering your background?" Afton asks.

His lips form a line. "That's no longer a rule I live by. I think intimacy is an important part of any relationship and if you and your partner are on the same page, something important to explore."

"Have you had your hoe phase yet?"

Luke snorts from behind the camera and covers his mouth.

"Wouldn't you like to know," Jonah says simply.

"I would. Are you here to mess around, or to find a wife?"

His eyes glint. "A wife."

"Would someone wanting to wait until marriage turn you off from pursuing a future with them?"

"Not at all. I completely understand that thinking and will respect that."

"But what about exploring that important part of a relationship?" she presses.

"Effective communication is more important to me. I want a partner who is able to be vulnerable in talking about wants and desires, and willing to keep having those conversations."

Good answer. Teenage Jonah wouldn't have been able to say desires with a straight face.

"How did you feel about Bea calling you a two-pump chump?"

He tilts his head to the side. "Not something I'm worried about."

Damn it. She is not going to overthink how he said that with the perfect amount of confidence so it wasn't cocky, but still sounds like he knows what he's doing. She drums her fingertips on her thigh, and he tracks it with his eyes. The corner of his mouth hitches. She frowns, and he full-on grins. He knows he has her flustered. He can't win here.

She's formulating another question to unbalance him under the guise of the interview when Chelsea comes sliding into the room.

"I've got news," she breathes.

CHAPTER ELEVEN

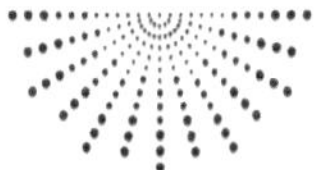

*W*ho has the audacity to be knocking on his door right now? He already dealt with the McKinlee disaster, reassured all the women, and then somehow managed to go on a date with Tage. All without Barb, the person he trusts most on set. Damn her appendix for almost bursting and taking her out indefinitely. He has nothing left to give to whoever's there.

"It's Chelsea. Open up," she calls as if reading his thoughts.

She's not the worst option, but he still has to hide a grimace before opening the door.

"You had a horrible day and we're going out. Do you want to join us?" Chelsea asks. She's standing with two PA's and Luke the cameramen from earlier today. He's almost blinded seeing them wear clothes with color.

"Is this allowed?" Jonah asks carefully.

"I'm making an executive producer judgement call. We're going to the bar, and we'll have you back in one piece."

He should say no and rest. But he hasn't had a casual conversation, much less with a guy, since showing up here. "Let me change."

He throws on the Yellowcard band tee he brought for non-filming days and jeans, then follows them out. The PAs introduce themselves, along with the cameramen.

"I need to talk about anything but love," Jonah says.

"We've got you," Luke says, clapping Jonah on the back. By the time they make it around the property to where everyone's parked, he's learned Luke microbrews in his tub, one of the PA's is a huge Premiere League fan, and the other is the Dungeon Master for their DND league. Luke promises to bring Jonah some beer to try and the PA's both text him lists of podcasts and groups to check out. Hopefully he remembers what they're for in six weeks when he gets his phone back.

They reach the driveway with the cars, and his heart stutters. Leaning against a black SUV is Afton, wearing a black fluttery skirt and an oversized band tee. Not just any band tee, but the same Yellowcard tee Jonah's wearing. She's typing furiously on her phone and doesn't see him. There's still time to turn around and back out. Yell that he's shit his pants or something. He'll lose even more of his dignity, but it'd be worth it.

"Did you both go to the same concert?" Luke asks, pointing between Afton's shirt and Jonah's.

Afton's head whips up and she spots Jonah. Her gaze rakes up and down his body, settling on his shirt before she closes her eyes for a beat too long. Is she remembering that he's the one that introduced her to Yellowcard? On that very first mix CD he made her in 8th grade? How she'd instantly loved them and demanded more of their songs for her next one? Had she been unable to listen to them for years because it reminded her of him? Then decided two years ago that they were too good of a band to miss out on the rest of her life and went to their concert?

"Chelsea and I saw them in Highland. When did you go?" Afton finally asks.

"Highland, with Henry."

She raises her brows, then forces her expression back to something neutral. She's not supposed to know who Henry is.

"Who's Henry?" Luke asks.

"My best friend from middle school. He flew out for the concert. He's watching my dog right now," Jonah rambles.

"Do any of you keep up with your friends from middle school?" Chelsea asks the PA's and Luke. They all shake their heads. "Me either. What are the odds you and Afton both still talk to your middle school friends, and that the three of us all went to the same concert? Do you two have any other weird coincidences? Where'd you go—"

"Come on, we're wasting time," Afton says, pulling on Chelsea's arm and leading her to the car. Chelsea hops into the driver seat and Afton takes shotgun. Jonah climbs into the second row with Luke, while the PA's scroll on their phones in the back.

They've barely started driving when Chelsea shoves her phone at Afton.

"There's an accident, direct me around it."

Afton stares at the phone, zooming and spinning it.

"Which way?" Chelsea demands.

"Hold on, it's freaking out."

"Do you need help reading that?" Jonah asks, leaning forward.

"No," Afton says.

"Yes," Chelsea says, handing him the phone.

He looks at the map, then directs Chelsea in the opposite direction. The bar isn't too far away.

"Fucking boy scout," Afton mumbles under her breath.

"I heard that," he says.

"I would have been able to read the map if I hadn't been so busy learning how to iron instead of life skills like you," she whines.

"Ironing is a life skill," Jonah says.

"Not when you're learning it so you can iron your husband and five sons' shirts for their important meetings one day. A dryer with an ice cube has taken care of all my wrinkle needs, thank you very much."

"I'll have to try that," Jonah says, unable to stop a smile.

"How did you know he was a boy scout?" Luke asks.

Jonah freezes. Did they just ruin everything?

"I grew up Mormon like Jonah. I assumed," Afton says cooly.

Luke's forehead scrunches. "Are you still Mormon?"

"Nope," she says, popping the p.

"What made you leave?" Luke asks.

She turns around in her seat, eyes quickly darting to Jonah, then back to Luke. "It always felt wrong to me, but I could never express why. Like a sweater everyone loves, but is itchy to you. When I was older, I realized it wasn't what I'd been taught it was."

"Like what?" Luke presses.

Afton raises a brow. "My therapist charges good money to hear that story. I'm not going to just throw it out there the first time we hang out."

Luke chuckles next to him. "Fair enough. Maybe by the time we get to the final week, I'll have earned it."

Afton turns forward in her seat. "We'll see."

Is she flirting with Luke? The cameraman she gets to spend all day with every day? Luke had been struggling not to laugh when they'd both been interviewing him today. Jonah focuses back on the map. He's here to find his wife. It's none of his business who Afton flirts with.

"Turn left, and then we should be there," he says.

Chelsea struggles to fit the SUV into the tiny parking spaces, so they all have to squeeze out. He hangs back to walk with the PA's into the bar. It's a total dive, stinking of stale beer with sticky menus.

"Do you want to go somewhere else?" one of the PA's asks.

Afton and Chelsea both emphatically shriek, "No!"

"Why?" the PA asks.

"Because this one has karaoke," Chelsea says, like it's the most obvious thing in the world.

The PA's groan.

"You don't have to sing. You're welcome to sit and talk with people like you would at any other bar," Chelsea says.

Afton splits off from the group and goes to the front of the room to talk with the DJ. Chelsea and Luke settle in at a high tabletop with red bar stools. His eyes track Afton as she moves through the bar, returning from the DJ stand.

"What do you want to drink?" Chelsea asks Jonah.

He hates this. He's still learning about alcohol and doesn't know exactly what he likes. Everyone else figured this out in high school or their early twenties. He's in his thirties.

"Whatever Luke suggests," Jonah finally says.

Luke smiles and goes to order.

Afton appears at the table, grabbing a menu.

"Shot of whiskey?" Chelsea asks her.

"Ooh, and the mango margarita."

"Got it! Save the table," Chelsea says, walking off with the PAs.

"I'll get them," Afton calls, but Chelsea doesn't hear her, leaving the two of them alone at the table.

"I'm perfectly capable of saving the table by myself," Jonah says.

A woman approaches one of the sides and starts to grab Chelsea's empty barstool. Afton quickly slides onto the leather seat. Her skirt rides up her legs, exposing a few inches of thigh. He snatches a menu, studying it instead of her skin.

"This one's taken," Afton says sweetly.

The woman apologizes and walks away. A single finger pushes his menu down.

"You were saying?" Afton smirks.

He presses his lips together. Why does she still have to be funny? "That I'm not capable of protecting the table."

"You'll get there. Is this your first time in a bar?" She sounds genuinely curious, not judgmental.

"No. It is my first karaoke bar though."

She gasps. "Karaoke bars are my church."

"Why?"

"Singing is the only thing I miss about theatre, and church for that matter. Here, I get to perform without all the stress of rehearsal and auditions."

"What happened to the musical theatre degree?" he asks.

She drums her fingers on the table. "I was good for our high school, but not good enough to make it professionally. I thought working in television production would be the safer choice career wise." She snorts. "What'd you end up studying?"

He's having this conversation with Afton. In a karaoke bar. What is his life? "My mission president worked in HR and convinced me it was the best field, so that's what I studied. I'm in recruiting now which is less soul sucking than your typical HR gig. I like it."

"I'm happy for you," she smiles.

Everyone returns to the table with the drinks. Afton thanks Chelsea before sipping her margarita.

"It's better than I imagined," she moans, licking the salt off the rim.

That noise and the sight of her tongue do something to him. He takes a long pull from the beer Luke hands him. Thankfully he doesn't grimace like the first few times he tried beer, but it's still not a Coke. He keeps sipping, determined to acquire the taste.

The DJ calls out Afton's name.

"Are you singing something by Yellowcard," Luke asks.

Jonah barely stops from snorting. He might not know much about this version of Afton, but he'd bet money she still doesn't like doing what she's told.

Afton grabs her shot of whiskey from the table.

"No way," she says before throwing it back.

Luke chuckles, and Chelsea claps. Afton clinks the glass on the table, then pushes her margarita toward Jonah.

"Here's a fruity little drink if you want to try it. No pressure." Then she bounces all the way to the stage.

When she has the microphone in hand, the opening notes of "Before He Cheats," play. With the first "right now," she transforms into a completely different person. Her voice is deeper, sultry. She could be mistaken for Carrie Underwood herself. She moves around the stage confidently, swinging her hips and flipping her hair over her shoulders.

"Right now, he's probably buying her some fruity little drink because she can't shoot whiskey," Afton croons, pointing at their table.

Did she seriously order a fruity little drink and whiskey for this moment? He shakes his head and laughs.

Luke leans in close to Chelsea, smiling. "She is a force."

Chelsea bumps him with her elbow. "I *told* you. She tortured herself learning to like whiskey purely because of this song."

Jonah tries to ignore the two of them, focusing back on Afton. He went to her musicals; he heard her church solos. They rocked out to his car radio, but he's never seen her like this. A confident woman owning the stage, the entire bar. The crowd is belting out the chorus with Afton, and she's feeding that energy right back to them. He's mesmerized. Purely in the exes to mutually beneficial acquaintances who can appreciate each other's talents sort of way.

The song finishes and Afton takes a bow. She skips back to their table, energy radiating off her as she twists her damp hair into a knot at the base of her neck. Chelsea wraps her into a huge hug, while Luke and the PAs compliment her.

She slides into her stool and reaches for her margarita. Jonah slips it out of her reach, locking eyes with her as he takes a sip. He holds back a grimace as the aftertaste burns his throat.

"What do you think?" she asks.

"About you or my fruity little drink?"

"Both." Her nose ring flashes as she tips her head.

"Surprisingly delightful."

She raises a brow and reaches for her drink. He lets her have it this time.

An older man with a deep rumbly voice is singing a slow country song. People start flocking to the middle of the dance floor and swaying. A dark-haired woman approaches the table and taps Luke on the shoulder. They chat for a moment, and then Luke walks away with her to the middle of the dance-floor.

"Would you have danced with him if he'd asked you?" Chelsea asks Afton.

His throat burns. It's probably from drinking so late. He pulls Afton's drink back and takes another long sip. More alcohol to soothe the burn of alcohol.

"No. We work together."

The burning stops. See, it worked.

Chelsea lays her head in her arms on the tabletop. "You're insufferable."

Afton grabs Chelsea's face in both her hands, forcing her to look up. "I'm not your job. I'm fine."

What's that about? Is there a reason Chelsea is worried

about Afton? The two of them stare for a long moment before Chelsea finally dips her chin.

"Speaking of work, do I get a new producer while Barb's gone?" he asks.

Chelsea turns to him. "We're discussing that tomorrow morning. Any preferences?"

"Anyone but Richard. He set McKinlee on me, didn't he?"

Chelsea doesn't confirm it, ever the professional. Afton nods emphatically from behind Chelsea's head.

"Noted. Can I ask, what's the weirdest part of being the Fiance-to-be?" Chelsea asks.

He takes another sip of Afton's drink. "Having you two watch me make out with people." He's only half kidding.

Afton groans. "How many times do I have to tell you; we're not watching. We have better things to do."

"Sometimes I watch," Chelsea says, shrugging her shoulders.

Afton punches her in the arm.

"I know how to fix it," Chelsea says, face brightening.

"How?" He's interested to see what a buzzed Chelsea thinks is a good idea.

"We'll go around the bar and kiss strangers while you watch us," Chelsea says.

He gapes at Afton in horror. Surely, she'll say no. She wasn't even willing to slow dance with Luke, someone she knows.

The corners of Afton's mouth creep into a smile. "I love it."

He shakes his head. "No, you don't have to do that. I was joking, I don't care..."

"No, I absolutely do," Afton says, standing and linking her arm in Chelsea's before coming over to Jonah and yanking him off his stool. He plants his feet and refuses to go forward.

"I was kidding. Don't do this."

"I've always wondered what it's like to kiss strangers back-to-back. When will I ever have another chance to do this?"

"You could be the lead next season," he offers.

"As if," Afton laughs. She lets go of his arm and starts toward the DJ stand with Chelsea. He groans before following after them, staying a few paces back as Afton approaches the DJ. When the DJ looks Afton and Chelsea over appreciatively, Jonah steps closer.

As the current song ends, the DJ grabs the microphone. "Attention everyone. These fine women here have a request. They'd like to kiss as many people as possible in the next three minutes. Kissing only, nothing extra. If you're interested, come line up here."

"Kiss Me" by Sixpence None the Richer starts playing. Chelsea pulls out a tube of lip gloss and smacks it dramatically on her lips.

No one moves at first. Afton and Chelsea look around the room dramatically, hands on their brows. Then Afton turns around to the DJ and points a finger between them. He presses another button on his setup. A disco ball comes down from the ceiling and showers the room in weak glimmering light.

The DJ jumps over his setup, then holds out a hand. Afton grabs it and he spins her into him, dramatically dipping her before running a thumb across her jaw. When he finally leans down to kiss her, the crowd goes wild with cheering. Chelsea laughs and claps next to them.

A pit forms in his stomach. It's concern, nothing else. He's worried for his coworkers' safety. People aren't their most reasonable when drinking, and they might try to push Chelsea and Afton's boundaries, that's all.

The DJ finishes kissing Afton and Chelsea is kissing a guy in cowboy boots. A new man approaches Afton, saying something in her ear. She laughs then walks over to the wall. He stands in front of her and flips his baseball cap backward, then leans an arm above her head. Her face is surprised delight as he leans in for the kiss. Jonah tracks her hand as it wraps around the back of his neck, pulling him closer.

The next man picks her up and she wraps her legs around his waist. The third he catches a glimpse of her tongue. He closes his eyes. Does Afton feel like this when he's kissing the women? She never seems affected. What's wrong with him?

He focuses on Chelsea who's also kissing strangers. Some are quick, and some men she lingers with. All he feels is awkwardness for glancing; they deserve privacy.

Jonah turns to go back to their table. Everyone is being surprisingly respectful. They don't need him here as backup. Then he sees Luke making his way through the crowd. He expects him to stop and stand with him, but Luke walks right past Jonah. The pit in his stomach becomes a cavern. He should not care. Afton is an adult and can decide for herself.

Luke approaches Afton. She stands up on her tiptoes and whispers something in Luke's ear. Then she kisses him on the cheek, and pats him on the shoulder. Luke doesn't look at all bothered, disappearing back into the crowd.

Afton walks over to the DJ who hands her the microphone wordlessly, turning down the music.

"Thank you, everyone. Our lips are tired, and our souls are happy. Have a good night," she says.

The crowd starts clapping and hollering, and then the next song is announced.

Afton links arms with Chelsea and they walk over to Jonah.

"Better?" Afton asks him, eyes blazing.

Worse. "You're ridiculous."

She giggles and the sound cuts through a layer of his defenses. Coming here tonight was a bad idea. He was supposed to see the bad sides of Afton and finally let go of the idealized version of her in his head. Not slip right back into this comfortable banter.

He should have faked the diarrhea.

When the girls are safely back at the table with the PAs, he walks over to the bar trying to clear his head. There isn't a line and he makes awkward eye contact with the bartender.

"Can I get a water?" He's barely drank but he doesn't want to risk a headache tomorrow. "Actually, make it three."

He hugs the waters to his chest and brings them back to the table, setting the others in front of Afton and Chelsea. Afton studies hers, forehead furrowing.

"Aww, you're always the one doing that for us," Chelsea says to Afton.

"Thank you," Afton says softly.

Why'd she have to say it like that? It's just water. He was getting some and saved everyone time by grabbing them in bulk.

Chelsea talks animatedly with the production assistants about… wrestling? He tries to follow the conversation so he can jump in, but he's truly lost. There's movement in his periphery as a man stumbles up to the table, stopping next to Afton. She stiffens, eyeing the man warily. Jonah slides off his barstool, standing in case he's needed.

"I want my kiss," the man slurs.

"Sorry, that's over."

"I want. My kiss," the man repeats, leaning in closer to Afton.

Afton slides backward off her barstool as Jonah steps toward her so she's pressed against him. Everywhere they touch, his skin instantly warms.

"It's my boyfriend's bedtime. Let's go home," she says, tilting her head backward and meeting his eyes.

He hesitates, then wraps an arm around her shoulders, pulling her in even closer. "Goodnight," Jonah says firmly to the man before leading Afton toward the exit. The drunk man stays next to the table, his eyes glazed. She's silent the entire walk to the SUV.

"Chelsea has the keys," she says when he pulls on the door handle.

The door to the bar opens and she flinches underneath his arm. It's not the man, but she still seems spooked. He leads her out of view to the side of the building where there's an alleyway. Surprisingly, there's no one out here. She ducks out from under his arm, moving to the opposite side of the alley and leaning against the wall. The September air chills where she'd been pressed against him.

"Sorry about that. I hate the whole damsel-in-distress thing, but it's the fastest way to get a guy to back off. They respect another man's property more than a woman."

"No—"

"Don't you dare say that I asked for it with all the kissing. That had a very defined start and end," she says, waving a finger at him.

Jonah puts his hands up. "I wasn't going to say—"

"Or about how I deserved it for being in a bar in the first place."

She's not going to let him get a word in. He crosses half the alley in a single step. It works; she stops and stares up at him. Her hair is mussed, her eyes are wild, and she smells of perfume and a hint of sweet sweat. He involuntarily takes another step, only a foot between them now.

"I wasn't going to say any of those things," Jonah says, voice surprisingly low.

"The old you would have," Afton says.

"I'm not him anymore."

She crosses her arms, but he sees her eyes flit to his lips. "Then who are you?"

"Why don't you find out?" He comes closer, stopping when

his feet bump hers, waiting to see what she'll do. One heartbeat. Two. He starts to step back, obviously having misread this, but she fists his shirt and pulls him back. Her chest is pressed against his and he can feel each of her rapid inhales. They hover there, their lips a hairsbreadth apart, every exhale tickling his skin.

One of them inhales sharply enough to close the distance, her lips finally brushing against his. It's so light he could have imagined it except for the heat that races down his spine, and her breathless gasp. He brushes his lips against the entirety of her mouth, memorizing the ridges of her cupid's bow, the fullness of her bottom lip. When he reaches the right corner that always hitches up when she's fighting a smile, he lingers, pressing the gentlest of kisses.

She tilts her chin, teeth scraping against his top lip as she captures his mouth with her own, kissing him fully. No more hesitation, no more teasing. His hand wraps around her neck, fingers tangling in her hair. She moans, fisting his shirt and pulling him with her until her back is against the wall of the alley. She presses her hips against him and his brain glitches. He slides a hand down her sides, past the hem of her skirt, to her bare leg. His fingers wrap around her thigh and he lifts her leg up, bringing her closer to him. She gasps, her fingernails digging into his shoulder.

"Jonah," she breathes, the word… Panicked?

That's all it takes. To remember who he is. Where he is. When he is. Afton isn't his. They're coworkers and the last thing they should be doing is exploring each other in an alley. He lowers her leg back to the ground. Once he's sure she's steady, he steps backward, running his hands through his hair.

What has he done?

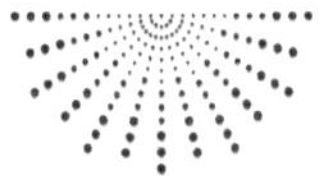

CHAPTER TWELVE

James Partridge passed away from a brain aneurysm while sleeping the last week of May. Afton sat in the overfilled chapel as Jonah's family members shared memories from the pulpit. Jonah was slumped in the front row, his arm wrapped around his mom's shoulders as she openly wept.

Afton's mom whispered to her dad, "she'll see him again. There's no need for that."

Anger filled her belly. How dare they judge Carrie for crying? Maybe it was because, unlike them, James and Carrie had the kind of relationship where they were best friends who couldn't get enough of each other. That was the kind of love Afton wanted one day. Not what her parents had. If the families were switched, her mother wouldn't be crying.

Afton and her mother went to the church kitchen to help the other sisters prepare the luncheon for Jonah's family while they were at the graveside service. Afton dutifully carried salad bowls and individually wrapped pats of butter for the rolls to each table. When the funeral potatoes and ham were served, she and her mom walked home, not wanting to intrude on the Partridge family in their grief.

At home, her middle brothers whined that they were hungry while her dad watched a baseball game with Dan. Her youngest brother, Noah, stood at her legs, pulling on her skirt and crying until she picked him up. Lately he only wanted her. To put his shoes on, hold him, and tuck him in bed. She helped him whenever possible, trying to prevent his crying before it started.

Afton balanced Noah on her hip, then on her back piggyback style, as she helped her mom prep sandwiches for everyone. Her chest ached as she thought about the Partridges. How could James be gone? She'd debated *Twilight* with him at the dinner she'd been invited to not even a month ago. Carrie and James had explained point by point how Edward and Bella's relationship wasn't healthy, while also praising how Meyer was able to write such an addictive story. James and Carrie always made her feel important, like her opinions mattered even if they didn't agree.

She couldn't imagine the devastation Jonah felt right now. She wanted to take away the pain, but there was nothing she could do.

"Lunch is ready," her mom called and her brothers and dad came streaming into the kitchen. Afton helped Noah sit at the table. Only food could make him let go of her. She quickly threw together her own sandwich as her dad settled at the table across from her mom.

"James Partridge was a good man," he said.

"He really was," her mom repeated.

"All I ever heard you do was complain about how much of an idiot he was," Dan said.

"Dan, that is not true," her mom snapped. "Take that back."

Her dad's cheeks went red. Was it in embarrassment because what Dan said was true? Or anger that Dan had said it? Whatever it was, she didn't want to be here. She grabbed her sandwich and slid out of the room and through the front door unnoticed. She headed down the street toward the park where there were picnic tables.

There was a lone figure at the park sitting on the swings. Afton knew it was Jonah, even from this far away. She could always locate him—whether in a crowd at school, in the halls at church, or from a block away. She kicked up the gravel as she approached so he had ample warning.

"Hey," she said quietly.

He looked up at her, purple rings under his bloodshot eyes. "Hey," he murmured.

"I'm here if you need to talk," Afton said.

Jonah nodded, but stayed silent. She sat on the swing next to him, swaying back and forth in the quiet.

"We're going to stay with my grandma in California for the summer. We might move there," he finally said.

Her heart clenched. "I'll miss you."

"I'll miss you too," Jonah said. And then he was crying.

What was she supposed to do? All she could think of was to slide her swing next to his, and wrap an arm around him.

"He'd want me to be the man of the family, but I can't do it," he whispered.

Afton rested her head against his, squeezing harder. She knew a taste of what that was like, expected to be a mini mom to her little brothers. At the end of the day though, she still had two parents.

"Your dad was an amazing man, and so is your mom. You are half of him and half of her. You can do this."

Jonah started crying harder, and Afton kept holding him.

"I didn't get enough time. Everyone keeps saying we'll see him again, but I want him now. Not later."

The scripts she'd collected Sunday after Sunday, lesson after lesson, popped into her mind. This was all God's plan. Endure to the end. We're never given something bigger than we can handle. The lines stuck in her throat. Jonah knew all those things; there was no reason to repeat them. So, she simply squeezed him harder.

SHE STAYED busy that summer volunteering at the library handing out prizes for the summer reading program with Naya. Afton signed up for as many shifts as possible, much to her parents' disapproval. When they complained saying they needed help with her brothers, she reminded them of the service hours she needed for her young women's award. That made them stop complaining for the most part.

Afton and Naya quickly became friends with Sadie, a black girl who'd be going to their high school. Sadie's family was Baptist and had moved to Utah from Texas the year before for her dad to be a pastor. Afton had tons of questions and was fascinated by the differences between Sadie's church and hers. Sadie's dad had actually gone to school to be a pastor, and it was his full time job. He wasn't called by God for a short while and still expected to work another job like bishops. Sadie always answered her questions kindly, her and Naya joking that Afton was their adopted white Mormon girl whom they loved in spite of it.

Sadie's neighborhood had a pool and she invited Afton and Naya to swim whenever they weren't at the library. The first time Afton asked to go, her mom said no, claiming the Holy Spirit warned her something bad was going to happen. Afton was sick to her stomach the whole day, terrified one of her friends was going to drown. Or have an aneurysm. She kept calling their cell phones and neither of them answered.

When Naya finally answered at 6:30, Afton almost screamed at her. "Are you okay?"

"Of course, why wouldn't we be?"

"The Holy Spirit told my mom something bad was going to happen."

"Well, nothing did," Naya said.

"Maybe it was going to happen to me, and since I stayed home, that's why it was okay."

Naya was quiet for a moment. "Or your mom just didn't want you to go to the pool, so she used that as an excuse."

"She would never do that. That's horrible."

"You're probably right. We're fine though. I wish you could have been there."

It happened a second time. Afton asked to go, the Spirit said no, and she worried all day while her mom stayed in her room and left Afton to take care of her brothers. The tiniest bit of doubt creeped in. What if it *was* an excuse to keep her home? When her friends were fine once again, she decided to do an experiment. If God really was warning her mom about her safety, then He would tell her mom that Afton was lying.

Afton approached her mom in the kitchen with all of her swim supplies shoved in her backpack. She announced she was going to the library. Her legs shook as she waited.

Her mom sighed, then agreed.

And so, Afton went to the pool. She sat with her arms wrapped around her legs on a lounger, terrified to get in. She'd been taught Satan controlled the water. What if God stopped protecting her the moment she touched the water because she'd lied to be here?

Sadie and Naya splashed at her, begging her to join them. Only when they promised to stay in the shallow end did Afton carefully slide into the pool one inch at a time.

She didn't drown.

She had a blast.

After showering off the pool smell and blow drying her hair completely, she returned home, once again an anxious mess. She waited for her parents to confront her about her lies. Instead, it was a normal night like any other. They didn't know. The Spirit hadn't told them anything.

She did it again. And again. Every time waiting for the Spirit to tattle on her. It never did. She learned how to make sunscreen tattoos from Naya and the best way to jump off the diving board from Sadie. They talked about books, which boys at the pool were cute, and what they hoped high school would be like.

"I wish all of the Mormons were like you," Sadie said one day while sitting on the loungers.

"What do you mean?" Afton asked.

"You haven't tried to convert us," Sadie said.

"Or called us a, what is it? A Leonite?" Naya asked.

"Lamanite?" Afton asked.

"Yes, that one! Do you really believe that we have dark skin because we're cursed?" Sadie asked.

"What?" Afton had no idea where that came from.

"It's in your scriptures," Sadie insisted.

Sadie's dad must have been lied to at his school. That night she pulled out her scriptures, trying to find what they might be talking about. It didn't take long to find the passage. The Lamanites were cursed with skins of darkness. The righteous Nephites were white, and when Lamanites accepted Christ, they too became white.

Why didn't she know that was in her scriptures, but her friends did? Did her parents know about it? The scriptures took place thousands of years ago. Why would people still think this applied, or call her friends Lamanites? She desperately wished Jonah's dad was still here. He was the only person she'd trust to ask these questions. Definitely not her parents. When they looked at her friends, did they think of that verse?

THE WEEKEND before high school started, Afton saw a familiar van in the Partridge driveway, along with all the windows in the house open. They were back. She immediately started pulling things out of the fridge. There wasn't a lot to work with so she made spaghetti, but with rotini to make it special. She heated up meatballs, and even roasted broccoli.

"What are you doing?" her dad asked.

"Making dinner for the Partridges. And us. I felt a prompting by the Spirit."

Her dad beamed at her. "I'm so proud of you serving others and learning how to understand those promptings."

"Thanks," she said, the guilt from the lie overshadowed by the excitement of seeing the Partridges. Her hands filled with aluminum tins, she kicked awkwardly at their front door instead of knocking. When nothing happened, she kicked it again. Finally, the door swung open and Sarah was standing there. At least, that's who she thought it was. This girl was almost as tall as Afton now and had sun-bleached hair halfway down her back.

"I brought you dinner," Afton said.

"Is it spaghetti or potatoes?" Sarah asked. "Because we're tired of those."

Afton deflated.

"Sarah," Carrie chastised, coming up behind Sarah. Her eyes lit up. "Afton, it's great to see you."

"I brought you dinner, but I'm sure you're tired of spaghetti. I should have–"

"Thank you, we're hungry after settling in all day. Come in,"

Carrie said. As soon as Afton crossed the threshold, Carrie wrapped her into a hug.

"You grew this summer," Carrie said, pulling away and looking Afton over.

Had she? She didn't think so.

"Do you want to have a girls' night with us and watch *Ready for the Ring*?" Carrie asked.

"I don't want to intrude," Afton said, copying what her mom always said.

"It wouldn't be. Jonah's out with Henry, and I need someone who won't complain about the kissing," Carrie says.

There was going to be kissing on this show? And Carrie was okay watching it? She settled down next to Carrie and her daughters, watching as a spacious mansion with a handsome man came into view.

Her little brothers were so chaotic at church the next day, she forgot to look for Jonah in the chapel until he was standing right next to her with the sacrament tray. She let out a little squeak. If Carrie thought Afton had changed over the summer, what had happened to Jonah? His hair had been lightened by the sun and was long, swooping over his forehead and almost covering his eyes. His skin was tan and the suit that had been baggy on him at the beginning of the year actually fit now. And, she could smell him. He was wearing some sort of cologne, and it wasn't the Axe spray all the boys came out of the gym locker room stinking of.

She'd been staring at him way too long, so he bumped the side of her arm with the sacrament tray. She was supposed to be focused on how the bread was the body of Christ, and how He'd died for her sins. Yet all she could think about was Jonah's body.

He was hot. This was bad. Very bad.

He bumped her arm again with the tray and she quickly took a piece of bread before passing it to her brother.

She tracked him around the room as he passed the bread from row to row. What was going on? This was Jonah. Her *friend*. The one who'd only started talking to her a few months ago because he'd been so freaked out after that meeting. She couldn't think he was cute, not now.

The other girls were tracking him, too. A pit of… something formed in her stomach. Why couldn't she have gotten hotter this summer? She still didn't have boobs, and her chin was covered in scabbed over zits.

Jonah came back with the tray of water. She grabbed a tiny plastic cup, something she'd done every Sunday since she was three and never had a problem doing before. Except for today. As she tipped the cup, water dribbled down the front of her light blue dress, landing in the middle of her lap.

"You peed," Noah snickered, pointing to the spot.

She leaned forward, trying to hide the spot while grabbing the tray from Jonah. It bumped the back of the metal chair in front of her, the clang filling the silent chapel. People turned around reflexively, searching for the source of the sound. Jonah stood next to her, hands clasped together in front of him, staring forward.

If there was any chance that he might have thought she'd grown up and was interesting after his summer away, it was gone now. There was no coming back from this.

CHAPTER THIRTEEN

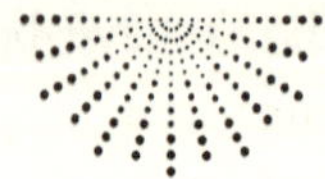

*A*fton knocks on his door, louder than she normally would. She hasn't slept the past two days, she's pissed off, and the door happens to be there. When she doesn't hear movement inside after counting to ten, she pounds.

The poor door. It's not the one lying to everyone, making it impossible to turn down a work promotion to Jonah's personal producer without causing suspicion.

"It'll get you away from the women and having to talk about Mormonism all day," Chelsea beamed when she told Afton. "It was you or Richard, and Jonah made his opinion on Richard pretty clear."

After that kiss in the alleyway, she needs more space from Jonah than ever. As his producer she'd be with him all day, every day. On flights, in cars, checking him into hotels. If there was ever a time to come clean, it was now, before she was going to be alone with him for long stretches of time. When given ten minutes alone, he'd pressed her against the wall of the alley and kissed her senseless.

It was the hottest kiss she'd had in, well, ever. She's had

dozens of kisses over the years and multiple in the bar right before Jonah, but nothing had prepared her for *that*. The feeling of being out in the cold and finally getting next to a fire. A desperate gasp of air after being underwater too long. The first taste of something foreign, yet familiar. All followed by the slap of remembering this is the worst thing you could possibly be doing.

She weighed the cost of confessing now. Chelsea might look suspicious having just recommended Afton for the position. The little trust Jonah has been building with production after his night one shakeup would be completely gone. She won't risk Chelsea's career any more than she already has. Plus, the faster she gets Jonah wifed-up, the easier it will be to close that chapter of her life. She's made it this far; she's going to see this all the way through.

That doesn't mean she has to be happy about it.

"Open up or I'm using my key," she yells at the door.

"Hold on," Jonah says, flinging it open.

She looks him up and down. He's shrugging on a t-shirt, but he didn't have a chance to find pants. She looks away from his navy boxers, smirking as she walks inside the room. He grabs a pair of sweatpants from a chair and hastily pulls them on.

"What are you doing here?" he asks, voice grumbly.

"I've been assigned as your new personal producer," she says, eyeing his room. There are only a few things out, so he must have packed the night before. She grabs his suitcase and wheels it closer to the door.

"Let's go. There's a crash, so we need to avoid traffic."

He gapes at her, mouth wide open. She's tempted to reach up and push it closed, but that would mean touching him which is a *horrible* idea.

"Very funny," he says.

"I wish I was joking."

Jonah closes his eyes and pinches the bridge of his nose. "No."

"You told production you didn't want Richard so, here I am," she says sweetly, feeling anything but.

Jonah inhales and exhales slowly before opening his eyes.

"Fine. Let me take a quick shower and I'll be ready."

"There's no time for a shower. Brush your teeth and let's go."

If he stinks, that will help with operation 'Stop Thinking Inappropriate Thoughts About Jonah.' Like the fact that even though they dated for two years, she never got to see him in the morning. She had no idea his voice was so quiet and grumbly, or that the sides of his hair stuck up adorably. She has the urge to run her fingers through the rest of his hair and mess it all up…

Stop it. It was one kiss.

This is going to be harder than she thought.

He shuts himself in the bathroom and she focuses on searching for anything left behind. There are no chargers or phones to find, and everything else is already packed. When she hears the shower running, Angry Afton™ is back.

"I told you we didn't have time for that!" she yells.

"What're you going to do? Come drag me out?"

The bathroom doorknob has the standard circle lock that she just so happens to have a master key for, in case anyone locks themselves in a bathroom and production is afraid they're going to hurt themselves. If Jonah doesn't get out of the shower and onto the road, he's in danger of *her* hurting him. She unlocks the door, opening it a few inches.

"You have until the count of five." The water keeps running so she starts counting. When she reaches one, the water is still going. She waits a few more seconds, hoping Jonah will come to his senses. Does he think she's bluffing? Rolling her shoulders, she reminds herself it's nothing she hasn't seen before and flings the bathroom door open. Jonah is brushing his teeth at the counter; a towel wrapped around his hips.

Her eyes dart around the room. The shower is still running, the curtain drawn. There are stray water droplets on his chest, his wet hair plastered to his head. Jonah grins at her, toothbrush sticking out of his mouth.

"Did you take a shower?"

"Told you I could be quick," he says.

"That's what Mckinlee said."

He rolls his eyes, then spits into the sink before throwing his toothbrush in his toiletry bag. He hands it to her before shutting the shower off and pulling on his t-shirt. He's fully dressed by the time she's shoved his toiletries in his suitcase and deposited it next to the door.

"I'm perfectly capable of carrying that on my own," he says when she starts rolling his bag out the door and up the path to the main driveway.

"Wouldn't want the talent to break a nail," she says, continuing to the waiting SUV and throwing his suitcase in the back. For some reason he's still standing right behind her.

"Do you need me to open your door for you too?" she snaps.

"Why are you mad at me?"

Normally she'd lie, but she's been telling too many of those. "It's your fault we're in this situation."

His eyebrows shoot up. "How?"

"You told them you didn't want to work with Richard, so I was the only option to replace Barb."

"When? I haven't talked to Karl and Hannah in days."

"At the bar," she hisses.

His forehead crinkles, trying to remember. "I said that to Chelsea in passing. It's not like I went to the higher-ups and threw a fit."

"Well, here I am." She waves her arms for emphasis.

He frowns. "Are you going to be like this the whole time? If so, I'd rather fess up."

Her legs wobble. "You can't. Chelsea vouched for me to get this position."

"So your first lie of not knowing me is spiraling out of control in ways you never imagined? Color me shocked."

She flips him off and he chuckles. She covers her face with her hands and silently screams, a high pitched squeak the only sound. She can't do this. He knows all the ways to get under her skin and that's before you factor in what happened in the alley.

"Look, I know things are weird after—" Jonah starts before focusing in on something above her head.

"Don't close the trunk," Luke calls out, running across the grass with one of the PAs from the bar.

"Could I talk to you for a moment?" Luke asks when they reach her.

This is not the conversation about the bar she wants to have. She desperately needs Jonah to finish whatever he was going to say. They're about to fly across the world together and she doesn't know how to do this. How to occupy the same space as him. How to keep her thoughts in check. How to stop reacting to the mere brush of his skin.

In the alley she'd been the first to realize what they were doing, but Jonah was the one who'd immediately rationalized it. It was a simple mistake. They were both slightly buzzed, Afton had just kissed a bunch of strangers, and Jonah was encouraged to kiss women whenever he felt like it. They had history, they were adults, and they'd both thought about kissing at the same time. It didn't mean anything.

She'd made a joke about how they were coworkers who'd kissed before, they'd just kissed more recently now. He'd laughed, then walked her back to the car where he easily chatted with the others on the drive home. He'd been completely unaffected. Yet here she is, an angry mess of a person who doesn't have the energy to talk with Luke in case she's going to have to turn him down. Again.

She feels Jonah watching as she steps to the grass where Luke's waiting. She gives him a small nod, trying to communicate she's fine. She'll get this conversation with Luke over with so she can focus on more important things. Like how to get through today.

Luke runs a hand over his hair. "I wanted to apologize for approaching you at the bar. I was told the interest was mutual which is the only reason I did. I never want to make someone feel unsafe at work, "

The only person who would say something like that is Chelsea. Chelsea's lucky that she and Hannah have to stay here for meetings instead of going to Mexico with the rest of the crew.

"I'm sor—" she starts.

"Don't apologize, you did nothing wrong. It won't happen again. I was assigned to ride to the airport with you, but I can switch cars if you're at all uncomfortable."

Damn it. Why does Luke have to be so caring and thoughtful? Most men go through the world never thinking about how their actions make women feel unsafe at work, a place they can't just leave. If he wasn't her coworker and her head wasn't such a mess, maybe she would go for him.

"It's fine, I don't mind at all. Let's pretend the other night didn't happen."

"Deal," he smiles, then opens the SUV door for her. Jonah already climbed into the third row with the PA and they're talking about Dungeons and Dragons. Multiple backpacks take up the shotgun, so Afton is forced to sit next to Luke. Thankfully her phone buzzes.

UNKNOWN

When's the next time you'll be in Utah?

WHAT THE HELL? What does Noah want from her? Two years ago he was screaming at her to leave the family alone. How does he go from reminding her that all she's done is let him down, to then wanting to know the next time she'll be around completely out of the blue? Does he somehow know she'll be in SLC next week for work?

Not sure. Probably Christmas. Why?

Just curious. It's been a while.

SHE CAN ONLY HANDLE four days home for Christmas every year, so it's not like she's been gone longer than usual.

I know. How've you been?

Better than I have in a long time.

SHE BITES HER CHEEK. When she's seen Noah at those Christmases, he'd seemed fine. Laughing while playing with their nieces and nephews. Messing around with their brothers. There are the occasional muttered words under his breath, but he always gives her a cordial hug and tells funny stories from his job as a wedding photographer. Does she deserve to ask why he's better now when she had no idea there was something wrong?

She's so stuck in her head they're almost through security before she realizes Jonah is rolling her carry-on through the airport.

"Wouldn't want you to break a nail," he says when she tries to wrench it back. She could fight him, but that would cause a scene, so she lets it go. For now.

Hannah and Chelsea were able to transfer their business class seats to Afton and Jonah so they part ways with Luke and the PA at boarding.

"Luke can switch seats with me if you want," Jonah says as they're walking down the airplane aisle.

"Why?" she asks carefully. Has she been that much of a jerk to him that he can't stand sitting by her for the flight? It can't be because he's uncomfortable around her; he's been Mr. Collected since the kiss.

He stuffs her suitcase into the overhead bin, his shirt rising and revealing a sliver of his stomach. "If you like him, you should go for it."

He's trying to hook her up with Luke. Her guilt is instantly gone. She might be single at the moment, but she isn't so desperate she needs her ex-boyfriend to try and hook her up with a coworker.

"You know men and women are allowed to talk to each other without secretly wanting to fuck, right?"

He jolts and she uses his distraction to snatch his suitcase and lift it up into the bin. When she looks at him, he's blushing.

"I was just saying if you want to switch seats, go for it."

She drops down into her slightly larger business class seat. "My life is too big of a mess already; might as well sit with the mess I know."

He puts his hand over his heart. "That's the sweetest thing anyone's ever said to me."

"Oh, I know," she winks.

His forehead wrinkles, but he doesn't press it. They're quiet as they settle into their seats and get through takeoff. She's reaching down to pull out her laptop when he turns to her.

"What do you mean your whole life is a mess?"

She jerks away from him. "None of your business. Watch a movie."

He taps his chin. "Not really in the mood for a movie. It's good we have a deal where you have to answer my questions, isn't it?"

She glares at him, radiating frustration. He waits, completely unfazed. Fine. He wants the mess? He can have it.

"For starters, the world's a shitshow."

"I already knew that; continue."

She rubs her chest. "You already know about the web of lies I made. Even if I get through this without getting caught, it doesn't guarantee I'll have a job after this because people are always getting cut. I'm never home so the only friends I have are Chelsea, Naya, and Sadie, all of whom I'm letting down. Chelsea thinks she has to parent me. Naya literally planned her baby shower around my old work schedule so I could be there. Sadie's flying out so we can all have one last hurrah before the baby, and I haven't had the heart to tell them that I got fired and am 93% sure I'll miss it."

Jonah opens his mouth, but she cuts him off.

"Oh, and Noah has started randomly texting me and I don't know what he wants. Maybe simply to remind me that I messed up his childhood. Who knows?"

He chews on his bottom lip and she readies to tell him all about Noah and their falling out.

"Do you like being a producer?"

The air is sucked from her lungs. "I'm good at it."

He raises a brow. "That's not what I asked. Do you like it?"

She rubs harder at her chest. "I fought to be here; you have no idea."

"Still not the question."

She'd loved being a producer at first. The travel, getting to meet unique people, learning how they ticked. The thrill of figuring out the right question to ask to make them act. Seeing everything behind the scenes and knowing exactly who was talking shit about who gave her the tiniest taste of what a god must feel.

She moved her way up, got invited to new rooms. She peeked behind the curtain. And she realized once again she was part of an organization that wasn't what it seemed. The higher ups would always say that cast members' physical and emotional health was their number one priority before making television, but it wasn't. Food, sleep, and sometimes even water were rationed. People were isolated in vulnerable states. The heads of networks and even show-runners were abusive to their own staff.

Afton tried to fight back. She'd advocate for her casts. She'd disobey the rules. Try to manipulate storylines to give assholes less of the spotlight. At the end of the day she was one cog in a machine, and if she couldn't do her job, then she'd be replaced. She started looking for new jobs, but two years ago her mom called to tell her one of the middle brothers was in jail.

Afton flew home, hoping to help. Instead she'd found a despondent mom in her room, a dad convinced the arrest was all a misunderstanding. Dan who was too busy with his own family, another brother high out of his mind, and Noah? Noah was angry. At her.

"Why are you here? You broke our family when you left us. Go back to your life out in the world," he'd said.

She'd come home to the life she'd fought so hard for. Her worldly, sin filled life. Where she had sex once a month if she was lucky to be in the same time zone as her boyfriend. A drink or two on the rare nights she saw her friends. Grocery shopped on Sundays because that was the only time she could squeeze it in. Swore, listened to smutty audiobooks, and supported her LGBTQ+ friends and neighbors.

She ignored the numbness crawling through her veins. Accepted it when her boyfriend dumped her because of her schedule. Did what she was told at work. Until that day she'd snapped on set and called out that abusive asshole. She has no idea why he was the one to set her off; he wasn't even the worst of them. A piece of her blinked awake in that moment, and it refused to go back to sleep.

Everything is different now. She's on an established production, has a better job, and gets to work with her best friend. But that familiar numbness has been creeping back in…

Is she having a heart attack? A blood clot? Her breaths are shallow and she tries to take deep, slow ones, but her chest aches so hard she physically can't breathe. She's thousands of feet above the ground. The air is thinner up here. She can't get enough oxygen in her lungs, and never will again.

"Hey, you're okay," Jonah says, leaning forward to look at her.

She's had panic attacks before, but nothing like this where her chest is contracting against her will.

"Can't. Breathe," she gets out.

Jonah grabs the vomit bag and presses it into her fingers.

"Breathe into this."

His words are a jumble and she drops the bag. That's not what she needs; she needs a medic to cut her neck open and shove a pen cap into it. Her fingers claw at her neck, trying to open it. If she was at karaoke she'd sing "Harder to Breathe" by

Maroon 5 which would piss Jonah off. Why can she think of jokes but can't make herself breathe?

Warm fingers wrap along her jaw, turning her face until she's looking into steady brown eyes. She scans them desperately, trying to hold onto something but her vision blurs. Jonah holds the bag up to her mouth with his other hand.

"You're hyperventilating. Your body needs carbon dioxide. Breathe into this bag. I've got you."

Her shallow breaths continue into the bag as Jonah holds it to her lips.

"There you go, keep going. In and out."

He starts taking exaggerated deep breaths in and out. Something primitive inside her brain locks onto the rhythm. Her next breath is the tiniest bit deeper. Slowly, ever so slowly, her chest starts to expand. Jonah keeps breathing with her and she stays completely focused on him.

"Good, you're doing great."

When her breaths finally match his, he pulls the bag from her mouth and watches as she takes a deep breath. His thumb strokes her jaw softly before he pulls his hand away. She immediately misses the pressure.

"Are you okay? Can I get you anything?" a flight attendant asks from the aisle.

"No, I'm fine—"

"Could she have a Diet Coke, if possible?" Jonah asks.

The flight attendant nods and disappears. Afton leans against the seat as a shudder goes through her like an aftershock. Jonah reaches for her hand, his thumb massaging her palm.

"How'd you know what to do?" she asks quietly, focusing on his touch. It keeps her from obsessing about every other sensation in her body.

"Naomi used to hyperventilate any time Mom left us home

alone after Dad died. Our grandma drove her to the emergency room the first time it happened, and then we all got good at getting her through it after that."

She pictures young Naomi experiencing that and instantly wants to hug her. "That was terrifying. I never want to do it again."

His thumb presses harder into her palm. "If it ever happens again, you know what to do and you'll get through it."

The flight attendant reappears with the diet coke and Jonah drops his hand so she can grab it. She sips, settling back into her chair, trying to relax. Trying to forget the feel of Jonah's hand in hers.

"I'm going to take your reaction to mean that you don't like your job," Jonah starts.

Her chest immediately tightens. How dare he bring that up right as she's starting to calm down. Is this revenge? Getting her to have panic attack after panic attack while they're confined here together?

"Which is great because you happen to be looking at someone whose job is figuring out how people's unique skillsets could best be used," he finishes.

"What?" she manages to get out. He's a recruiter for a specific company that she definitely doesn't have the skills for.

"If you want to get out of reality television, I can help you figure out next steps. I do this every day for people."

"I can't just up and change careers. I've put in a decade here."

He grins. "Yes, you can. People do it all the time. Usually multiple times."

"They have better job skills."

"You have great job skills. It's all about how you word it on your resume."

"But—"

Jonah leans in close. "We all have this one life. You don't

need to spend the rest of it in a career you hate because it's what you wanted when you were twenty. We're all allowed to change our minds, and then change them again. I'm not saying you have to do anything, simply offering to help if the fear of change is what's holding you back."

She pulls her legs up and wraps her arms around them. Is that what this is? The fear of change? That can't be right. When she was eighteen, she left everything she knew and completely remade herself. She knows how to do it.

Exhaustion overcomes her. Her body has been through too much in the past ten minutes.

"We can talk jobs whenever, but I plan on being a menace when we land, so you should probably rest up," Jonah says, popping his earbuds in.

Right. Her job, as the producer. She's supposed to be the one holding it together, not Jonah.

"I'm sorry for all of that," she starts. "That was unprofessional."

Jonah points to his earbud. "I can't hear you on account of you're being ridiculous. Go to sleep."

Fine. She'll take the nap and be back to her professional self by the time they land. No one will ever have to know how good it felt to have someone else take care of her for once.

CHAPTER FOURTEEN

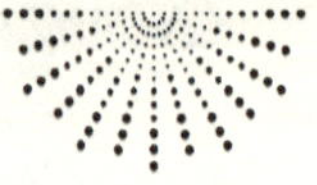

"Don't shoot the messenger," Afton says, leading him down the hotel steps to the awaiting car.

Jonah does a quick once-over of her. She's back to her traditional black, wearing a romper today. There are no dark circles under her eyes, and she's breathing normally. No signs of the panic attack on the plane from yesterday. He feels horrible for inducing it, but something shifted on the plane. Instead of feeling afraid of her and where his mind will go, he has a problem to solve—figuring out potential career paths for her. Using his work skills feels good, unlike the coil of dread weaving through him now as they're about to venture into the city.

"You were supposed to do a one-on-one with Tessa today, but she drank the water and is sick."

He winces, knowing how awful that is from his mission. "Is she okay?"

"Yes, we took her to the hospital early this morning for fluids. She just needs to rest and let her body get all the bacteria out. But..." Afton trails off.

The coil tightens. "Just tell me."

"Rileigh and Maylee turned on each other during the flight here, and they're causing so much drama in the hotel that immediate action needs to be taken."

"Okay," he says slowly.

"It's your first double date. To Isla de los Munecas. And you have to get there by kayak."

He blinks. "I've always wanted to go there. And you're saying I have to do it with the two most annoying women?"

"Yes," she grimaces. "Let's have a codeword if you need me to intervene. I'm really good at intervening."

He believes her. "Pineapple."

Afton snorts. "It can't be that. Everyone will think you're a swinger. They probably already do."

"Didn't you hear, it's part of the church's new branding," he teases.

"Pick something else."

"If I bring up my mission, get me out."

She raises her brows. "We're in the literal city you served your mission, and you're going out with two of the most judgmental Mormon girls we could find. That's bound to come up within thirty seconds."

"Exactly," he deadpans.

He's back in Mexico City. The familiar smell of horno de tierras and burning trash along with the humidity have him stepping back in time. His fingers keep going to his breast pocket, feeling for his name tag. When he sees his reflection in the car window with hair that's way too long, he jolts, expecting a clean-cut missionary to be staring back.

Every new person they pass, he's scared to see a familiar face. He loved the people he'd served when he was here. Now that he no longer believes what he taught then, he's embarrassed. He'd been an eighteen-year-old kid telling these families that he knew better than them. That he could teach them truths that would completely fix their lives. And when it didn't, that they needed to try harder.

Most had ignored him, but there had been those few families that had given the church their everything. Their limited time. Ten percent of their income even when they already couldn't feed their children. Those people were willing to starve over what he taught them. And now here he is on the other side: comfortable, fed, traveling to find love. Leaving the church has been painful and heartbreaking, but he'd never given up what these families had. No matter who he runs into from the past, he'll let them down.

If he sees any of them, he doesn't know what he'll say. Some still attend, sending him updates on their families and what they're doing in the church. They seem happy. If it's working for them, then he doesn't want to tarnish their joy with the fact he's left. For the families who didn't stay, who were hurt? He'll apologize and hope they can forgive him.

The person he's most terrified to run into is his mission president. The odds are next to nothing; they only serve in a place for three years. President Thompson was the closest thing to a father in Jonah's life since his dad passed. He and his wife cared for him when he was sick, cried with him when he was overwhelmed. They checked in with him every few months after he'd gone home, and always answered when he called seeking career and life advice. Now, he's done the worst thing they can imagine. Turned his back on eternity.

"What's it like being back here?" Afton asks.

"Weird."

She doesn't push him to explain, thank goodness.

The car turns into a long driveway with signs advertising various attractions. Jonah rolls his neck, trying to get back into pleasant Fiance-to-be mode. Double dates are always to settle drama. There's usually one woman the viewers will be rooting for, but even still, his Fiancé-to-be predecessors always come off caring and empathetic to both. He silently prays for strength to get through this, not caring if anyone is listening.

The car stops and Afton turns to him. "You're going to do fine. I'll make sure you get time alone to see the dolls."

Why is she being so nice to him? How bad is this going to be?

Pretty bad. There are only two kayaks available, so he's forced to ride with Maylee since the two women couldn't be trusted not to sink each other. Rileigh started complaining about an old volleyball injury halfway there, insisting they switch kayaks. When they all almost fell in the river, Rileigh finally started paddling herself again, quite well for someone who was supposedly in too much pain to continue only minutes earlier.

On land, they're approached by a tour guide, and Jonah shoves his hands into his pockets so no one can try to hold them. Maylee and Rileigh settle for hugging his arms instead which is worse. He can barely focus on the guide telling them the story of the man who found a drowned girl in the water, then decorated the island with dolls to memorialize her and later to appease her ghost.

The dolls are in worse condition than the pictures he's seen. They hang in the branches, sun bleached and moth-eaten. Despite the film of dirt and decay, their eyes are clear, watching his every move. There's a doll hanging on a low branch missing half of its hair, staring into his soul. He shudders.

"It's so sad," Maylee says from his right, staring up into the trees.

"It really is."

"People do strange things when they don't know the truth," she adds.

"What do you mean?" Jonah asks. He wants to give her the benefit of the doubt.

"You know, about the gospel. If he'd known about the next life, maybe he wouldn't have gone crazy with the dolls," Maylee whispers.

He stiffens. He's made it clear from the first moment that he doesn't believe in that anymore. Why would she say that to him? Who's he kidding, he can guess why she's saying it. Maybe hoping he'll feel the Spirit and want to come back to church. Or to reassure herself that she has all the answers. Whenever she's reminded of the uncertainty and suddenness of death, she can cling to the answers she's been given. He's heard it all before.

"My dad passed away when I was fourteen," Jonah says. "He was a great man, and I've spent my life trying to be a fraction of who he was. When I lost him, everyone kept telling me not to cry because we'd be together again.

"That was the worst thing someone could say to me. It made me shove everything I was feeling down. I didn't actually grieve for my father until my mid-twenties. Feeling sadness at loss is a natural reaction, and we shouldn't judge how others express it."

Maylee stares back at him, her mouth a wide o.

"Yeah Maylee. Stop trying to make yourself feel comfortable by shutting down other people's emotions," Rileigh says.

Is she using the story about his dad to look better than Maylee? When she literally whined the whole way here?

"I'm hungry. Why don't we go have our picnic? I hope there's pineapple," Jonah says. They've only been on their tour for ten minutes and haven't gone inside the building yet, but he's done. He walks past the women to where Afton is waiting behind the cameras.

"I can't do this."

"We've got a beautiful set up on the mainland for you to break up with them. Their cars are waiting there to take them back to the hotel." She starts to reach for his shoulder, then stops halfway there, fiddling with her headset instead.

"Do you want to do a quick in-the-moment?" Luke asks from behind his camera.

Jonah's nails dig into his palms as he fists them next to his sides. He's scared of what will come out if he has to talk right now.

Afton shakes her head. "We'll do them on the mainland. I don't want to disturb any spirits more than we already have." Afton leads them to the tiny boat. They squeeze two cameramen, a sound guy, Afton, Richard, and both women on board. It's so small he's forced to sit with his legs pressed against Maylee and Rileigh's.

"Don't talk right now. The engine is too loud for us to get any useable audio, and we can't miss anything," Afton instructs. "Look longingly out at the water as the wind blows dramatically through your hair."

Richard looks like he's going to argue with Afton, but the engine starts, drowning out anything he might say. Jonah uses the short ride to calm down. Once they're back on land, Richard pulls the women aside for interviews while Afton takes Jonah to his picnic. A rich spread of fresh fruit, meats, and cheeses sits there. He hates that he doesn't actually get to eat it.

Maylee eventually joins him, taking her time to smooth out her dress prettily as she sits next to him on the blanket.

"I want to apologize for what I said earlier. I didn't know about your dad, and I can see how hurtful my words were." She looks genuine. But it's not enough.

"Thank you for saying that. Being here, hearing that story, it brought up a lot for me, and is helping me put things in perspective."

"Me too—" Maylee starts.

"Which is why I think I should be honest and end this now.

It's been great getting to know you. I know you'll make someone else very happy, but I don't see a future between us. I don't want to waste any more of your time."

Her eyes bulge. "What? We've barely spent any together."

"I know that. But from the time we have, I can tell we want different things from life."

Maylee starts tearing up. He's not trying to be cruel, but he needs to make it clear it's over.

"Well you need to know about Rileigh—"

"Thank you for your concern. Don't worry, I know what I want. Can I walk you out?"

When she nods, he stands and pulls her up, walking her slowly to the car. At the door she slips off her promise ring and tries to drop it in his palm, but it falls to the ground. He scrambles to grab it and almost gets hit with the car door as she pulls it shut.

"We need more than that," Richard yells the second the door's closed.

"We can't reshoot it; she's already crying. We'd have to redo her makeup for continuity," Afton says.

Richard clenches his teeth, his face turning red. She doesn't budge. Is she going to get in a fight with Richard simply so he doesn't have to talk about this anymore? Is she going easy on him, or is the thing about the makeup true? He doesn't want her to coddle him, but trying to redo a breakup sounds awful.

After a beat, Richard walks to the other side and climbs in to the SUV to interview Maylee.

Jonah ambles back to the picnic setup and waits for Rileigh to appear. She smiles prettily at him as she sits.

"Are you okay?" Rileigh asks, leaning forward to try and hold his hand. He wipes his sweaty palms on his shorts instead.

"I'm feeling confused. If you really did have an injury, I would respect that, but that seems like something you would have mentioned previously. You were willing to risk all us falling into the river just to try to get more time with me."

"I thought I'd be fine, but my shoulder started acting up halfway there," Rileigh explains.

"Okay. It also felt like you were using the story of my father's death to make yourself look better."

Rileigh shakes her head. "That's not what I was doing. I heard what Maylee said and it needed to be called out."

Maybe she means it. Maybe it's all a spin.

"I've also been told repeatedly the hurtful things you've said to the other women. That's not a trait I want in a partner, and honestly I don't see a future between us."

Rileigh opens and closes her mouth. "What have they said? I can explain…"

"You could, but it wouldn't change my feelings. Can I walk you to the car?" He holds his hand out for her like he did Maylee. Rileigh gets up without him and storms off. When she reaches the SUV she rips the promise ring from her finger and chucks it at Jonah's head. It bounces off his forehead as she flips him off before climbing in the SUV. Richard practically throws the opposite door open and they all hear Rileigh yelling nonsensically.

Jonah interlaces his fingers on the back of his head. "Wow."

Luke moves in closer, Afton beside him. "What are you feeling right now?"

The faster he feeds the camera the sound bites they need, the sooner he gets out of here.

"I was hoping for a fun day exploring Mexico City and getting to know each of them better. I'm disappointed in how today went, but I feel one step closer to finding my wife."

"What about your dad?" Afton prompts.

"Going on this journey has me thinking of my dad more than ever. I wish I could have his advice right now. He died when I was young, and I never got the chance to ask him about what makes a good partner. How to find that incredible kind of love he and my mom had."

His voice chokes up, and he presses his palms into his eyes. He turns away from the camera and takes a few steps.

"I need a moment." He presses harder, trying to shut down the onslaught of memories and emotion. He loves his dad so much and misses him every day. The grief never leaves, but he's gotten stronger to carry it. It's always there, especially in the big moments, each another milestone his dad missed. He hates that whomever he chooses will never meet his dad; will never know the kind of man he aspires to be.

There are voices murmuring around him, and then they disappear. A hand rests lightly on his back.

"Want to talk about it?" she asks.

He hates that her touch grounds him. "No. I scheduled a meltdown for tonight; I don't want to spoil it."

"The cameras are gone. You can talk to me. Your wellbeing is my job after all."

He rubs at his chest, as if he can reach that ache where he carries his grief. Knowing that cameras aren't watching right now instantly lessens the pain.

"I'm good, promise."

Afton studies him, eyes narrowing.

"Why are you being so nice to me? It's weirding me out."

She scoffs. "I'm doing my job."

"Yeah, but you weren't this nice last week."

"It wasn't my job to be nice to you last week."

He rolls his eyes. "Treat me like normal, I don't like this."

Her eyes spark. "Deal. Your breakups with them were way too short, but I'm positive Richard got enough footage to work with. Grab a torta and follow me."

Back with the rest of the crew, Afton turns to Luke.

"I don't think we got enough B-roll of the island."

Luke tilts his head. "You're right, we didn't."

"Oh darn, I guess we have to go back and take an actual tour of the island," Afton says, eyes gleaming.

"No, that's a waste of time," Richard says, appearing out of nowhere.

"You were worried the breakups weren't long enough, and he broke up with both of them ahead of schedule. We have plenty of time," Afton argues.

"I really need more footage," Luke says to Richard.

Richard huffs. "I'm not going."

"I get it, the dolls scare even the best of us," Afton says sweetly.

Richard harrumphs and gets off the boat.

Back on the island, Afton instructs Jonah to walk around solemnly. He circles the perimeter with his hands in his pockets, staring up into the branches. He shivers as the remains of the decomposing dolls sway in the breeze. When he sees something moving among the branches, he backs away, hoping he imagined all the legs.

"Do you want to go inside there?" Afton asks, pointing to the hut in the center of the trees.

"That's where the talking dolls are," he says conspiratorially.

"Let's hear what they have to say."

He waits for the crew to follow him, but Luke is still getting shots of the trees and the other PAs are taking selfies. He and Afton go into the hut alone. Shafts of sunlight sneak through old wooden boards just enough to illuminate the dolls, and the spiders skittering across the floor and up the walls as they enter.

Afton lets out a high-pitched screech, wrapping her arms tightly around herself and ducking her head. She presses against him and he instinctively wraps an arm around her shoulders. That's something coworkers do when they're scared, right?

"You're scared of spiders?" he teases.

"No. This is their home; I'm trying to be respectful."

"By screaming at them?"

"By giving them space," she squeaks. When the spiders seem resettled, she takes a tiny step forward, still tucked in close to him. He can feel her body relax against him.

"Which doll is your favorite?" she finally asks.

"That one," he says, pointing to one wearing sunglasses.

"Mine is the red devil baby with wings outside," Afton says. "It speaks to me."

"Of course it does."

"Do you hear anything?" she asks.

They stay perfectly still. There's the rustling of leaves, slapping of the water against the sides of the boat, and the hissing of cicadas. But no voices.

"Nope."

"I stopped believing in these kinds of things a long time ago, but sometimes there's a bit of hope something might happen," she says.

"Hey dad, if you wanted to make an appearance, now would be a good time," Jonah says into the room.

There's no response. He didn't honestly expect one. So why does he feel disappointed?

Afton spins so she's looking up at him. Her arms are still wrapped tight across her chest, creating a barrier between their bodies. A shaft of light cuts across her face, making her left eye glow.

"Your dad would be proud of you."

An electric current zips through him. "Because I'm so desperate for love that I'm on reality television?"

She shakes her head, that golden eye glittering. "Because you're a good man who is kind and cares about others. You're willing to be vulnerable. Instead of letting Maylee's comment slide, you took the time to educate those women, and later our viewers, on why saying things like that is hurtful. I bet someone will think twice when talking to someone who's grieving, and it will make a difference," she pauses.

"The older I get, the more I realize that our parents were just winging it. Your dad probably didn't have this sage advice that would have fixed all your problems. I think he would have listened to you, and then helped you realize you can make this decision all on your own. I see so much of him in you, and I know he'd be proud."

Tears start freely flowing down his cheeks and there's no chance of holding them back.

"Damn it, Afton," he croaks.

With no warning she stands up on her tip toes and wipes a single tear away. She studies the tiny droplet on her finger. Then she looks back and forth between her hand hovering next to his cheek before slowly lowering it.

"Sorry. Old habit."

She steps out of his arms, and he fights every instinct to pull her back in close to him.

"Take the time you need. I'll make sure you have privacy."

She looks down at the ground as she turns to the door. "I'm leaving now, spiders. Please don't touch me." She shrieks the entire run back into the light.

He stares at her retreating back until he's alone in the dark with the dolls. He remembers the family dinners Afton came to, joining in on discussions with his parents about books, mythology, and history. How after six months of coming over, Afton started teasing his dad, making him laugh so hard the corners of his eyes had watered. He can picture his dad standing next to him, telling Afton that the spiders are more afraid of her than she is of them and turning it into a metaphor.

None of the women he's dating will get the chance to meet

his dad. But Afton did. For the briefest moment, he lets himself picture it. A future with Afton. Not the white picket fence version he'd wanted in his youth. One where they sleep in on the weekends until Millie wakes them up. Where they explore together: cafes, bookstores, and cities across the world. Where she's happy in her job, and his sisters barely talk to him on their weekly FaceTime calls because they want to catch up with Afton more. Where he finally feels home.

He knows it isn't possible. They have too much complicated history between them. She may have forgiven him, but it's still there. He's the one on a dating show, and she isn't a contestant. He wraps the fantasy with a final image of them holding hands and rocking on a porch together, their skin age worn. Then he leaves it in the dark with the dolls and spiders.

When he finally returns to his hotel room after stuffing himself with street tacos, he freezes. Something is floating in the dark. He pats his pockets for his phone, but it's locked up somewhere. He fumbles on the wall for the light switch, heart hammering. When he finally turns the light on, he jumps.

There's a tiny little hand reaching out from between his pillows. He waits for it to move. It doesn't. He slowly approaches, then pulls back the pillows. There's a doll lying underneath, its hair cut in a wild pattern. It's otherwise clean and pristine, unlike the dolls on the island. It's wearing a kid's t-shirt that goes all the way to its feet like a dress.

With a whale on it.

"Afton," he laughs. He told her to treat him like normal, which for her means pranks wrapped in inside jokes. He doesn't regret it.

CHAPTER FIFTEEN

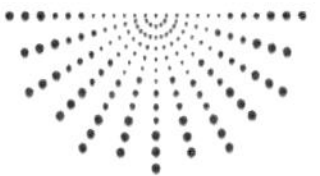

EIGHTEEN YEARS AGO

*A*fton discovered the magic of extracurriculars. Extracurriculars meant hanging out more with her friends, spending less time at home, and dreaming about leaving Utah after graduation. Naya, Sadie, and her made a pact to all pick one thing for the group to try together.

Sadie chose the student council. She had dreams of making the school more inclusive, and figured being involved in leadership would help. Naya chose a book club where they fought over love triangles. Afton dragged Naya and Sadie to the fall musical auditions. Afton made it into the chorus, while Naya and Sadie were invited to join the stage crew. They didn't, and Afton was okay with that.

Between school and extracurriculars, she still made time to watch reality tv with Carrie and Jonah's sisters. Jonah was rarely there, bouncing between sports, Boy Scouts, or to play video games with Henry. He'd always say hey to her before running out the door. It was the perfect amount of time to see that he was indeed still hot, and she had no idea how to talk to him.

Things were going great until her dad was called into the

bishopric. He was one of three men tasked with leading their church congregation, which meant being gone. A lot. On Sundays he had early morning meetings, leaving Afton and her mom to fight her brothers to get dressed for church. Dan couldn't be bothered to help.

During church, her dad sat on the stand with the other men, leaving Afton to wrangle the younger boys and keep them quiet. He was gone on Wednesdays for youth group with the young men, and Saturdays for camping trips with the Boy Scouts.

The more her dad was gone, the more her mom fell apart. They had a family meeting one Monday night where her dad announced that everyone needed to chip in more. A new chore chart was divvied up.

"Afton, we need you to be home more on school nights to help with dinner," her dad said.

"I can't, I have theater practices and book club. And the student council events I volunteer for."

"Yes, but those are extras. We need you here," her dad said.

She panicked. Those clubs were her freedom away from here. It wasn't her fault God thought her dad should spend all of his time elsewhere and her family was falling apart. If they were Baptist like Sadie's family, her dad wouldn't spend all day at work then disappear for the few hours he had for the family. Being at school was her lifeline.

"I need those to get scholarships for college. The prophet said all girls need to get degrees in case their husbands die and they have to provide for their families. Maybe I could make all the boys' lunches instead?"

Her parents couldn't argue with the prophet, so making her brother's lunches it was. Dinner usually came out of a microwave which was fine with her. When she'd come home every night, Noah would be waiting for her and she'd read him stories before tucking him in. Her middle two brothers only acknowledged her if they didn't like what she'd packed them.

In January when everyone's schedules changed, Afton had a free period with Naya and a few of her theater friends. They crammed at a table in the student center, working silently on their homework to get ahead before rehearsal.

"Hey, can I sit with you?" a voice asked, cracking halfway through. It was Jonah.

"Well, well, well," Naya said.

"Sure," Afton said, scooting down on the bench to make room for him. Her theater friends looked up in interest, and Jonah introduced himself.

"My mom said to tell you *Ready for the Ring* premieres this week, so TV Friday's are back on."

Afton frowned. "I have to babysit every Friday night now so my parents can go on a date."

"What nights are you free?" Jonah asked.

She pulled out her planner and checked. "Tuesdays until we get to tech week."

"I'll tell her to do Tuesdays. What's tech week?"

Her theater friends cut in, explaining everything he'd never asked to hear about theater. She was honestly surprised he returned to sit with her the next day. They did their homework in companionable silence, or he'd listen while Naya and her vented. Until early March.

"I have a weird question for you two," he said.

"Spill. Now," Naya demanded.

"You're still friends with Sadie, right?" he asked.

Afton's swallowed hard. Was he about to ask if Sadie was interested in him?

"Henry has a crush on her. Do you think there's any chance she feels the same?"

Wait, Henry was the one who liked Sadie?

"I don't think Sadie even knows him," Naya said.

"They have Government together this semester," Jonah said.

"We'll find out," Afton said.

They reported back the next day that Sadie had no idea who Henry was.

"We should figure out a way for them to spend time together," Afton suggested.

Jonah's eyes lit up. "My parents used to play this game called 'Bigger or Better.' They'd start with a clothespin and go door to door asking people if they had anything bigger or better than that they were willing to trade. Whoever had the coolest item by the end won."

"We could do that and make Henry and Sadie partners," Naya said.

"Exactly!"

When they approached Sadie with the idea, she wasn't excited. "That's weird."

"It's an excuse for Afton and Jonah to be partners," Naya said.

Afton glared at Naya.

"Why didn't you say that in the first place? I'm in. Are you going to kiss him?" Sadie asked.

"She can't until she's sixteen," Naya reminded everyone.

"I've definitely seen half the ninth-grade kissing, and they're not sixteen. Do you want to kiss him?" Sadie asked.

Of course she did, but that didn't matter. Jonah only saw her as a friend. He was handsome and he could have any girl in the ninth grade he wanted. There was no way he thought about kissing her as often as she did him.

Sadie wouldn't shut up about kissing, even sending text messages with tips. *Tongue the alphabet. Tilt your head to the right.* Afton was fed up and decided to get revenge. She found a giant moving box in her garage and got to work assembling a glitter bomb. Then she delivered it to Naya's house, knowing they weren't allowed to go on their own streets. Odds were good Sadie would visit Naya's house, and this box would definitely be the biggest item. Naya's parents agreed to give the box only to Sadie if she showed up.

The night came, and Naya 'randomly' drew names out of a hat for the pairings. Sadie seemed indifferent when Henry was announced as her partner, but winked when Afton and Jonah were announced. Naya was paired with a girl from book club she'd invited. Afton went and stood next to Jonah, both of them trying to watch Sadie and Henry inconspicuously. Poor Henry looked like he was going to faint when Sadie started discussing what street they should start on.

"He better pull it together," Afton hissed.

"We practiced making conversation all week, but he's choking out there."

"It's a good thing you know CPR," Afton said.

Jonah snorted. "The Heimlich is for choking."

"I wouldn't know." Her dad had been gone an entire Saturday morning to go with the young men to get CPR certified. She'd asked if she could go since the class was technically open to anyone, but had been forced to watch her younger brothers while her mom laid in bed.

"I'll show you what I learned," Jonah offered as they started walking over two streets to start.

"Okay."

"The Heimlich is for choking. You're going to put your hands in a fist like this, and, uhh. Can I demonstrate it on you?" Jonah asked.

Afton nodded. He stepped behind her, one of his legs going between hers.

"You want to stand like this in case they pass out," he said, his breath tickling the back of her neck. He wrapped his arms around her middle, his hands interlocked. She barely repressed the shiver that ran through her at his touch.

"You go two fingers above their bellybutton, and then pull in and upward, like this."

He did the move gently, her stomach lurching with the force. He did it once more before unwrapping his arms from around her and stepping away. She debated playing dumb and asking him to show her again, but Jonah was walking up a driveway, about to knock.

"Do you want to do the honors?" he asked.

She knocked on the door, and they waited silently until an older man opened it.

"Hi Brother Smith, we're playing bigger or better, and wanted to know if you have anything bigger or better than this clothespin you'd be willing to trade with us?" Jonah smiled.

Brother Smith narrowed his eyes at Jonah before relaxing.

"You're that Partridge boy, the one whose father died," Brother Smith said.

Jonah's face immediately fell, but he bobbed his head.

"How's your mom doing?" Brother Smith asked.

"She's fine," Jonah said.

"Do you have anything we can trade?" Afton cut in.

Brother Smith seemed surprised to see her there. "Let me look." He disappeared back inside.

Afton and Jonah stood in uncomfortable silence until he returned, holding a tiny snow globe of the Salt Lake Temple. Jonah handed over the clothespin and thanked Brother Smith, who reminded Jonah to take care of his mom. Afton bristled. Why did Brother Smith feel the need to remind Jonah of that fact? It's pretty hard to forget, and he didn't need to be reminded of it. Especially from how melancholy he seems now.

"You taught me choking, what about CPR?" Afton asked.

Jonah's face scrunched. "That's not exactly something you can teach while walking."

She looked at the houses on the street. The next one had all of its lights off. Afton ran over and laid on their lawn.

"What are you doing?" Jonah hissed.

"You better come teach me," she replied.

"Someone will see."

"Then you better hurry."

"Get up," Jonah said.

"Do you really want me to be unable to save the next unconscious person I come upon because you were too embarrassed to teach me a lifesaving procedure?" Afton asks.

Jonah groans. "Let's go to the park. At least that's neutral grass."

"That's fair." Jonah helped her to her feet before they walked down the street to the park where Afton immediately laid in the grass again. Jonah sighed.

"First you want to make sure they're truly unconscious. You can yell at them, shake them, or do…" His eyes flitted down to her chest, his cheeks coloring.

"Do what?" Afton asked.

"A sternal rub. Let me be unconscious, and I'll walk you through it." Jonah laid on the grass next to her, his arms and legs bumping against hers. She turned her head and looked at him, pretending it was the meadow scene from *Twilight.* She could practically hear the pianos playing above them before she got up and kneeled next to him.

"Take your knuckles and rub them against my chest, like this." He demonstrated rubbing his knuckles down the middle of his chest. If he'd done it to her, it would have been right in the middle of her breasts. That's why he wanted to switch. Now her face was hot as she brought her own knuckles down the center of his chest.

"Harder than that, you're not going to wake anyone up."

She pressed against the fabric of his hoodie until she felt flesh and bone.

"Oww," Jonah moaned.

She immediately pulled back.

He smiled encouragingly at her. "That's good. Next, you're going to interlace your fingers together and press down on my heart thirty times."

"How do I know where your heart is?"

"It's in-between the nipples, slightly to the left."

She full on blushed then. Thankfully, he pointed to where his heart was and she placed her interlaced fingers above the spot.

"Lock your arms straight and press down hard. When you're really doing it, you'll probably break a rib which is normal. Please don't break mine though."

Afton straightened her arms and stood as tall as possible on her knees before pressing down where his heart was, lightly, thirty times.

"After that you'll tip my head back."

Afton obeyed, the movement making his Adam's apple more prominent.

"Pinch my nose."

She held her fingers above his nose and he nodded for her to do it. She pinched.

"Lean down," he said, voice nasally.

She laughed and leaned so her face was a good six inches above his.

"Then blow two slow breaths into my mouth."

His mouth was inches away, waiting. Was this simply about learning CPR? Or was he trying to kiss her? He could have sat up and simply told her about the breaths, but he'd stayed here. Waiting. Did he feel like she did for him? That the tiniest details—a vein in an arm, the bob of a throat, the tiniest inch of stomach that showed when he stretched—were infinitely fascinating and new? That she wanted to collect as many moments with him as she could have?

They weren't sixteen yet. God would understand though, right? It was just a kiss, the brushing of skin against skin. What was the difference between her lips brushing against his and her bare arm bumping his? She steeled herself, then started to lean down.

Jonah rolled over, sitting up when he was no longer underneath her. "Those are all the steps for CPR. You'll keep doing that until help arrives. Come on, we need to go find something bigger or better than this snow globe."

Afton was momentarily stunned. She was about to kiss Jonah, and he rolled away. Could he tell what she was about to do and didn't want it? Was he disgusted? He still helped her to her feet again. Was he standing farther from her than earlier? She couldn't tell. Her head hurt from analyzing each of his actions as they went from house to house, trying to figure out if he knew she'd been about to kiss him.

This was Sadie's fault. She kept hyping Afton up, telling her that she should kiss Jonah. If it hadn't been for that, the thought wouldn't have popped into her head in the first place.

When they met up again with their friends, Henry and Sadie proudly carried the giant glitter bomb with them. Naya and her friend had a giant robotic toucan that said, "Polly want a cracker?"

Jonah and Afton had a broken electric mixer.

They all gathered around as Henry set the box on the ground and Sadie opened it. Glitter sprayed out, covering both of their faces. Everyone burst out laughing.

"Naya, why did your parents have a glitter bomb lying around?" Sadie screeched.

"You got that at my house?" Naya asked.

"Yes! They had it sitting by the door and everything. As if they knew I was coming."

Sadie and Naya slowly turned to Afton.

"Gotcha," Afton smirked.

Jonah raised his eyebrows in surprise.

Afton swore he said "impressive," but it was hard to know for sure because Sadie ran over and dumped the entire box of glitter on her.

CHAPTER SIXTEEN

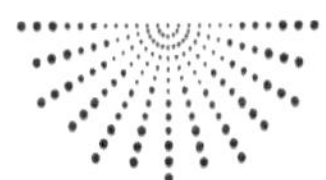

*I*f Afton's phone doesn't stop buzzing, she's going to throw it across the airport. Then she wouldn't have their boarding passes, they'd miss their flights, and oh darn, she'd have to stay in Mexico instead of going to Salt Lake City. Whoopsie.

She settles for throwing her still vibrating phone into a security bin, glad for a moment's reprieve. Whoever invented group chats needs to be included in one filled with women who decided they should change the baby shower to a nesting party and want ideas for themes besides birds.

A red light goes off as Afton's suitcase goes across the scanner, and an agent pulls it to the side to inspect. Her heart hammers, and she fumbles to grab the rest of her belongings from the bin. She knows the red light green light system is completely random, but what if she accidentally packed something illegal and forgot about it? Or they think that her MiraLAX packets are actually cocaine? She paid three times more to get the labeled single servings to try and avoid this.

Jonah waits next to Afton, his own suitcase in hand, as the

agent unzips her bag. She will not be embarrassed about the MiraLAX. Everyone has occasional irregularity when traveling for weeks on end. The agent opens the flap and Afton jumps. Frozen doll eyes stare back at her, tiny lips in a pink pout. The disheveled black hair she'd lovingly cut is filled with thick white flakes. How the hell did the doll she bought Jonah develop dandruff?

The agent picks the doll up carefully, and more white powder falls off in a mini snowstorm. The agent's eyebrows rise, taking in the mess. He starts talking hurriedly into his radio, and someone else approaches at the same time a security officer moves within arms reach of Afton. The agents swab the white powder and place it in a vial.

"What's this?" the first agent asks.

Afton's about to explain that her laxative must have exploded, when Jonah starts talking in Spanish. The agents' faces soften as they listen to him. He's been using Spanish all week when talking with locals. Jonah points to a flash of color tucked between her folded clothes. With gloved hands, the agent pulls out an opened bag of Muddy Buddies Afton had been eating last night in her hotel room. She'd meant to stuff it in her backpack, not her suitcase.

The agents wordlessly take the bag over to a table behind them, taking more samples. Afton wipes at a bead of sweat on her brow, hoping the security officer doesn't take that as a sign of her guilt. She's always hot in airports, even when she's not in danger of going to prison over a creepy doll that she definitely did not put in her suitcase this morning.

A third agent approaches with a dog and a whimper escapes her lips.

Jonah's head whips to her. "What's wrong?"

"Dogs love peanut butter, and chocolate is poison to them. It's going to alert and I'm going to jail."

The corner of Jonah's mouth twitches. "Do you think you're the first person to travel through an airport with peanut butter and chocolate?"

"Is this funny to you?"

"It's going to be okay," he reassures her.

"It better be because this is *your fault*," she whispers. He just had to try and top her prank the same day she left an open snack in her carryon. She pulls her phone out of her pocket and unlocks it before passing it to him. "Call Sadie. She's a lawyer; she'll get me out of here."

He bites his bottom lip, fighting a smile. Then he leans forward and shoves the phone back into the side pocket of her leggings, his fingers lightly brushing her leg.

"You're going to be fine," he murmurs.

She just might believe him.

The agents bring the suitcase back over and start talking to Jonah in Spanish again while placing the doll back inside. Why is it kind of hot, even now, when he's not taking her predicament seriously?

Jonah laughs and thanks the agents before grabbing her suitcase off the counter and wheeling it away with his own.

"What the hell was that?" Afton hisses, catching up to him.

"They were impressed with my Spanish for a gringo. If only they'd asked me to bear my testimony, then I really would have had them."

"Congrats on your gift of tongues, what about my bag?"

"I was getting you back for scaring the shit out of me the other night. How was I supposed to know you had incriminating white powder in there?" Jonah asks.

"Oh, I don't know, by not sticking the doll in my suitcase in the first place" Afton huffs.

People are staring at them. Jonah leads her over to a table out of the way.

"I'm sorry. I never would have done it if I thought that would happen. I'm horrible at pranks."

"You think?"

"I'll never try to prank you again. Are you okay?" he asks, seeming genuinely worried.

"I need a minute by myself. Sit over there and don't move," she says, pointing to a row of chairs. Once he sits, she takes off through the airport. It's small compared to others she's been in, so she laps around the little restaurants and shops, trying to calm down. The more steps she takes, the slower her heart gets.

She doesn't want to get on this plane. They're headed to SLC, and the closer it gets, the more she's filled with dread. The odds of someone recognizing both her and Jonah and posting online are much higher. And there's Noah's random texts. He hasn't said anything since he asked when she was coming to Utah. What if they randomly cross paths while she's there?

Chelsea is waiting in SLC though, and Afton's anxious to see her. Every time Afton checked in and asked how the meetings were going, Chelsea said she'd tell her in person. Afton worried that the truth about her past had come out, but Chelsea used her normal amount of emojis. If Chelsea was mad, the emojis would warn her.

When she tells Chelsea about the doll incident, Chelsea will do her deep belly laugh that ends with her running to the bathroom bent in half. It's an absurd story. It is Jonah's best prank, and she's objectively proud of him for upping his skills. It just so happened to coincide with her dread over their next destination and the constant buzzing from the group chat. Which is still happening.

She pulls up the group chat to mute it, when a new message comes up from Sadie only.

SADIE

Who is this friend of Naya's and what is her problem?

I met her once and she kept making snide comments about my Walmart cheese tray.

You could have at least gone to target.

Or Whole Foods.

Aren't you supposed to be super bougie?

My bank account didn't get the memo.

😂 SAME.

Can't wait to see you at the baby shower.

Excuse me- NESTING party.

AFTON SPINS her nose ring round and round. She should just admit odds are she won't make it because of work, but she can't bring herself to yet. She's not ready for the "that stinks, next time 🙁 " texts. How many times until they stop inviting her altogether?

"I'm sorry," Jonah says, startling her.

"I told you to wait over there," she grumbles.

"Yeah, we've got a problem," Jonah says.

She slips her phone back in her pocket, instantly back in work mode. "What's wrong?"

"My mission president is on our flight," he whispers.

"What?" Why would his mission president be here?

"He's sitting next to where we board. What do we do?" Jonah looks over his shoulder, running a hand through his hair.

"What exactly is the problem?" she asks. If she's going to fix this, she needs specifics.

"He's going to want all the life updates; specifically what I'm doing for the church. I don't want to go into the whole leaving the church thing with him right before we get onto a four-hour flight where he could be sitting next to us."

"He'll find out when he watches the show," Afton says.

"I won't be standing next to him, seeing how disappointed he is."

"Was he a good president?"

"He's like a second father to me," Jonah says quietly.

Her parents have been constantly disappointed in her since high school, and even though she expected it, it still hurts. She can only imagine how painful it would be for Jonah to have that confrontation with his mission president right now.

"We have two options. You can get really good at lying in the next few minutes, or we get you a disguise and wait as long as possible to get in the boarding line," Afton says.

"Option two," Jonah replies.

"To the gift shop!" she says with a flourish.

Jonah snorts, even though he's obviously stressed.

Inside the store, she goes straight to the hats. "These are back in style," she says, throwing a bucket hat at him. He tries it on and she's immediately taken back to middle school. Jonah takes the hat off and grabs a baseball cap.

"Let's be honest, this is the only one you'll buy for me."

It says Mexico City on it with embroidered dolphins on either side.

"Dolphins aren't whales, even my niece knows that," Afton scoffs.

"You have a niece?"

"Three nieces and one nephew. They're all Dan's. I won't be surprised if they announce they're expecting another at Christmas. Dan says he wants six kids to beat my parents."

Jonah grimaces. "How's your sister-in-law?"

"She says she's happy, but she seems overwhelmed and miserable. Dan barely helps with the kids, just like our dad," Afton says bitterly. Every time she sees her brother, she wants to scream. Her heart breaks for her oldest niece who'll be expected to parent her younger siblings, just like Afton did.

Jonah places the hat on his head backwards and all thoughts of her family disappear. She immediately understands why all the Booktok girlies are obsessed with this. She stands up on her tiptoes and immediately flips the hat around, covering his face with the brim.

"No one will recognize you like this."

He readjusts the hat. "I can't see."

She turns and grabs a pair of sunglasses. He slides them on and she immediately laughs. "You look suspicious as hell."

"I draw the line at sunglasses indoors," he says, reaching over her shoulder to put them back.

She scans the shop. There are reading glasses next to the books and magazines. "We could pop the lenses out of one of these," she suggests. Jonah doesn't answer, scanning the books.

"Great idea. You could pretend to read a magazine and cover your face with it."

"Can I get a book instead?" he asks.

"You're not allowed to have books," she reminds him. It's part of the deprivation process to make people more willing to fall in love so quickly.

He grabs a book with a dragon on the cover from the rack.

"I snuck you a dragon book. It's time to repay the favor," he says with wide puppy eyes.

He looks ridiculous, especially with his dolphin hat.

"If you're expecting *Eragon* you're in for quite the surprise."

"Great. It'll be better than the same few movies on the plane. Pretty please?" He makes a pouty face now.

"You do remember that you almost got me arrested only minutes ago, right?"

"I won't do it again, promise."

She hesitates, trying to make him sweat. He kneels down in the middle of the store, no care for what might be on the floor, and grabs both her hands in his.

"Afton, will you do me the honor of buying me this dragon book? I'll Venmo you back once I have my phone."

People are staring at them. "Get up."

"Not until you agree to buy me the book," he says.

"Fine, I'll get it for you."

He shoots back to his feet, handing her the book. She immediately swats him with it. He laughs before running to the fridge and grabbing two diet cokes, a bag of Twizzlers, and a fresh bag of Muddy Buddies. Their favorites in hand, they find a place to hide until boarding.

"I've been thinking about your job," Jonah says, offering her one of his Twizzlers.

She takes it. "Are you trying to distract yourself from your problem with mine?"

"Exactly," he grins before biting into his own.

"I have plenty of other problems we could talk about instead. Do you have any theme ideas for a nesting party?"

He tilts his head slightly. "Definitely going to circle back to whatever a nesting party is."

"How dare you use corporate lingo to blow me off."

"I know you're terrified to talk about this so just listen while I tell you my thoughts."

Fine. She doesn't have to engage. She'll simply be here as words fall out his mouth.

"You're great with people. You can read them in a way others can't. You could look into being a therapist or social worker."

That's his brilliant idea? She'd already thought of those paths. She *would* be good at them. Yet the sheer idea of them has a tension headache starting in her temples. As a child she'd promised to bear one another's burdens and comfort those in need of comfort. Those were still important things to do no matter what one believed. But she didn't want to carry people's burdens as a therapist. It was a big part of why she was stuck. All the in-demand jobs like nursing, teaching, and social work? They required that specific brand of selflessness that she lacked.

"HR is always an option. You're great at interviews; maybe journalism, the news, podcasts. You're creative and already have connections in the industry, maybe a writer's room of some sort. I could also see you in event planning. If you partnered with a local venue, you wouldn't have to travel. There are quite a few positions in city government you'd thrive in too. Why are you looking at me like that?" Jonah asks.

She gapes. "Do you really think I could do those things?"

He looks at her, confused. "Yes. That's why I'm saying them."

"With my current career experience?"

"If we can get you to the interview phase, absolutely. I can help you with your resume of course."

He has more ideas. Lots of them. And he knows how to navigate the application and interview process. The tiniest seed of hope takes root in her chest, and she doesn't immediately smother it.

"Boarding group A for flight 265 to Salt Lake City can start lining up now," a voice announces.

That's them. "We just need to get into our seats without getting spotted and you'll be fine."

Jonah blows out a long breath, tilts his hat over his eyes, his book at the ready. As they approach the gate, Afton searches for his mission president. She spots him immediately, standing next to the stanchions for boarding. He's an older white man wearing a suit and tie that screams Sunday best. She can never name what it is but there's something about the way Mormon men wear their suits that stands out in a crowd of other professionals. Is it the fit? The fabric? The lived in look, since they're brought out multiple times a week? Either way it's obvious it's him.

They hover at the end of the line. Jonah's mission president stays where he is, not getting in line yet, but only feet away from the counter. They'll have to pass him to get on the plane.

"New plan. We wait for him to get on, then we'll go," Afton says.

She barely sees Jonah's nod in confirmation over his disguise. She pretends to be interested in everything in the terminal while keeping an eye on the older man. After he boards with the B group, she leads Jonah onto the plane. They've almost pulled this off. Except, Jonah's mission president is sitting in the row ahead of theirs.

"You sit down, I'll put the bags up," Afton whispers to Jonah.

"No," Jonah protests.

"I am a strong, independent woman. I've got this."

Jonah ignores her, pulling his cap ridiculously low before grabbing both of their suitcases to shove in the overhead compartment. She watches helplessly as his mission president strains in his seat to look at Jonah's face.

"Jonah Partridge?" the man asks.

Jonah closes the compartment and straightens, slowly readjusting his cap so his face is visible.

"President Thompson," Jonah smiles. It doesn't reach his eyes.

The older man stands, bringing Jonah in for an embrace.

"It's Elder Thompson now. I was here on a seventy visit, and

I felt a prompting I'd run into someone at the airport. I'm so glad it was you," he says, holding Jonah at arm's length and inspecting him.

"Excuse me, can you clear the aisle?" a flight attendant asks.

Jonah quickly sinks into his seat directly behind Elder Thompson. Jonah and him start speaking rapidly in Spanish. She tries to follow the conversation, understanding a few sentences that seem to be about Elder Thompson's family, but she's not entirely sure. Afton hates this. She can't manipulate this situation in any way to help Jonah. All she can do is sit here and be with him.

Elder Thompson finally turns to Afton. "Where are my manners? I'm Elder Thompson. I was Jonah's mission president."

"Afton." She shakes his hand awkwardly between the crack in the seats.

Elder Thompson raises his bushy brows. "The Afton? It all worked out after all." Elder Thompson focuses back on Jonah and claps him on the shoulder.

Jonah opens and closes his mouth, his cheeks going red.

Elder Thompson knows who she is. Jonah talked about her enough over a decade ago that this stranger remembered her name. Considering her behavior back then, it probably wasn't a good thing.

"You're very lucky, Afton. I could tell Jonah was a spiritual giant from the moment I met him. The Lord works in mysterious ways and I'm glad to see he finally brought you two back together."

He thinks they're together. Jonah straightens, opening his mouth to correct him. She acts quickly, leaning into Jonah's shoulder and interlocking her fingers in his.

"I'm incredibly lucky. So much so that I already miss him." She pouts up at Jonah who's staring down at her incredulously.

Elder Thompson smiles. "How long have you been married?"

"Two weeks. I don't want to go back to the real world and have to be away from him," she whines, nuzzling her head against his chest.

"I remember those days. Can I share the best piece of marriage advice I've learned?"

"Please," Afton says. Jonah elbows her lightly in the side and she digs her nails into his hand in response. How dare he try and ruin the performance of her life right now when she's trying to get him out of an awkward situation.

"The best way to keep your marriage strong is to spend every morning and night on your knees together."

Afton buries her face in Jonah's arm. She's horrible. This man is trying to give them advice to pray together as a couple morning and night, and she's too immature not to make it into a sex joke.

"That's wonderful advice, we'll have to remember that," Jonah says, voice tight.

Her expression under control, Afton pulls her face from Jonah's arm. "We should get a sign that says that and hang it above our bed," Afton suggests.

Now Jonah's the one pressing his lips together, trying not to laugh while Elder Thompson smiles serenely at them.

"That's a great idea. I'll let you two get back to your newlywed bliss," Elder Thompson says, finally facing forward in his seat.

The flight attendants start their speech and Afton follows along on the emergency handout, doing her best to hold in her giggles.

"You are horrible," Jonah says, voice low. His lips brush the shell of her ear and she shivers.

"I have one minor suggestion to his advice."

"Afton," Jonah murmurs, voice a warning.

The flight attendants finish demonstrating how to inflate the life vests, and make their way to front and back of the plane. Elder Thompson slips a pair of headphones over his ears.

"Has anyone told him it's more enjoyable when you take turns getting on your knees?" Afton finally says into Jonah's ear.

"Afton," he groans, covering his face with his hands.

She bursts out laughing, unable to hold it in any longer. When Jonah removes his hands, his face is serious.

"You didn't need to get me out of that conversation," he says. "I could have handled it."

"I know. It was fun though."

"Pretending we're married?" he asks, face unreadable.

Was it that? Imagining them being on a flight back from a trip they'd taken just for them? Not for work or to find a wife? Getting to snuggle in close and touch him whenever she wanted?

"No, lying to church leadership," she says instead.

Jonah's face instantly relaxes and she feels a flash of annoyance. What, it's stressful that she might have liked the idea of being with him?

"You've been lying non-stop since I met you; maybe you should get that looked at," Jonah teases.

"I only lie to authority figures, I'll be fine."

He snorts. "Yeah, that justifies it."

Afton's quiet, parsing through all the truths and lies. Since he's come back into her life, she *has* been lying. A lot. It's like she's reverted back to her high school self.

"Do you think I have a problem?"

He seems surprised by her question. "Do you lie in all other areas of your life? Or just since your job was on the line?"

"Just the job." Unless you count the little lies every day. Like staying silent when Chelsea dreams about the next steps in their television careers. That it's just another party she's missing with her friends and not a big deal. That thinking about her family doesn't still hurt. That work hasn't felt quite as bad this week and it's purely because she gets to talk to Jonah. That she hasn't been replaying her kiss with him over and over, secretly wondering what it'd be like to be with him.

That she liked when he was hers, even if it was only for a moment.

If she was at karaoke, she'd sing "Sinner" by The Last Dinner Party.

"Do you lie to me?" he asks.

"You're not in a position of authority."

He rolls his eyes. "Just get through this and then you can get back to your truth telling ways. We're almost halfway through this process, right?"

He's right. After their week in SLC, they'll be exactly at the halfway point of this journey. Her time of lies and spending every day with Jonah are slipping away faster than she anticipated.

"Is now a good time to circle back to whatever a nesting party is and why it needs a theme?" Jonah asks after a few minutes sitting in silence.

Despite her fears of returning to her home state, her moral dilemmas, having no idea what to do with her career, and dread about the passing of time, she laughs.

CHAPTER SEVENTEEN

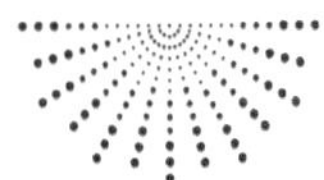

"Jonah? Are you listening?" Tage asks, waving a hand in front of his face. He's zoning out. Again. He tugs on the sleeves of his suit jacket, wishing he could have worn something warmer. After being in Mexico, the dry Utah air bites more than usual.

"Could you repeat that?" Jonah asks the older gentleman standing in front of him and Tage.

"Never go to bed angry. It's always worth staying up and figuring out your problems," the older gentleman says again.

Tage writes it down in her tiny notebook, then they keep walking. They're in the middle of Temple Square on a Tuesday morning and there are wedding parties galore spread across the perfectly manicured grounds. Would a show so heavily featuring Mormons be complete without a shot of its most recognizable landmark, the Salt Lake City temple?

Originally Jonah and the eight women on the group date all walked together, but it was impossible to maneuver through the crowds. Plus, he didn't think it was the best look for him, a single man, to walk around with eight women trailing. Hello, polygamy jokes. Hadn't anyone thought of the optics? The women broke into two groups and he bounced between them, careful to give everyone one-on-one attention as they asked people for their best marriage advice. With all these weddings happening, people are more than happy to share. So far, it's all been contradictory or plain awful. None of it has been as funny as Afton's interpretation of being on your knees.

"What are you humming?" Tage asks as they walk hand in hand, looking for someone else to talk to.

"'Teenagers' by MCR. It got stuck in my head in the car."

From Afton, who had been humming the chorus over and over as their driver took them from the hotel to here. When he'd gotten annoyed and asked if there was a reason in particular she was humming it, she explained when she's nervous she reminds herself that she's one of the teenagers MCR was afraid of. When he'd asked what she was nervous about, she hadn't answered.

He glances to the edge of the grass where the film crew is gathered; a cloud of black in a sea of sage and blush bridal parties. Afton is flipping through a stack of papers while talking to Chelsea. She looks fine. He turns so his back is to her, giving the women who are here for him his full attention.

Bea and Tessa approach him with their own notebooks in hand.

"I can't believe how many brides are here. The building is gorgeous, but it feels so rushed," Tessa says, waving to the grounds.

"That's what she said," Bea says.

Tessa rolls her eyes, but Jonah snorts.

"Have you gotten any good advice?" he asks.

"Go to bed angry and solve your issues when you're fully rested."

Tage laughs. "We were just told to do the opposite and stay up until it's settled."

"How can you settle something if you're exhausted? Most people are irrational then," Tessa says.

"Exactly. The second worse advice was to 'always fight naked.'" Bea makes a gagging noise.

"So you're all team fight when you're calm and rested, and don't be manipulative to try and win arguments?" Jonah asks.

Tage, Tessa, and Bea all nod.

"Glad we're on the same page." This advice might be horrible, but it's helping him learn more about what's important to everyone. It's reassuring to hear they think similarly in these regards.

"Let's try him, I bet he has better insights," Bea says, pointing to a lone photographer who's leaning against a tree with his equipment bags covered in colorful pins. One is a rainbow. The man who looks up in interest as they approach.

"We're looking for our future partners, and as a photographer, I'm sure you have some good relationship advice," Bea says.

The man laughs and Jonah freezes. He has brown hair and eyes, but it's the shape of his mouth that's familiar, along with the sound of his laugh. It sounds so similar to his sister's. He looks to be early twenties, so this has to be Noah. Afton mentioned him in passing when claiming her life was a mess, but he hadn't pushed her on the details after her panic attack. Is this why she was so nervous today? She knew he'd be here?

He needs to warn her. Her brother can't see the two of them together. He turns to where he last saw her with the production team, but she isn't there. Neither is Chelsea. He scans the grounds for the two of them. They should be easy to find in their all-black outfits, but that's the universal uniform of wedding photographers too, of which there are plenty. Maybe she saw Noah and is lying low.

"I can tell you all the red flags during wedding planning, but unfortunately I don't know how to have a healthy marriage," Noah says.

"How long have you been a wedding photographer?" Jonah asks.

"I spent four years as a second shooter in college, now I'm on my own," Noah says, studying Jonah a beat too long. "Do I know you?"

"I'm not sure," Jonah says, toeing the line. Noah was only seven when he and Afton broke up.

"He's the Fiancé-to-be," Tage says.

Noah accepts that answer. "Sorry I can't be much help," Noah winks.

"Can you tell us some of your wedding day red flags?" Bea asks.

"Absolutely." He starts listing them, most having to do with uninvolved or controlling grooms and brides who only care about the day.

Bentley and the other women on the date approach and ask Jonah to join them as they continue getting advice. He hesitates, wanting to hear everything Noah has to say. *Stop it.* He's on a date, not here to figure out the mystery that is Noah and Afton. He follows them across the lawn to talk to a redheaded man with a pregnant blonde wife who's wrangling two kids. Jonah tunes them out, not caring what a man who doesn't help his pregnant wife has to say.

"What's going on over there?" Bentley asks, pointing behind him.

Jonah whips around. Afton is standing with her hands up, facing Noah who is waving his arms dramatically. Jonah has never been more grateful for his Covid hobby of running as he races over to them. He stops a few feet away, ready to step in if they need him.

"I don't know why I expected anything more from you," Noah snaps.

"I'm here for work, not to visit family," Afton says.

Noah rolls his eyes dramatically. "Semantics. Sorry that I wanted to reconnect with my sister."

Afton huffs. "How was I supposed to know that? You text me from a random number, insinuate I'm an uncaring piece of shit, and then you want to know when I'll be in town?"

"I don't have to insinuate it if it's the truth."

Afton recoils as if he slapped her. Jonah moves to stand next to Afton.

"That's enough," Jonah says.

Noah regards Jonah, then lets out a single laugh. "No, it's not. It's Afton's MO to run whenever something isn't convenient to her. Everything was fine until she blew up our family after high school and never looked back to see the destruction she left behind."

"Your family was messed up long before Afton was forced to leave," Jonah says, voice low.

Noah's forehead furrows. "How can you even say that? You weren't there."

"Yes, I was. I lived three houses down from you, and I know that Afton is the only reason you and your brothers were okay. Your dad was never home and your mom was depressed. Afton made sure you were fed, that someone read you bedtime stories, and your homework was done. All while working, keeping up her GPA, and extracurriculars."

Noah's face cycles through emotions. "That's not... Still. She cut us all off. She didn't care about us."

"I wasn't allowed to come visit," Afton says quietly.

"That's not true," Noah shakes his head. "We needed you. I needed you, and you didn't come."

"I tried after the arrest, but you made it very clear you didn't want to see me," Afton says.

"I was gay and trapped at BYU. I hated myself and I had no one," Noah yells.

People on the fringes start coming in closer, curious.

Afton's expression completely changes. "Noah, I didn't know. I would have been there for you..."

"No, you wouldn't have. You can't even commit to getting a coffee. You definitely wouldn't have been there for the darkest moments of my life."

"What's going on?" Chelsea asks, breathless. The crowd around them has grown exponentially, and people have phones pointed at them. The rest of the crew is approaching, along with the women. They've run out of time.

"I've got to go," Noah mumbles. Afton reaches for his arm, but he sidesteps away from her.

"Let's keep talking," Afton says.

"I need some space to think," Noah says, then walks off briskly, his equipment bags whacking his legs.

"Are you okay?" Jonah asks Afton.

She's gone completely still, staring at nothing. "I left him all alone," she whispers.

It's pure instinct to wrap his arms around her. She clings to him as he strokes the nape of her neck with his thumb.

"It's not your fault."

"Afton?" Chelsea asks, alarmed now.

Afton slowly disentangles herself from him, one limb at a time. She doesn't meet his eyes before walking away with Chelsea. He rubs a hand over his chest, empty and cold where she was pressed against him.

"What's going on?" Bea asks.

Jonah snaps out of it, facing the film crew and the women. They're trading glances, brows raised, fiddling with their promise rings. Bea may have been the one who asked the question, but everyone wants an answer. Including Richard, who's standing right behind the cameras with narrowed eyes.

He runs a hand through his hair, trying to come up with an honest answer that doesn't include him knowing Afton way better than he should.

"I saw that man yelling at a producer with no one else around, and I just reacted. I would hope that someone would do the same for my sisters, or any of these women."

When he doesn't say more, Richard crooks a finger in silent command. Jonah follows Richard to a secluded bench underneath a tree with heart shaped leaves. Luke stands next to Richard, camera ready to capture everything.

"You want to explain yourself?" Richard asks.

Jonah braces himself with his elbows on his knees. "I heard yelling and reacted like I would for any friend."

"Friend?" Richard asks.

"I've become friendly with quite a few crew members. We spend all day together, how can you not?"

Luke catches his eye from behind the camera and dips his chin.

"Would you call that hug friendly?" Richard asks.

"Yes," he says, hiding the shiver that crawls up his spine. Would he have hugged, say, McKinlee like that? No. But McKinlee was not, and would never be, a friend to him. He would never tell McKinlee about his worries and fears. He wouldn't enjoy simply sitting in an airport with her.

"Bullshit," Richard says.

Jonah stands up and approaches Luke. "Bring it in."

Luke snorts, setting the camera down, and Jonah embraces

him, even bringing his hand to the back of Luke's neck. Then he claps Luke on the back and pulls away.

Richard is not amused, scowling at both of them. "What are you going to say to the women? They seemed upset."

"I'll listen to their concerns, tell them the truth, and hopefully we can focus on what we're here for."

Richard keeps prodding, but doesn't get the reaction he's hoping for from Jonah.

"I'm going to have Afton reassigned elsewhere," Richard finally says, the camera still rolling.

"Whatever you feel is best," Jonah replies, keeping his face blank.

Richard squints at him, waiting for something. Jonah refuses to give it to him. After moments of silence, Richard finally walks away.

Jonah tries not to worry when neither Afton nor Chelsea show up to escort him to the dinner portion of the date. He needs to play nice with Richard and keep up the pretense that earlier meant nothing. But he's never seen Afton like that, not even the night she broke up with him forever ago. Then she'd been furious. After her confrontation with Noah she'd seemed… defeated.

The SUV stops in front of a swanky jazz club, jarring him from his thoughts. *No more thinking about Afton.* It's not fair to these women who are here for him. They're halfway through this journey, and his decisions are getting harder. He knows who he'll send home this week; women he barely gets to interact with on group dates and cocktail parties. As for knowing who he might propose to at the end of this? Afton's face flashes in his mind, making his temples throb.

That's a future problem. There's no use thinking about it right now. He'd assumed he'd have some inkling by now. Is he doing this all wrong?

"Make sure to reassure the women about what happened earlier, then steer the conversation elsewhere in case we choose to cut all the footage of the incident," Richard tells him as he holds the door open for Jonah.

Jonah's eyes struggle to adjust to the dimly lit club. Golden sconces on the walls illuminate the black and white posters of musicians on the walls. The women are gathered on velvet sofas with dramatic arms, martini glasses in their hands. Their laughter reaches him over the sound of saxophone and bass, but immediately stops when they notice him approaching. He pastes his trademark smile back on as he settles into a spot between Tessa and Tage.

"It's so good to see you all again. I know things ended on a weird note earlier, and I wanted to see how you're doing."

The women exchange looks.

"The whole thing was weird. Especially the hug," Bea says.

Everyone else nods in agreement.

He drags his fingers down his jaw. "I was trying to comfort someone who seemed shaken up. I never want to make any of you uncomfortable, and I apologize for that." He respects and likes these women. He doesn't want to hurt them in anyway, but... He's enjoying having Afton back in his life, and it's starting to feel like he can't have both. Richard said she'd be reassigned; maybe it's for the best.

"Do you know if she's okay?" Tessa asks. "It seemed like she knew that photographer we were interviewing."

Jonah glances over at Richard for some sort of direction here.

"Let's move on from the whole scenario," Richard starts.

He's interrupted by the door of the club opening up. A

woman stands in the doorway, backlit by the sun. Head held high, messy bun bouncing as she bounds down the steps, Chelsea glares at Richard.

"I know we all saw a little altercation back at the temple. One of our producers ran into someone from their personal life unexpectedly, and things got a bit loud. Everyone is fine and Afton will be back tomorrow."

"Thank you for letting us know," Tage says, pointedly glancing to where Richard is pouting behind the cameras.

The evening gets back into its usual rhythm of Jonah talking one-on-one with the women. Tessa drapes her legs over his lap, wanting to know how he prefers to deal with disagreements. His arm rests on Bea's shoulders as they discuss their beliefs about gender roles. Tage leans against his shoulder while debating the wedding planning red flags Noah brought up.

Bentley rips a straw wrapper between her fingers with her legs tucked underneath her. She won't quite meet Jonah's eye.

"Being on the temple grounds today had me thinking about my future and I realized something," she finally says.

"What's that?"

She takes a deep breath. "I thought I didn't care about it, but I do want a temple marriage."

"I can't do that," Jonah starts, face growing hot.

"Which is why I'm telling you now, the moment I realized it. You're a sweet guy, but my heart isn't here, and I don't want to waste either of our time," Bentley explains.

Despite the fact she's ending things with him, a wave of affection surges. "Thank you for being so honest with me. It takes courage to realize what you truly want and to go for it."

"I wish you all the best," she says before leaning forward and wrapping him in a quick hug.

"Can I walk you out?" Jonah asks.

"Of course."

The club goes silent as Jonah walks Bentley out the door. He watches the car drive away, envying her. She knows exactly what she wants. He, on the other hand, feels more confused than ever. Tage is younger and has a strict family. She says she's open to a mixed-faith relationship now, but what about when she's home and has the voices of her family in her ear? Will they convince her this is a mistake? What about if they have children? Will he be okay with his child being baptized into something he wholeheartedly doesn't believe?

He loves his conversations with Bea. She's funny and has a nuanced view of the church. Of anyone, being in a mixed-faith relationship with her seems the most feasible.

Tessa is intelligent and deeply feeling. She doesn't come with any ties to the church so they can start off fresh. She has three older brothers and is used to a large family. He can see the two of them walking around downtown Chicago holding hands, her showing him all the best places to eat. The fantasy stops there. Does he know enough about her to commit to the rest of his life?

She isn't here tonight, but Emily is the other woman at the top of his list. She exudes confidence and has a quick wit. Whenever they kiss it's electric. He feels her holding back from him, which is completely valid considering how they've met. If he were to get sick or face a crisis, he feels she would be there with solutions and support. Will the two of them be able to build the type of trust where she'll let him be there for her in return?

Afton... *No.* She's not an option, yet his chest warms. A life with her is easy to picture. He knows how she deals with stress. How strong she is. Life is fun with her around. He feels peace for the first time all day. What if there was a way...

He goes through the motions for the rest of the evening until he climbs into his own black SUV.

"We need to talk," a woman's voice says from inside.

CHAPTER EIGHTEEN

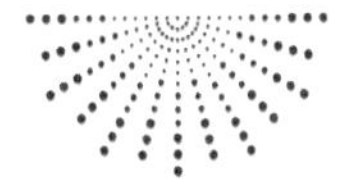

SEVENTEEN YEARS AGO

On her first official date two months after turning sixteen, Afton looked into Jonah's eyes and was infuriated.

"What sizes do you need?" Jonah asked, looking at a spot over her shoulder.

"Eleven," Brennan and Dan replied.

"Six," Dan's girlfriend said.

"Eight," Afton said.

Jonah grabbed the bowling shoes and slid them across the counter, still not meeting Afton's eyes.

This was all his fault. If he'd had the courage to ask her out, she wouldn't be on a double date with her brother and his best friend in the first place. She'd anxiously counted down the days until her birthday; she'd been promised if she followed the prophet's council, she'd be blessed. But Jonah hadn't asked her out. Instead he'd started acting weird around her, frequently clearing his throat or walking off mid-conversation.

When her parents asked during dinner last week if anyone had asked her on a date yet, Dan informed everyone that

Brennan wanted to go out with her. She was instantly brought back to the feel of his fingers on her underwear during her first dance, and said no. Which ended in a lecture about how hard it is for a boy to ask someone out, so you should always give people one chance.

If Jonah didn't feel the same way about her, fine. But he came to all her performances. He talked to her every time he saw her in the hall, even if he'd be late for class. They texted horrible jokes back and forth, and talked about his dad. She'd caught him staring at her sometimes, then looking away. Weren't those all things someone who liked you did? If Jonah had asked her out, then her parents would have left her alone, and she wouldn't be on her first date with her *brother.*

Now she felt his gaze on her back as she walked to their lane. Was he realizing that maybe other people might want her too and he'd missed out? Or did he not care at all?

Bowling was fine. Trying to ignore Dan and his girlfriend making out on the couch opposite her was not. Who was this person and what had he done with her brother?

"Is he always like this?" she eventually asked Brennan.

"You get used to it after a while," Brennan smirked.

Most of the girls from church would love to be here with him. He was a senior and objectively cute. She couldn't spend her whole life hung up on Jonah Partridge. Maybe he did deserve a chance.

Unconsciously she checked the front and caught Jonah staring in her direction again. She scooted closer to Brennan who wrapped his arm around her shoulders. The weight was unfamiliar and heavy. She glanced back at Jonah who was blatantly staring, his mouth in a little o. Was that jealousy? Good.

She endured the weight of Brennan's arm until it was her

turn to bowl again, wriggling out with relief. It was short lived; when she returned he pulled her in even closer.

She couldn't breathe under the weight of him, so she counted to ten before excusing herself to the bathroom. She watched her reflection take deep breaths in the mirror. What had she done? Brennan thought she liked him when that was the farthest thing from the truth. She needed to get out of here.

When she finally left the bathroom, ready to complain about a stomachache, Brennan was waiting outside the doors.

"Are you okay?" he asked.

"Yep." Her voice was high pitched and squeaky.

"Is it because Dan is here?" he asked, looking genuinely concerned. "He's barely paying attention to us."

"I'm fine," she said, trying to step past him.

He grabbed her wrist lightly. She could pull away if she wanted to, but the touch was unnerving.

"I'm having a great night with you," Brennan said, stepping in closer to her. She swallowed. How was he having a great night with her? They'd barely talked. He'd simply sat next to her on a bench and put his arm around her shoulders.

He started to lean in and she froze. He was about to kiss her. In the bathroom hallway of the bowling alley. Did she even want this? All her friends had been kissed already and it'd been weeks since she turned sixteen. She could get this over with and not have it hanging over her anymore.

Brennan pressed his lips against hers, light and uncomfortably wet. He tilted his head, pressing harder against her mouth. Then the tip of his tongue flicked against her lips and she recoiled in disgust.

"What are you doing?" she asked.

"Kissing you," Brennan said, stepping back.

"Were you trying to French kiss me?"

"Yeah?"

"We're not supposed to do that," she whispered.

Brennan rolled his eyes. "It's not a big deal; everyone does it."

"Why? You were licking me like a cat."

Brennan's cheeks turn red, his expression instantly changing. "Was that your first kiss?"

She didn't reply.

Brennan snorted. "I could tell. Hopefully you'll get better.

Shame seeped through her.

"Lots of girls would have loved to take your place tonight," Brennan adds.

He meant it to hurt her, but he sounded like her brothers when the middle two don't want to play together and one claims that they never wanted to play with them anyway. It's never the truth; they just want to have the upper hand. The realization gives her strength.

"Once they hear how horrible of a kisser you are, I'm sure they'll come to their senses."

Brennan's eyes flared and he opened his mouth, but she walked right past him and the shoe rental, flinging the front doors wide open. It was cold and dark outside, but she didn't care. Anything was better than spending another moment in that bowling alley.

Her breath puffed in clouds before her as she replayed Brennan's expression. She'd seen right through him. Her, a nobody sophomore against Brennan, a popular senior. She laughed, and then immediately started crying.

Why'd she gone in the first place? Why hadn't she immediately run out of the bathroom hallway so Brennan hadn't had a chance to corner her and kiss her? Was it her fault for snuggling into him to make Jonah jealous? Why could she attract the attention of Brennan, a guy who made her insides slither, and not someone like Jonah?

Sadie and Naya made kissing sound magical. Defining. Even

though they weren't with those people anymore, they still talked about them fondly. Yet Afton has waited until she was supposed to, and it had been *that*. For the rest of her life whenever someone asked about her first kiss, she'd have to remember that moment with Brennan.

She reached the park down the street from her home and wandered over to the swings. She couldn't go home yet; if she got there before Dan there'd be too many questions she didn't want to answer. She pumped her legs back and forth, the chains creaking. She closed her eyes and focused on the sound, trying to empty her mind.

Another squeaking joined hers, slightly off rhythm. She opened her eyes to Jonah swinging next to her. She planted her feet.

"What are you doing?" she asked, voice scratchy from crying.

"I love swinging in the dead of winter in the dark," he said.

She glared at him, unamused.

"I came to see if you're okay."

"Why?" she asked flatly.

"You looked really upset after… everything."

"What's everything?" she asked. She needed to know exactly what he saw.

"After Brennan cornered you next to the bathroom and kissed you, and then you chewed him out."

Great. So, everything.

"You were incredible. I would have clapped for you if you hadn't looked so upset."

"I'm glad my horrible kiss could amuse you," she deadpanned.

He winced. "That's not how I meant it."

She sighed. "What do you want?"

"To see if you're okay."

"I'm fine."

"No you're not."

"Why do you care?" she asked.

He stared at her incredulously. "Because you're my friend."

"Got it." She stood up to leave.

"Wait," Jonah said.

"I just want to go to bed." She couldn't deal with this right now.

"Please, talk to me." His eyes were pleading.

She settled back onto the swing. "You want the truth? I thought if I waited, my first kiss would be magical. Instead it was with Brennan—who gives me the creeps—next to a bathroom. And I'm mad at myself."

"For what?"

She's going to say it. She'll regret it in the morning, but out here in the dark on this swing, she doesn't care.

"I leaned into him to make you jealous. I don't like him at all, but that's probably why he went for it."

Jonah stops swinging.

"Sorry. I shouldn't have said— "

"It worked. I was jealous."

She clutched the chain of the swing so tightly it cut into her palm. "Why?"

"Why? Isn't it obvious?"

She shakes her head vehemently. "No, it isn't. I have no idea what you think about me. One day you're being sweet, the next you're quiet."

"Because you make me nervous. Because I can't stop thinking about you. My sisters and mom keep giving me conflicting advice and I don't know who to listen to."

"You've been asking them about me?" She would rather die before telling her parents about her crush on Jonah. Yet he felt comfortable talking to his entire family about her?

"Of course I have. I had this whole plan to surprise you on

your birthday, but you weren't home, and I thought maybe it was a sign."

He'd had a plan for her birthday? "A sign of what?"

He ran a hand through his hair. "That it was a bad idea. That I was going to mess things up."

"What is there to mess up?" she asked.

He waved his hands in the air. "Everything. What if you didn't want to kiss me? What if I suck at it?"

"According to Brennan I'm a horrible kisser, so I wouldn't know," Afton joked.

"He's an idiot," Jonah said, planting his feet in the gravel before leaning over in his swing. She leaned to the side, matching him, and finally, finally, their lips met. It was soft and sweet, electricity coursing through her.

Jonah gasped, and her eyes fluttered open in time to see him being swung in the opposite direction from her so fast, he banged his head on the metal frame of the swing set.

"Jonah!"

The force of the hit brought him back in her direction and she stood, catching the chain and stopping him. He rubbed the back of his head, looking dazed. His fingers were covered in blood.

"Let me see your head," she ordered, reaching up and turning him. There was a little gash, glistening in the dark. Thankfully it wasn't gushing, only trickling into his hair.

When he turned back to face her, he was smiling. "That was amazing."

Was he serious right now? "That's the concussion talking."

Jonah snorted. "That was not a concussion, I'm fine." He swiped the back of his head and came back with more blood. He fumbled around with his backpack and pulled out a beanie, pressing it against the wound.

"Let's get you home, we need to take care of that," she said.

"It's just a scratch; a little bit of pressure and I'll be fine."

"You don't know that," she started.

"I'm an eagle scout; I've taken a million first aid classes." He pulled the beanie away and peered at it. "See? It's already stopping."

She checked the back of his head and he was right; the bleeding was slowing down.

"How did you even hit the frame?" she asked. The physics weren't adding up.

"I…" He took a deep breath, as if he needed it for whatever he was about to say. "I've been imagining what it'd be like to kiss you for years. It was so much better than I dreamed it would be. I forgot to keep my feet planted and the swing flung me sideways."

"What do you mean you've been imagining that for years?"

His cheeks flushed even more despite the cold. "The first time I thought about it was when you told me you hoped Eragon and Princess Arya ended up together. It's been popping into my head ever since."

"That was a week after I met you."

He nodded.

"Why didn't you say anything?" she asked, exasperated.

He looked down at his feet, still pressing the beanie to the back of his head. "Because you're one of my best friends. I didn't want to mess it up, especially if you didn't feel the same."

She stepped closer to him. "You're one of my best friends too, and your friendship means so much to me. But, I've been thinking about kissing you for years, too."

His whole face lit up. "Should we do it again? Or pretend it never happened?"

They were on a precipice. They could go back to the way things were. The wondering of what it was like to kiss each other would be gone, leaving room to think about other things.

Could she go the rest of her life with only that kiss from him? Nothing more? Starting something could go horribly wrong and she's have to see him all the time. They might regret it forever. Or, it could also be the beginning of the rest of their lives.

She stepped up on her tiptoes, pressing her lips to his in reply.

CHAPTER NINETEEN

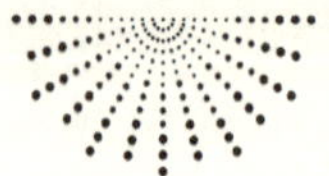

C helsea sits in the driver seat, motioning for Jonah to climb into the shotgun. Once he's buckled, she jerks the car forward.

"What did you want to talk about?" he asks carefully, heart hammering.

"What's your deal with Afton?"

His heart beats even faster. "Like I said, I would want anyone else—"

"Cut the bullshit. No one else is in the car and there are no mics here. I want the truth. Now."

"How long have you known Afton?" Jonah asks.

"You're not in a position to be asking questions," Chelsea practically growls.

"What would you do to protect Afton?" he presses.

She turns to look at him, passing headlights illuminating her face. Her eyebrows pull together.

"I've known Afton since freshman year of college. She's my best friend and I'll do anything to protect her. That's why we're having this conversation."

"Anything?" he presses.

"What did you two do? Kill someone? I'm not helping you bury a body."

"Of course not!"

"Sleep together?" she asks, keeping her head forward.

Jonah sighs, rubbing a hand down his face. She's Afton's best friend; she should be hearing this from her.

"Seriously? I'm gone for five days and she fucks the talent?" Chelsea cries.

"No, we didn't sleep together. At least, not in this decade," Jonah says.

Chelsea turns on her blinker, pulling into a strip mall parking lot. "Explain. *Now.*"

Afton might be mad, but he doesn't see a way out of this. Production is suspicious of them after the hug. If Chelsea loves Afton as much as Afton loves Chelsea, she'll be able to help.

"I've known Afton since we were eleven. She was my first love. I hadn't seen her since high school until I ran into her on set."

Chelsea squeaks. Then waves her hand, telling him to continue.

He summarizes their past and how they ran into each other. He emphasizes multiple times that Afton did the things she had to try and protect Chelsea while still having a job.

"I am in so much shit," Chelsea moans, head in her hands. "Why didn't she tell me?"

"Plausible deniability?"

"I'm the one who suggested she be your producer after Barb got sick. I could tell she was getting burnt out and thought it would help. Instead I ruined the show."

"It was one hug," he huffs.

"Yeah, among a shit ton of unresolved sexual tension."

He's still trying to come up with a response to that when

Chelsea turns in her seat, facing him. "Do you still love her?" He starts to say no, but she points her finger inches from his eye. "Be honest."

"As a friend."

She snorts. "You two started off as best friends and look where that got you. If she was a contestant on this show, would you keep her or send her home?"

He pictures her moving from behind the camera to stand with the women. "I'd keep her."

Chelsea laughs. "I knew it. We're all fucked."

"Why do you keep saying that?"

"Because either we all come clean right now, she gets fired and blacklisted from all productions, and they tell you to pretend she never existed and pick from your actual contestants. Or, we pretend there's no history, you two keep growing closer, you quit trying with your actual women and give us a boring show, then get caught fucking in the bathroom. Afton's still blacklisted from the industry, and you go down in history as the man who only wants what he can't have."

"You have no idea that's what would happen. I'm developing real relationships here," he starts.

Chelsea raises an eyebrow. "A relationship with someone you just met versus another chance at the woman who got away? I'm Afton's best friend; I know what a catch she is."

He swallows. "There has to be a way to get through the rest of the season without getting Afton blacklisted and ruining the show."

Chelsea rubs her temples. "If you can keep it in your pants for a few more days, I'll try and think of something. Can you do that?" Chelsea asks.

"I'm not a dog; I am capable of self-control."

Chelsea raises a single brow and he sighs.

"I'm not going to sneak off and sleep with Afton."

"Good. I'll try and figure some way out of this mess you two created."

"Thank you." If anyone can think of a solution, it's Chelsea. She's a powerhouse and he's slightly afraid of her.

"Is Afton okay?" he finally asks.

"She says she is, but she's a known liar." Chelsea glares at him again.

"Can I see her? Just to make sure she's okay."

Chelsea blinks at him before looking around the empty parking lot. "Maybe I will have to bury a body."

"I'm worried about her. I won't be able to focus unless I know she's okay."

"Boohoo, poor you."

Chelsea would get along great with his sisters.

"Maybe I'll have to knock on every single hotel room until I find her," he muses.

"That'll totally help your cover story of not being obsessed with her."

Damn it, she's right. He has no leverage here. Chelsea starts driving again, headed back to the hotel.

"Why'd you do it?" Chelsea asks after a few minutes of silence.

He startles. "Do what?"

"Get her thrown out of her house."

He hangs his head. "I'd been told what we'd done was a sin next to murder. I couldn't eat or sleep, and I was supposed to leave for my mission soon. My family was so different than hers, and I underestimated how they'd react. I've regretted that decision more than you'll ever know."

Chelsea's quiet for a moment. "You honestly believed consensual sex between two eighteen-year-olds was nearly as bad as murder?"

He nods.

"Did confessing make you feel better?"

"Instantly. It was this enormous weight off my shoulders and I could breathe again. Even though everyone knew what I'd done, I didn't care. I took my punishment gladly, ready to be clean again."

"What do you think about it now?"

He looks out the window, the steeples of the temple back in view. "If we hadn't been raised that way, I think we would have slept together and looked back on it fondly. It would have been no one else's business. We would have both gone to college in California, and who knows what would have happened after that."

"You're lucky you didn't have to meet my college self," Chelsea muses.

Jonah laughs, picturing a young Chelsea and Afton. They would have kept him on his toes. At the red light, Chelsea starts fiddling with her phone on the dashboard. Then she sighs.

"She's been dodging my calls all night, and frankly I'm pissed at her for lying to me about you. Which is why I'm going to send you in there to get her out. Do not make me regret trusting you. You've got twenty minutes." She pulls the SUV into a parking spot in front of an older brick building with a sign that says Bar. Chelsea reaches into a tote bag in the backseat and pulls out a yellow baseball cap, shoving it low on his head.

"Pretty sure this will attract more attention than if I just went in there."

She sighs again and yanks it off. "Nineteen minutes left."

He hurries into the bar. It's only half full and melancholic piano music blasts from the speakers. He searches the groups for Afton, finally finding her at the back of the room standing on a stage as she sings the opening bars to "My Immortal" by Evanescence.

This is bad.

He finds her jacket on the back of a barstool, and takes the seat next to it. Goosebumps cover his arms as her quiet, mournful voice starts to rise with the chords of the piano. When she gets to the chorus, her voice climbs in volume. Her eyes are closed and she's swaying, her arm outstretched as she sings about wounds that time hasn't erased. What does she think of when singing those words?

He's a mess of chills by the final note which she holds longer than he thought humanly possible. The crowd goes wild clapping and cheering. She swipes under one eye as she leaves the stage and makes her way back to her jacket. Some people try to catch her attention as she walks through the bar, but she ignores them, singlehandedly focused on her seat.

He turns to face the bar, using the menu to shield his face. When she raises a hand and gestures for the bartender, he thinks he's pulled off his disguise.

"You need to leave before someone recognizes you," she says, leaning in.

He drops the menu. "Not yet. I want to sing a duet."

She sighs. "Jonah, please. It's been a day."

Maybe this wasn't as good of an idea as he'd thought. "Chelsea brought me here. I have twenty minutes to get you out."

Afton frowns before looking down at her phone. "I'm going to stop sharing my location with her."

"Don't. I wanted to see if you were okay," he says.

She sighs before ordering a rum and coke from the bartender. He orders two waters. Afton drums her fingers on the bar top, swiveling back and forth in her chair.

"Why are you looking at me like that?" she asks with narrowed eyes.

"I expected to find you in here absolutely wasted, puking in the corner."

The corner of her lip quirks. "Typical Mormon thinking, that everyone who has a sip of alcohol is a sloppy alcoholic. I'll have you know that I make an effort not to use alcohol to numb my feelings."

"What do you use to numb your feelings then?"

"The gym. My sobbing in the shower playlist. The occasional edible," she shrugs. "What about you?"

"Running. Blasting emo music. Calling my sisters. Occasionally they're helpful, but usually they just roast me."

She's about to take a sip of her drink and snorts. "What've they called you lately?"

"They told me I chew like a millennial right before I left. I'm glad the dinners are fake for filming because it's yet another thing to be self-conscious about."

Afton snatches the menu from in front of him. "We need to investigate this immediately."

"I only have eighteen more minutes to get you out of here," he reminds her.

"Can we get some pretzels?" she calls out to the bartender.

"If we're doing this, I need to pee first." He heads toward the bathroom, taking a quick detour before returning to where Afton is waiting with a bowl of pretzels. Her phone is propped against her water glass, the camera facing them.

"The only way to do this is to see if we chew the same since we're both millennials," she explains.

He wouldn't do this for anyone else. He scoots in close to her so they're both in frame, then pops a pretzel in his mouth. She does too, then presses record. They both stare at the screen as they chew. It's like they coordinated this, the way their mouths move in sync. She quickly swallows then bursts out laughing. The sound is contagious.

"Your sisters are on to something."

"Technically we need to find some Gen z people and see if they chew differently," he says.

Her eyes light up and she's already halfway off her stool. "On it."

He tugs gently on her arm, stopping her. "Are you okay?"

"I'm not drunk; I would want to solve this mystery even if we weren't here."

"You know what I mean. Are you okay after today?"

The light in her eyes dims and she takes a long sip of her rum and coke.

"If you want to talk about it, I'm here," he tries.

Afton stops drinking. "I went to therapy in college to deal with," she waves her hand in a circle, "everything. I thought I'd moved on, but seeing Noah today shows I haven't."

"How so?"

She folds her arms on the bar, resting her chin on top of them. "I chose the selfish route. I could have taken my parent's deal. Or stayed closer so I could keep an eye on things. But I chose me. The moment I had the freedom to finally be myself I wasn't willing to give it up."

"Afton."

She straightens. "I know it all. I was a kid and I shouldn't have been put in that situation in the first place. My brothers' happiness isn't my responsibility. It's okay for me to want things for myself. I know all those things logically, but I can't get past the little voice saying if only I'd stayed, things would be better. Noah wouldn't have felt abandoned. My other brothers wouldn't be in and out of jail.

"When I look at what I abandoned them for, a career in reality TV that I don't even like anymore, it all feels so useless. Maybe the world would have been better if I stayed."

His jaw clenches. "Afton, no. You're allowed to be happy.

You're allowed to try things and change your mind. What happened with your family is not your fault. Your mom needed more support and your dad ignored that. They were doing what they thought was expected. If you want someone to blame for your family's pain, blame the systems that failed them. Never you."

"But Noah blames me..."

"He's twenty-two and needs a good talking to," Jonah practically growls.

Afton narrows her eyes.

"You two can talk and both explain your sides. It's obvious he wasn't told the truth."

She inhales slowly, letting that sink in. It's that moment the DJ announces over the speakers, "Afton and JJ."

He stands, holding out a hand. "That's our cue."

"What?" Afton says, looking alarmed.

"Come on," he says, tugging her. "I said I wanted to sing a duet."

She studies him, then gets to her feet. "JJ?"

"Trying to stay anonymous."

"By singing on stage?"

Yes, that. He'd momentarily blacked out when he'd gone over and signed them up. He'd been so focused on cheering her up that he forgot about the singing part. Nerves slam into him as they step onto the stage and are handed two microphones by the DJ. More people have filtered into the bar since he first arrived, dozens more eyes to see how horrible he is.

Afton's hand squeezes his, anchoring him. "What are we singing?"

"I can't remember," he says honestly. What had he told the DJ? It'd only been minutes ago. The room is unbearably warm out of nowhere. Is he going to pass out?

She laughs, the familiar sound breaking through. "It'll be over in two minutes, and I promise the majority of them aren't even watching. I've got you." She squeezes his hand again.

He's said those words countless times during dates for the show. Before BASE jumping, walking on a tightrope, and scenic helicopter rides. He's admired each of his dates for facing their fears with him. Now he needs to face his own fear.

A guitar rift starts and he's brought straight back to high school. Oh yeah. *This* was his brilliant song choice. Afton gapes at him, almost missing the opening notes to "Ocean Avenue." Almost. She shifts into a different version of herself, shaking her hair and bobbing to the beat. Her voice perfectly matches the tone, so different from the melancholy from earlier. Seeing her this close is mesmerizing.

The verses are shorter than he remembered and the chorus is starting. She looks straight at him, nodding encouragingly for him to join. Eyes locked on hers, he starts to sing. He's practically whispering, but Afton smiles, and he sings louder. Their voices mix together and it's like they're back in his beater car from high school, jamming in the front seat. He relaxes, singing only for her.

When the next verse starts, she inclines her head, telling him to take it. He barely has to glance at the screen, the words coming back from all the times he sang it, hoping it would bring Afton back to him. In Mexico City when he had no idea who he was. When he started school at BYU and everyone was too serious. At the Yellowcard concert where they finished with this song and he looked at the moon, wondering if it was night wherever she was and if this song reminded her of him.

They'd both been at that concert, and they're both here now, baring their souls to each other. There's no denying it anymore. This thing between them isn't simply a byproduct of their past. It's growing, changing, new.

Chelsea was right when she said they're all fucked.

CHAPTER TWENTY

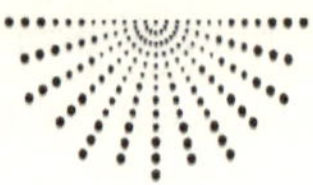

*D*id he purposefully look through these lyrics, figure out which verses would hit her the hardest, and divvy up the song that way? Why did she have to get this bridge, talking about the look in his eyes when she says goodbye and he's begging for one more night? She focuses on the screen, trying to ignore Jonah right next to her, singing all the oh's.

She used to sing this song constantly after their breakup, but rarely sang this verse out loud. She was the one who told him goodbye; Jonah was the one begging her not tonight.

Somehow, she gets through the verse, and they're on the final chorus. She faces Jonah and gives it everything. He would only ever sing when they were alone in the car as teenagers, no matter how hard she begged him. Now he's singing karaoke with her, willingly, in front of strangers. She loves the way their voices mix, how his eyes are focused solely on her. She could live in this moment forever.

They sing the final 'away' and she breathes hard as the violin echoes through the bar. The clapping from the crowd startles her, reality crashing in. She's in a public place singing with

Jonah. The Fiancé-to-be. Anyone could be filming right now. She yanks on his hand, leading him off the stage and back to their jackets. Her phone vibrates in her pocket.

CHELSEA

I have an emergency meeting. Can you two manage walking back to the hotel without taking your pants off?

You and I have A LOT to talk about.

Jonah mentioned something about Chelsea giving him twenty minutes to get her out.

"What's this?" she asks, showing him her phone.

His eyes dart across the screen, smile fading. "She ambushed me in the car and I may have told her some things."

"Some things?"

"Like that we know each other."

Her stomach bottoms out and the walls close in. When did it get so unbearably hot in here?

"Let's get some air," Jonah says, grabbing their jackets and leading her to the door.

Outside she breathes in the cool night air, relishing the way it hits her flushed skin. The high of the stage has faded completely. They cross the street over to a green area that snakes between tall windowed buildings, settling on top of a stone retaining wall.

"Are you okay?" he asks.

"Why'd you pick that song?" she blurts out. It's the least important of the questions spinning through her mind, but she needs to know.

"Answer my question first and I'll tell you."

She kicks her legs back and forth. "I was until you told me Chelsea knows about us. Is she going to kill me?"

"She very specifically told me she wouldn't help bury a body, so I don't think so."

"Why were you talking about burying bodies?" She needs to get back to the hotel and talk to Chelsea. Or flee the country. Except Chelsea would hunt her down and be even more pissed

"I asked if she'd do anything for you and she said that was her line. I only told her after that. She knew there was something going on and wouldn't give up."

"What'd she say?"

"Irrelevant stuff about me keeping it in my pants, and that she'd figure a way to get us out of this mess."

There's no way that's all that's going through Chelsea's mind. She needs to get back and apologize to her best friend. Except Chelsea's now in an emergency meeting…is it about her?

"I picked that song because it reminds me of you. Of us. I used to listen to it over and over after we broke up. I got in trouble once for humming it on my mission," Jonah says.

All thoughts of Chelsea evaporate. "No you didn't."

He tilts his head. "Pretty sure I did."

"I was singing that song too. So you couldn't have been."

"Why? You're the only one allowed to sing it?"

"No. We couldn't have been in separate parts of the world singing the same song, both thinking of each other."

He's shaking his head, the tiniest smile on his lips. "Yes, we could have. We're meant to be together. Can't you see that?"

She scoots away from him. "No, we're not. I don't believe in that stuff anymore." She'd prayed over and over, begging God to give her some way to make this all work. To have Jonah *and* the life she wanted. One away from the church he'd been so devoted to. All there had been was silence, so she'd chosen herself.

He hops off the wall and moves so he's standing in front of her, his thighs brushing her shins. "You were my best friend. The love of my life. Even with all the odds against us, we found our way back to each other. I've tried to get over you, believe me. Do you know many times I've grabbed my phone wanting to text you about a reality tv villain, one of our favorite bands reuniting, or that my mom went on two dates with a man named Chad?"

"Oh Carrie. Once can potentially be forgiven, but twice?"

Jonah's mouth twitches, but he continues. "I'm dating a dozen women right now and every time I ask them questions, I'm thinking about how you would answer them. I'd rather spend my time waiting in airports, sitting in traffic, and facing my past with you than going on the most romantic dates television can buy. When I'm with you, I feel like I'm home. I've vowed not to waste any more time, and I want to be with you."

No. No. No. This can't be happening. He can't say the sweetest things she's ever heard.

"You like being with me because I'm familiar. Picturing a life with a near stranger is full of unknowns. You *think* you want me because I'm less scary."

He shakes his head. "You're the scariest choice. You broke my heart and disappeared. I know what it'd feel like to lose you again. But I know what I want."

Tears blur in her eyes. "How can you want me when I'm such a mess?"

"Who isn't a mess? That isn't a prerequisite for someone loving you."

"I just..." Her thoughts are sticky and she can't untangle them.

He takes the tiniest step back, his leg no longer pressing against hers. "Unless you're not interested."

She's told so many lies lately; she won't tell another. "That's not it."

His brow furrows. "Is it because of what I did? I understand if you can't get past that."

"You were doing what you were taught you had to. I forgave you a long time ago," she says.

"Then what is it?"

She can picture it. Running off back to California. Going for a walk on the beach with him and Millie. She could apply for new jobs on his couch while he made dinner. She'd bring him to Naya's nesting party, and hold his hand as she tried reconnecting with Noah. Christmas could be with Carrie and his sisters. It'd be perfect, until the thrill of reconnecting wore off and he started to wonder if he'd made the right choice.

"There are so many amazing women here, and you're only halfway through your journey. I don't want to get in the way of that for you." She shouldn't even be here for him to consider. If she'd done the right thing and excused herself from this season, he'd be focused solely on the others. Her selfishness changed his journey; she doesn't deserve to have him consider her.

He steps forward, pressing his legs into hers again. "It would be unfair to them when I've already made up my mind."

"You barely know this version of me."

"I know the important parts."

She sighs. "No, you don't. You still know my favorite snack, and how to make me laugh. We both romanticized one of the best songs of our generation, but that doesn't mean it'll work."

He takes a few steps back, running his hand through his hair. "Why do you think I'll be able to get to know any of the other women better than that in this amount of time? Tell me what I don't know. I'm not scared."

"For starters, I don't know if I want to get married." She

expects him to walk farther away, or be shocked. All he's talked about while filming is how he's looking for his wife.

"Do you not want to be married because you don't want to be monogamous, or because of the legality of it?"

"The legality. I've seen so many women get burned by it and you can never guarantee you won't get divorced."

He nods. "I'm okay with not getting legally married." She must make a face because he continues, " I know what I'm supposed to say for the show. I'm here for a life partner, not specifically a wife."

"What about kids?" she asks. He's had that conversation with all of the women, but she needs to hear it said to her.

"I truly would be okay going either way with that. If it happens with the right person, I'd welcome it. If it doesn't, that's perfectly fine. I don't see them as a way to try and fill some void in myself."

"If you did have them, how many?"

"Two max."

The corner of her mouth ticks upward. "Same. I've seen our generation put more thought and care into parenting that my parents simply couldn't because of how many kids they had. And because they put the church first. I think I could do a better job. But it's not my dream or the only thing I think I'm good for."

His smile is devastating. "If it happens, you'd be an amazing mom, I know it."

The image of a baby with her eyes in his arms slams into her, unbidden. It doesn't feel like the daydreams of her youth, absolutely suffocating. She wouldn't be forced to have that baby because it was her only option. It'd be something they carefully chose. He wouldn't be torn away by church duties, abandoning her with multiple screaming children. It'd be a partnership. She'd still be her own person, not just a mom.

Who is she kidding? She still hasn't told Naya she won't make the baby shower because she's scared of her reaction. There's no way she's ready to have a relationship, or be a mother. She jumps down from the wall.

"I have to quit. It's the only way."

Jonah steps in front of her, his cold fingers lightly wrapping under her jaw, tipping her face up to meet his eyes.

"I'm not letting you walk away from this because it's hard. If you truly don't want to be with me, then I'll accept that. But if it's because you're feeling overwhelmed with decisions that we don't have to make tonight, then I refuse. I let you push me away before. I'm not going to this time."

She anchors herself in those eyes that truly see her. "I lied to be here for selfish reasons and imposed myself on your journey. I'm worried you'll look back and regret not following this process through to the end because of me."

His lips press together. "Fine, let's finish the process. You're a secret contestant. I'll ask you the same questions I ask the women, and you'll ask me yours. I'll weigh your responses with everyone else's, then choose who I feel is best for me. If that happens to be you, you have to trust me. I turned my back on everything I was raised to believe. I'm more than capable of choosing which life path is best for me."

She bites her lip. "If it's not me?"

"Then we get much-needed closure, we look back on this time fondly, and go our separate ways."

"You could do that?" she asks.

He licks his lower lip. "Can you?

She wouldn't have to say goodbye to him yet. Or feel guilty for the emotions roiling through her every time he's near. For secretly imagining being with him.

"Yes."

"Thank god." His voice is low and gravelly.

She tugs on his shirt, bringing him closer and his mouth crashes into hers. Their kiss in the alley had been tentative, whisper soft. Something that could easily be denied. Now they're fevered, stealing as much as possible. His tongue parts the seam of her lips, claiming her mouth. She slides her hands up his chest and around his neck, threading her fingers in his hair, holding him here. Making sure he doesn't disappear. He grips her hips, pulling her closer.

She nips his bottom lip and he's spinning them, walking her backward until she bumps the retaining wall. His hands move under her ass and he lifts her up until she's sitting on top of it. Their mouths separate; she's a good head taller from up here. She scoots to the edge of the wall and hooks her legs around his middle. His cold fingers slide up the nape of her neck, chills racing down her spine before fingers tangle in her hair. He grabs a fistful and yanks upward until her lips are back within reach. His other hand dips beneath her sweater, palming her breast. She gasps into his mouth as he rolls her nipple between his thumb and forefinger.

She tries to reach for him, but the wall is in the way.

"Not tonight," he breathes into her ear.

He tugs on her hair again, the pain delicious. She groans in frustration, trying to grind against him, but she's too high up. He lets go of her breast, his hand sliding down her belly, over her jeans, until his palm presses against her clit. She gasps as he starts to make slow circles, pressing the seam of her jeans into that perfect spot. When she gasps again, his lips trail from her mouth, pressing kisses against her jaw, underneath her ear, down her neck. He keeps up the circles with his palm; his long fingers wrapped under her and pressing her entrance. Her walls flutter, needing more. She swivels her hips with him, the seam of her jeans adding friction everywhere.

He pulls her hair to the side, baring her throat and the spot at the base of her neck that always drove her crazy. His teeth scrape against her skin and he sucks gently. Pressure builds in her belly, her spine. Is he actually going to get her off, fully dressed, out in public? She's going to get arrested…

He lets go of her hair, hand slipping back under her sweater, pinching her other nipple while sucking harder on her neck. Her head rolls back as he replaces his palm with his thumb, pressing tighter, faster circles on her center over her jeans.

She gasps. "I'm so close."

He presses harder, keeping the rhythm. "Let go for me," he murmurs into her neck.

Pleasure shoots down to her toes then back up her spine. Her core clenches and he swallows her cries with his mouth, kissing her deeply through the contractions. He keeps circling until her gasps turn to whimpers, body spent.

"You're incredible," he smiles into her lips.

She slumps against him, catching her breath before jumping down from the wall. Her legs are shaky and she fists his shirt for balance, before spinning him so he's pressed against the wall now. She slides her hand down his firm chest and stomach, all the way to the top button of his pants. He grips her wrist.

"Not tonight," he repeats, lips swollen from kissing.

She pouts. "You've learned some new tricks. I want to show you mine."

"I promised Chelsea I was capable of self-control. Let me maintain some so I'm not completely lying to her."

"Don't talk about her right now. I want a turn—"

"If you touch me, I'm going to come in my pants and I still have to walk through the hotel lobby where I might be recognized. Let me have some dignity," he says, voice low in her ear.

Oh. "I guess that's fine."

He smiles, then leans down, his teeth lightly tapping against her nose ring.

"What was that?" she laughs when he pulls away.

"Sorry, I've been wanting to do that since I first saw you. The nose ring is sexy as hell."

"Because it's forbidden?"

"Because it's you." Then he kisses her, sweet and slow. Every time they start to walk back, one of them steals one last kiss, then another. When she shivers from the cold, Jonah finally pulls away.

"Take my coat."

"It's only two blocks. I'll have to take it right back off again."

He frowns, sliding one arm out of the coat, then pulling her flush against him so he can wrap the coat around the both of them. It's a warm cocoon of his cologne and soap. She inhales deeply, trying to memorize the smell for later. For her reckoning with Chelsea.

CHAPTER TWENTY-ONE

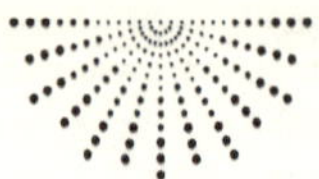

*J*unior year was about planning for the future. Her homeroom classes were spent in the computer lab researching colleges, dreaming of all the possible lives she could live outside of Utah. Away from her family and the constant worries about juggling her brothers' needs with her wants. Most often she looked at schools in California, then balked at the tuition every time. Naya and Sadie wanted out of Utah too, and they created a spreadsheet of scholarships and grants to apply for.

Jonah loved the idea of California too, especially with his extended family living there.

"We'll do freshman year together, then I'll join you again after my mission. You'll graduate before me though, hopefully you won't be too embarrassed," he teased.

She could picture it. The two of them walking around a new campus, studying under palm trees. Going to the beach on the weekends.

She made the mistake of leaving college materials out at

home and her dad came into the kitchen while she prepped her little brothers' lunches, a pamphlet in hand.

"Why would you want to go out into the world where they'll fill your head with lies, when you could go to college with people who are all living the same standards as you?"

"I'm looking at all my options, they're just brochures," Afton said.

"We'll only pay if you go to BYU. It doesn't make sense to waste all that money when you have an affordable option already."

She hid all the pamphlets after that and got a job at the movie theater. Every popcorn splattered theater she cleaned was one step closer to getting away.

Then there was her relationship with Jonah. She spent every spare moment with him. Jonah and Henry merged with her friend group, hanging out before school and always teasing each other. Afton was so happy she thought she would burst having all her favorite people get along.

Carrie was thrilled the two of them were dating. She told Afton she wasn't allowed to go upstairs anymore, but otherwise she didn't care when they sat next to each other on Reality TV nights, or if Afton came over to do homework on the rare afternoons Jonah and her were both free.

It took six months for her own parents to realize she was dating Jonah exclusively. They pulled her into their bedroom one night for a talk.

"The prophets have counseled that you shouldn't date exclusively when you're young. You should be dating lots of people to get to know them and realize what you do and don't like in a partner" her dad said.

"When you're with the same person long term, Satan will tempt you more to be physical before marriage," her mom added.

"You need to break up with Jonah and start dating other people."

Panic squeezed her lungs. "I don't like anyone else."

"You haven't gotten the chance to know them," her dad said.

"Yes, I have. They're all jerks, or they're out partying or drinking." It was true. Even in a place like Utah where the majority of kids were members of the church, it wasn't cool to follow the rules.

Her dad perked up. "Who's out partying and drinking? Kids in the ward?"

If she told him, he'd tell the bishop and everyone would hate her. "They don't invite me to their parties because they know I'm not interested," she said carefully.

"I'm glad that's your reputation," her mom said.

Her dad nodded. "You still need to break up with Jonah. If you go on dates with others, you can go with him every once in a while."

She called her friends, sobbing. Naya and Sadie promised they'd figure something out. Her heart hurt too much to call Jonah, and she wouldn't be able to get the words out even if she did. She dreamt of him kissing other girls and telling her he liked them better.

Sadie and Naya waited for her before school the next morning.

"We've got a solution, but you have to promise us something."

"Anything," Afton sniffed.

"You need to start spending more time with us again. I'm not letting you become one of those girls who drops everyone else because of a boy," Naya said.

It had been a while since she'd hung out only with them outside of school. She'd been lost in a world of kisses and laughter with Jonah.

"Deal."

So began the game of charades. Whenever she and Jonah wanted to go out, she'd pretend she was going on a date with Sadie or Naya's dates. Their dates would come to her house and receive the talk from her dad. Once they were out of sight of the house, they'd switch back to their original partners.

It was going great, until a weekend when Naya was supposed to bring a date. When Afton was double checking she was still on for it, Naya pressed trembling lips together.

"What's wrong?"

Naya shook her head and tried to speak, but no words came out.

"Are you okay?"

Tears trailed down Naya's cheeks. "I can't do it."

"The date? That doesn't matter; I'm not mad. Don't cry."

Naya covered her face with both hands and began sobbing. Afton pulled her close and held her until Naya's breaths began to slow.

"I don't want you to stop being my friend," Naya said into her shoulder.

"You're my best friend; that would never happen."

"Not after I tell you this."

Afton pulled gently on Naya's hands. "There's nothing you could say that would change my mind."

Naya looked at Afton for a moment, then took a deep breath. "I think I like girls."

Afton's face scrunches up. "What do you mean?"

"I'm a lesbian. Or bi? I don't know. I used to think your brother was cute, but I think it was more the idea of someone liking me? Every time I go out with a guy and he kisses me, I feel... disgust? Like a little bit of my soul is dying? I've been trying; I really have. But this isn't going away." Naya covers her face again.

Afton felt sick. Naya had been forcing herself to go on these dates so Afton could be with Jonah. "I'm so sorry; if I'd known I never would have asked you to do those dates."

Naya's removes her hands from her face. "You don't think I'm bad?"

"Why would I?"

"Because your church thinks it's a sin to be gay," Naya says flatly.

It hits Afton then, why Naya was so scared to say something. The Proclamation to the World. The lessons about marriage being between a man and a woman, and how inspired that document was for its time. To love the sinner but hate the sin.

How could they be talking about Naya? She *knew* Naya. Afton could be herself with Naya; she never worried that she was being secretly judged. When Afton thought of the Savior, she wanted Him to be more like Naya than the church members always watching for her to make a mistake.

"I know you, and I don't care who you like. Unless it's Jonah."

Naya cringed. "Definitely not Jonah."

"Then we're good. I love you Naya, always will." She wrapped Naya into a hug.

JONAH WALKED her home after her late shifts at the movie theater. Often it was them and two others in the building, giving them privacy. They'd sit in the dark, tonguing the alphabet in each other's mouths. The thought of French kissing with Brennan had been disgusting, but she loved it with Jonah.

Once as she shifted in her seat trying to get closer to him, her hand brushed across his lap and felt something hard. She pulled back, confused. It was dark in the theater, but she could see from the lights on the stairs that Jonah's face was flushed.

Oh. *Oh.*

"I'm so sorry," she whispered.

"It's okay." His voice was tight.

"Does it hurt?"

"The exact opposite."

"Does it happen a lot?"

"Just every time we kiss. Or I see you. Or I think about you."

"Really?" The thought of her could do that to him? She felt powerful. She'd always wondered if she was pretty enough, cute enough, funny enough. Merely walking into a room did that to him?

A year after they started dating, Jonah's hands wandered down from her neck, inching closer to her chest. She inhaled sharply, her breasts tingling. She arched her back, bringing them closer to him. His fingers froze for long seconds before finally cupping her left breast in his hand. Heat shot down to her stomach, lower. She wanted more.

Her own hand slid down his chest to his lap, feeling his erection. She ran her hand back and forth, fascinated by the hardness of him.

"We should stop," Jonah said through gritted teeth, letting go of her.

She jerked away. What had she done? They'd just been kissing, and then they were touching each other's privates.

That was a sin. One they'd have to go to the bishop for. She instantly felt sick. Jonah looked the same. They were both silent the whole walk home.

Afton felt dirty. Disgusting. Her parents had been right; the prophet had been right. If she'd been on a double date, if she hadn't been kissing him so passionately, her hand wouldn't have wandered. She wouldn't have known that could happen in the first place and been curious. But she had. And she'd liked it, until she'd remembered how wrong it was.

She didn't want to go to the bishop to confess. He worked with her dad, what if he told him? Even if he didn't, she wouldn't be allowed to take the sacrament, in plain view of her family. Everyone would know. Her parents would lock her away, never let her see Jonah again. She'd be the new object of their scrutiny. She pleaded with God every night for forgiveness. To take those feelings of disgust away.

Her prayers didn't ease the guilt. When she saw that she got the second lead in the school musical, she couldn't muster an ounce of joy.

"That's it, time for an intervention," Naya said, dragging her behind the stage where Sadie was waiting.

"What's going on? You don't seem okay," Sadie said.

"I'm f–"

"Don't you dare say you're fine. Not to us. Tell us," Naya said.

She did. Every sordid detail about what happened in the dark of the theater, and how she wasn't going to be with her family in eternity now. Her friends just blinked.

"That's it?" Sadie asked.

Afton swiped at her tears. "It's a sin. I have to confess, but if I do–"

"Afton, everyone does that. Even your church friends. I can't tell you how many times I've caught guys with their hands down girl's pants at the arcade," Sadie said.

"I've caught people trying to have sex in the showers at the pool," Naya said.

"If I'm being honest, I've done those kinds of things. It's normal," Sadie said.

Naya simply blushed.

"But I feel horrible. It's eating me alive," Afton said.

Naya chewed on her lip. "Do you think it's because you've

been told your whole life it's bad and that's why? That if you hadn't been told it was, it would have just been a fun night?"

Afton desperately wanted to think it was that. But she had the gift of the Holy Spirit to tell her right and wrong. It was screaming at her day in and out, "WRONG. WRONG. WRONG."

Jonah felt equally as bad, and together they gained the courage to go to the bishop. They had to confess by themselves, so she sat outside his office, tracing the floral pattern of the couch while Jonah was inside talking. When the door opened, Jonah came out with an odd expression, not meeting her eyes as Afton filed in.

"I heard you had something you wanted to tell me," the bishop said, hands steepled on top of his wooden desk.

She stared at the black hairs on his knuckles as she gathered the strength to speak. Spots danced in her vision as her heart sped faster.

"I messed up," she breathed.

"Can you tell me what happened?"

Why did she have to say it? Jonah had just been in here and told him everything. "I… touched Jonah inappropriately."

"Was it over or under the clothes?" he asked.

She peeked at his face, staring intently into her hers. Why did he need to know that? Why did the presence of fabric make a difference?

"Over."

"Did you let him touch you?" he asked.

She nodded.

"Above or below the waist?" he pressed.

"Above."

"Over or under your clothes?"

If she truly wanted the atonement to work, to be forgiven for this, she needed to confess everything. "Over."

"How many times has this happened?"

"Once."

"Thank you for telling me. The Lord is pleased with you for confessing." He pulled out his scriptures and started to read, reminding her about the steps of the repentance process, and how her sins would be forgotten once she completed it.

"You won't be eligible to take the sacrament for six weeks, to pray at church, or to give a talk. I also think it would be best if you and Jonah broke up and stopped seeing each other."

"No," she said reflexively. She'd suffered godly sorrow and confessed every detail. He couldn't take Jonah away.

"You two have gotten too serious, and if you keep dating, you'll only be tempted to go farther. I'd also suggest telling your parents what has happened so they can help you avoid temptation."

"Do I have to tell my parents to be forgiven?"

The bishop was quiet. "Your parents are good people. They only want what's best for you."

No, they didn't. They only liked her when she was taking care of her brothers and staying out of the way. Her dad rarely made it to her plays, and her mom was always complaining about the content of them. They wanted her to be a good little robot, go to BYU, then get married and start having her own babies. Tears finally broke through and she started sobbing.

The bishop pushed a tissue box across the desk to her. "It's going to be hard, but you can do what you need to be forgiven. The Lord loves you and is pleased with what you've done today. He will comfort and guide you through this process."

"Do I have to tell them to be forgiven?" she blubbered through her tears.

The bishop sighed. "No. But you need to read the scriptures I assigned you, abstain from the sacrament, and take a break from Jonah."

She kept sobbing, her entire body shuddering. Jonah was her best friend and she loved him. Now it was all ruined from a moment of curiosity. As she walked out of the bishop's office though, the overwhelming sense of disgust and despair had lightened, confirming she'd done the right thing.

Jonah waited for her outside the building in a little alcove. "Hey," he said as she approached.

"Hey," she said, voice hoarse. Then she started sobbing again.

Jonah reached for her and held her together. "He told you we have to break up?" he whispered.

"He said take a break," she managed between sobs.

"That's probably best."

"I don't want to lose you. I love you, Jonah. I only want you."

"I only want you too," he breathed.

She started sobbing even harder. "What if you change your mind in a few weeks and start dating someone else?"

He unwrapped his arms so he could look her in the eyes. "That's not going to happen. There's only you. We'll take a break. Cool things down. But it's still you for me Afton."

"Promise?" she asked.

"Always."

CHAPTER TWENTY-TWO

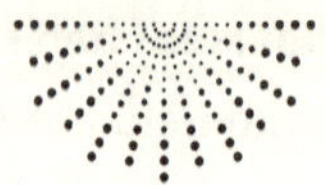

*R*ichard keeps an eagle eye on Afton after the hug, but there's nothing for him to see. She treats Jonah as she would any other crew member, until they're alone driving to locations. To anyone looking in, they'd see two people talking. Inside, they were going deep; firing questions at each other.

Whatever hard-hitting conversation he had with one of the women, they'd go over the same things off camera. What were her spending and saving habits like? Exes? What values were most important? How would they handle meddlesome in-laws? Mental health and health crises? Do they face the toilet paper up or down?

Chelsea was asleep the night Afton came back from karaoke with Jonah, and gone in the morning for yet another emergency meeting. She wouldn't elaborate any further over text and said she'd explain everything when she got back. Afton distracts herself from worrying about Chelsea, and the relationships Jonah is building with other women, by finding creative places to hide the creepy doll and applying for jobs. Ones that aren't in television. She doubts she'll get a call back, but it's something she's never done before. She feels hopeful for the first time in a while.

They're in the middle of filming a funeral-potato-cook-off in Toronto when Chelsea finally returns, wind blown out of a black SUV. Afton runs to the door and Chelsea throws her arms wide for a hug.

"I missed you, bitch."

She's happier than Afton expected her to be with everything unsaid hanging between them.

Chelsea surveys the industrial kitchen they're in, the women in pairs putting together dishes.

"What are they making?"

"Funeral potatoes."

Chelsea raises a brow. "We're in Canada. Land of poutine. And they're making funeral potatoes? What are those? Did someone die?"

"No. You'll take that back once you try them," Afton says.

Emily is teamed up with Jonah and says something that has Jonah's deep laugh filling the room. Last week they had a romantic date touring cathedrals in Spain where they kissed passionately in the street afterwards. Despite her experience helping others stay calm in jealousy inducing situations, she's struggling. Especially since no one can suspect what the sound of someone else making Jonah laugh does to her.

Chelsea frowns. Afton must not be doing as good of a job as she thought because Chelsea drags Afton outside to the SUVs. They get inside and Chelsea searches the sides for any rogue microphones.

Afton braces for impact. It's time.

"I know I've been gone at back-to-back emergency meetings, but now I can finally tell you why."

"Why?" Afton asks tentatively.

"I pitched a show idea to Hannah and she loved it. We've

been working together and meeting with executives. The show was just green-lit," Chelsea says, biting on her bottom lip.

"Wait, what?" That wasn't the lecture she was expecting. A show?

"You're looking at one of the new show-runners for a Mormon specific dating show. We'll be exploring the different spectrums of how people practice Mormonism, and the consequent dating complications. I thought of it the first night when some women left because of Jonah's faith, but for others that was a non-issue."

Chelsea's getting her own show? "I'm so proud of you!" Afton squeals. Chelsea's been dreaming of this since they first met and it's actually happening.

"Thank you! We've finally made it."

"We?"

"I want you to be my EP. More like I *need* you. You have insights into different angles I won't even know to explore. Hannah has been impressed by the touches you've added to this season and is on board."

Afton gapes open-mouthed at her.

Chelsea grips Afton's hands. "We've sweated, suffered, and worked our way up the ranks. Now we're here. I couldn't have done this without you."

"Yes, you could have."

Chelsea frowns. "Why aren't you excited?"

"It's a lot to take in. I'm so happy for you…"

"For us. This is exactly what you need. You've been burnt out, and then this whole mess with Jonah? It's a cry for help. I found our next project and I can get us away from here."

Annoyance spikes. "I told you discussing Mormonism all day was bringing up old stuff for me; now you want me to be on a show where that's the only thing they talk about?"

"It'd be different. You wouldn't be doing one-to-one interviews anymore, dealing with everyone's drama. You'd be behind the scenes, coming up with higher level ideas."

"And those ideas would be digging into topics I don't want to explore."

Chelsea blinks. "It'd just be for this one show. The next one could be about something different."

Afton cringes, which is Chelsea's last straw.

"What the hell? I have always been there for you. In college when you didn't know what a hangover was, I was there. When we had to sleep in the back of a truck because the only hotel we could afford had bed bugs? Right there, taking shifts on watch. For everything with your family, I've been there. When you got fired, I immediately had solutions. So help me understand why when your ex-boyfriend was announced as the Fiance-to-be, you didn't think I'd be there for you?"

That's what Chelsea thinks? "That's not it at all. I was trying to protect you."

"By leaving me in the dark so I accidentally make things worse?"

"By giving you plausible deniability if my connection with Jonah came to light. I wasn't thinking clearly. I genuinely thought I could avoid him all season and no one would have to know."

Chelsea scoffs. "I don't buy it. We could have easily gotten you a spot behind the scenes, or on something else. We're all in this mess because you're incapable of having hard conversations."

Afton recoils. Chelsea covers her mouth.

"I'm sorry, that came out harsher than I meant for–"

"It's what you think of me," Afton says. She's surprised at how steady her voice is. In all their years of friendship, Chelsea's never said something so blunt before. Neither has Afton. How many times has she heard that being able to argue and resolve conflicts is a sign of a healthy relationship? Yet here she is. She's been avoiding Chelsea. Naya. Sadie. Noah. Jonah. Herself.

"I'm stressed–"

"Let's have a hard conversation. You're mad at me, which you have every right to be. But you also treat me more like a child than your best friend."

Now Chelsea's the one who flinches. "How can you say that?"

"You were weirdly trying to make friends for me here; you told Luke I was interested in him. When I mildly complained about work, you found me a new role. Instead of talking to me about this project you're working on, you just dropped it at my feet, like it's already decided I'm doing it."

"I didn't want to mention anything about the new show in case it didn't work out. But honestly, I do have to act like your mom sometimes. You've been floating through life lately; all you do is work and sleep. I'm one of your only friends and I barely see you. I hoped getting you a job on your dream show would help, but it hasn't."

Afton pulls her feet up in her seat, turning so she's fully facing Chelsea. "It's not your job to make me happy; that's mine. I've been burnt out which is scary. I left everything I knew to go to school and create a new life, and it's terrifying to think that I might want something new again."

"So it's not that you're tired of me?"

Another shot to the heart. Her choices made Chelsea feel like this? "Of course not! I could never be tired of you. You're one of my favorite people in the whole world."

Chelsea swipes at her eyes. "I know it's ridiculous, and I can practically hear what my therapist will say already, but I keep thinking that I used to be enough. Our little life together used to be enough, and now it's not. Then you have your ex back in your life, and I'm worried you're changing for him to have that perfect white picket fence life you never had."

Afton reaches across the center console, wrapping Chelsea in a hug. "It has nothing to do with you, or him. I've been stuck for a while now and scared to make changes. Starting over when my parents kicked me out was so hard. I had to fight for every little thing, and it would have been so much easier to go back home and give in. I don't know if I have that fight in me still."

Chelsea pulls back so she can look Afton in the eyes. "It's not going to be anything like last time. Last time you lost your family, your home, your first love, and your entire worldview. Now you have a bigger support network. You don't have to decide if you think going to the store on Sunday is sending you to hell. You don't have math homework."

Despite the tears freely flowing down Afton's cheeks, she laughs. Not having homework *is* an advantage this time. She doesn't have to start completely from scratch.

"I love you. I'm so sorry for all the shit I've put you through. I don't deserve you."

Chelsea shakes her head. "Shut up. I wouldn't be here today without you either. I think we both deserve one massive mistake a decade. Remember when I assured everyone it was fine to skip the final walkthrough on our house since we were out of the country?"

Afton groans from the memory of raw meat left in an unplugged mini fridge, floors littered with dead moths, and unknown rust covered splatter on the walls. The only positive was that a swab from the police revealed the blood wasn't human.

Chelsea laughs. "Exactly. This will be your mess-up for the decade. You'll have to get creative to top it in ten years."

They reminisce on all the things they tried to get the smell of the meat out of the walls, eventually having to paint every inch with Kilz.

"Now what?" Afton finally asks.

"We wait for my face to calm down because I'm the world's ugliest crier, then go duet 'You're My Best Friend?' at karaoke?" Chelsea asks, face still blotchy and swollen.

"I meant about Jonah, and I was thinking 'You Raise Me Up' by Josh Groban."

Chelsea cackles, then grows serious. "That. Do you love him?"

She doesn't even have to think about it. "Yes."

Chelsea nods. "Is he worth it? The risk of getting destroyed financially, socially, and career-wise?"

Yes, her heart impractically screams. She's already unhappy in this career. Her three best friends aren't going to leave her over this, and there's not much financially to ruin anyways.

"It is to me. I can't speak for him."

Chelsea holds up a finger. "Don't you dare doubt yourself. Anyone would be lucky to be with you, and I'm not saying that because I'm contractually obligated to as your friend."

"If I'd told the truth from the beginning, he would be with someone else." There's no avoiding that fact.

"Potentially. Or maybe you two would have run into each other at the airport and he wouldn't have been able to get you out of his mind and fully commit to anyone. Just because he came on this show doesn't mean he was going to find true love."

"Do you think I'm ready for this? With my past?" Noah's hurt face pops in her mind. She was supposed to be there for him, and she let him down. What will she do to Jonah?

Chelsea squints. "Have you secretly been murdering everyone you've had feelings for?"

How is that at all related? "This is serious, don't joke."

"I'm not joking. Unless you've been hiding that from me, I

can't see anything from your past that says you're not ready to love and be loved."

Afton sighs. It's exactly like what she told Jonah. Logically, that makes sense. But practically? There's that nagging voice saying she's not worthy.

"I might need another round of therapy," Afton admits.

Chelsea picks up her phone and starts typing. "Just sent you a link to a great practice. If you come to work on my show, I'll make sure you have time for your appointments, just saying."

Afton side-eyes her.

"Here's the deal; if you stay, production is going to find out, and they're going to sue you both for breach of contract. They have powerful lawyers, and they will make your life hell just because they can."

"We've kept it professional this far," Afton says. Well, except for after karaoke. Both times.

"Maybe, but the chemistry between you two is obvious. There's also the risk that someone snapped a photo of you two while traveling, or escorting him to a date. All it takes is one person from your past to recognize you in a photo online and it's over."

Afton holds her head in her hands. She's known all of this, but having Chelsea lay it out makes it real.

"I know you're done with TV. Why don't you join me on my new show as an excuse to leave without production getting suspicious? This isn't me trying to be manipulative or trap you, only to help. You can job hunt and find something more your speed while Jonah finishes his season. You both avoid a lawsuit and live happily ever after."

Afton blows out a breath. Maybe it's not that she shouldn't be with Jonah, it's just they shouldn't be together yet. They've been apart for over a decade. What's a few more months?

What if while she's gone, he decides to be with someone

else? *That was always a possibility,* she reminds herself. She wants him to consider all of his options and what's best for him.

"I'll let you know tomorrow," she finally says.

Chelsea squeezes her hand encouragingly. "Sounds good. Now come on, they probably need judges for those funeral potatoes. They better live up to the hype."

They do. Afton's stomach is churning too much to eat different variations of cheese, cream of condensed soup, and potatoes, but everyone else loves them. She steals glimpses of Jonah while everyone eats, wondering what she should do. Does she stay, or should she go?

CHAPTER TWENTY-THREE

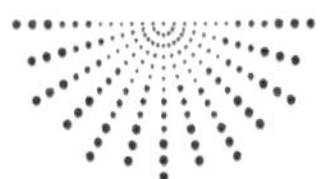

Chelsea was lulled to sleep by the soothing sounds of the Monday Night Raw announcers yelling, so only Afton hears the crackle of the radio a little after 11pm.

"Whale song," a low voice says.

Has she been thinking about Jonah so much, she imagined hearing him use the emergency radio code they came up with?

"What was that?" another voice asks over the radio.

It wasn't her imagination. She waits to see if Jonah repeats the call, but he doesn't. Is it because he doesn't want anyone else to know he used the radio, or because something is preventing him from doing it? She grabs her emergency backpack and shoes, running into the hallway in her oversized t-shirt and sleep shorts. Is he bleeding? Having a stroke? Food poisoning? She races up the emergency stairs, not willing to wait for the elevator.

What if she waited too long? What if this was the only time they got together and she wasted it?

She missteps, clutching the railing for dear life so she doesn't plummet down the stairs. No. She cannot think like that right now. She'll be no help to anyone if she gets lost in her thoughts before she even reaches him.

She reaches his floor, yanking so hard on the door she flies backward when it stays closed. She bounces back and pulls again, and again, but the handle won't even wiggle up and down. Would it be faster to run back down to her floor and grab the elevator, or call the front desk and see if they can unlock it somehow? Phone in hand, she looks for the floor number, then notices the tiny black card reader to the side of the handle. She taps her room-key on it and the door clicks, unlocking.

She sprints down the hall to Jonah's suite, backpack slamming against her back with every step. When she's about to knock, the door opens. Jonah is standing there, shirtless. He's conscious, so that's good. She scans his body for blood or any other signs of emergency. Other than holding the book she bought him, there's nothing.

"What's wrong?" Afton breathes, heart still racing.

"You didn't tell me this ends on a cliffhanger," Jonah huffs.

"What?"

He taps on the book. "This ended on a cliffhanger and I'm not going to be able to sleep. I need the next one."

Her erratic heartbeat starts to slow. He's not dying. He's okay.

"You used the emergency radio for that?" Afton asks.

"Yes. It was an emergency," Jonah says stone-faced.

Now she's mad. "I got stuck in the stairwell and worried those extra seconds could mean the difference between your life and death."

The color drains from his face. "I'm so sorry, I didn't mean to scare you. If it'd been a real emergency, I would have said what was happening on the radio. I thought you'd know that."

"Well, I didn't. Why else would you be using the emergency code?"

"Because I was reading to distract myself from everything, but I finished the book and…" he trails off.

"You decided to terrify me and demand I get the next one even though you know that's impossible right now?"

"And I figured out what I want," he says simply.

Her heart starts hammering again. "What is it? Some exotic food I need to scour the gas stations for? A meeting with some hockey stars? Did you realize you're almost done filming and want the full diva treatment while you have the chance?"

"You. I want to rant about books in the middle of the night. I want to problem solve with you. Stand with you. Laugh with you, cry with you, go to the gas station with you."

She holds up a hand. "I can't deal with this right now." She's still breathing heavily from the run. "You can't seriously be doing this right now."

He steps into the hallway, wrapping his arms around her. The feeling of him instantly grounds her. "I'm sorry for scaring you. I'm here. I'm safe."

His chest is warm against her face and she inhales the smell of his deodorant and skin. Her heart finally slows, along with her thoughts. He's here.

"You're okay?" she asks, leaning up to look at him.

"More than okay. I know what I want with my life and couldn't wait until morning to tell you."

She swallows. "What do you want?"

"You. I love you. I want to spend my life with you, if you'll have me."

She pulls away, shaking her head. "No, it's too soon."

He frowns. "I've known you the majority of my life, it's definitely not too soon."

"Didn't we agree two weeks ago that you were going to finish this thing, then decide? You're early."

"I'm even more sure now. I'll tell you again in two weeks if it makes you feel better, but it's you for me. Why are you fighting this?"

She laces her fingers behind her head like her teacher taught her in gym class, trying to get more oxygen. Running up those stairs, she'd worried he was gone. That she'd wasted the time they'd been granted. Jonah's insistence that time is our most valuable resource will undoubtedly become a joke once his season airs because of how often he says it. But it's true; there was no warning before his dad died. Something could have randomly happened tonight. She'd pictured a world with him no longer in it in the stairwell, and just the thought was enough to almost destroy her.

Why is she holding back? Will he actually change his mind in the next few weeks? Probably not; the majority of couples from this show don't last more than a year, and many contestants have confessed they knew night one who they were choosing. Will waiting two more weeks make Jonah's words more true to her?

No. It won't. Because she'll still be scared then like she is now. Scared that she's too messy. That the hurts of their past are too much to overcome. That they'll get back home and into the rhythm of normal life and she won't be enough. Or, that she'll finally open herself all the way and lose him tomorrow.

"If you've changed your mind that's okay–"

"I'm scared," she whispers.

He tilts his head. "Of what?"

"That I'll lose you." That's what it all comes down to.

He steps forward, brushing her cheek with the backs of his fingers. "Me too. But it's worth it to me."

It is to her too. No more holding herself back because of

fear. She surges forward and kisses him. He's still for half a second, pulling back, his eyes darting between hers.

"Is that a…" he trails off.

"It's worth it to me too. I want to be with you, as long as you'll have me."

The smile is slow, creeping across his face until he's entirely lit from within. He wraps an arm around her legs, picking her up bridal style. She shrieks in surprise as he carries her into his suite, depositing her on top of the white comforter and pillows. She bounces and laughs.

"I have a few important questions," Jonah says seriously, standing at the foot of the bed between her legs.

The nerves are instantly back. "Like what?"

"Is this okay?" he kneels, wrapping his long fingers around her bare calves.

"Mhmm," she hums.

His hands rub up and down, each time going slightly higher. He kisses each of her knees, then tugs gently on her legs so she's sitting on the edge of the bed. His wandering hands move to her thighs now.

"Still okay?"

"Yes."

He kisses his way up her thighs and she trembles each time he gets closer and closer to the edge of her sleep shorts. When he reaches the hem, his fingers go to her waistband.

"This?" Jonah asks, meeting her eyes.

She nods quickly.

He grins, pulling her shorts and underwear down in one fierce tug. She lifts her hips so he can pull them to the ground. His eyes rove over her, and she swears they darken.

"Beautiful," he breathes before pressing a kiss to her hip bone. He drags his tongue down the crease of her inner thigh, the scruff on his cheeks scratching the sensitive skin. He kisses his way back up, repeating it with her other hip. His fingers rove, a thumb pressing gently against her center. When she hisses, he smirks up at her, then tugs her even closer to the edge of the bed. He throws her feet over both his shoulders.

"Still okay?" he checks.

"Yes, everything. Please."

His smile is predatory before he leans in and kisses her center, pressing his tongue flat against her before circling with the tip. She falls back against the mattress when he gently sucks. Her hips buck, getting the angle just right and he moans against her, rewarding her with a gentle nip. Together they find the perfect rhythm; him licking, sucking, and gently biting at her clit while she grinds against him.

He slips a finger inside, then moans. "So wet, just for me?"

She tries to think of a smartass response, but his finger curls.

"Fuck," she gasps.

He rewards her with another finger, then circling with his tongue again.

Her gasps grow closer together, energy building low in her stomach. She leans up on her elbows, looking down at him. His eyes track her and he smiles before sucking, hard, sending her over the edge. Her head falls back as waves of pleasure crash through her, one after another. He keeps going, her body contracting until her thighs are shaking. When they ebb, he trails kisses across her stomach until she tugs on his hair.

"Yes?" he asks, amused.

Somehow, she manages to sit up and tugs on his shoulders until he stands, towering over her. She sits up on her knees so she can reach his mouth, her tongue meeting his, tasting herself. Her hands roam across his bare chest, tracing the ridges and lines of his skin. She scratches his pecs with her nails and he moans into her mouth, biting her lip. Her hands go lower, reaching for his waistband. He grabs each of her wrists, lightly pulling her away.

"It's still my turn," he says, voice low.

"No, mine." She needs him. All of him pressed against her, inside of her.

"I've never gotten to take my time before. I'm taking it," he says, tugging on the hem of her t-shirt, slowly lifting it up and placing kisses on the newly exposed skin. He finally reaches her breasts, nipples peaked against the cold air. His eyes drink her in before tugging her shirt completely off. He traces her collarbones with his tongue. He kisses down her chest, dragging his teeth against the top of her breast. Kissing. Nipping. Sucking. Everywhere but the peak. The stubble of his cheeks scrapes against her nipples, but it's not enough. She whimpers and he smirks up at her before finally swirling his tongue around her nipple. He moans, then finally sucks it into his mouth.

"I've despised my past self for not doing this years ago when he had the chance," he murmurs when he frees her breast, nose nuzzling her sternum.

"Hmmm?" she manages.

"They're so much better than I imagined," he says, kissing her right breast and giving it the same amount of attention. When she's clawing at his back in frustration, he lays her down on the bed, his eyes sweeping over her body, pupils dilating.

"So beautiful," he murmurs again.

"Come here," she whines, reaching for him.

She breaks whatever spell is over him and he steps out of his sweatpants, then tugs down his boxers so he's finally bared to her.

"Beautiful," she says, taking in the entirety of him. The broad shoulders, muscled thighs, defined ass. The constellation of moles and freckles strewn about his skin from days spent shirtless in the sun. The dark hair below his belly button leading lower... her walls flutter in anticipation.

He leans in, cupping her cheek. "Stealing my compliment? You must be frazzled."

Frazzled? She'll show him frazzled. She reaches for the length of him that's finally in reach. He shivers as she pumps him once. Twice. He steps away to the nightstand, pulling out a foil wrapper. She sits up and watches as he rips it open and slowly rolls it on.

"Can you believe we forgot that the first time?" she muses.

"I have nightmares about it," he says, coming back and cradling her face between his hands. "Is this okay?"

"Yes. Stop making me wait." She grips his shoulders and pulls him onto the bed. He flips onto his back and she straddles him.

"So bossy," he smirks from beneath her. She grabs his head and his eyes flare. She tilts her hips, pressing him at her entrance, meeting his eyes. She spent her entire adolescence fearing this. Tiptoeing closer and closer to it. It broke them once. Will it again?

He cups her cheek. "You're mine."

It's all she needs. They aren't those eighteen-year-olds anymore. They are in control, and she's not letting him go. "Mine," she repeats before joining their bodies one slow inch at a time.

"Fuck," he breathes.

"I love it when you swear," she whispers, slowly grinding against him before pushing up and coming down again.

He opens his eyes and watches her, his expression a mix of awe and something unnamable. She leans down and kisses him, nice and slow to match the pace of their hips.

"Afton," he murmurs before wrapping his arm around her

back and rolling them so he's on top now. He looks down at her, hands on either side of her head.

"How is this real?" he asks quietly.

She reaches up and brushes his cheek with her fingertips. "I don't know."

He thrusts into her, deliciously slow, friction in all the right places. He pulls back and she cants her hips so he hits that sweet spot, over and over.

"I can't get close enough," she breathes.

He grabs her knee and gently slides her leg up the bed, the angle changing so he's even deeper.

"Better?" he murmurs against her neck.

"Oh. *Ohh.*" She's almost there. He thrusts again, grinding and giving that perfect friction and…

"That's my girl," he says, kissing the base of her neck as her muscles spasm harder than before, bending her in half as she cries out. Waves of pleasure surge up and down her body, one after another. She rides through each wave and spasm, a passenger in her own body as Jonah keeps encouraging her.

As they die down, Jonah's pace becomes frantic. She meets him thrust for thrust until he moans "fuck" into her mouth. He presses his forehead against hers, then shudders. Her walls spasm again, their bodies wringing every last ounce of pleasure from the other.

They cling to one another, catching their breath before Jonah rolls to his back, pulling her with. She settles into her old favorite spot just below his shoulder, able to hear his racing heart.

"That was," he starts.

"Incredible," she finishes.

He kisses the top of her head. "Better than the last time?"

She rolls her eyes. "You definitely picked up a few tricks since then."

"You can thank late night scrolling and the algorithm for that."

"So it wasn't from lots of practice?" It wouldn't matter if it was; she's genuinely just curious.

He shakes his head. "A few, but mostly I'm just a student eager to please. It helps to have such a responsive partner." He nips the top of her ear.

"I love you," she tells him.

"Because I know where the clitoris is?"

She bites his bicep lightly and he chuckles. "Because you're you. Even if all we did tonight was talk, that would have been enough. You're my favorite person."

"You're my favorite person too." He kisses her slowly. "Stay. We've never gotten to sleep together."

"I can't— "

"I'll wake you up before sunrise. My call time tomorrow isn't until nine so no one will be looking for me. Please?"

It's beyond reckless and dangerous. Chelsea will kill her if she finds out. If she leaves with Chelsea though, this could be the last bit of time they have for a while. Or forever.

"I finally talked with Chelsea," she says.

Jonah stiffens. "And?"

"She's starting her own show and thinks I should join her as an excuse to leave so production doesn't get suspicious."

"But you want to get out of television," Jonah says.

His first worry is about her wants, not about him. Her chest warms. "I know. I'd only be there while applying for something new. I've actually submitted a few applications already."

"I'm so proud of you." He presses a kiss into her hair. "Are you going to do it?"

"I wanted your thoughts. I don't want to presume you're choosing me..."

"I am. I've made up my mind."

What if you forced him to by being here? Who would he have chosen if you'd left? that tiny voice asks.

"I should go then and give us the best chance of getting out of this without being sued. After you've finished, and if you haven't changed your mind— "

"Afton," Jonah warns. "I know this is all moving fast. But it's you. I knew it in Salt Lake, and I know it more with every day."

"We can stay on the down low until you're done with the press tour after your season."

He's quiet, and she counts the rises and falls of his chest as he thinks.

"Do you promise you'll be waiting when I'm done? You're not going to disappear again?" he asks, voice soft.

She sits up on her elbow so she can look directly into Jonah's eyes. "Yes, I promise. We're not in high school anymore. We're in control of our lives. No one else gets to tell us what to do or who to be."

"Except for the network until my NDA expires in seven years," Jonah says.

"Except for that. I'm not going anywhere," Afton says.

"Me either."

She nuzzles into his chest, finding a more comfortable spot to rest, and sleeps better than she has in months.

CHAPTER TWENTY-FOUR

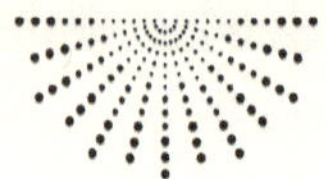

FIFTEEN YEARS AGO

Afton scanned the list of names for *Beauty and the Beast* fully expecting to be Mrs. Potts. For some unbelievable reason, her name was at the top next to Belle. She slowly turned around to where Naya, Sadie, Jonah, and Henry were standing. "I got the lead," she breathed.

Naya and Sadie jumped up and down. Jonah surged forward, wrapping his arms around her and swinging her in a circle.

"I knew you would!"

He hadn't so much as held her hand for five months. Even though they finished the repentance process three months ago, they'd been terrified of messing up again and agreed to only be friends. Here in his arms, his face pure joy as he spun her? It felt like home. She placed her hands on his cheeks and met his eyes. He gave the tiniest of nods and she kissed him.

"Can we be together again?" she whispered once he finally pulled away for air.

"We'll be careful. Do the things we've been doing," he breathed.

"Of course."

"I couldn't take the tension between the two of them any longer," Sadie said loudly.

Afton brought Jonah in for another kiss, purely to annoy her.

WHEN THEY TELL you to apply everywhere for college, they fail to mention that each application costs money. Through careful research she narrowed down her applications to: the BYUs for her parents, USU as a safety, Barstow Community College, and CSUDH. CSUDH was her dream school. Its theater program claimed freshman and sophomores had better chances of being in productions than at bigger schools. Her odds of being a professional actress were next to nothing, but she wasn't ready to give up theater yet. She could major in communications and media studies, and minor in theater. If she didn't get in there, she could get her associates degree at Barstow Community College, then transfer to a bigger university.

Jonah applied to the same schools as Afton, along with a few other California options. Carrie was thrilled by the idea of Jonah being closer to their extended family. Naya applied to California schools as well, along with Washington and Oregon. Sadie applied all over the country, including the east coast. Afton daydreamed of weekends spent at the beach, lying in the sand.

Dan left on his mission and something snapped in Afton's mom. She was angry. Afton would eavesdrop on her parents' fights late at night, catching phrases like "I don't know who I am." "My job is over." "I gave up everything for you." "What dreams?" And "I have nothing." Afton could never hear what her dad said in response, but whatever it was, it always made her mom sob.

Her mom had dreams? What were they? Had she researched and prepared as much as Afton was right now? She'd always said all she'd ever wanted was to be their mom.

Beauty and the Beast had three performances. Afton stuck flyers on the fridge, her dad's desk, and even in the car. Usually she pretended not to care if her family came, but she was the lead and proud of this production. The sets were gorgeous, the costumes fun, and she truly felt like a princess. She reminded her parents to get their tickets, preferably for her first performance. That way, if something came up, they'd have two more opportunities.

"We got them for the last show. Isn't that always the best one?" her dad winked.

Jonah came to opening night along with Naya and Sadie, all of them carrying bouquets of flowers for her. She couldn't stop smiling as she went to bed, the flowers perfuming her entire room. Being on that stage singing with people she loved cheering for her? It didn't get better than that.

Jonah's entire family came to her second performance. Carrie gave her the biggest bouquet of flowers she'd ever seen, along with an even better hug.

"You have a gift and we were all lucky to be here to experience it," Carrie whispered.

Tears filled Afton's eyes and she tried to blink them away.

"Your makeup looks normal on stage, but freaky up close," Naomi commented.

Jonah elbowed Naomi in the side, but Afton was thankful for a reason to laugh and stop the tears from falling.

For her final performance, she kept her eyes off the audience until her bow. She didn't want to know where her family was sitting and watching her, especially for the kiss at the end. She wanted to savor every last moment being Belle.

It took a bit, but she finally found Jonah and Henry sitting in the crowd, along with her mom and Noah. Her dad was nowhere to be found. She didn't even try to hide her tears.

"I'm always sad after the final performance too, let's go cry at Denny's," her cast-mates said before running off to change into street clothes. She didn't bother going out to the lobby to hug everyone who'd shown up to see her. She found a hidden alcove backstage and curled into a ball.

Jonah eventually slid down on the ground beside her. "What's wrong?" he asked softly.

"Why won't I ever be enough for him?" Afton got out before being overcome with body wracking sobs.

Jonah wrapped her in his arms, holding her together as she cried.

"He always makes it… to the boys… basketball games… They don't even… play the whole… time," she hiccups. "But he's only… made it to… four of my shows."

Jonah's brow scrunches. "Why?"

"Church. Something *always* comes up. Someone got bit by a dog and wanted a blessing, someone's furnace broke and the apartment hadn't fixed it yet and they wanted him to look at it–"

"Isn't your dad an accountant?" Jonah interrupted.

She waved her hands in the air. "Exactly! But he's in the bishopric, so maybe God will give him divine inspiration on how to fix a furnace. The other times were for meetings, young men campouts, and trainings. No matter how big or small it is, when he has to choose between church and me, he always chooses church."

Jonah frowned. "My dad always said it goes God first, family second, work third, church fourth. All of those things someone else could have done; it didn't have to be your dad specifically."

"I think he was glad to have an excuse not to come. He hates plays and musicals, but sports? That's his thing. Why make yourself miserable supporting your daughter's silly little play? It's not like I'm going to be a famous actor. The greatest thing I can do is pop out a bunch of babies and clean up for some mediocre man so he can attend *his* church meetings."

Jonah winced.

Afton wriggled out of his arms and faced him. "What was that about?"

Jonah's face turned red. "It's just…"

"Just what?"

"I would never treat you like that. I would support you in your dreams, and I wouldn't put meetings or trainings before my family."

Afton was speechless. She heard her mom's words echoing in her head. *What dreams? I gave up everything for you.*

"What if everyone says that before they get married, but then it never happens?"

"We're different from everyone else. I love you so much it hurts sometimes. I can't picture a future without you in it."

When she thought of the future, he was always in it too. But hearing him talk about putting his family first? That would be her family. Their babies. And no matter if he did put her first or not, there would be nights where he had meetings to go to, and she would be the one stuck at home with the kids.

She didn't want to think about kids, or church, or how the men in her life would always be pulled away from her by it. She wanted to still be here in high school with no worries.

"Do you want to go cry at Denny's with the rest of the cast?" she asked.

Jonah blinked, an odd expression flitting across his face before he smirked. "You mean be slightly embarrassed while you all sing show tunes in the middle of the restaurant?"

"You secretly love it."

He stood and helped her to her feet. "Yeah, I do."

IN OCTOBER the age for boys to leave on missions was changed from 19 to 18, and for girls from 21 to 19. All dreams of spending freshman year with Jonah in California were gone. Jonah could turn his mission papers in now, able to leave shortly after graduation.

"Maybe you could go on a mission too, and we'll get back within a few months of each other," Jonah suggested.

She'd never thought about going on a mission, ever. Only girls who weren't married by twenty-one went. Now, all the girls at church were claiming they'd always wanted to go, and rearranging their plans accordingly. She didn't want to leave school for two years, completely cut off from friends and the secular world. Thankfully she had another year to think about it, unlike Jonah who was meeting with the bishop to start submitting his papers and attending a mission prep class.

Every week pieces of Jonah were replaced with a new version of him. He'd turn the radio station if there was a swear word in a song. He stopped reading his fantasy books, replacing them with the Book of Mormon and *Preach My Gospel*. When they were watching reality tv at his place, she'd catch him reading the scriptures on his phone during kissing scenes. He got into a full-on debate with his mom on how inappropriate the overnight episode of *Ready for the Ring* was.

"It's time for them to ask the important questions they can't on camera. Who cares if they're having sex, it has nothing to do with you," Carrie said.

"God does," Jonah said, his cheeks burning.

Carrie rolled her eyes. "Yes, it's a sacred thing to share with the person you love most. But many of the church's teachings on it are harmful. In no universe do I believe it's a sin next to murder to have consensual, premarital sex. Spousal and child abuse are much more serious in my book. Just because you believe something doesn't mean you have the right to impose your beliefs on others. I don't see my Jewish friends wanting me to adhere to their dietary standards, or my Muslim friends expecting me to wear a hijab."

"How can you say that? If this is the truth, we need to share it with everyone. That's why I'm going on a mission."

"The church is headed by imperfect men and we believe in continuing revelation. Just because something is wrong now, doesn't mean it won't be changed later. Look at the priesthood ban for black members. That was finally changed in 1978."

"Because the world was finally ready–"

"Oh, bullshit," Carrie said.

Jonah recoiled, staring at his mom in utter horror.

Carrie pressed the heels of her hands into her eyes. "Your dad was so much better at explaining these things."

Jonah ran up the stairs to his room wordlessly. Carrie started crying.

"I wasn't supposed to do this by myself; he was supposed to be here with me. I'm messing this all up," Carrie said.

"I think you're doing great," Afton said, then tentatively walked over to Carrie and gave her a hug. Carrie hugged her back fiercely.

"You should go talk to him. Just leave the door open," Carrie said.

Afton slowly walked into Jonah's room where he was sitting at his desk, staring blankly at the *Preach My Gospel* manual and his scriptures next to the fantasy book he'd abandoned. Afton went up to the desk and leaned against it, looking down at him.

"I'm going to be a horrible missionary," he whispered. "I couldn't even convince my own mom, who's a member, about the truth."

"Maybe you should relax on the mission stuff for now," Afton said carefully.

His eyes met with hers, wary.

"You only get to do senior year once. You still have classes to pass and projects to finish. Missionaries don't have to worry about any of that extra stuff."

"I need to start preparing now to be the best missionary I can. If everything goes to plan, I could leave in six months."

Six months? She was going to be sick. They were supposed to have eighteen more. Time was slipping away and no matter what she did, she couldn't slow it.

"You could do all your mission prep on Sundays, and then focus on everything else the rest of the week."

A smile slowly crept onto his face. "You're right. I need to finish school strong and get those AP credits so I can graduate college earlier and be a provider." His face brightened. "And I probably didn't know what to say to my mom because I haven't been set apart as a missionary yet. When I am, the Spirit will whisper what I'm supposed to say. I'm so lucky to have you." He wrapped his arms around her middle, resting his head against her stomach.

She didn't tell him that what Carrie said made sense to her.

ACCEPTANCE LETTERS FILED IN. To her utter shock she was accepted into all of her choices. The years of extracurriculars and keeping up her grades had paid off. CSUDH offered a substantial grant and scholarship package, but it wouldn't cover everything. She did the math and had her friends check her figures. As long as she worked hard this summer, she'd be able to afford it without her parents' help. Then she'd get a job in California to replenish her savings.

On a Friday night while babysitting her brothers, she stared at the webpage to accept her spot. This was it, the moment she'd worked so hard for. She inhaled deeply before clicking on accept. She did it. She was going to California.

"Afton?" a tiny voice asked from the stairs. Noah stood there with tearstained cheeks.

"Yeah, buddy?"

"I had a nightmare," he said quietly. Afton rubbed his back while he drifted to sleep, staring up at his ceiling. Her heart was breaking. Going after her dream meant she'd have to leave Noah. Would her mom be patient enough to cuddle with him after his nightmares? Or too lost in her own misery?

Jonah received his mission call to the Mexico, Mexico City South mission. Because of the influx of missionaries, he wouldn't leave until October 1st. They'd still have the summer together, and he could even come to drop her off at college.

Spring arrived and with it, prom. Afton relished every moment of picking out her dress, getting ready, and posing for photos. Jonah came to her house and she did the dramatic walk down the stairs. Carrie and her mom stood at the bottom snapping photos while her dad silently wiped away a tear. She struggled to pin the boutonniere to Jonah's jacket and they both laughed and laughed.

She danced with her best friends, sang at the top of her lungs, then twirled in Jonah's arms. As the night went on, their bodies pressed closer together. He removed his suit jacket and rolled up the sleeves of his dress shirt. She ran her hands up and down his chest, and spun so her back was to him. Tentatively, she ground against him like the other girls. He was still for one. two. Three seconds before moving along with her. Her skin tightened and her stomach dropped.

After a few beats Jonah spun her back around. She readied

herself for him to remind her to be careful, but instead he started kissing her, deeply. Like they were running out of time.

"You're so beautiful tonight. I can barely breathe," Jonah whispered between kisses.

"It's so sexy when you roll your sleeves up," she whispered back.

He raised an eyebrow and rolled them once more so they were above his elbows.

"Nope, now you look like a jerk. You might as well tie your tie on your head."

He rolled his sleeves back to where they were, and the music turned to a slow song. She wrapped her arms around Jonah's neck while both of his hands rested on her hips. They swayed together, staring deeply into each other's eyes.

"If only I could tell that eleven-year-old boy just how special that girl who barely helped him unpack his room would be," Jonah said.

She laughed. "You said it was okay for me to read in the corner."

He smiled. "It was. You made the funniest little faces every time something happened. I couldn't stop watching them. I'll never be able to stop watching you."

She wanted to beg him not to leave. To delay his mission a year and go to California with her. To never go.

That would be unfair. Her leaders kept reminding her and the other girls it was their job to encourage the young men to go on their missions. That God needed them not to be selfish and hold them back. Afton couldn't bring herself to encourage Jonah to go, but she could keep her mouth shut. She rested her head on his chest, listening to the soothing sound of his heart as they swayed.

The limo dropped them off at Sadie's house. Everyone took

turns going into bathrooms and changing into their street clothes for after prom at the bowling alley.

"I forgot my clothes at home; can you walk with me to grab them?" Jonah asked, still in his suit.

"Sure."

"Why don't you keep that dress on a bit longer? I love it," he said.

She walked with him in her bare feet, the train of her dress hooked over an arm. It rained while they were at the dance and the world smelled perfect. Orbs of yellow light twinkled in the few puddles on the sidewalk. When they passed by the park, Jonah suggested they swing. She grabbed his hand and started running, laughing when she accidentally splashed in a puddle. He splashed her right back. Her entire body tingled; he truly was her best friend.

When they finally approached the swings, a flickering light caught her eye. Dollar store tea lights were arranged in the shape of a heart on the ground next to the swings.

In the middle of the heart was a cork-board with pictures of Afton and Jonah over the years. Some from when they were eleven, twelve. There were none from thirteen, but plenty from fourteen onward. She hadn't seen some of these before, sneaky ones Carrie must have snapped.

She whipped around to where she left Jonah. He'd taken a step backward.

"What's going on?" she breathed. They'd already gone to prom; there was no need for an elaborate setup. This couldn't be what it looked like. They were still in high school. He was leaving in five months.

Jonah swallowed, his Adam's apple bobbing. Then he slowly knelt down before her.

"Afton Hayes. Since the first time I met you, whenever I enter a room, I'm searching to see if you're in it. At first it was because you intrigued me. You were the only one I wanted to talk to. Then it was because you were always the most beautiful girl in the room and I wanted to steal as many glances as possible. Now it's because you carry my heart and part of my soul.

"I'm grateful to know that there is an eternity, and that it can be ours. Because that's the only amount of time that will be enough to spend with you. I can't leave for two years without you knowing that no matter what, I am coming back for you and my heart will always be yours."

Her own heart pounded so hard she could barely hear.

Jonah reached into his pocket and pulled out a velvet box, revealing a thin silver band covered in tiny diamonds.

"I know our parents won't approve of us being engaged yet, and I don't want you to have to fight with them. So, I got you your wedding band to wear for now and I'll swap it with an engagement ring when I'm back from my mission. I figured you could wear it in your right hand until you get to California."

She stared down at the ring. She'd been told what her future would look like her whole life. There'd been countless activities where she cut out pictures of dresses, wedding decor, and rings. They'd written letters to their future husbands and tucked them away in boxes. There was a lace doily covered hanger sitting in the bottom of her closet to hold her wedding dress. She'd learned to cook, clean, feed a baby, change diapers.

To wait.

She'd have to wait two years while he was on his mission, only able to email him once a week. When he came back, they'd finally go to the temple. It wouldn't be long until they had a baby. How would she finish college? Would she be forced to wait until her kids grew up? Stuck at home, waiting for Jonah to get back from work and church duties while their babies wailed?

She'd be exactly like her mom. Absolutely miserable, waiting for the next life–eternity– when she could finally be happy. But only if she endured now.

She started crying.

"What's wrong?" Jonah asked, still on his knees.

"I love you. I love you with all I am. But I can't."

He didn't register it at first. "What do you mean?"

"I don't want to be like my parents."

He stood up. "Who said we have to be like your parents?"

"I don't want to have a million kids, and spend my whole life waiting for you, and give up everything to be a mom."

"Those are our decisions to make. We decide how many kids to have, and when to have them. We won't be anything like your parents. Your hopes and dreams are equally as important to me, and I would never put the church before you."

She shakes her head. "That's not true. You're going to leave for two years. And you'll change; you started changing when you were taking your mission prep classes."

His eyebrows furrowed. "What are you talking about?"

The tears fell faster. "You stopped reading, listening to music, and were judging everything. It was scary."

"Why didn't you tell me?"

"Because I'm supposed to support you. I'm supposed to want that version of you. But I don't. I don't want to wait for you for two years. That's two years I'll be alone, unable to be held, or even hear your voice if I have a bad day."

Jonah stood up. "Do you think I want to leave you? No. I *have* to. God commands all worthy young men to go out and serve Him for a short time, but then we'll be blessed. It will be the hardest thing we do, but it's worth it for an eternity together. Don't you want that?"

Her head was swimming, vision blurry, lungs on fire. This mission was just the beginning of a life where God's will came first.

"I can't do it," she whispered. She tried to take a step back, but ended up tripping over her dress. She started falling, bracing for the ground, but Jonah's arms wrapped around her. He was always there to catch her. Who would when he was gone? Her entire body went weak and she couldn't catch her breath. Wordlessly he lifted her up and carried her back to his house. She wrapped her arms around his neck and held tight.

On his porch she slid down to the ground. He wrapped an arm around her and she leaned into him, still feeling like she might fall apart. Crying so hard, saying those words she'd been holding in for so long? She was exhausted.

"Mom," Jonah yelled when they entered the house. There was no answer. Jonah went around flipping on lights as Afton collapsed onto his couch. Jonah reappeared holding a note.

"She dropped off my sisters at a sleepover, and is out with friends. Should we change and then head to after prom?"

Oh yeah. That's what they were doing before that pit stop at the park shattered everything. Somehow in all the drama, she'd kept her little string backpack with her spare clothes on her back. She stumbled into the bathroom, but her teeth started chattering, body shaking. She wasn't wet, why was she shaking? Fighting with the zipper on the back of her dress was impossible.

Jonah eventually found her clinging to the bathroom sink, trying to get the shaking to stop.

"Are you wet? You need to get out of these clothes."

"I c-c-can't."

"Can I help you?" he asked.

She managed a nod.

He tried tugging down on her dress, but it didn't budge. She gestured to the zipper on the back, and he yanked on it, getting it caught in the fabric. It took multiple tries for him to get it down. She shimmied and stepped out of the fabric pooled at her feet.

Jonah set her jeans on the ground so she could step into them, then helped pull them up her body. She fumbled with the button and zipper, but somehow managed. Then she held her arms above her head and he helped her into her shirt. His eyes wandered down her body for a millisecond and then were back on her face.

"Thank you." Her teeth weren't chattering anymore, but she still shivered every few seconds..

"Let's warm up before we walk over," he said, leading her over to the couch and wrapping them in a blanket. He turned on the TV, *Miss Congeniality* playing.

"I liked your dress better," Jonah said as Sandra Bullock changed into her own gown.

She kissed his cheek. "I love you."

They kept watching. Once the shivers were gone, she took a deep breath, needing to address what happened.

"I'm sorry about earlier."

Jonah looked alarmed. "No, I'm sorry. That was a horrible idea, I shouldn't have done it."

That felt wrong. "It's not that I'm opposed to being engaged…"

"Just not right now?" he asked, eyes searching.

"Exactly."

He looked relieved. "On a scale of 1-10, how much did you like that proposal?"

She laughed, taking his face in her hands and kissing him. It was sweet and slow at first. But then the kisses became frantic. She tried to get closer to him, climbing into his lap. He was hard beneath her, and she shifted tentatively against him. He groaned, and she did it again. His hands held her hips, then slid underneath her shirt, his skin warm against her back. Slowly they slid upward. When his fingers grazed against the under-wire of her bra, they both froze.

"Don't stop," she whispered.

He studied her, his eyes a question.

She loved him with all that she had, and she was going to lose him. Before she did, she wanted to offer all that she could. She wanted to experience this with him, not with someone else. She pulled her shirt up and over her head, facing him in her bra.

His eyes ping-ponged from her face, down to her breasts, over and over.

"I want all of you. If you want me."

He started kissing her again, hungrily. His hands slid into her bra, tentatively cupping her. She reached backward and undid the hooks. He stared openly at her, mouth falling open. She slid her hands underneath his shirt and they broke the kiss to get it over his head. She felt the plane of his chest, the ridge in his arm where his biceps were, and the soft trail of hair above and below his bellybutton. He shivered.

"Is this okay?" she asked.

"Mhmm."

"Can I see where this goes?" she whispered, brushing the soft hairs.

"Mhmm."

Question after question, one article of clothing after another, they were both completely bare. Jonah cupped her face and slid her backward on the couch. Through awkward maneuvering, clumsy hands, and nervous laughter, they finally came together. It was sweet. Strange. But so right.

CHAPTER TWENTY-FIVE

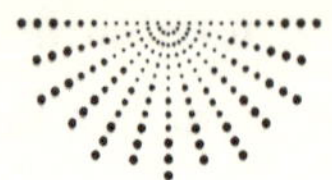

*H*e'd wonder if this was a dream if it weren't for his numb arm. Afton's curled next to him in bed, her face peaceful. He's seen her through puberty and every emotion under the sun, but never asleep. He memorizes the lines of her face, the sound of her breath, the feel of her skin. It'll be months until they can sleep like this again.

Last night he felt absolute certainty he was making the right decision. To be together though, they'll have to be apart one more time. The thought makes him sick. Afton said she'll be there when this is over. He just has to trust her.

Someone pounds on the door. Jonah tries to sit up, but his arm is still under Afton. *Shit. Shit. Shit.* He glances at the clock. 6:00AM. Not before dawn, but still earlier than anyone should be at his door. The banging continues and Afton stirs awake. She smiles sweetly up at him and he's stunned stupid. He's never seen this particular smile before. Sleepy and content before the weight of the world creeps in.

The smile is gone with the next knock. She's bolting out of bed, searching for her clothes. Jonah slips on his sweatpants.

"Hide in the bathroom. I'll see what it is," he whispers.

Afton nods and he turns to the door. Maybe it's the hotel staff, over eager to deliver him the breakfast he didn't order. A prank. A fire drill he somehow slept through. He opens the door and Tessa is standing there. Behind her stands Luke with his camera. Richard is further down the hall with a frowning Chelsea next to him. Chelsea's frown tells him everything he needs to know. They know, and they're going to get it on film.

"I heard you missed me," Tessa says, staring at him with adoration in her eyes. How long ago was it they had their first kiss outside the mansion under the fairy lights? That kiss had given him hope for this journey; reassurance he was headed in the right direction to find his future partner. So much has changed since then, and he's going to hurt her.

Tessa steps on her tiptoes, going for a kiss. Jonah doesn't meet her.

"Tessa, we need to talk."

Her face falls. "What's going on? Did you bring me up here to break up with me?"

"No, I didn't. I..." How should he do this? Do they know about Afton or not? Something soft brushes against his arm and he shivers, despite the warmth. Afton didn't hide in the bathroom. She's facing whatever this is with him.

Chelsea goes pale, both hands covering her mouth. Richard smiles gleefully.

"Oh, hey Afton," Tessa says, barely glancing at her. The fact that Tessa doesn't immediately suspect what's going on drives the sting of his guilt deeper. Why would Tessa think something was going on? Afton's his producer, so if they were going to film, it'd be normal for her to be here. Except Afton's in her pajamas.

When no one speaks, Tessa does a double take. "Why are you dressed like that?"

"I need to come clean," Afton says.

"About what?" Tessa asks slowly.

"It would be best if I told all the women at the same time," Afton says.

That's it? She's going to confess so easily after all these weeks? The network is going to sue her. They should call a lawyer. Didn't she say Sadie was one? Do they have the right to remain silent if they're not under arrest?

"Call Sadie before you say anything else," Jonah murmurs to Afton.

"Who's Sadie? Were you having a threesome?" Tessa asks.

"Whoa, no. Let's all slow down," Jonah says. This is quickly getting out of control.

Tessa shakes her head furiously. "You were supposed to be one of the good ones. I finally thought I could trust my judgement, but I guess I can't." Tears fall down her cheeks.

"Tessa," he reaches out for her, but she backs away with her hands up.

"Stay away from me," she says, voice shaking, before taking off down the hallway. Richard must have expected something happening because there's another camera already waiting down there. Luke keeps his camera trained on Afton and Jonah in the doorway together as Jonah hesitates. Tessa told him to stay away, and he doesn't know her well enough to know if that actually means, 'please follow.' Should he chase after her? Slam the door in everyone's face and lock himself away until hotel security comes up? That'd give him and Afton a few minutes alone to figure out their next steps.

The elevator dings in answer. Brian Tims walks out, fully dressed with his makeup already done. That means Richard had enough time to get Brian up and ready before coming up here to have Tessa confront Jonah. Brian dramatically looks up and down the hallway, tracking where Tessa is standing and crying with a PA comforting her.

"What's going on?" Brian asks, walking over to Jonah. "Why is your producer Afton here in her pajamas?"

Jonah drags a hand over his mouth. "That's a great question."

Brian comes closer. "Why don't we go inside and you can tell me everything."

Jonah glances at Afton, looking for a sign. What are they doing? They've just gotten back together and he's not going to ruin this like last time.

"Tell the truth," she says quietly. "It's time."

The elevator dings again, Karl pushing through the crowd in the hallway.

"We need to separate them. Take Afton back to her room," Karl orders Richard.

Richard doesn't bother hiding his smirk as he approaches Afton. She follows after him wordlessly, her fingers trailing against Jonah's arm as she passes. The last thing he sees is her small nod as she gets on the elevator. What the hell does that mean? That she'll be okay? That she's not going to run? That she wants him to actually tell the truth this time? He sizes up the distance between him and the emergency stairs. Can he get to them and race down to wherever Afton is? Then escape from an entire crew in an unfamiliar country?

He doesn't know what floor she's on. Or have his passport. They'd get nowhere.

"Shall we?" Brian says, gesturing for Jonah to follow him

Unless he's willing to get violent, he's out of options. Deflated, he goes back inside.

There's no extra chatter as an entire crew files into Jonah's suite, getting the room perfectly lit. He moves his arms robotically as a PA puts his mic on under his shirt. The furniture is rearranged, the armchair moved so it's caddy-corner to the couch where Jonah is told to sit. The cameras circle him like vultures, and Luke refuses to meet Jonah's eye.

Folding director chairs are brought in for the show-runners to sit on in the background. Chelsea leans against a wall; hands shoved in her pockets. Brian finally sits in the armchair, ready to interrogate Jonah under the guise of advising him.

Hannah enters the room, Karl at her side. Karl's face isn't red for once, but he radiates displeasure.

"I don't need to tell you how serious this is. We need you to tell us the truth. Don't bother lying. We have hundreds of hours of footage to comb through, if need be," Hannah says.

Jonah dips his head in response, and Hannah perches on her chair next to Karl.

"Let's start at the beginning," Brian says.

Jonah sighs. "I first met Afton when I was eleven." He summarizes their relationship, and how things ended when they were eighteen.

"She was the one who got away?" Brian asks, sympathetically.

"You could say that. I thought I'd moved on, but I always wondered about her. Who doesn't wonder about their first love from time to time?" He waits for Brian Tims to answer, but he doesn't. "Once I was here, I thought I was hallucinating her, until it was clear I wasn't."

"What happened when you first saw her?"

Jonah recounts their meeting and the deal to stay quiet, leaving out how she promised to give him insights. "She's worked hard to be here, and it didn't seem like it would be a problem."

"But then it became one?"

"She was assigned as my personal producer, and I started falling for her all over again."

"What made you fall for her?"

"Everything. She's hilarious; even the most mundane situations like being stuck in traffic are fun with her. She's loyal; always looking out for everyone. When we had the Jello wrestling date, she literally halted production because a few of the women didn't feel comfortable and ran to the store to get supplies so they could. She's creative, emotionally intelligent, willing to be vulnerable, and strong. There are pieces of the girl I fell in love with as a boy mixed with new layers that I want to keep exploring."

The host smiles. "That's beautiful. Were you two physical off camera?"

He's right back in a bishop's interview. But he's a man now, and this isn't about his odds of getting into heaven. It's about one or both of them getting sued. The whole world will know what he did, and there will be articles. His company said they fully supported him being on the show, but will they still want him around after this? Will he be relegated to selling weight loss teas on social media, unable to work until this blows over?

What about Afton? Will Sadie be able to help her or will she lose everything for him all over again? She said she was ready to be with him hours ago. Will that hold up under an impending lawsuit?

"We kissed twice before yesterday. Last night was entirely my fault. I used the emergency code on the radios and she came running, first aid kit at the ready. Then we started talking and I realized I knew."

"Knew what?" Brian presses.

"That she's who I want to be with."

Brian raises his brows. "Already?"

"Yes. I've had a lot of experience figuring out what I don't want, and I know Afton is the one I want to spend my life with."

The host leans back in his chair, drumming his fingers on the arms.

"Being the lead of this show and falling in love messes with people. It makes them doubt themselves and their judgement. This week you're about to choose four women to go and meet their families, and ask for their blessings to propose. The pressure gets to people, and sometimes they self-sabotage. Do you think your decision to ask Afton to your room was part of that?"

It wasn't self-sabotage; simply that he wanted to exist with her. "No, not at all."

"As your producer, the two of you spent significantly more time together than any of the women you were dating. If you'd spent a similar amount of time with the women, do you think you'd feel differently?"

"I don't."

"Did you seriously consider the other women once you saw Afton, or were you leading them along?"

Jonah rubs at his chest. "Not wasting anyone's time has been my priority this whole journey. I took every date and conversation here seriously, and my feelings were genuine for each of the women."

"How do you think they're going to react to this?"

Jonah blows out a long breath. "They're going to be hurt."

Brian asks him another question, but he can't hear it. The reality of what he's done hits him. He's betrayed all of the women who put their lives on hold to come here for him. People were always going to get hurt, no matter who he chose, but this wasn't what they agreed to. He didn't mean to fall for Afton again; it just happened.

Jonah focuses back on the room, where Karl and Hannah are now arguing.

"I knew from the first night we should recast him," Karl says.

"If you run with this, you could make this the most dramatic season ever," Chelsea says from her spot against the wall.

Everyone goes quiet, giving Chelsea their attention.

"A few seasons ago, a picture circulated online of a lead hanging out with his personal producer over New Year's Eve. The internet went crazy with theories, saying they'd fallen in love behind the scenes. People were sharing photos with them in the background from airports, etc. The franchise even made a statement saying they would support their leads on their journeys for love *no matter where that lead,*" Chelsea emphasizes each word.

"We have tons of footage of Afton in the background. Purposefully sprinkle shots of her through the season. Someone that went to high school with the two of them will spot it and say something, and then the fans will think they're solving a mystery."

Hannah's eyes are dancing. "The ratings and online chatter will be through the roof. It could work."

"We're still losing at least three episodes. The family visits, overnights, and the final episode with the proposal."

"You can fill an entire episode with today's events. You can go visit their families and still get a good episode, I'm sure their parents will have feelings about them reuniting," Chelsea suggests.

Karl's eyes narrow at Chelsea. "You're the one who recommended Afton to work here in the first place. Did the two of you come up with this idea so you could swoop in and save the show and get a promotion?"

Chelsea rolls her eyes. "I don't need a promotion, and I just learned about all of this too. I had no idea Afton and Jonah had a past, otherwise I never would have recommended her."

"We'll figure out the logistics of that later," Hannah says. "Right now, what do you want to do, Jonah? This is your journey. Do you want Afton to come on as a contestant? A lot of our leads know who their person is very early into the journey, but they still go all the way to the end to make sure. Adding a new contestant halfway through a season isn't unheard of."

Jonah blows out a breath. "I don't think that would be fair to the women left, especially since we were intimate."

Hannah chews on a pen, nodding absently. "We're going to go talk with Afton and figure something out. Hold tight."

Jonah is left with a single PA in the room, acting as his babysitter. It's the perfect opportunity to ruminate and second guess every choice he's ever made. Is he doing the right thing? Afton came and joined him in the doorway, ready to face this with him. Hannah and Chelsea are on his side, but will that be enough to go against the others? Those higher up than them?

What are they saying to Afton? *Was* he self-sabotaging when he called her to his room last night? That couldn't be it. He loves her, and he knows she's who he wants to be with. Yet, that feeling of absolute certainty from last night isn't there. All he feels is anxiety. The fact that he's doubting isn't a sign, is it?

ANOTHER MEETING AND AN ETERNITY LATER, Jonah sits in a conference room of the hotel. The crew did their best to make it look cozy, borrowing armchairs from the lobby, turning on the fireplace, and having the women bring their blankets. Jonah's glad he's wearing black to hide his rapidly forming pit stains. He'd thought he was nervous that first night when he announced he was no longer Mormon. That was nothing compared to the terror he feels now. He knows these women and started developing feelings for them. Now he's going to hurt them all.

A door opens and a tearful Tessa walks in. Emily stands and holds her arms out, and Tessa sinks into her embrace.

"What's going on?" Emily asks.

Jonah inhales deeply, probably for the last time today.

"When I was eleven, I moved to a new neighborhood and became best friends with a girl on my street. She was my first love. I even proposed to her after senior prom. She was wise for the both of us and said no. Soon after we broke up."

Everyone looks confused, as they should be. This will be the last moment where they can look at him with an ounce of respect.

"I didn't hear from or see her for over a decade, until I ran into her. Here. Where she was working as a producer."

The change is instant. Tessa starts sobbing again, Tage and McKinlee are murmuring, and Bea holds a hand over her mouth.

"You came on the show to try and get back with her?" Tage asks.

"No, I had no idea she'd be here," Jonah starts, but is cut off.

"So she came here to try and get back with you?" McKinlee asks.

"No. She's been a producer for years and was hired before I was announced as the Fiancé-to-be. She didn't speak up about our connection because she thought our paths wouldn't cross on a production this big. Then she was assigned as my producer and stuck in the lie."

"And none of us stood a chance," Emily says solemnly.

"That's not true. I took every date, every conversation seriously. I know you all put your lives on hold to be here. I didn't think it was possible, but I *have* been falling for multiple people at the same time. Until yesterday, I wasn't sure what I wanted. Now that I am, that's why I'm coming here today."

"Liar. You got caught in bed with her, that's why you're here," Tessa says, finally facing him.

"Damn," Bea says.

"I told you!" McKinlee says.

"Shut up, McKinlee," Tage and Bea say.

Everyone's talking, McKinlee's yelling. Jonah tries to gain their attention again, but it's a lost cause. A headache builds behind his eyes, their angry voices fueling it. As much as he wants to walk away right now, he can't. He created this situation; he has to ride it out.

Bea whistles, both fingers in her mouth. The noise dies down.

"I know we're all feeling angry and betrayed right now. If we want to get our questions answered and let Jonah know how we feel, we need to take turns. Let's go around the circle. McKinlee, you first," Bea points.

"You're like so many of the other boys I've dated. All you want is sex, but you want to pretend that you're still holy, so you have your innocent virgin girlfriend during the day and your sex buddy at night. I'm so glad I said no to you when you tried to sleep with me," McKinlee says.

That is the most shocking thing he's heard today, and it's been *a day.*

"McKinlee, you're the one who thought you had sex with Jonah and were more than happy to brag about it," Bea says.

McKinlee rolls her eyes.

"How often were you two messing around when we had to go back to our rooms for the night?" Tage asks.

"There were two instances where we kissed after hours. Last night was the first time she came to my room, and that's only because I called on the radio and she thought there was an emergency."

"When did you start developing feelings for her?" Emily asks. She still has an arm wrapped around Tessa.

Can he pinpoint an exact moment? There was the kiss after the karaoke bar, but he'd truly thought that was a one-time mistake.

"Mexico was the first time I started thinking about what a future with her might look like," he says.

It's Tessa's turn now. "I don't get how you can say you were falling for us, but be off sleeping with her behind our backs."

"I was falling for you. For all of you." Except for McKinlee. He was going to send her home this week. "I was prepared to meet your families and ask for their blessing to propose. I was considering a future with you, in Chicago, and what that would look like. How we would blend our lives, how I could support you during the school year. I was thinking about those kinds of scenarios with all of you, and trying to figure out which was best. Last night I decided which one I want."

Tessa sighs. "Were you thinking with your brain or your dick? You've heard of oxytocin, right? I wonder what you would have chosen if you'd made it to the overnights."

What the hell? He'd been ready to go home with Afton after Salt Lake City. He'd only kept dating the women because she wanted him to be absolutely sure in his decision. It wasn't the sex that made that decision for him; he'd known the moment he'd called to talk about the book with Afton.

But is he absolutely sure? He searches for that clarity he'd felt. A pit of uncertainty has replaced it.

"Jonah, you're a cool guy, and I had fun fantasizing about what a life with you would look like. You, and the entirety of America, missed out on seeing what a hoot my mom is. If I'm honest though, part of your appeal was the fact that you were choosing me week after week over other people. That feeling of being chosen by a man was intoxicating." Bea cups a hand next to her mouth conspiratorially. "Probably thanks to my daddy issues."

"We all need to look at why we're so mad. Were we truly in love with Jonah, or the idea of being the chosen one?" Bea asks, surveying the room.

Bea may be one of the wisest people he's met. When he himself was a contestant on *Ready for the Ring*, he swore he was falling in love. The tears in the SUV when he was sent home in third place were genuine; he felt devastated. But after a week at home, it was like coming out of a fog. All his feelings for the lead were gone. Probably because some of the appeal *was* about feeling chosen.

He's been cut off from all his family and friends. His job is to think, breathe, and sleep finding a wife. Can he trust anything he feels now?

Tage and McKinlee study their laps. Did Bea's words ring true to them?

"I was falling in love with you," Tessa says, meeting his eyes.

"I was too," Emily adds quietly.

He shouldn't be surprised. He felt the biggest connections with them, but they had no idea his heart was also exploring another path. How can he make this better?

"I was falling for you, too. You're all extraordinary women who deserve to be loved by someone wholeheartedly. I'm sorry that that person couldn't be me."

Tessa starts crying again and Emily holds her tight. He wants to comfort them, but he can't fix this.

The host appears in the doorway.

"Ladies, this is goodbye for Jonah. If you have any last words for him, now is the time."

McKinlee approaches him, then slaps him across the face. His cheek starts to throb as she walks away, head held high. Richard trails after her, eager to get that in-the-moment interview. He'd gladly take the slap from any of the other women, but McKinlee? All he did was kiss her.

Tage approaches next. "You okay?" she asks, tentatively touching his cheek.

"I'll be fine. Are you?"

She bites her lip, thinking. "I will be. I'm glad I came here and met you and the other women. This journey has cleared up things for me."

Before he would have asked what things were clearer. He doesn't deserve to know now. "I wish you all the best," Jonah says, holding an arm out tentatively. Tage gives him a quick hug before leaving the room.

Next is Bea. "You didn't deserve that slap. I hope you've found what you're looking for, even if it wasn't me."

"Thank you for always keeping things honest and real. I can't wait to see where you end up," Jonah says.

"Watch out world," Bea jokes before wrapping her arms tightly around Jonah's neck in a hug.

Emily disengages from Tessa to walk over to him. "I'd be lying if I said I wasn't feeling hurt and betrayed."

"I'm so sorry–"

Emily holds up a hand. "Nothing you say right now can fix this. I hope you can truly be honest with everyone around you from now on."

Her words pierce him. He'd been proud of the growth he'd made in not confessing things. Instead his dishonesty is exactly what Emily's calling out.

Emily kisses his cheek, leaving before he can think of a response.

That leaves Tessa.

"I wish I'd never met you," she says simply before walking away.

Alone, Jonah crumples to the floor. He spent the first thirty years of his life obsessed with being enough. Kind enough. Obedient enough. Humble enough. Righteous enough. Christlike enough. He needed to be perfect so he could make it to the highest level of heaven and spend eternity with his family. To be reunited with his dad.

Leaving the church and reconstructing his beliefs was beyond difficult. He no longer had an easy answer for everything. A path to follow. He was out here alone in the world trying his best to be a good person. And obviously failing at it.

He'd thought not tattling on Afton was good exposure therapy for him in not confessing. Where would he be right now if he'd told the truth from day one? About to go meet Tessa, Bea, Emily, and Tage's families? Would he feel more confident in his choices? Did Tessa have any truth to her claim that he was thinking with lust instead of with his heart?

He'd been celibate from ages 18-30. He could wait when he wanted to. Lust didn't call the shots. If that'd been the case, he would have been married at twenty to the first woman he met when he got home from his mission. Or to the first woman he'd slept with after leaving. That wasn't it.

He desperately wants that feeling of rightness he felt last night. He wants reassurance he's doing the right thing.

Heavenly Father, he starts praying in his mind. Then pauses. Praying when he's stressed or distraught is practically muscle memory. He doesn't know if there's a higher power that prefers to be called Heavenly Father. If there isn't, he likes to think his own father exists somewhere out there, even if it's only the parts of him that live in Jonah.

Heavenly Father, I don't know what to do.

CHAPTER TWENTY-SIX

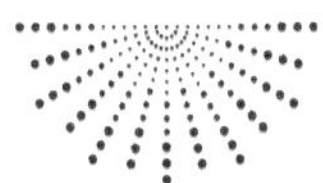

*A*fton swears several lifetimes pass before she's brought to see Jonah a little after 4:00PM. She woke up next to him at 6:00AM, blissfully happy to be in his arms. Then she'd been in panic mode, trying to hide from whoever was at the door. When she heard Tessa's voice out there, she knew what she needed to do. There was no reason for production to wake Tessa up that early and have her outside Jonah's door unless they'd figured out where Afton was and wanted to catch them on camera.

How had they caught her? Had there been a meeting this morning she hadn't shown up for? Did someone go to investigate what that noise on the radio was and saw Afton go into Jonah's room? Whatever it was, she was done hiding. She stood next to Jonah, ready to be the team they'd agreed to be.

When she'd been locked in her room with only Richard for company, he'd completely berated her. She recorded audio of it in case she needed proof later. She'd refused to talk until Hannah and Karl came to see her, one of their lawyers on the phone. The lawyer read the contract she'd signed verbatim to her, showing how she'd clearly violated it. She simply said she wouldn't be answering any questions without speaking to her own lawyer, infuriating Richard.

They'd left her alone again with a PA to babysit her. She snuck a phone call to Sadie in the bathroom, quickly explaining everything.

"Get out of there and come home. We'll figure this out, promise. If they threaten to hold you there or tell you you can't leave, ask them how they'd feel about an unlawful imprisonment or kidnapping charge," Sadie said. "Mention O.J. Simpson if you have to."

Hannah and Karl finally reappeared. There was yelling. Screaming. More berating. And then, a potential deal.

"If Jonah wants to choose you, then we need him to choose you. We're hoping you can help convince him he's done the right thing. If this all ends in a proposal, that would be ideal," Hannah said.

What did they mean she needed to convince him to do the right thing? An SUV drops her off at a Toronto park. When she thinks of Toronto, she's never thought of fall foliage, but the park is filled with color. She shoves her hands in the pockets of the cropped plaid jacket a PA handed her so she could look like an actual romantic interest, and not just a producer.

The leaves crunch underfoot as she approaches Jonah sitting on a bench. Whoever scouted this location did a great job, finding a bench underneath a maple tree that's leaves softly fall behind him. She bites her cheek. Everyone knows the truth about them now, and they're letting her talk to him in hopes of getting their happily ever after on film. It's finally their time. No religion, no parents, no secrets in the way. They can be together.

When Jonah turns toward her, she realizes why Hannah said they hoped she could convince him. His hair sticks up at random angles, as if he's been pulling at it. Stubble covers his face, and his eyes are red and bleary. Only the corners of his mouth come up in a smile when he sees her. What happened to him?

He regrets it. The thought stops her. Did spending the night together help him realize he didn't actually want to be with her? That he wants to be with one of the other women? Did Hannah send her in with false hope? Or did Karl and Richard worm their way into his mind? She glances over her shoulder, back to the car. Should she cut her losses and leave with some dignity?

No. She's not running from hard conversations. She's going to get through this, even if it's only to prove to herself she can.

"Hey," Jonah says, voice gravelly. He stays seated on the bench.

"Hey," she says, sitting down next to him. She keeps her hands in her pockets, unsure of what to do. "How are you?"

He huffs out a laugh. "I'm a mess. I told everyone the truth about us." He rubs at a red mark on his cheek.

"What happened?" Afton asks, reaching out and rubbing the spot gently. Jonah winces, then closes his eyes at her touch.

"Nothing."

"Jonah," she says sternly. She will find out. Did Karl punch him? She'll report him for assault. Or did he run into something trying to escape when they separated him?

"McKinlee slapped me."

"McKinlee?" Afton practically screeches. Anger courses through her at the thought of someone, especially McKinlee, hurting him. Because of her. "You didn't deserve that."

Jonah shrugs, staring straight ahead at the park. "Maybe I did."

Afton gently cups Jonah's face, turning him so he's looking at her. "Jonah, you didn't deserve to be slapped. You were nothing but kind and respectful to McKinlee, even after she tried to turn everyone against you."

"I hurt everyone," he says, voice breaking.

"You're on a reality dating show. There was no way not to hurt people."

Jonah closes his eyes, face still in her hand. "But I lied and hurt everyone. I could have handled things differently."

Afton swallows. "You did it for me. I shouldn't have put you in that position; it was unfair of me. I hate that you have to take all the blame for my mistakes."

Jonah's eyes flutter open. "I was okay with it if it meant I could see you."

"Yeah?"

"I wasn't ready to let you go. I came here thinking I'd finally moved on from you, and then there you were. I figured getting to see you now as an adult would help me move past that idealized version of you from my memories. It didn't. I fell for you all over again."

Afton can't help her smile now. She can't believe she almost ran from this. "I'm sure you could find something annoying about me."

He snorts. "Of course I could, and you for me. But I didn't find anything that was a dealbreaker. I fell for you all over again, and I'm scared I'm never going to get you out of my mind."

"Or you from mine. I hated how excited I got every time I saw you, or better yet, got to talk to you. This past month has been the happiest I've been in quite a while."

Jonah looks between her eyes, to her lips. She moves her hand from his cheek to the back of his neck, her fingers twirling in the overgrown strands of hair. She leans in to kiss him and he meets her. Each brush of his lips against hers is a gentle reminder that they're here, together. Despite all the odds, they're in a park in Toronto under a maple tree, red leaves falling around them in the crisp air.

Jonah winds his hand through her hair, his tongue flicking

into her mouth, deepening the kiss. When she meets his tongue with her own, he scoots in closer to her so she's against the arm of the bench, pressing as much of his body against hers as he can. His mouth moves urgently, taking as much as it can, as if they're running out of time.

He pulls away, chest heaving, and moves back to his original spot on the bench. He leans forward, his head in his hands.

"What's wrong?"

"I thought... I thought that'd help me know what to do."

She tugs on the neckline of her shirt. Since Salt Lake and their singing together, he's been adamant that he knows that he wants her. She was the one with hesitations, who wanted him to make sure. Yesterday she'd finally been ready to believe him. But now he doesn't know what he wants?

Hear him out. She will not panic until he explains what that means.

"What do you mean?"

He inhales slowly, then exhales. She reaches out and starts scratching his back. Whatever is going on in his mind, he's struggling. She'll be right here as he figures it out.

"Last night I felt so sure about being with you. I felt good about it. After everything today, that sure feeling is gone. I have no idea what I'm thinking or feeling. All I feel is awful. Like I'm a terrible person."

"Jonah, you are not awful. The farthest thing from it."

He shakes his head. "My brain is reverting to when I was a teenager. All of that progress I've worked so hard for is gone. I want that feeling of certainty I used to get, reassurance this is the right thing to do. For you and me. If I'm slipping back this easily, what else am I going to do?"

This isn't about her. It's about certainty, something she has quite a bit of experience with. She rubs a few more circles on his back.

"You're in an extremely stressful environment right now. It's completely normal to have some of your old thought patterns pop up. It doesn't negate everything you've done; it's a bump in the road."

His breathing stutters. "I've been in a bubble for over a month. How can I trust anything I'm thinking or feeling?"

She starts writing his name in cursive on his back with her finger. "Today has been hard. If it were me, I'd take the day to rest, and not even try to figure things out until tomorrow."

He runs his hands through his hair. "I don't know if that's enough. I need to get out of here. I need to go home to talk to my family and Henry."

In her meeting with the executives, there had been no mentions of his family coming. Normally he would get that before a proposal.

"I'm sure that can be arranged."

He shakes his head again. "I don't want them to visit. I want to go home. I can't do this anymore."

If she was here as his producer, she'd talk him down. Insist he go to sleep, then revisit the topic in the morning. Now she's here as his… Afton.

"If you need to go home, then go home."

He sits up slowly and she drops her hand from his back.

"I need to propose— "

"I don't want you proposing to me if you're feeling this conflicted. I want you to be happy, however that looks."

He frowns. "You don't want to be with me?"

Her skin bristles. "That's not it at all. I love you and I want to spend my life with you. If you asked me to elope today, I'd look up where the nearest karaoke bar is to go celebrate after.

"I selfishly forced myself back into your life, and I'm not going to let you do something that feels wrong because you think you have to. I want you to do whatever you need right now."

Jonah presses his lips together, his gaze searching. His eyes glisten and he squeezes them shut.

"I need to go home. I'm so sorry," he whispers.

Afton swears her sternum cracks, but she stays upright. A teeny tiny part of her is relieved. She'd been so worried he was going to choose her and secretly resent her for it. Instead he's choosing himself and what he needs.

"I'm proud of you," she rasps.

He reaches out and swipes a tear off her cheek. She does the same to him. He wraps her in his arms and they hold each other as they cry. Eventually he pulls away.

"I'm sorry— "

She covers his mouth with her hand. "No more apologizing. You're taking care of yourself which is hella hot."

Jonah makes a throaty sound that might have been a laugh. "This isn't goodbye."

"Okay," she manages, her throat unbearably tight. He can't promise that yet. She has no idea what he'll realize once he's out of this mindfuck of a reality show.

He stares into her eyes. His are a shade of amber in the afternoon sun. He blinks, then kisses her forehead before standing from the bench. She tries to memorize the sight of him with the leaves falling around with the sound of children shrieking with joy in the background. Just in case it's the last time she sees him.

Slowly he turns and walks away.

The cameras follow him and one stays to interview her.

"What are you feeling?" Richard asks.

"I'm proud of him. I love him so much. If this is all I got, I'm grateful for it. I feel awful for potentially ruining this for him." Her throat burns, trying to hold back her emotions. Being on this side of the camera is worse than she imagined. She always tried her best not to be cruel to people, but still. Her heart is breaking, and people are going to eat it up as entertainment.

"Does it feel worse breaking up the first, or second time?" Richard asks, eyes gleaming. Luke turns his head to glare at Richard from behind his camera. That was a low blow, but a blessing in disguise because there's no way to continue answering Richard's questions with the gut wrenching sobs breaking loose.

CHAPTER TWENTY-SEVEN

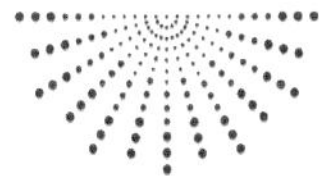

FIFTEEN YEARS AGO

$\mathcal{N}$aya and Sadie stood across from Afton at the concession stand, hands slapping the counter. "Why weren't you at after prom?" Naya asked.

Heat crept into Afton's cheeks.

"Did you two sleep together?" Sadie asked.

Naya gasped.

"Keep it down," Afton hissed before taking them into the break-room for privacy.

"Jonah proposed," she said.

Sadie and Naya's eyes bugged out. They both pulled on her left hand, holding it up. Afton wiggled her bare fingers for them.

"I said no."

"You two broke up?" Naya asks.

"No. I don't feel ready to be engaged— "

"I could cry right now, I'm so proud of you. Especially since you've been raised to be a child bride," Sadie said, wiping an invisible tear from her cheek.

Afton ignored that. "I got really shaky afterward, so Jonah took me back to his place to change, and I was shaking so hard I couldn't so he had to help me get dressed— "

"And instead he ravished you?" Naya asked.

"And then we cuddled on the couch for a bit and started making out, and then we…" Afton trailed off.

"Say it. Say it out loud," Sadie demanded.

"Had sex," Afton squeaked.

Naya and Sadie both shot to their feet, clapping and cheering. They pulled Afton up and hugged her fiercely. For doing something considered a sin next to murder, they sure were happy.

They wanted to know if it hurt, was it good, if she bled.

"How do you feel about it?" Naya asked.

Afton bit her lip. "I know I'm supposed to feel bad, but I don't. I liked being that close to him. Sharing it with him."

"Don't you dare feel bad. Not like when you got to second base. You two have loved each other for a while. Jonah literally proposed to you. Do not let some old white guys who can't get it up dictate how you feel," Sadie said.

"Sadie," Naya gasped.

"What? Tell me you haven't thought about it," Sadie said.

"Definitely haven't," Naya said.

"So it's okay that I wasn't ready to get engaged, but that I wanted to have sex?" Afton asked.

"Yes!" they practically screamed. She wished she could bottle up this moment and carry it around forever. Who cared what others thought when two of her favorite people were so happy for her?

~

JONAH WASN'T SITTING on the stand to bless the sacrament on Sunday. All the older boys took turns blessing it, so it wasn't an immediate concern. Until she saw him sitting with his mom, head bowed the entire meeting. When he hadn't texted much yesterday, she'd written it off as them both being busy with work. Seeing him today? This was bad.

She caught him before Sunday school. "We need to talk."

He was silent as she dragged him outside to the parking lot where they sat on the curb. "Are you okay?"

He shook his head. "We shouldn't have done that. I knew better, but I still did it. I wasn't strong enough and I'm so sorry."

His words stung. "Don't apologize. I loved being that close to you."

Jonah's expression changed to pure agony. He covered his face.

"Did you not like it? Did I not do it right?" Afton asked. It'd been her first time, maybe she was supposed to do more? Or maybe she...

"Of course I liked it. I liked it too much. I love you; I want to spend my life with you. But I know better. God gave us rules, and I broke one. I shouldn't have taken you to my house with no one there. I shouldn't have undressed you, or sat on the couch. I keep playing it in my head and seeing all the places I didn't stop. They warned us over and over, and I still gave in."

"I don't feel guilty about it. I love you and it felt like a new way to share that."

Jonah frowned at her. "You don't feel bad? Not at all?"

"Not until you told me how you're feeling."

He wrapped his arms around his legs, hiding his face.

She clawed at his arms, trying to get him to look at her. "Jonah, look at me."

He kept his head down, shaking with silent sobs.

She'd thought about this all night. "I think we feel so bad

because it's what we've been taught. What if it's not right? Sadie and Naya have never dealt with this guilt. If what we did was so wrong, wouldn't I have felt awful in the morning? I didn't. Remember what your mom said, that the teachings can be harmful? I believe her."

Jonah finally looked up, eyes gleaming with tears. She hadn't seen him cry since his dad's funeral. "They don't feel guilty because they haven't been taught the truth. We know it so God holds us to a higher standard."

"Then why don't I feel bad?" Afton asked. "Or your mom. We've been taught the truth too."

Jonah studied her. "Satan is sneaky and conniving. He wants us to believe what we did wasn't wrong so we will be miserable, just like him."

She'd been taught these things her entire life, but hearing them repeated by Jonah right now hurts. Does he really think she's being deceived? That she isn't capable of deciphering the Holy Spirit for herself?

"The guilt is eating me; I can't live like this. I need to confess to the bishop. "

Adrenaline shot through her. "Hold on, we need to talk about this."

"What is there to talk about?" Jonah asked.

"We've already messed up once, and the bishop told us we needed to break up. He said the punishment would be worse a second time. My parents will find out."

"He can't tell them, what you say is private," Jonah said.

Afton feels faint. "You don't know that. My dad is in the bishopric with him; plus he might make us tell our parents as part of our forgiveness."

Jonah blew out a breath. "I made a mistake; I can't go on my mission with this hanging over me. I'll do what I have to to be forgiven."

"Your mom is awesome, my parents aren't." She dug the heels of her hands into her forehead. She could only imagine what her parents would do. "I'm leaving for California in three months. You could wait to confess until I'm out of the house. You'd still have time to repent before your mission."

"Wait three months? I can't go on like this," Jonah said.

"Think about eternity. These three months will be a blip in time. Some people wait until their deathbeds to confess."

"I could die tomorrow, and then I wouldn't be eligible for heaven," Jonah said.

"That's not true. God knows the desires of our hearts. You could repent in Spirit Prison…" She tried to think of any other doctrine she could use to convince him to wait. "Please Jonah. I'm begging you. I need to get out of here, and then I'll confess to my new bishop in California. We're both at fault, we can get through this together."

Jonah took a shuddering breath. "I'll try."

JONAH WOULD BARELY TOUCH HER, much less kiss her, and was withdrawn. He didn't come to senior ditch day, instead going to class. He barely talked to anyone at the senior party. Getting him to smile for graduation was a legitimate nightmare. Now the guilt was hitting Afton. What they'd done was destroying the person she loved. They just needed to get through this, and then everything would be fine.

It was the second week of summer when Afton was pulled out of Sunday school and called to the bishop's office. She blacked out on the walk there and through the bishop making small talk with her before he asked the question.

"Is there something you need to talk to me about?" he asked.

She shook her head no, unable to form words.

The bishop let out a long sigh. "That's not what I've heard."

Blood whooshed through her ears and she crumpled in her chair.

Jonah had confessed.

She felt herself floating above her body, looking down as she answered the bishop's questions. Over or under clothes? Who initiated? Who kissed and touched where? Had she reached climax? When she asked what climax was, the bishop simply moved on with no explanation. He droned about the law of chastity and he made her read scriptures back to him. She zoned out when he listed her steps for forgiveness. She only re-entered her body when the door opened and her parents entered the room.

"What are they doing here?" she asked.

"I asked if you'd like my help to talk with them, and you agreed," he answered.

Afton left her body again, watching from above as the bishop talked, and her parents both cried. She drifted in and out until that night when her parents called her into their room after an afternoon of talking in there with hushed voices.

"We've failed you. We've given you too much freedom and you've used it to sin. We've prayed and the Lord has helped us come up with a plan to get you back on track," her dad said.

She didn't bother responding.

"You will no longer have a phone. You'll be in charge of running a morning and evening family scripture study for the family. You'll quit your job at the movie theater and stay home to take care of your brothers–"

"I need to work all summer to afford my first year of school," she interrupted.

"If you do what we ask, we'll pay for your entire tuition at BYU after you finish the repentance process," her dad said calmly.

"Why don't you pay me for taking care of the boys this summer? Then I could still go to-"

"You think you're still going to California after this? If you can't follow the commandments surrounded by members, what do you think you'll be tempted to do out there? You'll be having abortions in between drug binges. We won't allow it."

The walls were closing in. "I made a mistake and it won't happen again. Trust me, I've learned my lesson."

"We won't *let* it happen again. It's our job as your parents to make sure you do what's right. Otherwise the sins of the child rest on the parents," her dad said.

Afton tried to think of something to cling to, a loophole to get out of this.

"I'm an adult. You can't force me to do any of that."

Her dad's face started turning red. "If you're living under our roof we can."

"What are you saying?"

"If you don't agree to our rules, you can get out," he said.

Her mother started sobbing. "Afton, we're only trying to save you. This is your eternity on the line. Accept our help."

Their help?

"Your help is locking me up and treating me like an unpaid nanny for the children you're too overwhelmed to take care of," Afton said with her whole chest.

If her dad's face had been red before, it was practically purple now.

"I'll offer you one last time. You can do it our way, or you can leave."

She couldn't do this anymore. She had fought tooth and nail for every ounce of freedom in her life, and she wasn't going to lose it now.

Without a word Afton went to her room and started throwing her things in a duffle bag; trying to decide which items were most important for her new life. She didn't know if she'd be welcome back, so she shoved all her clothes and toiletries in. She glanced at her tiny bookshelf. On it was the copy of *Eragon* Jonah had let her borrow all those years ago. He'd given it to her for their one-year anniversary of dating. Before prom, it was one of her most prized possessions. Now it filled her with rage.

He'd betrayed her and hadn't even given her a warning. He got to feel better, and she was getting kicked out of her home. She didn't know where she was going to go, or what she was going to do. From how loud her parents were yelling from their room, she needed to get out of here and fast.

A duffel and suitcase in hand, she ran down the stairs. Her two middle brothers were zoned out playing a video game, but Noah was crying. Afton's heart broke. If she left, there would be no one to protect him from a mom who wasn't emotionally there and a dad who only loved you if you fit his mold. For a few seconds, she thought about staying. For him. She'd take care of him. Go to BYU. Marry the first boy who was interested in her. Have his babies, and be miserable forever.

She loved Noah, but not enough to give up herself. There had to be some way to watch out for him, even if she wasn't here. She wrapped Noah into a hug and whispered that she loved him. Then she walked out the front door.

She dragged her suitcase and duffle three doors down the street and rang the doorbell. Ruth answered the door. "Come in, dinner's almost ready."

"I need to talk to your mom," Afton said, shifting from foot to foot.

Carrie came to the door, brow furrowed. "Why don't you come in?"

"I can't. My parents kicked me out, and they're fighting right now. I was wondering if you could—" her throat was closing up with the oncoming tears. "If you could keep an eye out for my brothers. Especially Noah."

Carrie looked alarmed. "Afton, get inside. We'll figure this out."

"I can't. Just look out for my brothers."

"Where are you going? Who's going to look out for you?" Carrie asked.

"Me."

Carrie kept talking, but Afton turned on her heel and walked away.

Sadie's family agreed to take Afton in for the first half of the summer, and Naya's would for the second half until it was time for the two of them to go to California. Sadie and Naya held Afton as she cried, and cried, and cried.

Her parents had never taken the time to know who her friends were, so they weren't able to find where she was staying. When she wouldn't answer their messages, they shut down her phone. Naya's parents instantly added her to their family plan.

She stopped going to church and it was a confusing feeling. She didn't feel dread every Sunday morning. She had three—more like four hours —given back to her. She didn't have to hear how horrible she was, or how Naya was also a sinner, or whatever else the congregation decided to spew from the pulpit.

It didn't take long for people to start whispering about her and Jonah. She'd overhear them from behind the concession counter, while cleaning the bathrooms. They blamed her for tempting Jonah and delaying his mission. They called her a harlot, a slut. Said she was hardhearted and under Satan's control because she refused to repent.

She'd pray in the middle of the night when she couldn't sleep, pouring out her heart, searching for some sort of direction.

"I don't think what I did was wrong," she whispered one

night. Her entire body was instantly flooded with warmth, goosebumps trailing up and down her arms and legs. That was the tell-tale sign of the Spirit confirming something. She couldn't deny this feeling of comfort; it was the first she'd felt since prom. The Spirit wasn't supposed to lie, so why would it confirm the opposite of what she'd been taught? She didn't know, but she was going to find out.

It took three weeks for Jonah to finally corner her. He'd been stopping by the theater every day, but her coworkers always gave her a heads up and she'd hide until he disappeared. He'd come to Sadie's home a few times too, but her parents told him to stay away or they'd call the police. He'd left multiple letters for her, but she'd refused to open them.

He finally caught her when she was walking home one night.

"Afton!" he yelled.

The sound of her name from his lips made her ache. She closed her eyes and for a moment she was the girl she'd been before prom. The one who loved with her whole heart. That girl was gone now. She kept walking, but he caught up, breathing hard.

"Please, we need to talk."

"No, we don't."

He reached out and touched her arm. She let the touch linger for one second, two. Then she shrugged out of it.

"Let me explain," Jonah begged.

She whipped around, finally facing him. "There's nothing to explain. I asked you to wait to confess. You couldn't, and gave me no warning. Guess what? The bishop said that he could help me tell my parents what happened, then brought them in. They reacted exactly how I expected. My options were to let them lock me up, or leave. So I left. Once school starts in the fall, I'm never coming back here."

Jonah's mouth was agape. "I had no idea. He didn't bring my

mom in. I couldn't carry the weight of what we'd done, it was eating me alive."

"What we did wasn't wrong. Why can't you see that?"

"It was. I feel it in my soul. Now that I'm repenting, I can finally breathe again."

She looked him over. The boy who'd been her best friend, her first love. She thought he would be her everything. But he can't be. He might say that he'd never put the church before her. That their hypothetical family came first and he wouldn't desert her for meetings and activities. He would. He believed in the church so strongly that it made him physically ill.

"Good for you." She started walking again.

"Afton, wait. What about our relationship? You can't just shut me out."

She turned around slowly. "Jonah, we're done. I can't be with someone who feels so disgusted at the thought of being with me. You're going to go on your mission and come home. You'll meet some pretty girl at BYU who'd never sleep with you before marriage. Then have a perfect little life. I'm going to California and I'm going to find myself. I'm going to figure out what I believe without everyone around me telling me what I do."

He shook his head back and forth, tears streaming down his cheeks. "No. I love you and we can figure this out. What if we start praying together every day, doing scripture study? Go back to the basics. You can start feeling the Spirit again, I know it."

She reached up and brushed away a few of his tears. "I can't give you what you want. It's time to let go."

"No, we can fix this. You're my best friend, you're the one I want to spend forever with."

Tears trailed down her own cheeks. "You were mine too. But I can't." She stood on her tiptoes and pressed a kiss to his cheek. He wrapped her into a hug. She lingered for a moment longer than she should have, her already broken heart practically shattering. Knowing this was what she had to do didn't make it hurt any less. She pulled herself away from him, inch by inch. A child afraid to remove a band-aid, stretching out the agony. When all that was left was his fingers, featherlight on her arms, she stepped out of his reach. What was left of her heart shattered even further as she and walked away from him for the last time.

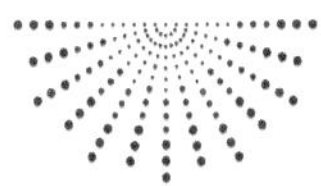

CHAPTER TWENTY-EIGHT

Afton walks up the steps of the townhome, awkwardly carrying the box of diapers and gift bag in her arms. Naya flings open the door before Afton can knock.

"You made it," Naya says, pulling her in for a hug. Naya's belly pushes hard into Afton, and she tries to maneuver around it.

"I can't wait to be able to hug people again," Naya says, pulling away and leading Afton inside.

They pass an elaborate archway wrapped in greenery. The kitchen table is covered in circles made of woven sticks. If they're nests, they're all missing the bottoms.

"What theme did your cousin settle on?" Afton whispers conspiratorially.

Naya smacks her lightly on the arm, peeking around the corner. Said cousin is busy talking with a group of women on the other side of the room. The cousin is wearing one of the bottomless nests on her head.

"Eucalyptus. Apparently, it's the shade of green we painted

the nursery and it symbolizes strength, protection, and purification."

"As long as I don't have to wear a nest, I'm good."

Naya's pulled away by more guests arriving, and Afton catches up with Naya's parents. They'd moved to California when Naya and Afton went there for school and became her second family, having her over for every holiday until Afton slowly started talking with her parents again. They live two hours away now and it'd been ages since she's seen them. When they ask about work, she keeps her answers vague, not wanting to worry them or take any attention from the shower.

Sadie arrives and squeezes Afton hard.

"You better get ready to spill everything," Sadie says.

"After. We need to help build this nest with protection and whatever else eucalyptus means."

Naya's cousin divvy's everyone up for the tasks. There are teams working on freezer meals, making postpartum pads, deep cleaning every nook and cranny. Sadie and Afton are assigned to help build the crib.

Naya's wife, Miriam, escorts them upstairs to the nursery. It's a mess with boxes everywhere, the one with the crib pressed against the wall.

"I've been meaning to get to this, I just don't speak whatever language this is," Miriam says, waving the instruction manual in the air.

Afton plucks it from her fingers. "The three of us and TikTok will be able to figure it out."

"I didn't even think to look there," Miriam moans.

Naya enters, clutching her belly and completely breathless. She settles into the rocking chair in the corner.

"You built this chair and that's all I care about. Most babies don't even sleep in their crib. It's a consumerist decoration if you ask me," Naya says, settling her legs on the ottoman.

"Your parents bought it for us. I'm not letting them down," Miriam says.

"Suck up. I swear they love you more than me," Naya says.

Miriam and Afton start pulling the pieces of the crib out of the box while Sadie takes charge of the instructions.

"So Afton, Sadie said you have quite the story for us," Naya says.

Sadie snorts. "Way to be discrete."

"I don't have time to be discreet. Spill, now," Naya orders.

"Today isn't about me. It's about you," Afton says. She's so grateful to be here; she's not going to bring down the mood with her messy life.

"If I have to talk to someone else about whether or not my cervix is dilated, I'm going to stab someone. All anyone wants to talk about is my body and the baby. Please, tell me all the juicy details," Naya says.

Afton scans the room. Sadie and Miriam nod encouragingly. So, she tells them everything. By the end she's a snotty mess with a pile of tissues next to her, holding a useless flathead screwdriver.

"So, you're in limbo right now? Not sure if they're going to pursue legal action and on call for anything they might want to film while Jonah figures himself out?" Naya asks.

"Exactly. While searching for a new job," Afton adds.

"You should create one of those skill-share courses on how to do good interviews. There are so many people with podcasts that have no idea how to ask a follow up question," Miriam says.

"Babe, you're a genius," Naya says.

That's a path Afton hadn't even considered.

"As for the lawsuit, I'll help you find resources to fight anything they throw your way," Sadie says.

"How do you feel about Jonah? I can't believe you didn't tell us any of this while it was happening," Naya says.

Afton cringes. "I was scared I'd have to miss your shower and didn't want to let you down. Again. And I didn't want written evidence that I knew Jonah in case the network found out."

Naya laughs, then winces. "Fake contraction," she hisses. Miriam walks over; face pinched with worry. Naya waves her off. "When did you get so paranoid, Afton?"

"If they played their cards right, they could subpoena her texts. It was a smart move," Sadie says.

Naya sighs. "I miss my pre-pregnancy brain. It would have known that. So what now?"

Afton swallows hard. "I put him in yet another impossible situation because I couldn't tell the truth. I can't change what I did, and if this doesn't work out... I'm glad it happened. I needed this to crawl out of the rut I've been in."

She feels like a failure to feminism that it took falling in love to finally muster the courage to make changes in her life. That's the special thing about love though, its ability to crack through the strongest of defenses.

"You did the best you could in the situation. But how do you feel about him?" Sadie asks, lying on her back to screw something in upside down.

Afton sags against the wall. "I love him. So much. I thought we had the timing right this time, but then he..."

"Panicked?" Miriam asks.

"Crashed out?" Naya suggests.

"Needed a moment?" Sadie says.

"Whichever of those it is. Now he's gone, I haven't heard from him, and I miss him."

She saw him every day for the past six weeks. Going from that to total radio silence has been a shock to the system. All day she thinks of things she wants to tell him before remembering why she can't. Maybe it's pathetic, but she's been writing them all down in a note on her phone, just in case.

"This is all going to work out, I know it. If it doesn't, I'm going to kick his ass," Naya says.

Afton remembers the red mark on Jonah's cheek from McKinlee slapping him. He doesn't deserve anyone's violence. "If it doesn't work out, it's my fault, not his."

"Stop with the self-blame. What happened happened. We'll be here for whatever is next," Sadie says. She rolls out from under the crib, and Miriam steps back from the side she'd been tightening.

"It's finished," Miriam says, helping Sadie press it against the wall

Naya starts sobbing from her spot in the chair, startling everyone. Miriam kneels in front of her, placing her hands on Naya's belly.

"Are these happy tears or overwhelmed ones?" Miriam asks softly.

"Terrified," Naya blubbers. "There's actually going to be a baby in there. I'm never going to be the same."

Afton and Sadie go to Naya, sitting on either side. Naya reaches for their hands and Afton squeezes in reassurance.

"Remember how cool I was in high school? And college? Now I can't even form a thought properly and I read that it's only going to get worse," Naya says between sobs. "The old me will never come to the phone again because she's going to die as soon as this baby rips itself out of my vagina."

"Don't tell me you think you peaked in high school as a closeted girl in Orem, Utah," Sadie says.

"Or as treasurer of your sorority," Afton adds.

Naya sniffs. "Delta Gamma's budget was never as balanced as when I was there."

"You hadn't met Miriam yet, started your career in copywriting, or learned that you have a knack for hosting amazing parties."

"Those are all things I need my brain for. I missed four comma splices in the last project I turned in for work. Comma splices! I forgot to remind my cousin to make sure there was a dairy free cake option today, and I need to be on my A game if I'm going to keep Miriam interested in me."

"Naya, I'm not going anywhere. If anything I need to up my game because you've always been out of my league," Miriam says.

"I'm going to lose myself, and then I'm going to lose you all as friends. I'll have to make all new ones at mommy groups and choose between the mom who asks what flavor of Mexican I am and the one who swears by unpasteurized milk because they'll be my only options." Naya devolves into sobbing again.

"We're not going anywhere," Sadie says gently. "Our friendship has weathered long distance, natural deodorant, and every change in between. I'm excited to meet the new you that emerges from motherhood."

"I'm settling down and getting a job that doesn't require travel, so you're going to have a hard time getting rid of me," Afton says. "I'll help you prank the racist moms at baby and me time."

Naya snorts at that.

"I'm not going to let you disappear in motherhood. We're in this together," Miriam says.

Naya leans forward and kisses Miriam before leaning and giving Afton and Sadie side hugs.

"How long are you in town for?" Naya asks Sadie.

"Two more days, why?"

"Because either I've been peeing my pants on and off the whole time we've been up here, or my water broke. I'm going to get this baby out before you fly home."

Everything devolves into chaos. Miriam helps Naya out of the chair and to the bathroom, yelling for the hospital bags. Her parents tell Naya she waited too long to have her baby shower, and Naya cusses them out. Naya's cousin tries to gather everyone for a picture next to the eucalyptus arch with them wearing their nest crowns, but Miriam yells at her while ushering a now contracting Naya out to the car.

"It's karma for all the annoying group messages about nesting themes," Afton whispers to Sadie.

Sadie cackles, and they help the rest of the guests prepare Naya and Miriam's nest for them to come back to, a family of three.

JONAH LIES ON THE FLOOR, drool falling on his forehead. And his chin? He opens his eyes to see Millie panting above him. Henry's daughter looks down at him, aggressively chewing a teether with a stream of drool dribbling down. He closes his eyes, but a tiny finger jabs him, trying to pry his eyelid open.

"Can't you let a man wallow by himself?" Jonah groans.

"This really is as bad as you said it was," a familiar voice says.

Jonah sits up so quickly, he almost takes out Henry's daughter. Millie jumps back, bouncing on her hind legs, ready to play. Jonah's mom stands in the doorway of Henry's family room, chewing on her bottom lip. He gets up and embraces her. She hugs him back fiercely, and it's like he's eighteen again, dealing with his first breakup with Afton. Except that time had been her call. This time it was all his.

"When did you get back?" she asks, looking him over.

"A few days ago," Jonah says, not meeting her eyes.

She frowns. "Why didn't you call me right away?"

He rubs the back of his head. "I was hoping to pull myself together a bit beforehand."

"You were avoiding your sisters, admit it," Henry says.

"I wanted to figure out my thoughts before facing them. You know how they are," Jonah says.

His mom only nods. "Go clean yourself up. I can't believe you subjected poor Henry to this. Then we'll talk."

A long shower and clean-shaven face later, Jonah stands with his mom on Henry's back deck, both of them taking turns throwing the ball for Millie. In California Jonah knows better than to dream of ever having a yard, and he momentarily feels guilty for depriving Millie of this. At least at home she has the waves to nip at and chase, though. He'd created a wall around the Millie shaped hole in his heart while filming, and being back with her has been healing.

Being with Henry has been good too. He's watched Henry's girls every night this week, letting Henry and his wife get some much-needed alone time. They love playing vet with Millie, who's all too happy to have the attention. When he returns, they sit on Henry's deck in the dark, sipping on beers while looking up at the stars. Henry hasn't pushed Jonah to talk since that first night when he told him everything, and Jonah's appreciated it. He needs to think about something besides Afton and his feelings.

"What happened?" his mom finally asks.

Jonah throws the ball again for Millie. "Afton."

His mom startles. "Did she apply to be a contestant?"

Jonah shakes his head, then tells her the whole mess, ending with his meltdown in Toronto and demanding to go home for a breather.

"How are you now?" his mom asks.

"I have no idea. Being forced to examine every single thought and emotion all day every day made for the perfect conditions for my OCD to creep in. Rumination, anyone?" Jonah jokes. "Falling for Afton again and then having everyone be upset with me brought up a lot of old stuff too."

His mom blows out a long breath. "I wish I would have noticed your struggles earlier and gotten you help as a teen. It would have saved you from so much pain."

He'd learned in college that Henry, and many of his roommates, had slipped up with the law of chastity as young adults. And while they felt shame, it was nothing compared to the outright depression Jonah slipped into. He'd been unable to eat or sleep, consumed with what he'd done. He'd written it off as the godly sorrow needed to be fully forgiven. The intensity he policed his thoughts and actions wasn't normal. His mom still clung to the church, blaming herself for his OCD, not the church for feeding it.

He grabs her hand and squeezes. "We all did the best we could. I shouldn't have accepted the role as the Fiancé-to-be in the first place."

Her nose scrunches. "Why?"

"I thought I was ready, but my OCD spiked and I hurt everyone, including Afton."

Millie brings the ball to his mom and she throws it. "What? Because you have it you aren't allowed to do things? Should all people with mental illness be disbarred from living?"

"No, that's not–"

"You were as ready as someone could be to fall in love on reality tv. You're in a stable place in life, you've worked through a lot of your past hangups, and you weren't in a secret relationship only wanting fame. People were going to get hurt no matter what you did. I know you don't believe in it anymore, but it seems like the universe, fate, God, something put you and Afton back in the same place at the same time again."

He side-eyes her. "You're just saying that because you've always wanted her as a daughter-in-law."

She laughs. "So sue me."

Jonah winces. "That's the other thing. If I don't propose to Afton, there's a chance the studio sues one or both of us for breach of contract and ruining their season. How can we both know what we truly want with that hanging over us? Or after falling in love in such a manipulated environment?"

His mom lets out a low whistle, which has Millie stop mid run to turn and cock her head.

"Your overthinking skills are impressive."

"Some might even say compulsive," Jonah grumbles.

His mom wraps an arm around his middle. It's never stopped being strange, being bigger than the person you always looked up to. "You're going to figure this out. Stop putting so much pressure on yourself. Take it one step at a time."

"What's a good first step?"

"Getting back to work. Sending a text. Going home and letting poor Henry's wife have her house back."

The thought of going back to work actually sounds doable. There are clear expectations. Things to occupy his mind besides his love life. He'll fly home. Take Millie on their walk to the beach. Get back to work and clear his head. Then he'll think about that text.

"Thanks, mom."

She squeezes him tighter. "Any time. I'll do my best to keep your sisters off your back, but I make no promises."

When it comes to Sarah, Naomi, and Ruth, that's the best anyone can do.

CHAPTER TWENTY-NINE

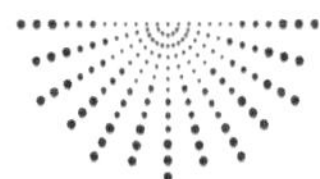

$\mathcal{A}$fton launches her interviewing masterclass the last week of October after working non-stop. Her background in media is helpful for once; she knows how to write a script quickly, film, and edit. The sales are slow, but she gets an email from a media production company that represents podcasts wanting to chat with her. She leaves the meeting with a job offer, even after she warned the executives that there was a good chance she would become public enemy #1 once the show airs.

"Great, we love humanizing people," the senior executive smiled.

She happily accepts after checking there's no travel. Officially her job title is as a producer, but she'll be jumping between multiple podcasts, along with hosting interview workshops for their hosts. As soon as her insurance kicks in, she books a much-needed appointment with a therapist.

After two sessions, she feels brave enough to reach out to Noah. Her therapist cautioned he might not want to talk about everything for quite some time, but Noah wants to hash out the past and move on. Their first phone call is three hours long, and Noah apologizes for his behavior at temple square and finally hears out why she left.

"I had no idea about any of that. I would have left too," Noah says at one point. Afton cries hearing everything Noah went through without her, including not understanding his sexuality until he was halfway through his degree at BYU. The following calls are filled with equal parts tears and laughter. She meets Noah's partner, Ian, over FaceTime and they invite her to stay in their apartment for Christmas instead of with her parents. She accepts.

She still hasn't heard from Jonah. The show will start airing in January, and with the holidays coming up, they're running out of time to film anything. He follows her business social media page though, and always views her stories. She's respecting his space, but it doesn't make her miss him any less.

WHEN JONAH ARRIVES FOR THANKSGIVING, his sisters tackle him in the doorway.

"Where's Millie?" Naomi asks.

"Who'd you pick?" Ruth asks.

"Why are secret sources claiming you left filming early?" Sarah asks.

Jonah whistles and Millie comes bounding up from his car. All three of them crowd Millie, fighting to be the first to kiss her.

"Do you have a backup career since being a tiktoker could be taken away any day for political gain?" Jonah asks Sarah.

"Do you need a chiropractor referral from all the whiplash from your on-again off-again relationship, Ruth? Most people say they want to be a doctor in elementary school; you couldn't get more creative Naomi?"

Jonah spent the entirety of the drive here coming up with those roasts.

The three of them look between each other, eyebrows raised.

"That was the best you could come up with?" Sarah asks.

"I thought HR had to be good at jokes so they don't get written up," Ruth says.

"Maybe we can stop by the library tomorrow and get you some joke books," Naomi says, patting him on the shoulder.

"Not dad jokes though. According to online sources he's nowhere near qualifying for them," Sarah says.

He pushes past them into the house, Ruth and Naomi whispering, "too far," as he closes the door.

They're right though. He's been too chicken to reach out to Afton. He opens the text with her name in it multiple times a day and stares. Then he watches her Instagram stories, trying to somehow parse from her business account if she's still single. If she'd still be open to him. He bought her interviewing basics course and watches the videos every night before bed. He's gone through it three times already.

Where did the Jonah from before filming go? The one who was ready to travel the world with strangers to fall in love? It's like the show leeched all the bravery out of him and he still hasn't regenerated it.

Jonah and his sisters work hard prepping all the dishes for Thanksgiving while his mom sets the dining room. He's carrying the mashed potatoes to the table when Naomi shrieks in front of him with the pretzel Jello salad.

"What is that?" Naomi points.

Jonah looks and sees someone already sitting at the table with shorn hair, sunglasses, and a whale t-shirt.

Their mom catches Jonah's eye, smirking. "This arrived in a box with specific instructions on what to do with it."

"What kind of bad juju did you get that someone would send you that?" Ruth asks, peeking around Jonah's side.

Jonah stares at the doll, hope blossoming. "The best."

AFTON'S WALKING up and down the hall with Naya's baby when the picture comes through from an unknown number. It's a picture of Jonah sitting next to the doll at his mom's table, doing a peace sign above the doll's head.

A second picture comes through with his whole family taking a selfie, crowded around the doll sitting in its seat. Sarah, Naomi, and Ruth are grown women now. Carrie smiles with wrinkles around her eyes and a grey streak of hair through her bangs. Afton's chest hurts seeing them. Today has been delightful with Naya's family, but she wishes she could have been there too.

She'd gotten tired of waiting for Jonah and decided not to waste any more time. The least they could do is talk once more and get closure. Now that he's reached out, she has no idea what to say. The cursor in the text box taunts her.

JONAH

You don't have to wait ten minutes to reply. I know you're cooler than me.

Well, now that that's been established...

How was your Thanksgiving?

SHE SENDS him the family photo with Naya's family, and then a selfie of her and the baby.

> She's adorable. Did you get a new job?

> You do realize Linked In tells you who views your profile, right? And Instagram stories?

> Busted. How's the production company?

THEY TEXT until 2am about work and their families. Jonah sends Afton a million pictures and videos of Millie and she can agree —Millie is the world's cutest dog. They move to phone calls and FaceTime's. She talks with Millie over the phone, and Jonah explains his theories for the rest of the dragon book series to Naya's baby. Their nightly calls are her new favorite part of the day.

Jonah must finally realize something because production reaches out and says they need her to fly to Utah the week before Christmas to film. She arrives at the airport and Richard escorts her to *the* park down the street from where they grew up. Her parents moved the summer she left home, too embarrassed by the church gossip. Carrie still lives just a block away.

The park is so much smaller than she remembered. She walks around with the cameras, recounting all her memories with Jonah here. Where she sat with him after his dad's funeral. Where he taught her CPR. Where they had their first kiss, and he later proposed.

Afterwards, she's brought to a safe house. Production always rents some for the engaged couples to meet a few times while they have to keep their relationship a secret until the season finale airs. She can barely breathe walking up the stairs to the unassuming home knowing Jonah is inside. They've been talking every day, but this is different. Now they're taking the next step in… whatever this is.

With cameras eagerly watching.

She knocks on the door, and it opens, a dog running out to greet her.

"Millie?" Afton asks, extending her hand for the dog to sniff. She's been worried that if given the chance to meet Millie, she wouldn't like Afton, ruining all chances at a relationship with Jonah. Dogs can sense bad people, right? What if Millie confirms her secret fears about herself? Afton's been working on that whole "accepting yourself" thing in therapy, but she still has a way to go.

Millie immediately nuzzles her head into Afton's leg, and Afton tentatively starts scratching her head. Millie sits, tilting so Afton can hit all the right spots.

JONAH WATCHES Afton from the doorway of the house, his heart about to burst. He'd reassured Afton that Millie would love her, but seeing it? It's almost too much. His two favorite girls are meeting. Afton finally looks up and spots him in the doorway, her face lighting up.

"Hey," she says shyly.

He crosses the distance and immediately wraps her into his arms. He spent all morning at the park, walking stoically and recounting everything that happened there with Afton. Then they filmed him talking with his mom and sisters, explaining his journey on the show. His mom deserves an award for how well she pretended not to know anything.

His sisters gave him shit for being so secretive and mopey

since coming home from filming. Then they shared some of their favorite memories of him and Afton.

"Bring her back home to us," Sarah demanded.

"Whatever you choose to do, we'll support you," his mom said.

Holding Afton in his arms now? It's right. He's had the space to clear his head, and to talk with Afton with no pressure for weeks. He grabs her hand and leads her inside to the couch. Millie follows after them, jumping up next to Afton and begging for pets. Afton starts stroking her back.

"I missed you," Jonah says.

"Me too. I'm glad you reached out," Afton says.

He rubs his hands on his jeans. "I'm sorry for the way I ended things."

"Don't apologize for that. You did what you needed to do, and I'm proud of you," Afton says, continuing to pet Millie.

Jonah swallows. "Thank you for that. That time to clear my head and realize that yes, I can actually trust myself, was invaluable."

"I'm glad. I needed to get some things in order, too. Like telling the truth," she says with a sad smile. She's told him about starting therapy, reconnecting with Noah, and her job. They don't need to rehash all of those details on camera.

Jonah reaches for her other hand. "Now that all of that is gone, where do we go from here?"

"I'm ready for a relationship if you are," she says shyly. "But if you're not I completely understand."

He leans forward, resting his forehead against hers. Millie gets up from the couch, giving them privacy.

"I'd love nothing more." Then he kisses her. She wraps her arms around his neck, practically clinging to him.

When they pull apart, Barb pulls Jonah into a separate room.

He's so glad that she's back from her medical leave. He didn't want Richard to taint these moments with Afton.

"So…" Barb says, trailing off.

"I'm going to propose to her. I know what I want."

Barb grins. "Perfect. I'll let the network know. They'll fit it in late January, early February after you're done promoting the premiere of the show."

"Sounds great."

"We'll get out of here so you two can enjoy your weekend," Barb says with a wink. She ushers the crew out and Afton and Jonah are finally alone. The door has barely closed before Afton practically leaps at him. She straddles him on the couch, kissing him fervently. She licks down the column of his neck, nipping at his shoulder. He's reaching to tug her shirt off, but she's sliding down his body until she's kneeling on the floor between his legs.

"Afton?" he breathes. She's undoing his belt, yanking it from the loops.

"Help me get these off," she murmurs, tugging on his jeans.

"You don't have to do that," he starts.

She glares at him. "Hips. Up."

He obeys and she yanks his pants and boxers off. She bites her lip and her eyes darken.

He hisses when she drags her tongue up the length of him, swirling at the tip. She explores every ridge of his head, before dragging her flat tongue up the underside of him. She cups his balls and he shivers. When she reaches the tip, she swirls her tongue before sucking his head into her mouth. He groans, throwing his head back on the couch as she slowly moves up and down, moaning softly around him. Somehow, he manages to open his eyes and look down at her. She's watching him, eyes dancing before she strokes his balls and sucks him in deeper.

"Fuck," he breathes.

She hums in approval and he blacks out for a moment from the new sensation. There's pleasure everywhere, and he can't think. He's going to come way too fast...

"Come here. I want a turn," he says. When she doesn't obey, he rocks backward, and she releases him with a pop.

"Is it not good?" she asks, brows pulling together.

"It's fucking amazing. But I want to touch you."

She pouts. "Not until I'm done. I want you to come on my tongue."

He'll have to ask where she learned to talk like that later because she sucks him back into her mouth, her other hand twisting at his base. The sensations are too much, too perfect. He fists her hair and she moans in approval as he pulls. His hips have a mind of their own, bucking up and down in the perfect rhythm as she works him. He's breathless, babbling encouragement, praises, he has no idea what, he's completely lost in the feel of her hot mouth, her tongue, her hands.

Heat builds at the base of his spine. "I'm so close," he warns, giving her a chance to let go. She sucks him even deeper, going faster. He thrusts into her mouth, once, twice. On the third thrust she cups his balls again, pleasure instantly racing down his spine.

"Afton," he moans, coming on her tongue, aftershocks crashing into him with each pull of her mouth. He sees stars. He blacks out. He comes back into himself and Afton is still there, smiling up at him with her eyes as she swallows.

He lays his head back on the couch, too exhausted to hold it up as he catches his breath. Afton settles next to him, laying her head on his chest.

"I can't understand why the church banned oral sex in the 80's, especially since it's run by men. Do you think it's because they didn't want to go down in return?" she asks.

He breathes out a single laugh. Of course she can make witty jokes right now. He inhales, trying to slow his heart.

"My turn. And I'm not done until you can't think straight," he rasps, pulling her mouth to his.

He meets his goal. More than once.

AFTON WALKS INTO THE BEDROOM, ready to climb into bed. Jonah is outside with Millie one last time before they go to sleep. He'd made her the best grilled cheese of her life earlier. She wasn't sure if it was the post-sex hunger, or if he somehow had magic powers to combine bread, cheese, and butter better than everyone else. They'd eaten them out on the back deck of the house, wrapped in a blanket. He'd pointed out the constellations to her as they ate.

"If they're wrong, we can blame Henry. He taught me when I was moping at his house after the show."

She'd nuzzled closer to him, still not able to believe this was real. They'd come back together for a third time. She finally felt ready to accept the love he offered her. She wasn't perfect, and knew she never would be. There's no way to know if you're the perfect match or if you'll last forever. All she knows is that she loves Jonah with her whole heart and soul, and she's not going to waste any more time staying away from him. She can have the hard conversations and won't resort to lying or hiding things. She's not going to be stuck in a job or situation because she's scared of change.

Being in a relationship isn't going to stop her from living a fulfilling life. She will not be her mother, and what happened with her parents and family isn't her fault. She's still working on figuring out how to include them in her life, but she's proud of the progress she's made with Noah. It's okay not to have all the answers now. She feels stronger by the idea of doing life with Jonah, not trapped.

The bed is still perfectly made, covered in a fluffy white duvet and knitted beige blanket at the foot. This is the one place in the house they managed not to visit. Limbs deliciously sore, she throws the duvet back. Then screams. Dead eyes stare up at her, a pair of sunglasses resting in their shorn hair. She presses her hand to her heart, trying to slow the beating. Then she bursts out laughing. Jonah is horrible at pranks. He didn't even get to see her shock at the doll because he's outside.

She'll teach him.

She picks up the doll, putting the sunglasses back over its eyes. Instantly it goes from nightmare material to weird souvenir. She smooths out the whale t-shirt dress, and pauses. There's something underneath. She reaches down under the shirt and pulls it out. It's a long silver chain. At the end of it hangs a thin diamond band. She gasps. She's seen this ring before. It can't be. She clutches the doll to her chest, needing to find Jonah.

He's in the doorway, on a knee.

"Afton, no middle name because your parents figured you'd make it your maiden name, Hayes. I have spent the majority of my life loving you. You've left an imprint on my soul. There are not many things I can say I know with absolute certainty. The fact that I love you and will keep loving you every moment I have breath is one of them. Will you do me the honor of letting me spend the rest of my life with you?"

"You're supposed to propose for the cameras," she croaks, her throat almost too tight to speak.

"When have we ever done what we're supposed to?" he asks. "I wanted to have this just for us. I know that the show will expect us to get married, but I know that you're unsure of marriage. I don't care what we do, as long as I get to spend my life with you."

Tears leak from her eyes, but they're nothing like the anguished tears of their first proposal. This time they're from being seen. Known. Understood. There are no expectations, no rules for how the rest of their lives will go. They can do whatever works best for them.

"Yes. Absolutely yes. Yes. Yes."

Jonah stands just in time to catch her as she crashes into him, wrapping her legs around his waist. He carries her to the edge of the bed, setting her down gently. He gently pries the doll from her hand, then pulls the necklace off.

"Is this the same ring from last time?" she asks.

"Yes. My mom saved it, just in case. I picked it up today." He pushes her hair to one side of her neck and she shivers at his touch. "Richard and Karl will literally kill us if you're spotted wearing this ring, even on your right hand. So I figured you could hide it with this necklace until the finale," Jonah says. She holds her hair out of the way for him as he fastens the necklace around her neck. The chain is long enough that the ring rests right above the space between her breasts. Jonah kisses the spot, before resting his forehead against hers.

"I love you, Afton," he says softly.

"I love you, Jonah. Let's do this life thing."

He interlaces his fingers with hers. "Together."

"Together."

EPILOGUE

(W)hen clips of Afton were sprinkled in the premiere episode with even more appearances in the second, the internet did what it does best. Speculate. Week one they thought it was an editing error. By week three, Afton's name hit the internet and it exploded. People from high school started popping up, trying to give another inside scoop into what was going on. Their senior prom pictures were shared over and over beneath stories about how cute of a couple they were.

Others honed in on the fact Afton stopped going to church and disappeared right after senior year. The most popular rumor was that she was pregnant and left to have their baby in secret, coming on the show to finally introduce Jonah to their child. That evolved into the theory their child was a girl who was adopted and accidentally applied to be a contestant on the show and kissed her dad. If people were capable of doing math, they'd realize that the baby would only be fourteen, and even if he and Afton conceived a baby with their prepubescent bodies on the day they met, that baby still wouldn't be old enough to come on the show.

Bea commented, "auntie?" on his sister Sarah's TikTok's, feeding the rumor mill. Bea's mom posted a graphic photo of Bea entering the world with a tiny heart over the most sensitive parts with the caption, "knock it off."

Afton worried all the attention would hurt her job, but her coworkers fought over who would get the first interview with her after the finale aired for the exclusive scoop. Afton joked she'd only accept the winner via a WrestleMania showdown. Her company loved the idea and she helped each of the podcast hosts decide on wrestling outfits and entrance songs to fit the themes of their podcasts. Current and past wrestlers came on each of the shows, teaching the hosts moves to use. He loved hearing how excited she was for work every day.

The crew snuck the two of them to a tastefully decorated barn in February to film their proposal. Afton was absolutely stunning in a pale blue satin gown, the chain of the necklace with the ring he'd already given her hidden beneath the neck-line. Even though the proposal was for television purposes, they both cried.

Rewatching the episodes got harder each week as each of the women confessed how they were starting to fall for him. Then, it was time to film the women tell-all. It was going to be a two-part episode, and he braced himself accordingly. Tell all they did, dishing on the stolen coffee pot and revealing they all thought Maylee hid it. Maylee swore she didn't. McKinlee played coy on whether she truly thought French kissing was sex. And then they let Jonah have it. He validated their pain, their hurt, and their betrayal. There were tears all around. The host finished by getting life updates from all the women. Bentley was engaged. Tage was getting married the day after the Toronto episode aired, finally free from her contract.

The episode in Toronto aired and Afton's parents finally reached out to her. They were confused and embarrassed. The whole world was now commenting on the two of them having sex when they shouldn't have been. Jonah desperately wanted to be there to hold her through this repeat of their past. Instead of hiding in shame, Afton leaned into it, making TikTok's with her coworkers to songs like "I Just Had Sex," "Wood," and even audio of church leaders cautioning about sexual immorality. Each one made him laugh and was a balm to the intrusive thoughts that the next article would be the one to break them. When he voiced that fear to Afton, she said, "we made it through a small-town Mormon community at eighteen, that internet can't get anywhere close to that."

The finale arrived. Henry and his family flew into town, along with his mom and sisters. The network tried to bring Afton's parents to the live recording, but they declined. Her oldest brother Dan and his wife asked if they could come instead. Afton had been shocked, unsure if they wanted to look good on TV, or if they truly wanted to support her. Noah and his partner Ian came as well, along with Sadie, Naya, and Chelsea.

Somehow Afton got them to sneak a bowl of whale cheese crackers into Jonah's dressing room. It was the exact boost he needed before going out in front of the crowd and explaining himself. Bea was announced as the next Fiancé-to-be before Afton finally joined him on the couch. The 3.25 carat engagement ring he'd selected for her sparkled under the stage lights, and the world finally knew they were together. As soon as the final cut was called, Afton ran through the crowd to where their loved ones were waiting, hugging his mom. She was crying, holding the back of Afton's head.

"You've always felt like my daughter, Afton. Now the whole world knows it."

Jonah had held strong the whole night, but that broke him. They only had a few more minutes with family before they were whisked to the airport to make it to the east coast by morning. He worried he'd be sick of Afton by the end of the constant talk shows and podcast interviews, but he wasn't. After being apart the past five months, getting to travel together was exactly what they needed; even if it was to talk nonstop about their journey.

The world was divided on their love, but they didn't care. He was too busy apartment hunting with Afton and packing their things. They found a cute place near her work and thirty minutes from the beach. There was a shelf in the living room just for their creepy doll. They slept in on the weekends when he'd wake her up with kisses across her chest where she always wore the chain and ring he'd gotten her. Afterwards they'd go for brunch where people always asked for selfies.

The world eventually moved on to new scandals, only remembering the two of them for premiers or "Which Reality Tv Couples are Still Together" articles. People always asked about their wedding plans which Jonah always coyly answered by saying he couldn't wait to go cake tasting. They did go cake testing, but they were for their birthday parties. Afton insisted they celebrate each and every one of them with the people they loved.

THREE YEARS after their season aired, Henry and his family came out for a spring break trip to Disneyland the same week Sadie and her boyfriend came to visit. It was a chaotic week of hosting dinners and showing their friends their favorite haunts. By Friday Jonah is exhausted, glad for the time with friends but ready to just sleep.

Afton frowns at her phone. "Sadie's flying home tomorrow and wants to have one last girl dinner before she leaves."

Jonah's phone buzzes with a text from Henry. "Henry wants to have one last dinner too."

"Perfect. Just one more day, and then back to our regular programming."

"Can't wait."

"I have a few things to finish up at the office, so I'll see you tonight," Afton says with a kiss.

Jonah dozes off and wakes to Henry banging on his front door. When he opens it, Henry's carrying two suit bags.

"What are those for?" Jonah asks.

"Your sisters got us a reservation at this fancy restaurant. I need to look nice in case we run into anyone famous. Make yourself presentable," Henry orders.

It had to be Ruth or Sarah who'd seen a place online and wanted to send Henry in their stead. Naomi was far too busy in her last year of residency and taking care of her nine-month-old son. "You should take your wife, not me."

"Humor me, it's my last night in town."

In the spirit of humoring him, Jonah throws on the suit. The jacket is navy and made of velvet. There's no tie and Jonah doesn't have anything that matches, so he leaves the top button undone, trying to look intentional. He restyles his hair, but when Henry demands he do another spritz of cologne, Jonah puts his foot down.

"Your odds of getting a selfie with someone aren't going to go up based on how I smell."

"No, but I don't want to be known as the best friend of someone who stinks. People love to post that stuff anonymously."

Jonah rolls his eyes, then does one more spritz.

"Can you believe we're here? Friends from middle school,

driving down the highway in California, both of us blissfully happy?" Henry asks as they drive.

Henry never talks like this. Was this trip something else? "Are you okay?"

"Yeah, why wouldn't I be?" Henry says.

"You never talk like this. Are you sick? Is this a last good-bye?" Jonah asks, his fingers white against the steering wheel.

Henry's expression completely changes. "No, nothing's wrong, I promise. The beach always makes me feel sappy."

"Promise on your playstation?" Jonah asks.

Henry rolls his eyes. "Promise on my playstation."

"Don't scare me like that" Jonah exhales.

"I will never express feelings of happiness to you again," Henry says in a deadpan.

The PCH which is actually moving for once and Henry exits before driving up a winding road, stopping in front of a beach cottage. There are only four other cars out front; definitely not the celebrity hotspot Henry was talking about.

"Did you get the address wrong?"

Henry looks at his phone. "No, your sisters said it's exclusive."

Did they send him and Henry to the middle of nowhere as part of an elaborate prank? That's something they'd do. Henry hops out of the car before Jonah can look up the location on his own phone. He follows Henry up the rickety wooden steps to the front of the cottage. When he opens the door, there's no hostess. Instead, his sisters all stand inside.

"You little shits," Jonah says.

They're all wearing flowing gowns in gold, deep orange, and burgundy, their hair in beachy waves.

"We're the colors of sunset," Ruth says, twirling.

"Good for you?" Jonah says, the words a question.

His mom walks into the room, holding his nephew in her

arms, wearing a violet lace dress to her knees. She's dabbing at her eyes with a tissue. He's seen this scene before in movies. He swallows hard. "What's going on?"

"Surprise," his sisters say, doing jazz hands. There's a clicking noise behind him. "You're getting married."

He staggers back a step and Henry claps him on the shoulder, holding him steady.

"What?" Jonah whispers.

His sisters groan. Henry holds a hand out. "Pay up."

Sarah pulls a $20 out of her bra and hands it to Henry. Henry grabs it with the tips of his fingers, then disappears to wash his hands. Someone steps out of the shadows, a camera on his shoulder. It's Luke from the show. Jonah frowns.

"I'm a wedding videographer now. Afton hired me. No one will see this except you two," Luke reassures him. Jonah goes over and embraces Luke, stroking his thumb on the back of his neck for old time's sake.

"How wasn't it obvious when Henry showed up and got you dressed?" Sarah asks.

Because they've never seriously talked about a wedding? Because he's utterly content with his life now? There have been hard moments the past three years, but they've gotten through them together.

"Be nice," his mom says to Sarah. His sisters disappear somewhere else in the cottage.

"Is this real?" Jonah asks his mom.

She nods, eyes sparkling. "Afton's been planning this since Christmas. I can't tell you how many times I almost texted the wrong group chat and ruined it."

Since Christmas? She has been suspiciously busy with work the past three months. His eyes water and his mom pulls out another tissue.

"Save your tears for when you see your bride," she says, dabbing at his eyes.

He hears the clicking noise again, and spots a photographer. This is happening. Afton planned a surprise wedding and they're getting married.

Henry reappears and hands him a tie. It's black with tiny dragons stitched into it with golden thread, matching his suit perfectly. Then there's the box of cufflinks which are tiny whales.

"Damn it," he laughs, and Henry helps him fasten them.

His mom leads him outside the cottage to where there's a small pergola strung up with fairy lights. There are two rows of white chairs: his sisters, Henry's wife, Naya's wife and parents, and Noah and his partner are already sitting. Chelsea stands at the end of the small beach, holding a small leather book. There's no arch, no hangings, only the sky, black rocks, and beach behind her. The view is absolutely stunning.

Jonah's mom grabs his arm, but he stops. The velvet suit jacket looks good, but this is a beach wedding. He removes the jacket and rolls up the sleeves of his dress shirt, sliding the cuff links in his pocket for safekeeping. There, the one thing he would have picked himself had he been consulted on the planning. He grabs his mom's arm again and leads her down the aisle to the front. The first chair has a framed picture of his dad on it. He swipes at his eyes and embraces his mom.

"He's ecstatic for you two, I know it. You both deserve all the happiness in the world," she whispers before taking her seat.

Jonah goes and stands next to Chelsea.

"I've been ordained for years; I didn't do it online at the last minute," Chelsea says.

"I'm sure it comes in handy working in TV."

"Exactly. I like you," Chelsea says.

"Good because we'll be seeing each other often."

Instrumental piano music starts playing and everyone turns back to the cottage. Henry and Naya's daughters appear, throwing flower petals down on the sand. They freeze halfway down the aisle, and Jonah squats down, holding out his arms for a hug. The girls go running to Jonah, crashing into him. He hugs them fiercely before they go and sit back with their moms'.

Naya and Sadie emerge from the cottage wearing sunset hued gowns. They link arms and make their way down the aisle. They both hug Jonah before going and sitting in the front row. Henry appears, Millie next to him on a leash. Henry unclips the leash and Millie comes bounding down the sand. She reaches Jonah and drops a small package at his feet. He chuckles, knowing he'll find that creepy doll contortion inside.

It's not the doll. Instead it's an old battered copy of *Eragon*. The one he gave to Afton all those years ago. There's a gauzy ribbon wrapped around it with two rings. One is a black band, exactly like he's always wanted. The other is the ring Afton's been wearing around her neck for over two years. Jonah carefully hands the book to his mom to hold.

That's when he spots the doll, sitting in the second row, sporting a new pair of bedazzled sunglasses and a bow.

He needs Afton to get out here, now.

The music swells and he freezes. What he thought had just been instrumental music is actually a piano cover of "Ocean Avenue." As the chorus starts, the cottage door opens and everyone rises to their feet. Afton appears in view and Jonah almost falls to his knees. She's wearing a deep V-neck lace gown with long flowing sleeves. Her hair is down in loose beach waves with the front braided back with baby's breath. Chelsea hands him a handkerchief and he wipes away his tears. The girl he's loved as long as he can remember is walking to him.

Afton finally reaches him. She hands her bouquet off, and grabs his hands.

"Wow," he breathes. He spins her around. The back of the gown dips low, mirroring the front.

"Are you okay with this?" she asks, forehead wrinkled.

He rubs the line with his thumb affectionately. He thought he'd never get to see these proofs of time passing. He can't wait to add more. "Okay with it? This is beyond anything I could have dreamed of."

"Did you not like the suit jacket?" she asks.

"I did, but someone once told me I look sexy with my sleeves rolled up."

It takes a beat, but then she laughs, remembering the comment from prom. He'll never get tired of that sound. He leans in to kiss her, but is stopped by an arm pushing him back.

"Let's get you married first," Chelsea says.

He holds Afton's hands as Chelsea goes through the ceremony. He barely hears her, lost in this moment. The ocean is crashing behind him. All of their loved ones are here. He's not sure what happens after this life, but he swears he feels his dad here with them.

It's time for the vows. "Jonah. It's hard to remember my life before you. Not because I met you at eleven, but because meeting you opened up my whole world. You snuck me books, you invited me into your family. For the first time I felt seen, and like my voice mattered. You were my first love.

"Circumstances and beliefs tore us apart. We were young and hadn't had a chance to find ourselves yet. Yet somehow the universe brought us to the same place, at the same time again. We've both grown and changed, yet the parts of you I fell in love with so long ago haven't.

"We've made so many speeches and declarations of love for the world. I want to make my vows just for you."

Chelsea turns off the microphone and Afton steps in close, her chest pressing against his. She holds his hand at his side, and then softly so only he can hear, she vows to make him laugh. To cherish him. To stand by him in good and bad. To always talk their way through things. To love him. And, to allow herself to be happy with him.

"I didn't have time to think of my own vows," he whispers.

"That's okay. Speak from the heart," she encourages.

She wipes the tears from his cheeks as he vows to be her family. To always support her dreams. To never cage her. To talk his way through things with her. And, to let himself be happy with her, too.

They step back and Jonah's mom brings the book to him. They unwrap the ribbon and repeat after Chelsea before slipping the rings on each other's fingers. Despite the fact he bought the wedding band as a teen, it matches perfectly with Afton's engagement ring.

"Now you may kiss," Chelsea announces before stepping out of the way.

Jonah snakes one hand around Afton's waist, the other to her face before he dips her. She squeals, and then kisses him right as the sun starts to set, the clouds a rainbow of color.

After dinner, they start the dancing and karaoke. Jonah somehow convinces Henry to sing, "The Boys are Back" with him. Everyone takes turns and his sides hurt from the ridiculous range they choose—from High School Musical to Bon Jovi. He snuggles with his nephew, dances with his sisters, and catches up with Luke before Afton brings him up to sing "Honestly I" by Yellowcard. The song is the perfect bookend for their journey.

People start leaving one-by-one, having to catch flights and put kiddos to bed. They finalize their plans to visit the east coast next month for Sadie's housewarming, and Utah in the summer. Once everyone's gone, he and Afton sit snuggled under the pergola, the fairy lights still twinkling above them.

"I know it's our wedding night, and karaoke always makes you horny," Afton starts.

Jonah chuckles, resting his chin on her head. He would argue it wasn't the karaoke; it was seeing her so happy and in her element, but there's no point.

"But I'm so tired. Rain check till morning?" she finishes.

"Whatever you need, my wife." He pulls her onto his lap, meaning to stand up and take her inside the cottage. But Afton sits up, looking him in the eyes.

"Say it again."

"Whatever you need, my wife?"

Afton groans. "I'm not tired anymore." She pulls the train of her dress up, then straddles him.

He raises a brow. "Oh?" His hands wrap around her back, feeling her warm skin at the deep v. She shivers.

"You better unzip that right now, husband."

Hearing her say that word unlocks something. He brings her mouth to his hungrily, hands exploring every last inch of dress with his hands. Especially where the dress doesn't cover. She brings his hand to the back, showing him where the hidden zipper is.

"You want to do this out here?" he teases.

"Yes," she says, loosening his tie and already starting on the buttons of his dress shirt.

"You're turning into a little exhibitionist. First the orgasm in the park, now this?"

"I'm nowhere near as bad as those couples who dry hump in the grass at BYU," she says, getting the last of his buttons and ripping his shirt open, exposing his bare chest to the air. She licks a line from his pec, all the way up his neck. The cool air hits the trail and he shivers.

"Only my wife can crack jokes while getting undressed."

Afton makes a noise in her throat, and he finally tugs on her zipper, baring her to him. Under the open sky with the crashing of the waves and the humming of crickets, they make love. They crawl into bed afterwards, their bare bodies curling against each other with the window open.

"I never thought I could be this happy," she whispers.

He squeezes her tight, waiting for a feeling of dread that this will be taken away. He inhales deeply, filling his lungs with the smell of Afton. Her shampoo mixed with floral perfume and a hint of the sea. The feeling doesn't come.

"I'm so grateful I get to be a part of it," he murmurs.

Before he would be afraid to feel so much joy. That it would be snatched away. He moves his hand to her heart, the rhythm synced with his own. Here with her, he's not afraid of the what ifs their tomorrows will bring.

ACKNOWLEDGMENTS

There are so many people who have been important to my writing journey as a whole, but this book is different. It wouldn't exist without my faith deconstruction and the people and resources who supported me along the way. Talking about my relationship with Mormonism is so complicated. I'm grateful for the people who are in my life because of it, many of whom are still dear friends to this day. I'm grateful for the community I was raised in. I wouldn't be the person I am today without it, and I'm proud of who that person is. But that doesn't erase the pain and hurt it caused for me, and for those who aren't as privileged as I was.

Leaving is scary. You're told that every good thing in your life will disappear. That wickedness never was happiness. That you'll no longer have divine protection and it'll just be you in this dark and dreary world. That's not the truth. I wanted to share a story showing people who have left experiencing joy. To show the entire spectrum of Mormonism and how differently people interact with it. I wouldn't have been able to have the courage to choose what felt right for me without hearing the stories of those who came before. Thank you to those who shared in places like Girlscamp and Mormon Stories. For Lindsay Hansen Park and A Year of Polygamy. For Chelsea Homer and Faith Journey Meetups. Every story, every comment, every piece of yourselves shared was another piece of strength. Another chance to feel seen and not alone.

A huge thank you to Brandi who went through this journey before me and sent me polo after polo of understanding, whether it's about the church, motherhood, or books. You've been such a light in some of the hardest times and I so appreciate you.

Amy, thank you for always pushing me to dig deeper and examine things in a way I never have before. For reminding me accomplishments deserve to be celebrated, and for being a fellow creative who just gets it.

Rachel, Kate, Bridget, Hayley, Sarah. I thought you were the coolest in high school and reconnecting as adults has been even better. Thank you for being the kind of friends you can always pick it up right where you left off.

Kelsey and Mallory for Bachelor Tuesdays which gave me the idea for this book, and for being supports during a hard time. To my library friends Amanda, Katie, Lucero, Chris and Kelly for accepting all the different versions of me. My rec coworkers—you are genuinely some of the coolest people who I'm lucky to call friends. Thank you for always supporting my writing.

Amanda and Josh, thank you for walking this crazy journey with us and being some of the most genuine people I've ever met. You draw in some of the coolest people and have expanded our world.

Sarah, I stayed way longer than I would have simply because I wanted to hang out with you and all the young women. If I had to make a perfect church, I would put you in charge. You are magic in human form.

Molly, this book wouldn't exist without you. Thank you for being not only a critique partner extraordinaire and cheerleader, but also a friend. I'm so excited to keep reading and writing with you!

Helen, my ride or die. Meeting you was worth a million

testimony meetings. Thank you for continuing to love me even though I'm such a picky reader. You are the person I immediately text whenever something funny happens or shit hits the fan. You're one of the only people who can make me cackle, and even after five years of friendship, I still learn more about you and go, 'hey! Me too!' You are my fire-breathing bitch queen and I'm so thankful to get to do life with you.

My in-laws, thank you for always loving me and treating me like family, even when we didn't agree.

My parents and siblings, I know it's hard when someone leaves the church. Thank you for always being respectful of my decisions and not letting it change anything in our relationships. I love you all dearly, and please know Afton's parents were not inspired by you in any way shape or form.

My boys—you are the light of my life. Being your mom and watching you learn and grow and become your own people has been such a privilege. Seeing these perfect little humans who are filled with so much light and wonder completely changes the way I view...well, everything. You are a big reason I made the decisions I did. You are worthy, loved, and whole just the way you are. You were born with inner wisdom and no one can take that away from you. You will make mistakes as we all do, but you can learn from them and keep trying again and again, and again. There is no such thing as perfection, so please don't go chasing it. Remember you are a part of this earth and no one has more of a right to be here than another, so we must share it and do what we can to better it. I love you, I love you, I love you.

Sammy, the love of my life. My best friend. The person I feel most seen by and am grateful to do every day with. The inspiration for this story came from the fear of what would have happened had I listened to the advice of others and written you off purely because you weren't a member of the church. I would have missed out on all of this and be a completely different person, all for something I stopped believing later. There were so many times when you could have said, "I'm out." You didn't. You believe people can grow and give them the space to do so. Thank you for being the one I get to grow with and laugh with as we navigate this thing called life.

While Jonah and all the other characters I write aren't your carbon copy, they're all infused with my favorite parts of you and will live on long after we're gone through these stories. I have no idea what's after this life, but whatever it is, I'm forever grateful I got to do it with you.

And thank you readers. You're the ones who make these dreams possible.

ABOUT THE AUTHOR

Kylee Summers grew up Mormon but made the agonizing decision to walk away at 27 (return to Saturn anyone?) She lives in Colorado with her husband and two boys. When not writing she can be found cross-stitching, making horrible "that's what she said" jokes, and dreaming about the beach. She writes mysteries as Kylee Awiech.

Find her at kyleethewriter.com , @kyleethewriter on TikTok, and @kylee.summers.author on Instagram.